To Cordelia-
Happy reading.

MOONBURNER

Claire Luana

Moonburner

Copyright © 2016 by Claire Luana

Published by Live Edge Publishing

ISBN-13: 978–0–9977018–1–4 (Paperback)

ISBN-13: 978–0–9977018–2–1 (Ebook)

Cover Design: Okay Creations

Interior Formatting: Integrity Formatting

To Mike,

for constantly reminding me that life is supposed to be fun.

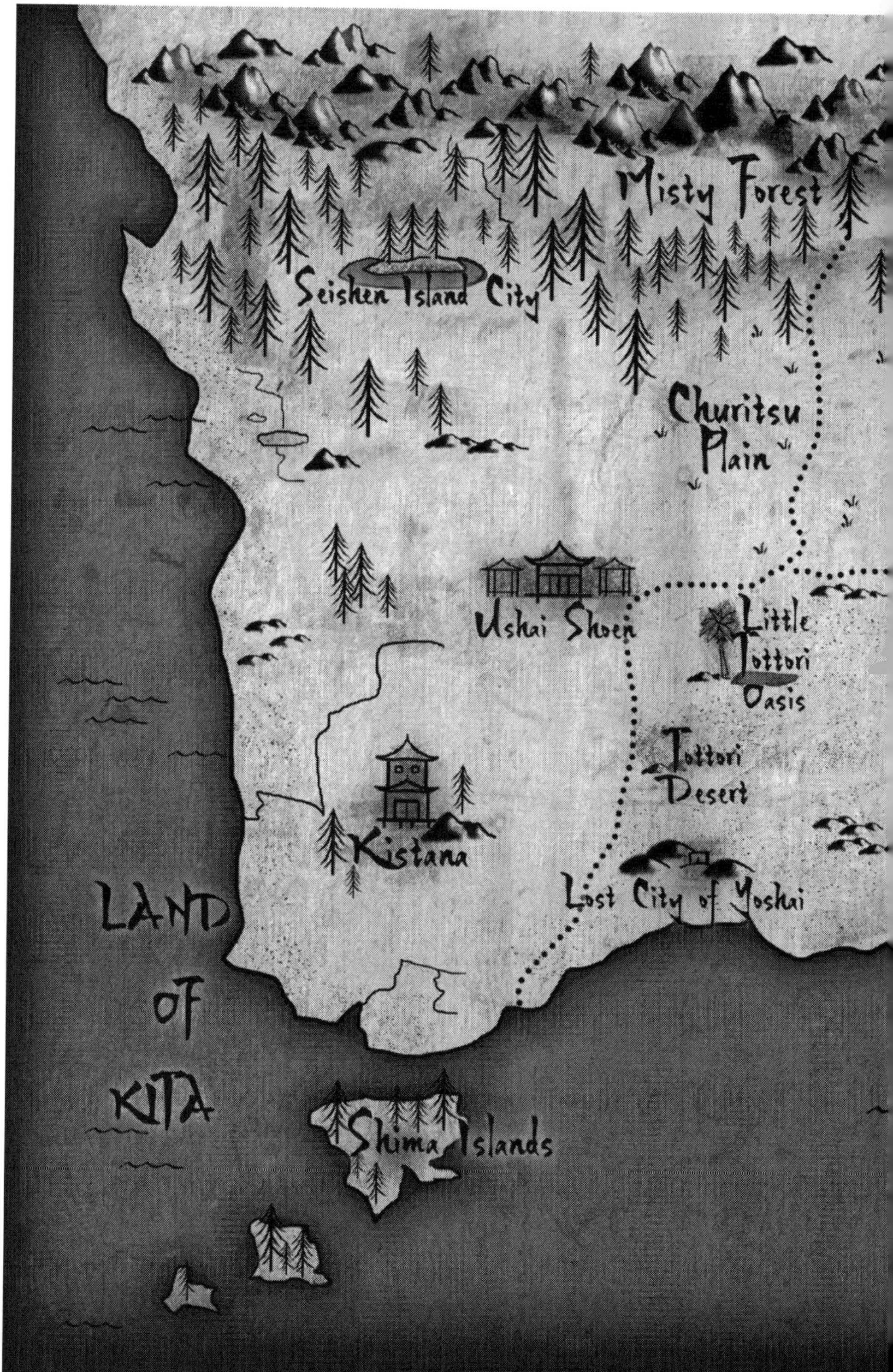

Misty Forest

Seishen Island City

Churitsu
Plain

Ushai Shoen

Little
Tottori
Oasis

Tottori
Desert

Kistana

LAND

Lost City of Yoshai

OF

KITA

Shima Islands

Akashi Mountains
Citadel
Kyuden
Nozuchi River
LAND OF MIINA
N
W
E
S

PROLOGUE

The thick woods muffled Hanae's anguished screams. Raiden had chosen this location carefully. They did not want anyone near when their child was born.

"It will be a daughter," Hanae had said. "And they will try to kill her."

Her mother's intuition came to pass. Hanae's labors were joined by the first wail of a new life—a perfect glistening daughter.

Raiden bathed their tiny child with a damp cloth and placed her in her mother's arms.

Just like delivering a calf, he thought, and then chided himself for having such a thought about his wife.

He bustled around the cabin, if it could be called that—only four ramshackle walls guarding a square dirt floor. He cleaned up the worst from the delivery and sat on an old wooden stool by his wife's side.

Hanae spoke softly to their daughter, entranced and oblivious to the danger that faced them.

"We need to perform the Gleaming ceremony," Raiden said, smoothing his wife's sticky hair back from her soft brow. "We need to know."

Hanae's arms tightened around the child. She didn't look at him. He could see that in that moment, she only had eyes for her daughter.

"She's weak—she's barely taken her first breath. Let's wait a little longer. Until she has a chance to gain her strength."

"My love. No daughter of yours could ever be weak. We talked of this. It must be now. We must know. Everything depends on what it shows."

Her eyes flashed and she jerked away from his extended hand. "No." Her voice was steel. "I won't let you hurt her."

"Hanae. We must. So they do not." He stroked her cheek softly. "We swore . . . that we would not let them do to her what they did to Saeko." Why they had named their first daughter, he didn't know. She had only lived two days.

Hanae's shoulders slumped, and the iron grip of her arms loosened. She turned back and offered him the bundle.

"You are right," she said, as a tear slid from the corner of her eye to her ear, leaving a trail through the dried salt of her sweat. "But I can't watch."

She turned away from him, pulling her knees to her chest in a ball.

He stood before the small basin of water, resting on a rickety table on the other side of the cabin and unwrapped their daughter. She was so beautiful. Even red and wrinkled, he could tell she had her mother's fine hands, delicate but strong. She had his square jawbone. He wondered whether she would be as stubborn as he was in his youth. But he was delaying.

He plunged her into the water and held her there, his own heart hammering in his chest like a wild beast desperate to be set free. He began counting. Ten. She flailed under the water, her tiny limbs no match for his strong calloused hands. Thirty. At sixty, he could let her up. And try to save her. Fifty. Relief and hope began to well in him.

And then a bright, white light exploded from his daughter. He stumbled back, throwing an arm over his eyes. She illuminated the cabin, shining silver light into cobwebbed corners and dusty crevices.

After a few seconds, the light died, and his daughter was herself again. Tiny, pink, floating on top of the water peacefully. He and Hanae locked eyes. She had turned over and was half sitting up on her cot. The look of helpless horror on her face was mirrored on his own.

"I knew she would be," Hanae said softly. "A moonburner. And a strong one."

"What do we do?"

"We hide her. We keep her alive."

CHAPTER 1

The breeze blew across Kai's face, cooling a rivulet of sweat that dribbled down the side of her neck. She closed her eyes, opening her senses to the heat of the sun, the fresh smell of grass, horse and leather, and Jaimo's gentle wuffing.

"Look sharp, Kai." Her father, Raiden, trotted by, sending her a pointed look. She shook herself from her reverie. Sitting and soaking up the sun upon your face wasn't very manly. She blew a stray lock of her shaggy hair from her forehead in a silent rebellion. That habit wasn't particularly manly either, as her parents constantly reminded her.

She nudged Jaimo's chestnut flanks and trotted to join her father. He sat astride their other horse, Archer, a feisty dun with a white marking like an arrow on his forehead. Her father sat with the grace of a man who had spent his life on horseback. He was muscular and strong, the skin on his face, neck and arms weathered from years outside. Laugh lines paralleled his wide mouth and strong square jaw, and he shared his easy smile often, revealing white teeth. Only the tightness around his eyes betrayed the stresses he had faced in the last few years. None of her family had been unaffected.

"They are looking good this year," she said, surveying the cattle herd. There were a number of calves that looked healthy and strong.

"Yes, Taiyo has blessed us," Raiden said.

Kai snorted. "Right. It was all Taiyo. None of the hard work, careful selection, or late hours we spent with the herd played any part in it."

"Do not speak such blasphemous things." Raiden lowered his voice. "At least where others can hear you. You know better."

"Somehow," Kai said under her breath, "I don't think Taiyo has much interest in blessing me."

Taiyo, the Sun God, was worshipped by all of Kita. His golden-haired sun-burners, who drew magic from the rays of the sun, were treated like royalty. Never mind that it was his war with Tsuki, the Moon Goddess, that had plagued their lands for hundreds of years. Never mind that it was his damn war that had forced her to masquerade as a boy for the last seventeen years.

Kai and Raiden joined the rest of the men: her father's old friend Aito and Tomm and Ren, brothers from their village. Handsome, perfect, Ren. They had reached a watering hole surrounded by tall, delicately-leafed ironwood trees. It was an oasis of color in the otherwise dull tan landscape—leagues after leagues of banu grass withering in the summer heat. The cattle were already heading to the edge of the water and reaching down to drink.

"We'll break here for lunch," Raiden announced. "I'm going to take a closer look at some of the calves. Save me something to eat, you animals."

Aito pulled lunch out of his saddlebags, spreading dried meat, fruit and cheese over a flat stump under the shade of one of the ironwood trees. He was the keeper of the food, as Tomm and Ren—renowned bottomless pits—couldn't be trusted.

The brothers were nearly identical—tall and thin but strong, like two acacia trees that refused to bow to the wind. Tomm was the older and more charismatic, with an easy laugh and a quirk in his smile. Ren was more reserved, as if he preferred to observe life around him before expressing his conclusions.

Kai found him observing her often, which was disconcerting, as it usually happened when she herself was trying to sneak a sideways glance at him. She didn't think he suspected her secret, but he must know something about her was not as it seemed.

Kai sprawled out on the ground next to the watering hole in typical masculine fashion, eating her lunch with gusto. She constantly felt that she was playing a caricature of a man, that her exaggerated gestures and mannerisms were painfully transparent. Apparently they weren't, as the villagers who lived around them hadn't discovered her yet. If the tables were turned, she supposed she wouldn't see reason to think twice about herself. She was short in stature for a man, but her lean figure, made strong by years of helping her father, was not unusual in this rural area. Food was not always plentiful during childhood. Her face was square like her father's, her skin tanned by the sun, a field of freckles across her small nose and cheeks. Her ears stuck out like her mother's, though her mother could cover hers with long hair. Kai's cheekbones were a bit high for a man's, and her eyes were hazel and almond-shaped, but those feminine features were balanced by a nondescript mouth, unruly eyebrows, and a close-cropped, unfashionable haircut. As a woman, Kai would never be more than plain, perhaps pretty if she really put some effort into it. She thanked Tsuki every day for her unremarkable features.

Kai only had to blend into the background for six more months and she could be free. Maybe. If she made it across the border and wasn't killed for a spy. It was the best she could hope for, a shadow of a future that could easily elude her. But as quickly as her emotions took a turn towards self-pity, she righted them. She knew she was lucky. By all rights, she shouldn't be alive at all.

Kai laid back into the dry grass and her mind drifted, imagining what it would be like if she and Ren were at the watering hole alone, as a man and a woman. Would he hold her hand or kiss her? Look at her softly?

A commotion by the water jarred her from her daydream, and she sat up.

"Kai! Come on, we're going swimming!" shouted Tomm, already stripped down to his underclothes.

Her cheeks grew hot as she watched Ren take his shirt off. His lean, tanned muscles shone with sweat. She tore her eyes away, not wanting to be caught staring. "No thanks," she called. "My father might come back any moment."

The brothers seemed to accept her excuse and dove into the water. She watched them splashing each other, floating, and doing lazy backstrokes across the glistening surface of the water. Just another slice of everyday life that she had to watch from a distance.

Kai closed her eyes and laid back on the grass again, listening to the light sounds of Aito's gentle snoring punctuated by the brothers' laughter. That man could sleep through anything. It grew quiet. A shadow passed over her, and she felt a drop of water on her forehead.

She blinked it away and opened her eyes to Tomm and Ren standing over her, mischievous grins on their faces.

"Come on!" Tomm cried. The brothers heaved her up, racing her down to the water to throw her in. She panicked, beating Tomm across the shoulders uselessly. She couldn't end up in the water, it would expose everything.

Kai's blind panic gave way to a spark of reason, and she acted quickly. She punched Tomm in the windpipe with a quick blow of her hand, trying to strike true despite the angle they were holding her. Luckily, it was enough, and Tomm doubled over in surprise, dropping her left side. Unsupported, she tumbled out of Ren's hands as well. She sprang to her feet, and with a mental apology, kneed Ren in the stomach. She raced up the bank, leaving the two of them spluttering and coughing.

"Wow, Kai," Tomm said when he finally caught his breath. "Can't you take a joke? What are you, a manga cat?" he asked, referring to the big felines that roamed the Tottori Desert that bordered their land.

"Looks like you two need to spend some more time in sparring lessons with Master Opu," she said, trying to turn the situation into a joke. They couldn't realize how deadly serious it was.

"What's this?" Her father chose that moment to reappear over the hillside. Her shoulders sagged as the tension left them. Playtime was over. She was safe. "You boys should know better than to try to take on my son, even two to one." He clapped her across the shoulders, giving her an inquisitive look. She nodded wearily.

Ren laughed. "He's right Tomm, we better adjust our plan of attack next time. We underestimated Kai."

"I bet you won't make that mistake again," she said, grinning.

The rest of the ride home was uneventful. Kai loved the peace of the open countryside, disturbed only by the soft creak and clank of tack and leather, the soft hoofbeats of the horses and gentle moos of the cattle. The land they rode through was yet untouched by the war. When she was out here, she could almost imagine it didn't exist.

As they neared their village, the reminders were obvious. Even the smallest towns were fortified, wooden and earthen walls and gates built to protect from an attack by Miinan soldiers and moonburners. Though if the moonburners really came, that wood and earth would do nothing to stop them. A few Kitan soldiers were stationed in each village, providing defense as well as intelligence back to King Ozora.

Her family's house was one of the few built outside the town wall. Officially, her parents had built the house beyond the walls in order to stay close to their livestock. Unofficially, they had wanted to be as far away from their neighbors as possible.

They rounded the cattle into the pens, and Aito, Tomm and Ren waved goodbye. She and her father watered the cattle and then saw to their horses, rubbing them down and filling their stalls with fresh hay and oats.

"Do Tomm and Ren suspect anything?" Raiden asked as they walked from the barn towards their small stout house.

"No. I handled it. They just think I'm strange." *They and everyone else in the village,* she thought. That was the price of keeping the entire town at arm's length.

"Be careful, my little fox. We are so close." It was her father's nickname for her when she was little, given to help a child understand and embrace the little-taught virtues of slyness and deception. They had made it a game for her. It didn't feel like a game anymore.

"I know we're close," Kai said. "But some days I don't think I can do this another six months."

"You are strong. You will. You must."

And there it was. She had never had a choice but to carry on.

They walked into the small wooden house and were greeted by the welcoming smell of a spicy stew on the fire. But when Kai saw who filled the room, she stopped in her tracks.

Raiden recovered more quickly.

"Prefect Youkai." He gave a respectful bow. "To what do we owe this honor?"

Prefect Youkai stood up from the kitchen table, his bloated stomach jostling the teacups set on top.

"I had a minor ailment and I was consulting your wife regarding a remedy. Her herbs and poultices always do the trick."

"Of course," Raiden said, eyeing his wife who was also standing at the table. "We are happy to assist."

Kita was divided into shoens, which were each ruled by a prefect appointed by King Ozora. Youkai, the prefect of their shoen, was a man of appetites. If he cared about the residents of Ushai at all, it was only for the tax revenue they represented. Today his massive girth was swathed in a colorful silk tunic embroidered with flowers, wrapped with a straining obi sash. His tiny dark eyes, set above a pencil-thin goatee drawn onto his quivering pale jowls, flicked to Kai's mother too frequently for comfort.

"Hanae," Youkai said, gathering the stoppered bottle she had given him. "I will try this. Thank you as always for your help." He nodded to Raiden and lumbered towards the door.

He paused at the doorway and turned.

"Raiden, be alert. I have received word of a raid on the next shoen by Queen Airi's moonburners. I think an attack here is unlikely, but we must be vigilant."

As soon as Prefect Youkai was gone, Kai's mother Hanae shuddered slightly and blew a few stray strands of hair off her forehead. Then she turned her attention to Raiden and swept him into an embrace.

Her parents' love for each other, after almost twenty years, was still embarrassingly intense. There were many nights Kai wished that their house was bigger, or at least had thicker walls.

"I don't like how he looks at you," Raiden said. "Or how often he comes to visit."

"I don't either," Hanae said, leaving Raiden's arms to check the stew. "But I am the village healer. I do not turn patients away."

"Even patients with fake ailments?" Kai chimed in. "His only ailment is being fat as a rhinoceros."

"Kai!" her parents chided her simultaneously.

"We must show him respect," Hanae said. "Even if he has not earned it."

After dinner, Kai and her parents sat by the warm light of the fire. Her father oiled a halter for one of the horses. While her mother ground herbs in a stone bowl, Kai studied her face in the firelight. It was no surprise that Prefect Youkai was interested in Hanae. She was strikingly beautiful despite years of hard work as a rancher's wife and the village's only healer. She had lustrous black hair, pulled into a bun at the nape of her neck, a few stray pieces loose around her temples. Her face, round and smooth like a doll's, was filled with perfect features: wide, striking light-gray eyes with long lashes, a small nose and a full button mouth.

The way her ears stuck out at the top seemed endearing, rather than awkward like Kai's. But more than that, her mother had a way with people. She treated each of her patients, from the poorest to the oldest, with kindness and humor, earning their trust and respect. The townsfolk worshipped her. Some days, Kai aspired to cultivate her mother's gentle strength, while others left her annoyed that she had a role model that she could never live up to.

Kai flipped through *The Rising Sun,* a children's fable about the formation of Kita that she had already read about a thousand times, before finally tossing it aside.

"Can we talk more about the plan?" Kai asked, breaking the silence.

"Not tonight," Hanae responded. "I have had a trying day."

"Please? I can't just sit here anymore. I need to do something, prepare, plan . . . something."

"We have been preparing you for this your whole life," Raiden said. "You are ready. You are strong. We just need to wait until you are eighteen. Then you will gain your full powers, and the moonburners will not be able to deny you."

"I know. But won't you tell me more about the moonburners? About Queen Airi? I need to know what to expect."

"Queen Airi is a calculating woman," Hanae said. "I do not relish entrusting you to her care. Her moonburners are only a weapon to her." Her mother pursed her lips. "But there is no other place for you. Now please, let us speak of this no more tonight."

CHAPTER 2

K ai awoke that morning from a hot, fitful sleep. She never slept well. It seemed that as soon as the sun set, her mind and body became energized and alive, like a taut bowstring itching for its arrow to fly. She opened the tight shutters over her window and sunlight streamed into the room.

The air in her room already felt heavy. It would be a hot day. The shutters were her mother's idea, designed to keep stray rays of moonlight from touching her, lest they awaken some hidden power she was unprepared for. In her seventeen years, her supposed powers had only ever once manifested, and at this point, she couldn't help but wonder if it was all a horrible misunderstanding.

If not for her hair. That was undeniable. She splashed water on her face and toweled it off, careful not to get her hair wet. A moonburner, a female sorceress who drew her magic from the light of the moon, developed her powers fully by age eighteen. Her magical maturity was marked by her hair turning entirely silver, a process that had already begun for Kai. Hanae carefully dyed Kai's short cropped hair dark brown once a week to cover the silver, but if her hair got wet in the meantime, the dye would wash out.

Sunburners, male sorcerers that drew their powers from the rays of the sun, were marked by the same distinct hair—except theirs turned the color of spun gold. And it wasn't illegal to be a sunburner in Kita. They were honored and revered, making up King Ozora's most elite fighting force. It would have been so much easier if she had been a boy.

She pulled on brown trousers and began the daily process of tightly binding her breasts so any trace of a feminine curve was gone. Not that there was a lot of curve to begin with. She pulled on a long white shirt and leather vest, followed by her leather work boots and broad-brimmed hat. Her costume as Kai, the cherished only son, was complete.

That day, they checked the cattle for illness and pests and branded the new calves. The day passed quickly as Kai and her father worked in companionable silence. As much as her situation grated at her, there was much she would miss about this life.

But there was no place for a moonburner in Kita. King Ozora had decreed years ago that all moonburners would be killed on sight. All female babies who were revealed by the Gleaming to be moonburners were left in the Tottori Desert to die; a gruesome sacrifice for Taiyo. No one ever said gods were civilized.

When her parents realized that she was a moonburner, they had pretended she was a boy to avoid performing the Gleaming in public. A king's ransom to the town surgeon had secured his silence in the matter, and even then, her parents breathed easier after he passed away a few years ago. They had somehow, miraculously, kept up the charade.

Kai and Raiden walked in from the outer pasture as dusk was falling. The last rays of the setting sun fell across the caramel-colored grass of the fields, seeming to set it on fire with its ruddy light.

The stillness was shattered by a piercing scream that sounded faint in the distance, soon followed by the sounds of broken glass and falling rubble. Kai and her father looked at each other in alarm and both started running towards the house.

"I'll get mother," Kai said, and her father nodded his assent. He split off from Kai, heading towards the closest gate to the village.

Kai flew through the front door.

"Something's going on in the village. It sounds like there could be injuries," Kai said, catching her breath. Hanae was already gathering her bag of instruments and herbs and Kai grabbed the knife and sheath her father had given her when she turned thirteen, tucking it into her belt.

They ran towards the village, one-tenth of a league from their house. Smoke was already rising from the buildings behind the stout wooden wall. Screams and explosions punctuated the scene. She could only imagine what was going on inside those walls.

"There are no attackers at the gate," Hanae said. "It must be someone from the inside."

"The inside? A rebellion? But who? Why?"

"I don't know. I don't understand," Hanae said breathlessly. "But the gate is closed."

"Maybe we can get in the Sun Door," Kai said, referring to the pedestrian entrance leading into the town market.

They veered to the left, flanking the high walls. Smoke was billowing higher now in the center of town, drifting over the side of the walls.

They reached the Sun Door and were almost bowled over by two women fleeing the burning town. Hanae grabbed the arm of one, who Kai recognized as the baker's wife. Her face was smeared with soot and her eyes were wild.

"What is going on?" Hanae asked, gripping the woman's arms as if willing her to shake off her daze through sheer force.

"Moonburners. Attack."

Hanae recoiled as if bitten by a snake. The women continued to flee and Hanae turned her iron grip to Kai.

"You cannot go in there. They might recognize you . . . what you are. You must run."

"I am not going to flee while you and father help save our village," Kai replied, square jaw set stubbornly. "I'm coming."

"Absolutely not. This is not up for discussion. There is no way I will—"

Hanae was cut off as a fireball hit the wall above their heads, the strength of the blast tossing them to the ground like discarded chaff. Kai tried to sit up and reeled to the side, a vision of the flames burned onto her retinas. A portion of the wall above them was alight and spreading fast. Her mother wasn't moving.

And then Kai saw the moonburner. She rode astride an enormous black bat, circling and flapping its membranous wings to stay aloft above the town. Kai had heard the legends, but had hardly believed they were real—moonburners or the giant bats. Did they breathe fire, too, like the stories said?

Kai's body felt strangely detached from her mind, as if she were floating outside of time, senses ringing and backfiring.

The woman sent fireball after fireball along the length of the village wall, systematically lighting it on fire, a grim smile on her face. Her long silver hair whipped in the wind and the heat; her eyes shone like comets blazing across the sky. She was beautiful and terrible.

The moonburner's gaze swept past Kai and returned, eyes narrowing as she no doubt realized that her prey had not been neatly dispatched. As the woman raised her arm to throw, Kai's mind slammed back into her protesting body, and she launched into action. She heaved her mother's unconscious body up into her arms and half stumbled, half threw them through the Sun Door. Fire exploded behind them, the intensity of the heat threatening to overwhelm her. But Kai managed to stay on her feet, gripping her mother's unconscious form over her shoulder.

Kai made her way into the center of the village, placing one heavy foot before the other. Her skin felt tight and painful, especially where the weight of her mother pressed her. People streamed past in panicked flight, oblivious to anything but their own survival.

Kai reached the first clearing in the market and nearly cried from relief when she saw her father. He was directing a team of men pulling buckets from the ornamental fountain, trying to make a small dent in the blazes that lit the sky around them.

"Father!" she cried, reaching his side and laying her mother down as gently as her aching muscles would allow.

They examined Hanae quickly together, reaching the same conclusion that she was unconscious, but alive and generally unharmed. She was already stirring.

Raiden drew Kai into a quick, fierce embrace. "Good job, my little fox," he said into her ear.

"How can I help?" Kai asked, wiping the back of her shirtsleeve across her forehead, no doubt leaving more grime than was there to start.

Before Raiden had time to respond, a woman stumbled out from a stone building to the left of the square, tripping and falling to the ground like a limp rag doll. The top floors of the building burned brightly, and debris was already beginning to fall. Kai ran to her side, kneeling down.

"Maiko!" Kai said, smoothing the tangled hair from her face. "Are you all right?"

"Sora is still inside," she sobbed. Maiko was Tomm and Ren's mother. Sora, their little brother, was eight. Sora with his brothers' same mischievous smile, Sora who loved chasing the calves in the field, sprinting after them until he fell to the ground, breathless and giggling. Kai's anger flared. How could someone do this to an innocent child?

"Where are Tomm and Ren?" she asked. "Are they inside?"

"No, they ran to help when the attack first came. I tried to get Sora, but his door was stuck, I couldn't get it open. Help him!" she pleaded.

"Kai!" She heard her father call. "You can't!"

But she had already plunged into the house.

The bottom floor of the house was smoky but not yet aflame. She used her knife to rip a patch off the bottom of her shirt and tied it over her nose and mouth. The smoke stung her eyes as she ran up the stairs, taking them two by two.

The air on the second level was almost suffocating. Flames licked the ceiling from the rooftop above. She passed two open doors, Ren's and Tomm's, she presumed. There. The closed door. Her eyes watered, blurring her vision. She tried the knob and screamed as her hand came away. The knob was red hot and angry. Blisters spread across her palm and fingers. She took a shuddering breath to steel her nerves and doubled over, coughing from the smoke.

She mentally shook herself. *Get this done or you will die in here,* she thought. She took a step back from the door and kicked with all her might. The door hardly budged, the impact reverberating through her entire body. She tried again. And again. The fourth time, the warped wood of the door frame gave and the door burst in. Sora lay on the floor curled in a ball, unconscious.

She lifted his still body; her burned hand screaming in protest. She turned to leave and was driven backward as a portion of the hallway roof gave way in a shower of embers and wood. The flames roared through the doorway, greedily making their way inside the room.

Kai looked back at the second story window, too tiny for her to fit through. The hallway was the only way. Tsuki be with me, she prayed silently to the moon goddess. She backed against the far wall and sprinted forward, leaping through the flames over the downed beams.

She had cleared it! Her elation died in a strangled scream as she felt flames continue to caress her body, up her shoulders and down her back. Her shirt had caught fire.

She pounded down the stairs and out the front door, straight for the fountain. She hurdled the low stone ledge and plunged into the shallow water with Sora still in her arms, collapsing sideways. Steam rose from her as she heaved Sora over the edge, lowering him to the ground gently. She had done it.

Kai dragged herself from the fountain, searching for Maiko in the crowd. The number in the square had grown. Even Prefect Youkai was helping quell the worst of the fires. She found Maiko, and it took her a moment to realize that Maiko's eyes did not register gratitude, but shock. Fear.

Confused, she searched for her parents. There they were; her mother had awoken. But the look on their faces . . . horror. She self-consciously wiped the soot from her face and her hand came away black. Not black from soot. Black from dye. Her dye was streaming down her, staining her shirt.

Oh no. Her shirt. It was nearly gone, charred and hanging in tatters. Her feminine form was unmistakable.

Prefect Youkai's eyes were large as saucers, his bovine face quivering with fear. He pointed a finger at her, accusing. "Moonburner."

CHAPTER 3

The cell was pitch black. The darkness swam in front of her, swirling into shapes that could only be her imagination. The cell was designed to hold a burner, so the lack of light was imperative. Never mind that she hardly qualified as a burner. She was probably the least dangerous burner prisoner that had ever inhabited this cell. She didn't even know how to use her powers.

With her eyes rendered useless, Kai's other senses heightened. She smelled the dusty floor and stale urine from a former inhabitant, felt the cool of the stone walls seeping the warmth from her. She strained to hear her parents; they had been taken to a holding cell as well. She didn't know if it was close by. She couldn't hear anything but the muffled sounds of King Ozora's soldiers guarding her door.

The door slammed open and Kai started awake, heart leaping into her chest. She must have fallen asleep. The light from the room beyond her cell illuminated the unmistakable bulk of Prefect Youkai, carefully positioned behind two soldiers whose yari spears were leveled at her.

The soldiers entered the room carefully, one pointing his blade while the other cuffed her in heavy iron manacles. Kai came compliantly, unsure what her strategy was. She needed to evaluate the situation. Escape seemed unlikely, but she would be damned if she just let them kill her.

The stairs from the cells opened into a corridor that led to the main room of the village hall. The early morning sunlight cast soft rays that seemed out of place, illuminating the harsh reality of the charred room. Blackened debris covered the floor; remnants of fine oriental rugs and elaborate carved wooden furniture littered the room, still smoking in places. One of the exterior walls leaned precariously inward.

"Admiring your handiwork?" Prefect Youkai asked.

"I did not cause this," she said, knowing it would do no good.

"We know you are complicit. All moonburners are evil."

Kai squinted as they walked into the main square in front of the village hall, shielding her eyes against the bright light. The square was filled with people, their whispers and muttering forming an angry buzz. Their clothes were covered in soot; dried blood and tear-stains marked the faces of many. The town had been devastated. The moonburner attack had been short but efficient, leveling many of the buildings. It would take years to rebuild.

"Go get the other traitors," Youkai said. The two guards disappeared back into the building.

The guards re-emerged with her parents in shackles. Raiden had been savagely beaten, his face purpling and swollen. Hanea looked unharmed, save for her wounds from the moonburner's earlier attack. She stood with a serenity that Kai could not muster herself.

"People of Ushai." Prefect Youkai held his hands up to quiet the crowd. "We are here today, in the wake of tragedy, to stand witness to the sentencing of three traitors who were living among us. Let this be a lesson to all of you to be vigilant and ever watchful against the plots of our enemies. Miina is not content to let us be. Queen Airi and her moonburners seek to destroy all of us!"

Prefect Youkai never missed an opportunity for fear-mongering.

"Wait," Kai said, voice hoarse. "Sentencing? Don't we even get a trial?"

Her parents both leaned forward and looked at her in silent censure.

What? She wanted to ask. It's not like she could make things worse.

"Yes, sentencing. King Ozora has decreed that all women who are born capable of moonburning will be put to death. There is nothing to consider. Do you deny you are a moonburner?"

She bit her lip. Her hair was a dead giveaway. No one would believe her now if she tried to deny what she was. "No, I do not deny it."

Angry whispers rippled through the crowd.

"But I am not a traitor. I have lived among you all my life. You are my friends, my neighbors. I had no part in this attack."

Youkai smiled cruelly as he saw his trap spring shut.

"You lied to us all your life! You have proven your word cannot be trusted."

Her shoulders slumped. He was right. She had no credibility here. At least she could plead for her parents.

"What of my parents? Don't they deserve a trial? Think of how many of you Hanae has saved. Norie, she found your son that rare herb when he was dying of cherry fever. It saved his life. And Ryota, my father has stayed up all night helping you deliver calves and foals who weren't going to make it. Don't punish them for my transgression."

Don't punish them for something that's not their fault, she thought. They didn't ask for a moonburner daughter. If they had never had me, they could have lived normal lives.

The harsh expressions on the faces of some of the village folk softened. She saw Maiko's face in the crowd. She didn't look angry anymore. But Prefect Youkai jumped in before Kai had a chance to garner too much sympathy.

"Hanae and Raiden have lied to us and deliberately disobeyed King Ozora's command. Perhaps some of you had a moonburner daughter, but did you hide her away? No. You complied with the law."

At this, a few heads nodded. None were spared the Gleaming, or the gruesome price to be paid if it revealed a daughter of the moon.

"The law is clear. By the power vested in me by King Ozora, I pronounce the following sentence."

Prefect Youkai paused and the crowd seemed to take in a collective breath. "The King has decreed that all moonburners shall be left in the Tottori Desert to die, as a sacrifice to our God Taiyo. Kai is sentenced to death in the desert."

Death by desert? It was one thing to leave a baby there to die, it wasn't truly aware of its predicament, and was no doubt picked off by predators before long. But to force a grown woman to slowly die of heat and dehydration? It seemed cruel, even by Kitan standards.

"For his crime of treason, I pronounce Raiden's sentence to be death by hanging."

"No!" Kai cried. "It's not his fault! I'm the moonburner . . ." Her pleas were cut off as one of the soldiers cracked his spear butt across the back of her legs. She fell to her knees and closed her eyes in disbelief.

"As for Hanae, a husband is the head of the house, and she had no authority to contradict her husband's treasonous words or deeds. Therefore, her punishment will not be death. She will become the property of King Ozora and serve Kita faithfully in bonded servitude. She will remain here to serve Ushai shoen. This is my decree."

Kai and her father's mouths dropped open in shock. Cold fury was written across her mother's face—her perfect doll's face a storm of anger. Prefect Youkai had played this one perfectly. Get rid of the husband and daughter and enslave the woman he had always desired. No doubt Hanae would be serving King Ozora as the personal slave of Youkai. Rage and hatred swept through Kai's body in a rush of heat. She had to live. She had to live to make him pay.

The blackness surrounded Kai once again, but this time she welcomed it. They had placed her back in her cell, utterly alone, any sliver of light blocked from view. She could finally let down her guard, drop the mask of strength and indifference that she had worn for Youkai and the crowd. Her fear and sorrow rushed over her in a tidal wave that threatened to sweep her away.

Kai laid on her side and cried wracking sobs, shoulders heaving, all dignity gone. Her tears mingled with the dust on the floor, muddying her face.

Her sentence was to be carried out at daybreak the next day. The village inhabitants had work to do, searching for the missing, burying the dead, making sure the survivors had food, water and shelter.

No time for an execution in that busy schedule, she thought to herself, as the last bit of grief drained from her. She felt empty. Hollow. The feeling came as a relief after the force of emotion that had been washing over her.

Kai pondered what her short future would hold. Ushai shoen bordered the Tottori Desert, a vast piece of desolate land that stretched for thousands of leagues. No one lived in the desert. No one survived it. As children, they had dared each other to walk into the shimmering expanse, taunting each other to see who could walk the farthest. The bravest among them only made it a few hundred feet; the oppressive heat and blinding emptiness of the desert played tricks on your mind.

At least she would leave this world a free woman, no longer hiding from the world what she was. That was something.

Hours passed. No one came. The guards didn't bring her food or water. Kai alternated between sitting against the cold stone wall and pacing the small cell. When her pacing through the darkness caused a stubbed toe and a smarting nose, she finally sat down again.

When the guards came for her, Kai was ready. She straightened her shoulders and held her head high as they shackled her and led her from the cell.

Her parents were shackled in the square outside the village hall and others had gathered to witness the spectacle. Kai's heart sank as she saw Tomm and Ren at the edge of the square. Tomm's face was black with anger. Ren looked pained.

Prefect Youkai addressed the crowd, reveling in the rapt attention.

"When we offer a moonburner sacrifice to Taiyo, we offer her as she came

into this world. No more." He approached her with a little smile on his face, a short blade in his hand. He grabbed what was left of her tattered shirt and began slicing her clothes off her.

She hissed as he pulled the shirt from her burned shoulders, taking some of her wounded skin with it. He cut her pants off next, until she was standing, naked, in front of the whole town. A flush rose up her body into her cheeks, and she blinked back hot tears. Her mother quietly sobbed while her father stood stone-faced, fists clenched by his sides.

"Walk," Youkai said, and a soldier prodded her forward with his spear. She began to walk, feeling the heat of the hard gravel under her feet. It was the better part of a league to reach the desert, apparently they meant for her to walk the whole way. She was nearing Ren now and she couldn't keep herself from looking at him, from silently pleading with him to meet her eyes, to understand that she hadn't wanted to lie to him, that in another life she might have loved him. His chocolate brown eyes met hers for a second before he looked away.

Tomm was not so delicate, spitting in her face as she passed by. She recoiled as his saliva flecked her cheeks. She shook her head and blew the hair and spit off her forehead as best she could. From that point, she only looked straight ahead.

Kai walked for what felt like hours before they reached the edge of the desert. The sun, watching unblinking from its high vantage point in the bright blue sky, told her that less than an hour had truly passed. Sweat dripped down her forehead, stinging her eyes. Her feet left a trail of bloody footprints from the rough terrain along the way. Her embarrassment over her nakedness had faded, overshadowed by the pain throbbing through the burns on her back in rapid tempo.

Prefect Youkai had ridden ahead on a sturdy tan Misa horse, as he was too fat to make the walk himself. He had ten mounted soldiers with him, armed with bows and arrows. He dismounted clumsily as she and her two escorts approached, a slow macabre parade.

"Moonburner," he sneered, taking in her naked form with a lecherous sweep. "This is where we say goodbye. I promise I will take good care of your mother."

An unexpected calmness settled over Kai. She looked him straight in the eyes and made him a promise, casting each word like a master smith pounding the dents out of a suit of armor. "Goodbye for now, Youkai. But I will see you again. And that day will be your last."

He shuffled back a step.

"These soldiers will be stationed at intervals across the Tottori border. If they get so much as a thought in their head that you might be trying to skirt the border and make your way out of the desert, they will put an arrow in your heart. If you make it that long, that is."

Well, there went her one plan. Kai began walking, but then paused, a surge of panic rising.

"Aren't you going to take my irons off?" She asked. She was as good as dead in the desert, but she was definitely dead if she was shackled.

"Maybe I will just forget that part," Youkai said, turning towards his horse and gathering its reins.

"You said it yourself. The sacrifice to Taiyo must be pure, as she came into this world. Do you risk his wrath by tainting your offering?" she said, praying he was superstitious enough for her entreaty to work. She held out her shackles to him.

Youkai's expression darkened.

"Unshackle her," he said to her escort and swung heavily back into his saddle.

The guard complied, and Kai rubbed her swollen wrists.

"Now walk."

CHAPTER 4

The hours sifted by like grains of sand. Or did they stand still? Kai wasn't sure. She was sure only of the oppressive heat and the agony of her body—agony that threatened to overwhelm her. The chorus of her pains sounded off in a round, her back, her hand, her feet, her sunburned skin. Sometimes they sang together, and in those moments, she stood and screamed.

She walked, but in which direction she wasn't sure. East, she figured, southeast if she was precise. Not that there was anywhere to get to. There was no final destination, no safe haven if she just made it far enough. There was only sand and death. So she walked, not because she had a destination, but because she was not quite ready to lay down and die.

She wasn't ready to be Taiyo's sacrifice. The shiftless sun god who had plagued her from birth. His war had lasted so long that it was all Kita knew anymore. It made up the sum of her country's identity. If he wanted her dead, he would have to work for it. So her mind turned to thoughts of survival.

Water was key, and she hadn't a clue of where to find it. She knew creatures lived in the desert. She had seen a thorny lizard scurry past, had caught sight of a crimson hawk soaring above. Life meant water. But maybe not soon enough for her. She would find it, or she would die.

Next, she needed shelter. The sun's rays beat down on her

relentlessly, and she had no protection. Her burns flared like fire when the sun hit them. Her luck turned a few hours into her trek when she found an outcropping of golden rocks that formed a rough-hewn wall. She settled down in its shade and nearly cried in relief. She had made it far enough.

Night fell, and the desert grew bitter cold. Kai wrapped herself in a ball and huddled at the base of the rock, grateful for the residual heat it radiated from the day. Her teeth chattered and she shook convulsively, making sleep impossible. How did such heat turn into such cold?

The only consolation was the stars, more than she had ever seen before, glistening pinpricks dotting a blanket of inky darkness. Her mouth hung open as she looked at them all.

When the moon rose, almost full, its presence illuminated the darkness of the desert. Kai should be almost at the height of her powers as a moonburner during the full moon, but she had never had anyone to teach her. Her mother seemed to know a lot about moonburner culture and teaching in theory, but professed to have no practical information about how a burner actually drew power. Plus, as Hanae would always lecture, it would be too dangerous. Kai thought wistfully about the night as a child when she snuck out of the house and ran into the fields, calling to Tsuki, to the moon, to the stars, to fill her with power. It only took Hanae dragging her back to the house and spanking her till she screamed to end that childish flight of fancy.

For the thousandth time, Kai wished she understood her powers. She had prayed to Tsuki so many times when she was a child, but had never received an answer. As she got older, it began to dawn on her that the goddess might just be cold and impersonal, content to ruin her life and leave it at that. Kai hadn't prayed in a long time.

I guess there is no harm in giving it one last try, she thought. Kai closed her eyes and bowed her head.

"Goddess Tsuki," she said, clearing her dry throat. "I come to you humble, as I came into this world." Goddesses want to be worshipped, right? She should throw in some of that. "Thank you for the wonderful gift you have given me, your power of the moon. But I do not know how to use it. Please . . ." Her voice cracked, sounding small in the emptiness. "Please, help me, so I can live."

She opened her eyes and started, catching sight of a white blur in the distance. Kai sat very still, straining her eyes in the darkness.

There it was again! Her heart hammered in her throat. What could it be? She catalogued the list of animals that lived in the desert that could kill her. Manga cats, sand dragons, and scorpion birds. Those were all supposed to be old wives' tales, told at night to scare the Ushai children into behaving. But, there was usually a grain of truth in stories, right?

She slowly picked up a rock from the ground next to her, its rough edge digging into her fingers as she gripped it tightly. Whatever it was, she wouldn't go down without a fight.

☾

Kai awoke with a start, brushing the gritty sand from her face and eyes. The rock had fallen from her hand in the night as she had eventually fallen asleep. She hadn't seen the blur of white again.

She stood slowly, leaning on the rock for support. A stiff back and neck had been added to her list of pains, but they were the mildest of the group. She lifted one of her feet gingerly to examine the damage from the prior day's trek and put it back down quickly. The sole of her foot was coated in packed sand and blood, her skin sliced beyond repair. Best not to think about that right now.

Part of her wanted to just sit by her rock shelter, and rest, and die. But she had to at least try to find water. Kai looked around, trying to get her bearings. The desert was deceiving, heat waves already rising off the hot sand. She knew the sun rose in the east, and so she set off, slowly, in the direction of Taiyo's rising.

After a few hours, Kai reached a stand of three scraggly dead trees. Trees meant there had once been water. She dug and dug at their base, hoping to find something that she could live on. Her hopes sunk as she found only more sand.

She stood, and broke off a narrow white limb of one of the trees. It would be a good walking stick, or weapon, if she needed to defend herself.

As she walked, Kai thought about her prayer the night before. Tsuki hadn't appeared to answer her. She wondered about the Gleaming. The powers of moonburners who were only a few hours old automatically reacted to save them when they were close to death. Was the same true of adult moonburners? Did she just have to get closer to death, and her powers would kick in to save her? Or were adult moonburners supposed to have learned to use their powers by now, so no more automatic reflexes would save them? She guessed she would find out soon enough.

Kai was shaken from her thoughts by a flash of white along the ground in the distance. She stopped and stood still, scanning the horizon where she had seen it. She shook her head. Nothing. Was she imagining things? How long did it take to go mad here?

Her slow walk continued, and the shadows of the day lengthened. Her thirst was becoming unbearable, her tongue huge and swollen in her mouth. Her tender skin blazed red from the constant sun and the burns on her back wept angrily.

Her thoughts flicked between her parents, marrying Ren and living a normal life, and killing Prefect Youkai. And then they fell silent, dulled by the fiery explosion of pain as she sank one foot after another into the hot sand.

Kai thought wistfully of her rock home from last night as the last rays of sunshine slipped over the horizon. A wind blew through the twilight, whipping fine sand against her body.

She closed her eyes to the grit and sunk to her knees where she stood. No further tonight. She dug a small indentation into the sand to shield her from the wind and curled into it, slipping into unconsciousness.

She woke when the moon was at its height. She laid very still, listening. She heard movement—the slippery sound of sand shifting down the side of a dune.

Footsteps. Sniffing. An animal. She saw her stick close by and reached for it slowly. The animal was coming closer. Her heart hammered in her throat.

Kai leaped up, brandishing her stick with a shout. She promptly staggered to her knees again as her head rushed with blood and pain. She was so weak and thirsty. She could hardly stand, let alone fight. She looked up wearily at whatever had come to eat her.

Two black eyes like marbles stared back at her from a silver face topped with pricked ears. It was a fox! It was as large as a medium-sized dog; much bigger than any fox she had ever seen. It was covered in pure silvery-white fur, the kind of fur that called out to be touched. Somehow she didn't think the fox would appreciate that.

"Well, the battle cry was impressive, but I don't know what you thought you were going to do with that stick."

Kai slouched back on her heels, dumbfounded. She had gone mad. They said the desert could do it, and here was the proof. A talking silver fox. She started to laugh, first just a bubble, and then she broke into peals of laughter that sent tears streaming down her face. Her laughter subsided into a fit of coughing as her dry throat reminded her she hadn't had anything to drink for two days.

The fox laid its ears back on its head and sat on its haunches. "That was rude."

"I'm sorry, Master Fox," she said, clearing her throat. "I've just never spoken to a hallucination before."

"I most certainly am not a hallucination. I am here to help you." She paused, mouth open, about to speak.

Wait. What?

"I'm your seishen."

CHAPTER 5

Kai didn't dare hope that he was real.

"My seishen? My spirit guide?" She had heard of them. Legends told of animal companions that accompanied the most powerful sun and moonburners through life. It was supposed to be a true sign of honor from the gods to be gifted with such a partner. They were said to be very mysterious and very powerful.

"Yes, your seishen."

"No offense, but how do I know you are not a figment of my imagination, or a dream?" Kai slowly inched her way towards him. She wanted to touch that fur.

"I am as real as you are." "Prove it."

He chuffed and blew out his cheeks in an adorable gesture that she interpreted as annoyance, but he approached her grubby outstretched hand and sat before her. Shaking, she drew her hand down the shiny fur of his back. He was warm and real. His fur was softer than the finest silk she had ever touched. She sprang forward and pulled him into a tight embrace, her arms locked around him tightly, her face buried in his soft fur. She rocked him back and forth.

"Kai . . ." a strangled voice came from beneath her chin. "Air . . ."

She released him and sat him down gently before her, embarrassed. His fur was askew in wild angles and she suppressed a laugh. "Thank you for coming."

He shook himself and leveled an inscrutable gaze at her. "My name is Quitsu."

Quitsu curled up in her arms in her little sand shelter to help her fall asleep. He had told her not to get used to it, but he would allow it tonight for survival purposes.

Kai had already begun to suspect that Quitsu's bark was worse than his bite. He radiated heat into her like the cheerful embers of a once-roaring fire and she soaked in the first measure of comfort she had felt in two days and two nights. She fell asleep quickly.

The morning sun rose blazing and undeniable.

Quitsu took one look at her and announced: "Water. We need water." Her lips were parched and cracking and her thoughts felt like they were swimming through thick sludge to reach her. She nodded to Quitsu and stood, leaning on her stick.

"Lead the way."

He trotted off in front of her. She focused her vision on his white form and focused her will on putting one foot in front of the other.

Quitsu was a gentle guide despite his gruffness. He frequently looped back to check on her and let her rest when she needed it. She didn't dare rest for too long, though, as she didn't know if she could get up again.

A few hours passed and the sun was almost at its zenith. They reached a place where the rolling sand dunes gave way to a flat, cracked expanse of hard-packed sand.

"This used to be a lake," Quitsu said, "before Taiyo grew so powerful."

"The desert is here because Taiyo is too strong?" Kai asked, her thoughts fuzzy.

"In a sense. The war has upset the balance of this land in many ways. The desert is but one example. The seishen are closely tied to the land, and we are sensitive to such disturbances."

Kai pondered what he said, turning the new information around in her head like a puzzle. She had always imagined Tsuki and Taiyo to be fictional, even though the powers of the sun and moonburners demonstrated otherwise. It was too hard to imagine there were real gods warring over their land.

She looked at Quitsu, her answered prayer made manifest. She'd better start believing.

Quitsu stopped suddenly and sniffed at a spot on the ground that looked indistinguishable from the expanse around it. He started digging and liquid began to fill the hole. Kai clapped her hands to her face and fell on her knees beside the precious water.

"Quitsu, you're a miracle!"

He sat back with his chest puffed out, daintily licking the mud from his paws.

She drank the gritty water greedily. Nothing had ever tasted so pure.

"Slowly," Quitsu cautioned. "Don't make yourself sick."

She alternated between drinking and sitting back, letting the liquid soak back into her body. When her belly was distended with water, they set off again.

Kai looked back longingly at the water glistening in the small hole in the dirt. Quitsu hadn't let her drink as much as she had wanted, assuring her that there would be more waterholes.

At first, Kai had felt reverence towards Quitsu, and held her tongue respectfully around him. That slowly wore off as they walked through the desert, and she began peppering him with questions.

"Where are we going?"

"A moonburner camp in the Little Tottori oasis."

"What is a seishen?"

"Every burner is deeply connected to the earth. Only through that grounding do you have the force to draw power from celestial bodies like the sun or moon. Seishen are the embodiment of that spiritual connection. Only strong burners have seishen because only those burners have a connection strong enough to take corporeal form."

"Where are you from?"

"The Misty Forest at the foot of the Akashi Mountains, in Kita."

"How do you know where the water is?"

"Spiritual connection to the earth, remember?"

"Have you been seishen to a moonburner before?"

"No," Quitsu said, pausing and lowering his voice. "I am connected to you, a part of you. When you die, I die."

Oh. She was touched. Quitsu had bound his life to hers.

"Well, I guess we better keep me alive then, eh?" she said with a grin.

Quitsu chuffed in mock annoyance, but rubbed his length along her leg before he trotted off ahead.

He returned bearing something in his mouth. He dropped it at her feet with a distasteful sound. She picked it up, cradling the small furry body of a desert dog, a little rodent that burrowed in the sand.

Kai looked around. There was no wood to make a fire. Her stomach growled and she fell upon it, tearing raw chunks of meat from the little body. The sensation of fur and blood in her mouth was vaguely unpleasant, but her body's overwhelming desire for nutrients overshadowed it. She had ravaged half the body when she looked at Quitsu.

"Do you need to eat?" she asked, offering him the bloody carcass.

"No, thank the goddess," Quitsu said. "I draw my strength from the moon and from you."

Kai considered this. "Like a parasite?" Quitsu's hackles rose.

"Like a parasite that's saving your hide!" He turned his tail to her and trotted off into the distance.

"Like a symbiotic parasite!" She called after him. She smiled, and turned her attention to finishing her disgustingly wonderful meal.

He'd be back. He had to keep her alive, he had said so himself.

The following day they set off, continuing east towards the Little Tottori oasis. He said they would be there by nightfall. With water and food in her belly, Kai felt more like her old self. She could feel her feet throbbing and hot, and suspected there was infection brewing. She would need medical care soon.

As they walked, Quitsu began a peculiar dance, moving from his usual spot trotting in front of her, to circling behind her, and returning. After the third time, Kai finally spoke up.

"What are you doing back there?"

Quitsu paced next to her, and spoke quietly. "I don't want to alarm you, but it appears we are being stalked by a manga cat. It has been following us for the last hour."

"A manga cat?" Kai asked, her voice shooting up an octave. "Are you sure?"

"Very sure."

"Can you do anything? Magical?"

Quitsu shook his head. "My powers, like yours, are strongest at night. I can act as a conduit to strengthen your power, but only when we can pull from the power of the moon, and only if you actually knew how to use your powers. Right now, we are as helpless as a normal human and a normal fox."

"Great," Kai grumbled. "We'll have to try to make it to the oasis. Maybe it is just curious, and won't attack."

"Maybe," Quitsu said, in a tone that implied that he didn't believe that at all.

They hurried towards the oasis as fast as they could with Kai's condition. Quitsu circled back several times to check on the cat's location.

"It's gone," he said, with breath of relief.

Kai thanked the moon goddess and felt the tension leave her. They would make it.

"Can we rest for a moment?" Kai asked, as they approached a small rocky outcropping. Her wounds were throbbing, and her sides heaved from the effort of their pace. She was feeling weak again.

"Just for a moment," Quitsu assented. "The cat could return."

Kai stepped into the shade of the rocks and was greeted by a inhuman snarl. A massive shadow leaped at her, its bulk throwing her backwards and flattening her to the ground, pushing the breath from her. Instinct had caused her to throw up her stick in front of her, and now massive jaws gnashed around the stick, seeking freedom.

The manga cat was larger than she was, spotted with the light tan and gold of the desert. Its yellow eyes, intent on its next meal, unnerved her.

Kai tried to roll to the side to heave the cat off her, but it was too heavy. Its claws dug into one of her shoulders and her breastbone and she screamed in agony. So this was how she would end. What little strength she had was leaving her, as her weak body gave out.

Quitsu threw himself on the cat's neck, a furious white demon tearing at its ears and eyes with his claws and teeth. The cat snarled and reared back, trying to knock the interloper off with its massive paws. She rolled to the side, out from under the cat, blood streaming down her front. The cat whipped its head to the side and Quitsu shot off its back, cracking into the nearby rock and crumpling to the ground.

"Quitsu!" she screamed. Rage and sorrow filled her and she ran at the cat, giving all she had to one last desperate blow. The cat leaped at her and she fell to her knees under it, forcing her stick upwards into its soft underbelly with all her force.

The cat screamed and tumbled over her, wrenching her stick from her grasp. She darted into the arc of its flailing paws and wrenched the stick out of its stomach before backing away. The cat lay on its side, blood running from its wound. It began to struggle to its feet. She aimed and shoved her stick into the cat's throat. It started, twitched, and finally lay still.

Kai closed her eyes and panted, her pain threatening to overwhelm her. She staggered over to Quitsu and felt his soft furry body. His eyes were closed, but he was alive. His breathing was shallow and fast.

"Quitsu. Don't die. Please."

She scooped his body into her arms, her blood dripping into his silvery fur. He was so heavy, but she would make it to the oasis. She had to.

She turned east and started walking.

INTERLUDE

Pura stood at the edge of the oasis, looking into the desert. The bright light of the falling sun had turned the high clouds into a rainbow of oranges, pinks, and reds. Some moonburners hated landing duty in the Little Tottori oasis. It was in the middle of nowhere, far from the action, too close to Taiyo's domain for comfort. Pura liked it. She liked the peace and the solitude. For a few days, she could forget the war.

She gazed into the sky, at a few early stars winking into existence. It would be a full moon tonight. The moon felt so big here in the desert sky, it was like Tsuki was right beside you.

Her gaze fell back to the desert before her, scanning for signs of threat. The oasis had never been attacked by sunburners, but one could never be too careful.

She paused. Was that . . . movement? She unsheathed her two swords, one short, one long. Yes, definitely. Something was coming towards her. She squinted into the setting sun, straining to make out what it was from the silhouette.

"Who goes there?" she called loudly. "Announce yourself." No answer.

She repeated herself, but her command was again met by silence.

Pura began walking slowly towards it, swords at the ready. As she grew nearer, the form took shape. A person on foot! The figure was moving slowly, staggering. As the interloper came into view, Pura stared in disbelief.

It was a girl with short cropped silver hair. She was naked but for the sand and blood that coated her. She looked near death. Cradled in her arms was a bloody animal, its silver fur unmistakable. A seishen.

"Help us," the girl croaked, and then collapsed.

BOOK TWO

CHAPTER 6

K ai blinked, her eyelids gritty and heavy. Above her stretched a tan sky.

Tan?

She craned her neck to get a better view of her surroundings and instantly regretted it. Her head exploded with pain, and her chest felt as if it was being stabbed with hot pokers.

"Stay still," a feminine voice said.

She felt a touch on her shoulder and turned her head slightly, opening her eyes. A face swam into view. The woman's silver hair was tied in a fishtail braid down over one shoulder, the end wrapped in black leather. Her skin was tanned but delicate, her face framing big brown eyes and long black lashes. It was a pretty face, one that showed warmth and concern. Kai felt like she hadn't seen the sentiment in ages.

"Water," Kai croaked, and the woman complied, dribbling the cool liquid onto Kai's lips.

She drank greedily, and the woman slowed her.

"Take it easy. You've been through an incredible ordeal. The goddess must have her eye on you, because you shouldn't be alive."

It all came flooding back to her. Prefect Youkai. The desert. Quitsu. The manga cat.

"Quitsu!" she cried, struggling again to sit up. "Is he alive? Where is he?"

The woman pushed her back down, overpowering her easily. "Calm down, he's alive. He's in the other room with another seishen. You need to regain your strength, so he can."

Kai flopped back down, relief mingling with the pounding pain in her head and shoulder.

"I feared he was dead," she said faintly.

The woman smiled. "You saved him. You should be proud. Now rest."

Kai opened her mouth to ask the woman her name, but was asleep before she could form the words.

The next time Kai awoke, she felt more like herself. Her caretaker was by her side. Her name was Pura, and she was the first moonburner Kai had met who hadn't tried to kill her. Pura had been standing watch and had carried both Kai and Quitsu in from the desert when she had collapsed.

Pura was tall, lithe and strong, with an easy laugh. She wore navy blue leggings and a navy high-necked tunic piped with silver thread and wrapped with a silver obi.

"It's the master moonburner uniform," Pura explained. "You will wear it once you pass all your tests and become a master. You'll kill to wear a dress after a few years in this, trust me."

"I've never worn a dress," Kai said, "so I doubt that."

Pura looked at her with a quizzical eye, but didn't ask.

Pura helped Kai bathe and dress, and then wrapped her arm under Kai's as they walked out of the tent into the hot sun of the oasis. Kai raised a hand to shield her eyes from the light as she took it all in. There were perhaps a half dozen master moonburners in navy and silver bustling about the green palms and foliage. There were two smaller tents and one big tent that Kai assumed was for eating and gathering. Kai started when she saw a giant bat resting in the shade of a palm tree.

"I never thought there could be a settlement all the way out here," Kai said. "Does King Ozora know about this?"

The desert, as the realm of the sun god Taiyo, was traditionally thought of as King Ozora's territory, although technically, it was politically neutral ground.

Pura chuckled. "No. Typical man, so prideful he doesn't see what goes on under his nose. We originally stationed moonburners here to rescue the Kitan babies that were left in the desert to die. About ten years ago, though, we started using it as a forward base, as well."

"You save the babies?" Kai asked, hope welling in her. The deaths of those children had always weighed on her. She didn't know why she had been fit to live when they had to die.

"Some of them. Nice of him to deliver them to us special, isn't it?" she said, with a wicked grin. "Goddess Tsuki's oracle tells us each time a new moonburner's power is invoked through the Gleaming. We know to perform a sweep for a child along the Kitan border within 24 hours. You, though, my dear, no one saw coming."

"Yes. I was a bit of a special case," Kai admitted. As she spoke, a silver blur leaped at her.

"Quitsu!" she cried, digging her fingers into his silver fur. He burrowed his face into her neck, cold nose stark against the heat of the desert. "Thank the goddess you're alive."

"Careful now!" Pura grinned. "Your mistress is still recovering. As are you," she scolded, and then caught herself, nodding her head to Quitsu.

Quitsu jumped to the ground, donning his usual reserved form. His tail continued to wag like a barn dog, ruining the look.

"Are you feeling up to walking a little further?" Pura asked Kai. "The Eclipse is here, and she wants to see you."

The brightly lit tent was littered with paper and weapons. The desert floor was covered by a thin woven rug colored with a faded ikat pattern of red, yellow and orange. A simple bambu wood desk nestled against the back wall, with mismatched chairs and cushions lining the edges of the tent. Practically every flat surface was covered with piles of tan paper or scrolls, with arrows or daggers being used as paperweights. Spears and longbows leaned against the wooden supports of the tent, and a wicked looking double-bladed masakari axe lay across the desk. A silvery bowl of water stood on a stand in one corner. A huge statue of a silver eagle sat on top of the tent's lone bookshelf, styled with its head tucked under its wing.

Odd.

A woman sat at the desk muttering, her back to them. Or at least Kai thought she must be a woman. She wore the navy blue uniform of the moonburners, but her arms were as heavily muscled as any farmhand's. She had close-cropped silver hair styled into a hawk's tail down to her collar, with a few thin braids hanging from behind her right ear over her shoulder.

The woman stood and spun around, her fluid movement lightning-quick. She had startling wide-set gray eyes covered in round spectacles, a unobtrusive nose and a thin set, serious mouth. Kai hurried into a respectful bow a beat too late, as Pura cleared her throat next to her.

"So." The woman removed her spectacles and put them on the table, picking up a silver dagger. She stepped close to Kai, so they would have been almost nose to nose, if Kai wasn't half a head shorter. She felt about as tall as the woman's shin.

"This is the moonburner who emerged from the desert two days ago. No name, no people, no story. Some are whispering that you are an operative of King Ozora, sent to spy on us before he attacks our little waystation. What do you say of that?" She peered into Kai's hazel eyes, as if she could pull the truth from them by force.

Kai swallowed. This was not the welcome she was expecting. "I am not a spy. I almost died out there. And I have a name. It's Kai."

"But isn't that exactly what a spy would say? How do I know you are not working for King Ozora?"

Kai's temper flared. All her life she had held out hope that these moonburners would take her in, and this was the reception they gave new recruits?

"I hate King Ozora," Kai exploded. "He is a tyrant and a coward. Because of his decree, I was forced to live my life in secret. His prefect killed my father and took my mother for a slave. He stripped me and left me to die in the desert. The only reason I'm alive today is because of Quitsu!" Her voice rose to a frantic pitch. She felt a comforting pressure against her shin and looked down at Quitsu. She steadied herself. "And why exactly would a sunburner spy have a seishen companion? I'm a little new to this moonburning thing, but I'm pretty sure the goddess doesn't send seishen out to just anyone."

Pura's mouth had fallen open and her eyes were wide.

The other woman, however, broke into a grin. She put her knife down on the desk. "I thought you must have a little backbone in you to survive the desert. I'm glad to see I am not mistaken." She crossed her arms in front of her, studying Kai. "And you're right. Seishen only bond with the most powerful and honored moonburners. Isn't that right, Iska?"

Kai jumped as a sharp caw answered from the back corner of the room. She whirled around and saw the eagle statue untuck its head and gaze at her with intelligent black eyes. It was a seishen. She hadn't even recognized it.

The woman seemed to share a moment with the eagle, before turning her attention back to Kai.

"Quitsu's presence, his very existence, vouches for you, as you cannot for yourself. He has told Iska what you two have been through in your short time together. The bond between you and he is strong indeed."

The woman continued. "I believe that the goddess has important plans for you. And it is my job to ready you for them. My name is Nanase, and I am the headmistress of the Lunar Citadel. Welcome to the moonburners, Kai."

CHAPTER 7

And so it was arranged that Kai and Quitsu would travel to Kyuden, the capital city of Miina, in two days' time. Pura, her unofficial nurse, had declared that Kai would be ready to fly by then.

"Fly?" Kai gulped. "How, exactly are we getting to Kyuden?" "You'll see," Pura said with a devilish grin.

As the sun set on their last day, Pura gave Kai fresh underclothes and a navy uniform trimmed in silver.

"When we get to the citadel, you will have to wear novice grays, but for now, this is all there is."

Pura left her alone to change. Kai fingered the fabric and the delicate silver threading with mixed emotions. Kai pulled on the uniform, stomach flipping nervously. She was actually doing this. Starting her new life. Kai caught her reflection in the silver tray used to hold medical implements on the side table and saw that the dye in her hair had washed out. Her hair was entirely silver. The uniform fit her well, tighter than any clothes she had worn since she was young. She tugged at it.

"How do I look?" Kai asked Quitsu, who sat on the cot in the medical tent.

"Good," he said softly. "Like the master moonburner you will be."

"I wish . . ." she started, the words stalling in her throat. She sat down on the cot besides Quitsu. "I wish we had all made it to Miina, how we planned. I was supposed to join the citadel with my parents safely settled somewhere nearby. Everything went so wrong."

"It's not your fault," Quitsu said.

"Isn't it? If I had listened to my mother and not gone inside the village . . . or listened to my father and not gone into the building after Sora, none of this would have happened."

"You can't blame yourself for doing what you thought was right at the time. You saved that little boy. You couldn't have known what would happen."

"That it would cost my parents their lives?" Kai said softly.

"You don't know that either. You are supposed to be dead, yet here you are. If what you have told me is true, your parents are smart and resourceful. Maybe they will find a way to escape."

Hope blossomed in Kai's chest, lightening the guilt that had been pressing upon her. She *had* survived the desert. Maybe her parents could find a way out of their predicament.

"I hope you're right," Kai said.

She swooped Quitsu up in her arms, too quickly for him. Her displays of affection seemed to mortify him, which only made her enjoy them more. "The best part of being a moonburner so far is you," she said jokingly, but grew serious. She placed him back down on the cot. "I wouldn't be alive if it wasn't for you," she said. "But it's more than that. I could never really have friends . . . when I was young. I had to keep everyone at arm's length. I don't have to do that with you. You're my first real friend."

Quitsu blinked his black-beaded eyes twice. "That is just about the most depressing thing I have ever heard," he said. "I never would have agreed to be your seishen if I knew you didn't have any friends."

He jumped past her to the ground, whacking her in the face with his tail on the way down.

"Hey!" she said, laughing. "I was opening up, and that's all the thanks I get?" She grabbed a handful of sand and threw it at his retreating form. She ducked out of the tent to follow him.

They walked out to the landing ground, where two huge bats dozed in the shade of a stand of acacia trees.

"They are koumori," Pura said, "Not bats. Although they share a lot of attributes with their smaller brethren."

"How did you . . . tame them?" Kai marveled.

"Moonburners have a close connection with the moon and all creatures of the night. I think they recognize that we both serve the goddess, and they assist us. But they are not our slaves, nor our pets. We must respect them."

"I have plenty of respect for them," Kai said, eying her mount nervously.

Pura explained the basics of the koumori anatomy and the flying harness that fit on her koumori's back under its wingbones. She taught Kai the basic commands she would need to control her koumori, a female named Peppe. "The main word you need to know is 'Appu.' It tells her to go."

"And how do I tell her to go down?" Kai asked with a shaky laugh.

"Da," Pura said, clapping her hand on Kai's shoulder. "But don't worry. Peppe will take good care of you."

Kai nodded.

"We've rigged up a smaller harness for Quitsu. He will be in front of you, so you can see how he is doing," Pura said.

Quitsu hissed and backed away.

Kai rolled her eyes, though she didn't blame him for his reaction. "It's this or walking, Quitsu. Up to you."

Kai gripped the harness with white knuckles as Peppe climbed off the desert floor. Her powerful wingbeats threatened to unseat Kai. Quitsu moaned quietly in front of her, strapped spreadeagled between Peppe's wings. It wasn't a dignified means of travel befitting a seishen, Kai had to admit.

As they reached elevation, Peppe leveled off, soaring after Pura and her koumori. Kai let out the breath she had been holding and peeked over a black wing. The sun was just slipping over the horizon, its long rays illuminating the golden desert. The moonburner camp was already disappearing in the mirage of the desert.

She gradually relaxed and felt her spirits soar. She was flying!

A line of green appeared on the horizon as they approached the edge of the desert. If Kai remembered her geography lessons, they were coming out into the Churitsu Plain, neutral territory between Miina and Kita. Despite being a fertile valley bounded by beautiful hills, no settlers lived there, due to the constant skirmishes between forces in the area.

As Kai's utter terror diminished, her wonder grew. The last glowing light of the sun illuminated bits of the landscape in a magical glow. Kai could see the contours of the foothills and the white-peaked crags of the Akashi mountains in the distance. She had never left Ushai province before; their yearly cattle drives had been the extent of her adventures. Now, it seemed as if the whole world opened up before her.

"Quitsu, can you see the Misty Forest from here? That is where you are from, right?"

Quitsu was flattened to Peppe, his claws digging into her tough black hide. "Foxes were not made to fly, not even seishen foxes," came his response.

She laughed as she saw that his eyes were glued shut.

Kai grabbed tightly to the harness handles as Peppe banked to the right, following Pura. Rough leather reins hooked into a tight-fitting collar around Peppe's neck, but Kai needed something more secure. The moon was rising and she could just see Pura and her koumori ahead of them. The cool crisp air felt heavenly after the heat of the desert. They were traveling northeast, towards the capital city of Kyuden.

She thought she could make out the lights of the city winking into existence in front of her. The silvery serpent of a river wound below her towards the inviting glow.

A flicker of movement behind her flashed in the corner of her eye. Kai turned her head, peering into the twilight.

She saw it again. A shadow passing through the twilight, a shimmer of something.

"Pura," she hollered into the darkness. "I see something."

A second later, a fury of feathers and claws bashed into her like a sledgehammer and she went tumbling into the night sky.

The sensation of falling was very much like flying. The wind rushed by her and the landscape below stood out in stark relief in the moonlight. It seemed a funny time to die, when she had just survived so much.

Kai struggled and twisted in the air, reaching out for something to cling to. Her mind grasped too—reaching for a lifeline it somehow knew was there. Just . . . there . . .

She felt a warmth growing in her, flooding her mind with awareness and lucidity. It was as if time slowed down, her mind sharpened to a knife point.

Live! She thought. *Do something!* The warmth grew. It was getting hotter. Uncomfortably hot. It kept growing until she felt like she was on fire from the inside. She had to release it!

And then, as if her silent, panicked thought was manifested, a power of radiant silver light burst out of her. A great gust of wind wrapped around Kai's body, then another, until she was caught in a whirling funnel of currents, slowing her descent, bearing her away. Was it one of Tsuki's miracles?

Kai's thought was cut off as the tornado abruptly ceased and she fell into the silvery wetness of the river. She hit the surface like a ton of bricks, her whole body stunned from the shock of the force and the cold of the water. The moment passed, and she began to move, sluggishly at first, and then with more force, kicking towards the surface.

She gasped for air as she broke the surface of the water and looked around, trying to get her bearings. Luckily, the current of the river was not strong; it did not impede her as she swam towards the nearest bank.

She collapsed on the ground with a cough, laying on her back, panting. What had happened? Had she been attacked? And where was Quitsu? And Pura? She scanned the sky for signs of the koumori. There! A wingspan!

"Pura," she cried, waving her arms. Too late, she realized that the wings were flapping like a bird's, not outstretched and soaring like a bat's. She looked around for cover and stumbled to her feet, heading towards a copse of trees. Something snared her legs, tripping her and bringing her to the ground. Wind from the backbeats of a huge bird's wings stirred up the dust around her and she closed her eyes to the grit.

Kai fumbled with the cords of the snare around her legs as the rider of the giant bird dismounted and approached. She grasped for a weapon and came up empty. Why didn't she have a knife? She always had her knife. Stupid fat Youkai, not even leaving her with a weapon.

In an instant, he was upon her. The rider's boot connected with her chin and she was thrown back onto the ground, dazed. He followed it up with a sharp kick to her ribs. She doubled over in pain, spitting blood onto the dark ground. The rider grabbed her hands and tied them roughly behind her back before throwing her to the ground once again. She couldn't even gather her wits to fight back. What was going on? Who was this man?

He knelt next to her and grabbed her by her hair, wrenching her head back painfully. He poured a vial of a bitter-tasting liquid in her mouth, which she coughed down involuntarily.

She could just make out his features, light close-cropped hair, heavy brows, a crooked nose that had seen one too many fights. His mouth was twisted in a snarl.

"Tell me where the facility is! Where is your whore queen keeping our brothers?"

Kai shook her head in silent denial, not understanding his questions.

"I . . . I . . ." she managed, head still spinning from her fall into the river and his blows. "I don't know what you are talking about."

"Liar," he exploded, landing a punch across the right side of her face, knocking her back to the ground. She couldn't even protect herself with her hands tied behind her. She braced herself for another blow.

"That's enough, Daarco," a calm voice said. Her assailant obeyed, standing up and stepping back.

A second man knelt down next to her and helped her to a seated position. Blood stung her eye from a cut on her forehead.

"I'm sorry about my friend. He is very . . . zealous about our mission." He pulled out a white handkerchief and dabbed it at her cut. She hissed from the pain and pulled away. He stopped his ministrations, putting his handkerchief down.

"Did you poison me?" she asked. The drink the other man gave her still burned her palate.

"No, just some lusteric to keep you from burning," the man said, "while we ask you some questions."

He continued, "I think you have probably deduced that we do not belong here," he began. "We are not here to harm you. We are looking for our friends. They have been taken and are being held by the citadel. We have heard some very . . . disturbing stories of how Queen Airi is treating her prisoners of war. We have heard they are being kept in a facility in this area. We only seek to find our fellow soldiers and bring them home."

He paused, gauging her reaction. Kai considered him in return. In the moonlight, she could see that he was tall and well-built. He had a handsome face with a strong jaw, a dimpled chin and gentle almond-shaped eyes. He had a well-educated manner and was clearly in a position of command over the other man. He had light hair pulled back into a short ponytail, in the fashion of the Kitan court. No doubt in the sunshine his hair would glow golden.

Merciful Tsuki, they were sunburners. She was as good as dead, despite his kind manner. She might as well tell him the truth.

"I am not a master moonburner yet. I was on my way to Kyuden for the first time. I don't know anything about what the queen does with her prisoners, or where she keeps them. I'm sorry, I can't help you."

"She is lying!" Daarco hissed. "Kill her. She will reveal that we are here."

The other man held up his hand for silence, and studied her.

"You burned. You called the wind to you. It was incredibly powerful. How do you claim to have such power without any training?"

"I don't know how I did it," she pleaded. "I just knew that I was falling and I didn't want to die. And so I didn't. You have to believe me."

"I don't have to do anything." His face hardened.

"It was like the Gleaming," she said, awareness dawning on her. "My power saved me, but I didn't do it consciously."

His penetrating gaze brought heat to her cheeks. All other sounds grew quiet but the urgent beating of her heart. She wanted to look away, but willed herself to hold his gaze, to show him her strength.

The man sighed. "Strangely enough, I believe you. Unfortunately, my companion is right, we should kill you." He drew a knife from his belt. She stilled, muscles tensed.

"And yet . . ." He moved quickly towards her, so fast she didn't have time to struggle. He deftly sliced through the binds around her hands and the snare around her feet. "I have had enough death for a season." He stood, an intense expression on his face.

"Do not make me regret this," he said quietly, before turning to walk back to his eagle.

"If you can't do what needs to be done, I will," Daarco hissed. He unsheathed his sword with a wicked ring of metal on metal and advanced on Kai.

Kai scrambled back away from the man, feet shuffling frantically in the dirt. But as his arm raised for a blow, a fireball engulfed him, sending him to the ground. He rolled from side to side to put the flames out.

The other man jumped onto his eagle as Pura heaved a fireball his way. His eagle made it off the ground in time to avoid her strike.

He whistled to the other eagle, which leapt into the air and swooped in to pick up a still-smoking Daarco in its strong talons. The two birds with their burdens winged off into the darkness.

Pura leapt from her koumori and ran to Kai's side. She pulled up short when she saw the blood dripping down Kai's face.

"I can't believe you are alive," Pura said, breathlessly. "I've never seen burning like that. I guess the goddess really has blessed you."

Kai laughed weakly, hardly believing her good fortune herself. She should have been dead at least four times by now, but here she was.

CHAPTER 8

Pura, Kai and Quitsu touched down in an open square inside what Kai assumed was the moonburner palace.

Her flight over Kyuden had awed her, despite her chattering teeth, wet clothes, and aching body. She had never seen so many buildings in one place. And that wasn't all. The city was beautiful. The main river split the city into two parts, spanned by graceful silver bridges that arched over it at evenly spaced intervals. The buildings appeared to be white, creamy tan and blue, set with mirrors that reflected the moonlight like a carpet of stars. The palace was surrounded by tall, delicate towers that reached for the heavens. She couldn't wait to see Kyuden in the daylight.

She helped Quitsu out of his harness, where he had remained securely fastened through her ordeal. He tumbled to the ground in a mess of fur and claws, seeming to cling to the ground for a few moments longer than necessary. She pretended not to notice, instead taking in her first glimpse of Kyuden from the ground.

Despite the late hour, there were people all around, bustling from place to place. Servants in silver and white livery ran out to take the koumori to their rookery.

"I will take you to the hospital ward first," Pura said. "You need to see someone about your injuries."

"I'm afraid that will have to wait," said a short, stout woman who had hurried up from the nearest entrance. "The queen wants an immediate audience."

Kai, Pura and Quitsu were led into the throne room by the tight-lipped woman who had summoned them.

Though she was filled with trepidation about meeting the queen, Kai couldn't help but gaze slack-jawed at the room. Her eye was first drawn to its sweeping ceilings. Tall gray marble columns rose gracefully and met at elaborate star designs from across the room. The panels between the marble stars were painted with scenes of the night sky—stylized constellations and the moon in its various cycles.

Orbs of white light hung in thin air throughout the room, the soft light illuminating both the room and the ceiling, making the celestial scenes glow. Kai's borrowed leather boots squeaked across the white marble floors, polished to a high sheen.

Pura dropped to one knee in front of the dais at the front of the room and Kai hastily did the same, bowing her head in imitation of the other woman. Quitsu daintily sat beside her, like a cat patiently waiting to be handed its saucer of cream.

"Rise," a soft, feminine voice said.

Pura and Kai stood, and Kai got her first look at Queen Airi, the woman whose name cast terror into the hearts of Kitan children.

She was tiny. Even standing two steps above them on the dais, Kai thought herself slightly taller. The queen's face was round and perfect, with delicate features and alabaster skin. Yet her figure was womanly—her generous bosom and thin waist accentuated by an impeccably-tailored periwinkle dress. Its high collar and silk seemed old fashioned, but somehow suited the queen perfectly.

Her silver hair was braided and piled into an elaborate design high on her head, pinned with silver crescent moon pins. She wore a thin circlet of silver, so bright that it seemed to glow on her brow.

Kai blinked, trying to reconcile the woman in front of her with the evil tyrant from Kitan bedtime stories.

Behind the queen, curled up on the throne on the dais, was a silver dragon, her seishen. It barely lifted its head to acknowledge the guests.

Next to the queen stood a tall shapely woman with long, loose silver hair and a navy moonburner uniform. Her face was fine-featured, with graceful arching brows, high cheekbones and a delicate chin. Yet her face held no beauty; her mouth was twisted in a grimace. It was a face that had been burned into Kai's memory from behind the fireball that flew at her outside the gates of Ushai.

Kai's attention snapped back to the queen as she swept down the stairs toward them, her gown and gate graceful and flowing like a river. She placed her hand warmly on Pura's shoulder.

"I thank you for rescuing this one and bringing her to us. It pains me to think of losing even one of our kind."

Pura bowed her head respectfully.

The queen turned to Kai. "I am Queen Airi Shigetsu. This is General Geisa." The queen motioned to the tall woman, who was staring frostily at Kai from the dais. "From what I have heard, you have been through quite an ordeal to get here, daughter. Words of your bravery and endurance have traveled before you."

Kai bowed her head, tongue-tied, blowing a loose lock of hair from her forehead. The queen paused slightly, cocking her head for a moment before continuing.

"But tell me, your wounds seem fresh." She looked at Pura sharply. "Were you not given medical care at our camp?"

"We were attacked on the way here, Your Majesty, " Pura explained.

"What?" The word cracked like a whip.

"They rode giant golden eagles," Pura said. "So I assume they were sunburners. The attack definitely happened on Miinan soil. Kai had the interaction with them. She might know what they were after."

"Tell me about your attackers," the queen commanded, turning her gaze on Kai.

Kai was mesmerized by the queen's ice-gray eyes. They were so cold. Kai felt as if they bore icy holes into the very center of her. Yes, she could see how this queen could live up to her reputation.

"Kai?" Pura asked, concerned.

They expected her to say something. Blushing, Kai found her tongue. "Yes. Eagles. We were nearing Kyuden when I was knocked from the harness. I did not see what caused it, but I assume it was one of the men. I fell, and would have died, but my powers saved me somehow." For some reason, Kai felt hesitant to share the full extent of how her powers had manifested. Her mother's words echoed in her head. *Her moonburners are only a weapon to her.*

"I fell into the river. When I made my way to the shore, there were two men. They had golden hair. They tied my hands behind my back, kicked me, and forced me to drink something bitter. They . . . they wanted to know the location of a facility, where they said you were was holding their brothers."

The queen jerked back almost imperceptibly, her nostrils flaring. General Geisa's dark gaze blackened further. There was something to the sunburners' questions, after all. The queen's seishen had risen from the throne and flapped its wings lazily, landing on the queen's shoulder. The way it moved through the air was eerie.

"What did you tell them?" The queen asked.

"The truth. That I knew nothing, and that I was not a master moonburner. They seemed to believe me, but one of them wanted to kill me, so that I could not report their whereabouts to you. And then Pura intervened. She hit one with a fireball, but they escaped."

"Thank you for your tale. We will find these lawless men and ensure no other citizens are attacked." The queen turned to Geisa. "General. See that it is done."

"Yes, Your Majesty," Geisa said, bowing slightly, eyes still on Kai.

The queen took Kai's hands in her own. They were as cold as ice, though the queen's words were warm.

"Transitions can be difficult. But the citadel is your home now. You need want for nothing here. If you do, please do not hesitate to call on me. I consider the moonburners to be my daughters," the queen said, squeezing Kai's hands.

"Thank you," Kai said, stifling her urge to yank her hands from the other woman and run from the room.

Kai slept through the following day and into the next night. In her fitful dreams, great beasts of the air clashed with claws and talons, and a man with golden hair chased her.

When she finally awoke, a white-liveried nurse hurried to her side, checking her wounds. Kai's ribs and face were sore, but the nurse assured her she had no broken bones. Quitsu stretched out on the foot of her bed, showing his sharp teeth in a big yawn.

"He refused to leave your side," the nurse said, chuckling.

Kai sat up in her bed and devoured a meal of rice, dried fruit and warm nutty bread.

"You look like hell," Quitsu observed, examining her bruised face.

"We can't all be naturally cute and fluffy," she said, mussing his fur.

"Isn't that the truth," he retorted, turning and smoothing his fur with his rough tongue.

A young woman in a light blue uniform sat down with a bounce on Kai's bed.

"I'm Maaya," the girl said. Her silver hair was gathered in two braids behind each ear, giving her a youthful look. She had big eyes, a button nose, and a grin on her face that spoke of mischief. She clearly had no shame in the gap between her two front teeth. Kai liked her immediately.

"I've been assigned to show you around," Maaya said. "I have heard so much about you, Kai. You are already a legend."

A legend? "All I did was manage to not get killed," Kai said.

"Yes, but that's pretty remarkable, don't you think? You survived days alone in the desert, killed a manga cat with only a stick, survived a fall from a koumori without a scratch and fought off two sunburners single-handedly? Pretty impressive," she said as she ticked them off on her fingers.

Kai considered this. "I didn't fight off two sunburners single-handed. If Pura hadn't been there, I'd probably be dead. And in the desert . . . I had a lot of help." She ruffled Quitsu's ears affectionately.

"But it's nice to meet you," Kai said. "This is Quitsu."

"I know. Your seishen is so handsome," she said, eying Quitsu wistfully. "You can pet him if you want," Kai said.

Maaya looked at Kai as if she had just offered to fry up Quitsu for breakfast.

"She most certainly may not!" Quitsu said.

Hearing Quitsu's voice, Maaya practically fell off the bed in shock. "I've never heard one talk," she said.

"What?" Kai asked, confused. "He talks all the time."

"Yes, to you. Seishen almost never speak when others can hear them though. Those without seishen are not deemed worthy."

"Is that true?" she asked Quitsu. He sat silently, unwilling to repeat his breach of decorum.

"Great," Kai said."He already takes himself way too seriously."

"I'm in charge of showing you around the citadel. I will show you to your quarters, to your classes and to the dining hall. Pura said I'm to make sure you have everything you need." Maaya grabbed Kai's hand and pulled her to her feet.

"Right now?" Kai asked. "It's the middle of the night."

Maaya looked puzzled for a moment. "That's right, they said you are from Kita. You wouldn't know. In Miina, day is night. As in, everyone sleeps. Night is day, when everyone works and we attend classes."

"That's crazy," Kai protested.

"No, it's not. Moonburners are nocturnal. It is when we draw our power, when we are closest to the goddess. Don't you ever have trouble sleeping at night?" Maaya asked.

"Yes," Kai admitted. "I just always thought I was strange. Doesn't everyone else mind sleeping during the day, though?"

"I don't think so. It's been like this for so long, I doubt anyone remembers any other way."

Maaya grabbed Kai's hands again with a friendly camaraderie that put Kai at ease. "Let's go."

Kai donned the gray tunic and leggings that had been laid out for her, and they set off.

Maaya didn't seem to mind being designated as Kai's tour guide. "I was excused from classes," she said, in a conspiratorial tone.

As they walked out of the hospital ward into the night air, filled with lingering warmth from the summer afternoon, Maaya happily spouted off an encyclopedia worth of facts about the Lunar Citadel.

"And that's a statue of Hamaio the Luminous, one of the first queens of Miina. She is said to be a direct descendant of Tsuki," Maaya said, pointing to a nearby marble figure.

Kai fell in behind Maaya and let her cheerful narration wash over her. The citadel was a massive white fortress, with dozens of white-walled and black tile-roofed buildings, stone walls, hidden gardens and cobblestone courtyards. It sat on an impressive hill nestled next to a waterfall where Kyuden's Nozuchi river plunged onto limestone rocks below. It was built, according to Maaya, in alignment with the phases of the moon.

In the center was the throne room and the queen's quarters, in a tall central tower that stood stark and white in the moonlight. The courtyard surrounding the tower was divided into sections: the Koumori landing grounds, a garden shrine to Tsuki with ornamental ponds, a sparring ground and gardens where food was grown for the citadel's inhabitants.

Then came a ring of buildings: libraries, residence halls, classrooms, stables, the dining hall and kitchen, and the Koumori rookery. Only one other tower stood as tall as the queen's, on the outer edge of the circle.

"That is the astronomy tower. The Oracle lives there," Maaya explained, her voice hushed. "I've never been up there, but it's supposed to be built in an astronomically significant spot."

"The Oracle. Pura mentioned her. Oracle as in, sees the future?" Kai asked.

"Oh yes. The Oracle has saved the moonburners in many battles and has forecast disease and drought. She is one of our most precious resources."

As they passed the sparring ground, Kai stopped, drawn by the movement. A round circular ring cordoned off in rope was illuminated by winking silver globes hanging unaided in the air. A group of girls in sky-blue uniforms like Maaya's stood around the ring, cheering on two combatants.

The two in the ring were locked in a bitter battle of hand-to-hand combat, landing punches and kicks that seemed like they would break bone. The bigger of the two girls finally finished her opponent with a knee in the stomach and a strong right hook. She turned from the fight and caught sight of Kai and Maaya.

"Can't wait to get in the ring, new girl?" she called, her chest heaving from the fight. "Do you think because you can take a manga cat down that you're too good for the rest of us?"

"We're fine!" Maaya called cheerfully, pushing Kai along. "Nice fight." "Who was that?" Kai asked, looking over her shoulder.

"Chiya," Maaya replied, walking briskly until they were out of sight of the ring. "She is the toughest samanera in our class. Everyone says she will go through her trials soon."

"The toughest what?" Kai asked.

"Samanera. It's the intermediate level of training. Novice, samanera, master. The trials to become a master moonburner are supposed to be brutal. Those who go through them are sworn to secrecy, so the samanera who come after them don't know what they will be facing."

"That sounds awful," Kai said.

"It is the highest honor a daughter of the moon can obtain. To serve her country and Tsuki, to be a master moonburner. You'll see. You'll want it. No matter what it takes."

A bell tolled in the distance, breaking off Maaya's explanation.

"That's the class bell. We have four classes each night. The third class just finished. I am supposed to take you now to the armory to meet the headmistress to get your schedule."

Maaya grabbed Kai's hand and they ran across the courtyard.

Kai left her meeting with Nanase with a list of four classes, a room assignment, and a charge to "serve the Goddess well." Nanase was just as intimidating the second time around.

"She and that bird of hers really need to lighten up," Quitsu said as they wound their way out of the maze of offices in the teaching wing.

"Quitsu!" Kai scolded, trying not to smile.

"Seriously. I cracked a joke and that bird didn't even ruffle a feather."

"What do you mean you cracked a joke?" Kai said. "You didn't say a word

in the meeting."

"Oh," Quitsu said. "Seishen can communicate with other seishen telepathically."

"What?" Kai stopped in her place. "You can read each other's minds?"

"No, thank the goddess, or that bird would have pecked my eyes out," Quitsu said. "We can project thoughts to each other. Only if we want to."

Kai started walking again. "What other super-secret seishen powers do you have that I should know about?"

"We can become incorporeal."

"Speak Kitan please."

"Well, technically, it's a Miinan dialect now."

"Whatever, Quitsu. " Kai rolled her eyes. "What do you mean?"

"We can walk through walls if we want to. Or become invisible."

"Wow." Kai said. "Anything else?"

"We can see in the dark."

"Okay, some of these might come in handy. Anything else?"

"We don't shed?" Quitsu offered.

"Duly noted."

After taking two wrong turns and pleading with a servant to show her the way, Kai and Quitsu finally made it to her room. It was small and windowless, but it was her own. It had clean white walls, worn wooden floors and a shaggy blue carpet set with a moon and star pattern.

A small bed was nestled in the corner and topped with a fluffy blanket of goose feather. Next to it sat a small wooden nightstand. A dresser with several sets of identical gray novice uniforms and a desk and wooden chair finished off the space.

The room was lit by two glowing orbs like those she had seen all around the citadel. She still hadn't figured out how they floated or stayed constantly lit.

"I guess this is home," she said, sitting on the bed, bouncing a few times to test it.

Quitsu jumped on the bed and surveyed the room disdainfully. "Where is my bed?"

"Hmm, yes, I'm surprised they don't have some sort of throne for you. I guess we'll have to share." She grinned. "Unless you want to take the rug."

"Maybe you should take the rug . . ."

"In your dreams, foxy," she said, ruffling his ears.

The last bell sounded, and Kai settled into bed, acutely aware that the sun was just beginning to rise outside.

"Sleeping in the daytime. This will take some getting used to," she mused.

"I guess that's why they don't give us a window," Quitsu said.

Kai murmured her assent before her exhaustion quickly pulled her down into slumber.

CHAPTER 9

The next evening, the ringing of the first bell woke Kai from her leaden sleep. Maaya had said that the first bell rang one hour before the first class of the day.

She and Quitsu wasted a precious ten minutes finding their way to the dining hall, but finally located it. As they entered the room filled with silver-haired women in gray, light blue and navy uniforms, heads swiveled their way and the buzz of conversation dimmed. The sound of whispering quickly took its place.

With Quitsu at her side and her face still bruised and battered, guessing her identity must have been easy for the moonburners in the room. Kai's heart thudded in her chest. She wasn't used to this. Her parents had always homeschooled her to keep her away from prying eyes.

Quitsu rubbed Kai's leg encouragingly, and she walked stiffly to the front of the room, wiping her sweaty palms on her tunic. The food was set out on a long table at the front of the room, and there were a few latecomers, like herself, filling their plates. Kitchen staff bustled through a nearby swinging door, bringing new dishes to replace what was running low.

The tables contained more food than she had ever seen in one place: fresh fruits, plump pastry dumplings of different shapes and sizes, grilled fish, eggs, juices, cheeses and rice. The moonburners must eat as well as the queen.

Kai filled her bowl with what looked like porridge and ladled in nuts, fruit and cream. It was about the only thing she recognized. She poured herself a cup of lemongrass tea and turned around to face the gauntlet of eyes once again.

"Hi!" Maaya stood before her. "Do you want to sit with us?"

Kai was so relieved, she could have kissed her.

Maaya led Kai to a long table in the section of the room that seemed, based on the color of neighboring uniforms, to be reserved for the samanera.

Kai looked over her shoulder at the tables of younger girls in gray. "Are you sure it's okay if I sit here?"

Maaya waved dismissively. "We segregate mostly, but its not a rule. All the novices are so much younger than you. You shouldn't have to spend all your time with them."

Kai smiled. "Thanks."

The two of them slid onto benches on either side of the table. Quitsu hopped up beside her, his furry tail hanging down almost to the floor.

"Plus, you have Quitsu," Maaya said. "So everyone knows you're special."

The girl sitting next to Maaya cleared her throat, and Maaya tore her gaze

from Quitsu. She had been staring.

"This is Emi," Maaya said. Emi was striking in contrast to Maaya's cuteness. Her long silver hair flowed in waves down her back, curling around her face in a nonchalant manner that Kai couldn't help but envy. She had a long, oval face, delicate features and eyes so dark they were almost black. She looked like she belonged on some nobleman's arm, rather than sitting on a wooden bench, eating rice.

"I'm Kai," Kai said. "And this is Quitsu. Nice to meet you."

"Nice to meet you, too." Even her voice was elegant, low and smooth. Kai blew her shaggy bangs from her forehead, trying to tame a few of the pieces that were still unruly after her night's sleep.

"What did you mean about Quitsu? And me being special?" Kai asked.

"Seishen are rare, especially among the students," Emi answered. "Usually, they only bond with royalty or other important burners, like the Oracle."

"There is only one other samanera who has a seishen," Maaya said. "Who?" Kai asked.

"Chiya," Maaya said, indicating behind Kai with a nod of her head. "The samanera who was fighting last night."

Kai looked over her shoulder and found the woman two tables down. She didn't look as intimidating sitting down. Her shoulder-length silver hair was pulled into a no-nonsense ponytail. Her face was plain, but could almost be pretty. Her body set her apart—ropey forearms and muscled biceps straining against her uniform. Kai's attention slid to the seishen at her side, sitting on the bench with its back to her. Its fluffy tail hung off the bench, but unlike Quitsu's, it was striped silver and white down to the tip.

"A raccoon?" she asked.

"Raccoon *dog*," Maaya corrected. "His name is Tanu. Or so I hear. He's not as friendly as Quitsu." Maaya beamed at Quitsu, who was doing his best to look bored.

"If he's anything like her, I'm not surprised," Kai said. "She seems like trouble."

"That's not a bad sentiment. You should probably steer clear of her for a while," Emi said. "She's the most powerful samanera, and the only student with a seishen, so she's been top dog for a long time. Now you show up, a novice, with a seishen, and all these stories about how you survived the desert and fought off sunburners before you even made it to the citadel? She will be looking to pick a fight."

The girls must have seen the dismay on Kai's face.

"It will be fine," Maaya said, shooting a warning glance at Emi. "They don't let student bouts get too rough."

"Speaking of, was there actually a sunburner attack near the palace?" Emi asked, lowering her voice. "It's impossible to get a straight answer from the faculty."

"There was an attack," Kai admitted. "One of them knocked me off a koumori. And then he did this." She pointed to her bruised face.

"My goddess! What were they doing so close to Kyuden?" Maaya asked. The two girls looked at Kai expectantly, eyes wide.

Kai shifted uncomfortably. "I don't know how much I am supposed to talk about it. I'm sorry."

Maaya pouted. Emi crossed her arms.

"I'll ask Pura, and tell you everything I can," Kai said.

"Oh no," Emi said. "Not necessary. Don't get a master involved."

"Can you at least tell us what they looked like?" Maaya asked. "I've never seen a sunburner."

"One was awful. The other had golden hair pulled back in a ponytail. He was a nobleman of some type. He was tall . . ." she paused, her face growing hot. "Tall and handsome."

"Ooh," Maaya said. "Sounds like you have a thing for this sunburner."

"Don't even joke about that," Emi scolded. "You know we can't think about such things, especially with a sunburner. You know what happened to Davina."

They both grew quiet. Kai looked from one to the other. "What happened to Davina?"

Maaya and Emi exchanged a look.

"She has to find out sometime," Emi said.

"Being a moonburner is not just a job. It's our life. It's who we are. We were chosen by Tsuki. We are hers, and must stay pure for her," Maaya said. "The queen is Tsuki's emissary on earth. The moonburners belong to Tsuki, and so by rights, they belong to the queen."

"What do you mean, *belong?*" Kai asked. "Like we are her property?"

"Yes," Maaya said. "We are hers, her weapons. She takes care of us and in

return, we give our lives to her, to the cause. We cannot marry, bear children or have a family. We cannot engage in . . . carnal pursuits. Davina was a samanera who fell in love. She tried to run away with the man. Her crime was punishable by death," Maaya finished softly.

"They killed her for falling in love?"

"I suppose falling in love isn't technically against the rules. But acting on it? Yes. They killed her for laying with him and for deserting," Maaya explained.

Kai was speechless. She knew her life had never been hers to begin with, but she had always thought that making it to the moonburners would mean freedom. It was bittersweet to escape one cage only to find herself in another. Would she never be free to live her life as she pleased?

"I know," Emi said with a harsh laugh. "You wish they were a little more up front about the job during recruitment. But the truth is, none of us ever had a choice in this. We don't choose the goddess. She chooses us."

Kai's first class of the night was Moonburning. Nanase had arranged a special tutor for Kai until she caught up with the rest of the novices.

Kai poked her head through the door of the dimly lit classroom and grinned when she saw Pura at the front of the room. She ran up to the older woman and stopped just short of throwing her arms around her. Pura wore her easy smile and fishtail braid.

Kai followed Pura to the center of the room where they sat down cross-legged on the floor. The room was remarkable. The octagonal walls and ceiling were entirely made of iron and panes of glass, allowing the soft glow from the moon and stars to shine in. The floor of the room sloped downward towards the middle and several circular sets of stairs littered with soft cushions made their way down to the center of the room, where Kai and Pura now sat. Moon orbs nestled against the walls and hung in the air, like constellations close enough to touch.

"Thank you for tutoring me. I am sure you have plenty of obligations," Kai said.

"I asked to tutor you, and the queen obliged," Pura said. "She agrees that you are very important, though we are not sure how."

"Important?" Kai asked, eyebrow raised.

"When I saw you dragging yourself and Quitsu out of the desert, I knew there was a reason you were alive. Tsuki has plans for you."

Kai shifted uncomfortably. "I know what you might think, but I'm just a girl." *And I'm not even good at being a girl,* Kai thought. "I don't know how to moonburn. Maybe Tsuki got it wrong."

"The goddess is never wrong," Pura said with a certainty Kai wished she could share. "But let's not worry about any grand destiny for now. The reason you cannot moonburn is because you are untrained. It is my job to fix that."

"As you know, moonburners draw our power from the moon, but more specifically, from its rays. We absorb it into our body, through our hair, our eyes, but mostly through our skin. We hold and store the moonlight in our spirit, called our qi. When the moon has not risen, or during the new moon, we can pull its power, but it is difficult, sluggish. It takes moonburners years to master this technique. When the moon is high, like it is tonight, and its rays fall on you, the power floods through you and it almost demands to be used. Often it manifests in tingling on your skin or the back of your neck, or generally feeling energetic—needing to move. Have you felt those sensations before?"

Kai thought back to the nights when she would run around the garden, opening her senses to the world around her. Or to the moonlight cattle drive when she raced off across the plain on her horse, leaving her father behind yelling at her that she had gone mad.

"Yes," Kai said. "I think I have experienced that."

"Good. Now, the next step is directing that energy through your qi into a focal point." Pura handed her a large silver cuff bracelet, mounted with a milky-white oval stone. "This will be your focal point. It is moonstone, an excellent conductor for burning."

Kai held the bracelet of hammered silver in her hands, examining the stone. She could see something swirling in its depths, like mist that clings to a field on a cool morning.

"Put it on," Pura said.

Kai did, finding the fine seam on one side of the bracelet and opening it. The bracelet felt heavy and cool in her hand, but when she snapped it closed around her left wrist, it grew warm, somehow molding to her arm. It was comfortable, like a second skin.

"We call these bracelets our links," Pura said, ignoring Kai's wide eyes. "When a student becomes a samanera, they are given a link as a symbol of their growing skill. We will practice with this one."

Pura rose and gestured for Kai to do the same. She took Kai's hands and led her to a spot in the room where moonlight was streaming through the glass ceiling and pooling on the floor like silver lava. Kai noticed for the first time that Pura was wearing a link that matched her own.

"Close your eyes."

Kai obliged.

"Now, first, quiet your mind. To moonburn effectively and safely, our mind must be still, a cool ocean reflecting the light of a moonlit sky. Imagine yourself as an island in a silent ocean. You are solid, and those still waters surround you."

After a time, Kai's heart rate slowed, and she began to feel the serenity Pura described.

"I think I'm there," Kai said, eyes still closed.

"If you think you are there, you are not there. You must know you are there."

Kai pushed down her irritation and set herself again to the task of quieting her mind. It was difficult. But finally, slowly, she sunk into the cool water of the ocean. It was as if she was floating in a dark place devoid of emotion or movement.

"I'm there," she said, sure this time.

"Good. Now feel the moonlight on your skin, filling your senses. Feel the pull of the moon on the water, like the tides. It washes against you."

At first, Kai felt nothing, covered by the heavy coolness of the ocean. But as she continued to concentrate, reaching her senses towards something unknowable, she began to feel it. There was energy in the water, movement. Her skin felt alive, full of pins and needles. She felt like she should be glowing.

"Wow," she said.

"Now this can be hard for novices, but once you get it, you'll always be able to do it. Imagine yourself gathering those feelings, those sensations towards yourself, like ocean waves against the shore. Once you've gathered them together into yourself, imagine yourself pushing them out through your arm into the moonstone. The waves are leaving you, but with a new direction, a new purpose. One you have chosen."

Kai took a deep breath and followed Pura's instructions, trying to reel in delicate waves of sparks and tingles and sensations. She gathered them inside her, and their warmth nestled within her, like the first sips of hot miso soup after a cold rainy day driving cattle.

She gathered her strength and moved to push the warmth out her arm, into the moonstone, willing the waves to leave her, to send their rhythmic pattern into the moonstone. But the waves wouldn't budge. They splashed against something firm and hard, a dam keeping the energy trapped. More waves of light entered her, joining the tingling sparking mass inside her. It was getting hotter. She inhaled sharply, the light now becoming painful with heat and pressure.

"I can't . . ." she said. She felt hot, as if she were catching fire from the inside.

"Something is wrong." Kai heard Quitsu's voice, but she kept her eyes squeezed closed, trying to keep her focus on the boiling mass within her.

"Kai?" Pura put her hand on Kai's arm and yanked it away. "Your skin is hot!" Pura pushed Kai out of the moonlight, back into one of the recesses of the room.

"Try to push the power into the moonstone," Pura said. "The moonstone is designed as a conduit. It wants to take the power from you."

A loud buzzing was filling her head, and Kai could hardly hear Pura. The heat inside her had become a raging furnace; sweat poured off her. Her thoughts were fuzzy and the room was growing dim.

"I . . . can't," she managed. "Won't . . . leave . . ."

"Open your mind, Kai." It was Pura's voice, distant and tinny. "Let me in."

Kai tried to do as instructed, but felt consciousness slipping from her. A foreign presence entered her mind, swimming through the fog. It was a vaguely unpleasant sensation, but compared to the inferno inside her, she hardly minded. The presence was determined, forceful. The presence tried to push the power from her, but was unsuccessful. The power continued to rage. And then, finally, Kai felt the magic draining from her, like water down a bathtub after the plug is pulled. Kai slipped from consciousness.

CHAPTER 10

Kai awoke to whispered voices around her. She cracked an eye and saw Pura and Nanase standing over her in hushed conversation. She stilled her breathing, feigning sleep. She felt Quitsu's comforting weight by her feet.

"She drew a tremendous amount of power. I could hardly manage it myself. No wonder the goddess chose her. If we can figure out how to break down the blockage, I suspect she will be the strongest moonburner in her generation," Pura said.

"Good. We need powerful burners," Nanase said. "What can you tell me about the blockage? I've never heard of such a thing."

"When I linked with her, I felt the moonlight trapped within her—walled in. I couldn't push it out through her. A regular burner's qi is porous; the light travels in and out of us freely. It was as if hers was a one way valve. The light goes in, albeit with more difficulty than a regular burner, but it does not come out. I had to pull the light into myself to keep it from burning her up, but even that was nearly impossible."

"And you have never encountered a student with these traits before?"

"No. I . . . I don't believe this is a natural phenomenon. I think someone did this to her."

"What?" In her surprise, Kai blew her cover.

Nanase turned her hawklike gaze to Kai. "Eavesdropping is frowned upon, child."

Kai looked up sheepishly, scooting up into a seated position. "I'm sorry. I didn't want to disturb your conversation."

"How considerate," Nanase said, arching an eyebrow. "But I suppose there is no harm. We would have needed to discuss this with you shortly."

"Will I ever be able to moonburn?" Kai asked.

"Of course."

"Oh yes," Pura and Nanase answered over each other.

Nanase continued, "We may be warriors, but we are scholars, too. We rarely come across a problem we cannot solve. I will put the mystery to the faculty and see what answers they find."

Kai was discharged from the hospital ward after Nanase's visit. Kai and Quitsu walked into the courtyard, flooded by warm yellow sunlight. She had been unconscious through most of the night and the morning. The courtyard was deserted, as most of the citadel's inhabitants were sleeping.

"I don't know why they bothered giving you a room," Quitsu remarked. "You've spent twice as much time in the hospital ward."

"Very funny," Kai said, aiming an exaggerated kick towards his hindquarters. It felt good to joke after the weight of Nanase and Pura's revelation.

"Let's not go back to our room just yet," Kai said. Despite her natural moonburner predilections, it felt good to be outside in the sunshine. And she was too wound up to go to bed.

Kai and Quitsu set off through the cobblestone courtyard and into one of the gardens. The sunlight filtered through leafy maple trees onto green grass. A pool filled with orange koi fish nestled against a cluster of rocks. She and Quitsu walked down the gravel path, taking it all in. Kai picked a familiar leaf off a low bush and twirled it between her fingers, breathing in its fresh scent.

"I used to play in my mother's garden behind our house when I was a child. Her menthe plant was my favorite," Kai said, as the memory flooded back. "My mother would always tear the leaves away from me." She smiled ruefully. "'No little boy lolls around smelling menthe leaves!'" Kai mimicked her mother's voice.

"It must have been hard," Quitsu said.

"I didn't know any different," Kai said. "It kept me alive. More than I can say for them." Tears temporarily blurred her vision as images of her parents swam to the surface unbidden.

"They could be alive," Quitsu said.

"My mother, maybe," Kai said. "But I don't know how my father could have survived Youkai's death sentence."

"Don't lose hope."

"He would have loved you," Kai said to Quitsu. "He would joke that he preferred animals to humans. Much more honest, he'd say."

"Smart man," Quitsu said.

"Do you think they would let me return to Kita?" Kai mused.

"For good? No, I don't get the impression that the queen would be too happy about that."

"No, just for a mission. To rescue my mother."

"I don't think so," Quitsu admitted. "But you could ask. At the worst, they would say no."

Kai rounded a bend in the path and slammed headfirst into another woman. She stumbled backwards from the force of the contact. She had been wrapped up in her thoughts.

"I'm so sorry," Kai said and then fell silent as she saw who stood opposite her.

She was one of the most unusual women Kai had ever seen. She was small and slight, like a child, with her silver hair cut short. But her face— her face was ageless, filled with mesmerizing dark violet eyes that seemed to swirl with ribbons of smoke. A tiny silver owl fluttered above her.

"Kailani," the woman said, using Kai's full given name, a name that Kai's parents had used only when she was in the worst sort of trouble. Her body stilled and her violet eyes gazed into the distance. The owl began to dart frantically to and fro above her head.

Kai took a step back.

As the woman continued speaking, her voice seemed to become two, three, a thousand voices in one.

"Daughter of Azura. Daughter of Miina. Hear these truths.

The moon cannot enslave the sun, nor make the day its mistress.

Or victory shall spell defeat, a crimson sky its auspice.

The sun and moon must shine as one, or all will be undone."

The hackles on the back of Quitsu's neck rose as the woman spoke.

If Kai had any, they would have done the same. It was a moment before Kai could articulate a question.

"How do you know my name?" Kai asked. "Who are you? And what do you mean daughter of Azura? My mother's name is Hanae."

The woman started, shaking her head as if to clear it, blinking rapidly. Her owl had calmed, landing on her shoulder, shaking its feathers.

"Hello," the woman said, her voice bright. She sounded like a different person. "I'm sorry, who are you?"

"What?" Kai asked. "You just said my name. I'm Kai. Who are you?"

"I thought it was obvious. I am Roweni," she said. "But most just call me the Oracle."

Of course. Kai felt foolish. She bowed slightly, hoping to make up for practically plowing the woman over.

"This is Giselli," the Oracle said, motioning to her seishen. "She tells me I just prophesied?"

"I think so," Kai said. "You went all stiff and said some strange things."

"Quite the honor. Some live for years at the citadel and never hear a prophecy. You never know when one is going to bubble up."

"I suppose not," Kai said cautiously.

"Come sit with me for a moment," the Oracle said, nodding her head toward a nearby bench.

They walked to it and sat down. The Oracle's gait was smooth and graceful, as if she was gliding. Kai felt ungainly in comparison.

"Normally my visions are reserved for the queen, but obviously, this one was meant for you. A time of great change is coming. You have a part to play in it."

"I can't imagine what," Kai said. She wished they wouldn't keep talking about great change, and the goddess choosing her, and all that. She didn't even know how to moonburn!

"Now what did I say?" the Oracle asked. "You don't know?" Kai asked.

"No, that is one of the more annoying parts of being an Oracle. I have never heard one of my own prophecies."

Kai tried to remember. "You called me the daughter of Azura. Who is Azura?"

"Your mother," the Oracle said.

"My mother was named Hanae," Kai protested again.

"We all have secrets," the Oracle said, and motioned with her hand for Kai to hurry up. "What else did I say?"

You talked about the moon trying to enslave the sun . . . but that they have to work together."

"Interesting."

"A crimson sky . . ."

"And that victory will spell defeat," Quitsu said.

"Yes, that's most of it." Kai frowned. "I don't understand any of it. My mother is not named Azura. And how could the moon enslave the sun? And how could victory spell defeat? Are you sure your prophecy skills are . . . you know, working correctly?"

The woman laughed, ignoring Kai's sudden stream of questions. "Oh, my child. There is so much you do not understand. Your mind is like a fresh piece of rice paper."

Kai bristled, not knowing whether to be offended.

"To know the future is a heavy burden. The goddess does not hand us an instruction manual on what is to come. What we mortals are gifted with is only a glimpse, sometimes a word, a sentence, an image. It is all we can be trusted with."

"Then what good is prophecy at all?" Kai complained.

For a moment, the Oracle sat still as a statue, but for the blinking of her charcoal violet eyes. The silence stretched between them.

"You will have to wait and see, little fox."

Kai looked up sharply. Only her father had ever called her that. Her voice caught in her throat. "How did you . . ."

"You will have to wait and see."

Kai knew a dismissal when she heard one. The Oracle would give her no further insight that day.

CHAPTER 11

K ai and Quitsu walked back to her room and managed to sleep a few hours.

The Oracle's words echoed in Kai's head, and she dreamt of crimson skies and the moon shackling the sun. She woke feeling more exhausted than when her head hit the pillow.

Kai attended her classes that night. Quitsu wanted to explore on his own and raced off across the courtyard into the cooling night air.

Kai felt uneasy about him leaving her sight, even though he was safe here in the citadel. He had become an extension of her.

Kai and Pura met in the glass and iron room once again, but Pura did not encourage her to moonburn. She showed Kai how to link to another burner, and Kai cast her consciousness into Pura's. Their class was blissfully uneventful, and Kai proceeded to her next class when it was over, rather than the hospital ward.

Kai's History class was the first she shared with other novices. She felt self-conscious as she sat among rows of gray-clad girls who all looked to be between twelve to fourteen years of age. Pura had told her that the staff would endeavor to help her move through her core classes quickly to allow her to catch up with the other students her age. Kai prayed it was true.

The teacher strode into the classroom and Kai had to stifle a smile. The woman was diminutive, wrinkled beyond belief. Her hair was white, even beyond the moonburner silver, and pulled into a severe bun. She wore robes of orange and an obi belt of scarlet, some of the first bright colors Kai had seen worn at the citadel. Maybe when you got that old, no one told you what to do.

A fresh-faced girl next to her leaned over and whispered: "We have a wager going on whether she lived through the first battles herself."

Kai snickered, trying to muffle her mirth. She looked up and started, as the miniature woman stood before her, dark eyes like iron.

"Our newest student. Already thinking herself too good for my lessons, I see. I am Mistress Furie. And you will be quiet in this classroom."

Kai nodded solemnly.

Mistress Furie walked back towards the front of the room, remarkably spry for her advanced age. "We were just studying the Fracturing and the beginning of the Burning War. Since you are obviously too advanced for my class, why don't you share with us what caused the Fracturing?"

Kai's face reddened. She had always been home-schooled. This situation felt uncomfortably new for her. Mistress Furie tapped her tiny foot. Kai cleared her throat. She did remember the history detailed in the The Rising Sun. That would have to do, though it was a fable.

"Yes . . . Mistress Furie. In the beginning, Tsuki and Taiyo were husband and wife. They ruled together over the heavens and there was peace. Tsuki had a wandering eye, though, and a handsome mortal man caught her eye. She laid with him and became pregnant. When she had the baby, the first moonburner girl, Taiyo became enraged, realizing her betrayal. He threw a fit and his anger spread across the earth. Tsuki and her lover fled, and while chasing them, Taiyo raised volcanoes that we now call the Akashi Mountains, and scorched the land, creating the Tottori desert. Tsuki, her lover, and their daughter stayed ahead of him and settled in a fertile land along a snaking river, creating their own land of Miina. Taiyo created the sunburners to track Tsuki and her progeny down and destroy them. They have been fighting ever since."

Kai finished, realizing she had been talking rapidly to compensate for her nervousness. But overall, that had been a pretty good telling of the history. She looked around. Mistress Furie and all of the other students stared at her aghast, mouths hanging open. Mistress Furie was the first to recover.

"Is that what they teach you in Kita? No wonder it is such a backwards place. No, child, I assure you that the Fracturing was not a result of any wrongdoing on the part of our goddess Tsuki. That snake Taiyo is to blame. Can anyone enlighten our new student about what actually caused the Fracturing?"

A freckle-faced girl with red hair streaked with silver shot her hand up eagerly, giving Kai a withering glance over her shoulder.

"You," Mistress Furie pointed at the girl.

"Tsuki and Taiyo were married. Tsuki traveled among the people of the world, helping them build and grow crops, healing them. She cared deeply for their human children, and those she healed began gaining special powers. Taiyo was a jealous, selfish god, who wanted all of Tsuki's attention for himself. He was sure that she was lying about what she was doing. He grew paranoid and thought she was raising an army to defeat him. He created a prison for Tsuki and created his own sunburners using evil blood magics. He scorched the Tottori desert surrounding the prison, so he could always keep his watchful eye on her. Her moonburners came to rescue her one night, and they escaped to Miina. Taiyo has been attempting to destroy Tsuki and her moonburners ever since."

"Very good," Mistress Furie purred. "That is an excellent recitation. Now who can tell me from the reading about the founding of Kyuden?"

Other hands went up around the room and Kai tuned out, lost in thought. She had always thought the story of the Fracturing seemed a little farfetched. Now hearing Miina's version, she was sure that neither were the truth. How could two countries hate each other bitterly for two different reasons? Thousands had died in the hundreds of years of the Burning War. Babies were slaughtered in Kita. For what? A lover's quarrel between gods? Neither version of the Fracturing seemed to justify hundreds of years of death and devastation. What had really happened?

Kai looked at Mistress Furie. Whatever the truth, she would not find it in this class.

Kai finished History class and made her way to Zoology. Mistress Adiru, who was also the rookery-mistress in charge of the koumori, was in the middle of a unit on the koumidi, tiny bats that the moonburners used to carry messages.

Mistress Adiru was a pleasant-looking, middle-aged woman with straight silver hair cut into blunt bangs and a bob just above her shoulders. Her navy uniform was covered with a leather jerkin, and she had one forearm wrapped in leather, to protect her skin from the koumidi's tiny claws.

Mistress Adiru was an engaging teacher, clearly passionate and knowledgeable about her subject. Kai found herself warming to the woman immediately and she felt almost comfortable by the time she and the rest of her novice class left the Koumori ground and made their way to the sparring ring for their last class of the night, Weapons and Combat.

The fresh-faced girl who she had sat by in History caught up with Kai and walked beside her. Though the girl was a head shorter than Kai herself and at least five or six years younger, she didn't appear intimidated.

"How's the professor for Weapons?" Kai asked, searching for a topic of conversation.

"Amazing. The Eclipse teaches us. She is remarkable. She could shoot a koumidi out of a dark sky with a bow and arrow," the girl said, with a touch of awe in her voice. "Not that she would."

"Nanase?" Kai asked. "I thought she was the headmistress of the school? I didn't know she taught classes."

"Nanase used to be armsmistress, and taught all the weapons and fighting classes. When the queen promoted her to headmistress, she didn't want to give it up. She does both."

"Why do they call her the Eclipse?" Kai asked, curiosity overwhelming her.

"You have heard about the Flare War, about twenty years ago?"

"Of course," Kai said. "Miina and Kita had almost signed a peace accord when it all fell apart. It was the worst bloodshed in two hundred years."

The girl nodded. "Well, they say that Nanase killed so many sunburners on the battlefield that the sun went dark in mourning when it was done."

Kai couldn't help but chuckle. "That sounds like a myth if I've ever heard one."

The girl sniffed. "There are several stories, and it's hard to tell truth from fiction. That story always seemed the most believable to me. If you really want to know the truth, you could always ask her."

"That sounds like a good way to get myself eclipsed," Kai said, trying to make up for offending the other girl.

She giggled.

As they entered the sparring ring, the other girls dispersed, moving into a loose formation. Kai mimicked their stiff, wide-legged stance, clasping her hands behind her back. She somehow had ended up with the freckle-faced redhead next to her. Kai inwardly groaned at the girl's arrogant stance, exuding feigned importance and maturity. Was the girl truly in such a hurry to be taught to kill? But then she blanched, her arrogance giving way to fear. The rest of the girls shifted slightly on their feet.

"Novices!" A harsh voice rang into the night. Kai's head whipped towards the speaker, and she saw Chiya shoving past a thin girl into the ring, causing her to stumble.

"Nanase has more important places to be tonight than teaching your sorry asses. So lucky me, I get to whip you into shape." Chiya's raccoon dog seishen scaled the large juniper tree that leaned protectively over the sparring ground, observing the group.

Chiya caught sight of Kai and smiled coldly. She walked over and stood before Kai nose to nose, a pillar of muscle. Chiya had a slight bruise on one cheekbone, no doubt from her latest sparring match. It only made her look more intimidating.

"Our newest novice. Normally, you know, the citadel doesn't take novices over fourteen. But apparently, you are special. Don't you feel special, learning to walk among these children?" Chiya asked, motioning to the other novices. If the other girls were offended, none was foolish enough to voice it, or so much as frown in displeasure.

"Or perhaps you think you are special because you have a seishen?" Chiya asked. She looked around. "But why isn't he here? Bored of you already?"

Kai struggled to keep her temper in check.

"I don't think I am special, or better than anyone. I am here to learn." Kai bowed her head respectfully, even though it felt contrary to every fiber of her being. She didn't need to antagonize Chiya.

Chiya stepped back and considered Kai, a frown on her face. She had clearly hoped Kai would rise to the bait. She turned to the class.

"Grab your staffs!" she barked. The girls scrambled to the side of the ring, picking up wooden staffs from a pile resting against the side of the nearest building.

"Formation!"

The girls quickly settled into evenly spaced rows before Chiya. Kai, watching the others, managed to find a place without too much difficulty.

Chiya took them through a set of exercises with the staffs. The novices had clearly done these exercises before, as they all flowed from move to move, knowing which was coming next. Kai found herself a beat or two behind on every move, as she looked around her to see what the other girls were doing. Chiya delighted in her tardiness and with each moved berated Kai.

"Kai, you call that a katana? Embarrassing!"

"No, left then right, Kai, are you blind and stupid?"

Kai grew more and more flustered under Chiya's taunting until she stopped, setting the butt of her staff down on the ground in frustration.

"Stop," Chiya hollered. She stormed before Kai. "Do you think yourself too good for these exercises, novice?"

"No," Kai snapped, eyes flashing. "But I have never seen the moves before. Of course I don't know what is coming next. Maybe give me one chance before you tell me that I am doing it wrong!"

"You want a chance, do you? Do you think a sunburner will give you a chance on the battlefield? Your slowness could be the death of you, or one of your sisters! You think you deserve special treatment, but it will get the rest of us killed."

"I don't think I deserve special treatment. I am just trying to learn. But I can't do that with you yelling at me every second!"

"You want to learn?" Chiya lowered her voice so only Kai could hear her. "I will teach you a lesson you won't forget."

Chiya stalked over to the wall and picked up two spears with curved blades on the end. She tossed one to Kai, who caught it in the air. As she looked at the blade, a memory bubbled to the surface. Kai and her father, driving cattle to market in the next town over, passing two handsomely armored sunburner warriors riding lion-horses. While Kai had ogled the immense feet and manes of the golden beasts, her father had explained every piece of armor and weaponry the sunburners possessed.

"Those curved blades are naganita spears. Best for slashing, almost like a sword," he had said. What she wouldn't give to have his gentle guidance with her now, she thought with a pang of loss.

"We aren't supposed to use real blades, Mistress Chiya," the fresh-face girl called out, her voice cracking.

"Thank you for reminding me of the rules, novice," Chiya said darkly, her eyes locking Kai's. "Kai doesn't mind, does she?"

"No," Kai said, straightening her shoulders. Her father had taught her how to fight. She had even been able to beat him, towards the end. And clearly Chiya was gunning for this fight. Kai needed to make a stand or the woman would never leave her alone.

"Clear the ring," Chiya said, and the novices scattered, leaving Kai and Chiya to circle each other. Kai twirled her spear in her hands, swinging it a few times, feeling its weight. Chiya was bigger than her, and likely stronger. But she didn't know Kai's skills, and she was cocky. If Kai underplayed her skill, Chiya might get sloppy.

Chiya lunged for her, spear forward. Kai stepped to the side, feigning a fall. She scrambled to her feet, and swiped her spear at Chiya's legs. Chiya jumped over her strike nimbly and thrust again. Kai threw her shoulder out of the way and Chiya's spear just missed her. She grabbed it and pulled Chiya forward and past her. She whacked Chiya across the back with her spear, and the woman stumbled, almost out of the ring.

Chiya rounded on her, nostrils flared and eyes full of malice. Cocky and prone to anger, Kai thought, revising her assessment.

Chiya stepped in with a barrage of hits that Kai barely managed to block. The woman was fast. The cracking of the wood staffs and the heavy breathing of the combatants echoed through the night.

Chiya moved into Kai's stance and shoved her with her spear, causing Kai to stumble back. Chiya cracked the butt of her spear across the side of Kai's head, and lights exploded behind her eyes. She fell to her side, ears ringing with the blow. Chiya advanced towards her, spear in hand, certain of victory. Had she forgotten that they were sparring?

Kai summoned her strength and spun her legs to tangle Chiya's. Chiya clearly wasn't expecting Kai to put up any more of a fight, and she fell backwards to the ground. Kai grabbed a spear and threw herself on Chiya's chest, gripping the spear like a dagger to Chiya's throat.

"Yield," Kai said, feeling blood dripping into her eyes.

"What in the name of the goddess is going on here?" A loud voice called out, filled with cold fury. Chiya pushed Kai off her and stood up, dusting off her tunic and pants. Kai laid back and gingerly set her head on the ground, trying to stop its spinning.

"I was sparring with the new novice," Chiya said.

Nanase stood with her hawk seishen on her shoulder and her hands on her hips. Their black eyes shone like two pairs of hard coals.

"Sparring with a novice on her first day with real blades? We need to talk about your teaching methods, child," Nanase said, placing emphasis on the final word. "Report to Mistress Adiru, I'm sure she has some extra chores she can find for you."

Chiya threw her spear down. "Class dismissed," she said. She shot Kai a look of loathing as she stalked off across the courtyard.

The novices stood silently for a moment, before they swarmed Kai, helping her up.

"That was amazing!" The fresh-faced girl said.

The praise was short-lived.

"Kai," Nanase said. "With me."

CHAPTER 12

Kai and Nanase entered a building Kai had not yet visited, weaving through wood-paneled hallways decorated with oil paintings of severe, silver-haired women.

"Former headmistresses of the citadel," Nanase said, without turning around. Kai furrowed her brow. How had she known Kai was looking at the paintings?

They turned into a brightly lit room with a high ceiling and windows lining one wall. It overlooked a garden filled with tall green bambu trees dancing gently in the wind. The window lent a green serenity to the room, which was otherwise a whirlwind of papers and books. Nanase's office.

"Sit," Nanase said, and Kai did, sinking into one of two large leather armchairs by the desk. Nanase leaned against the desk, crossing her arms, studying Kai with her intense gaze. Kai blew the hair off her forehead, fidgeting in her chair.

"Are you all right?" Nanase asked.

"Yes?" Kai said. She wasn't sure what Nanase was getting at.

"I would not have asked Chiya to cover your class if I had known her intentions." Nanase said, motioning towards the black eye Kai could feel forming. Kai touched her face gingerly, acutely aware that her other eye was already swollen from the sunburner's attack. Now she would have a matched set.

Nanase continued, "Chiya's bark is worse than her bite. Usually."

"It's all right. The moon does not heed the barking of dogs, right?" Kai said with a nervous chuckle. "Or . . . so my mother used to say."

"An unusual saying," Nanase said, frowning. "I've only heard one other use it. But aptly put in this circumstance." Nanase walked around the desk and sat in the worn leather chair behind it. "You handled yourself well. Your technique with a naganita spear was surprising. Where did you learn to use one?"

"My father taught me," Kai said. "We used to spar."

"Your father was a soldier?" Nanase asked.

"No. A rancher. Cattle."

"What else did you spar with?"

"Fists, knives, staffs, axes, both masakari and ono, and bows. And the cattle whip when he was feeling creative." Kai ticked them off her fingers.

Nanase's right eyebrow raised ever so slightly with each additional weapon Kai listed.

"Yet, you say he was not in the military? Before you were born, perhaps?"

"No." Kai was growing confused. "At least . . . I don't think so."

Nanase contemplated this information. "I will see about getting you moved up into a samanera weapons class," Nanase said.

"Thank you."

"Dismissed."

Kai stood to leave.

"Oh, and Kai?" Nanase said.

"Yes?" Kai paused at the door.

"Put something on that eye."

☾✦

Though exhausted, Kai tossed and turned through the day, mind racing through the events of the past hours. Finally, she gave up on sleep and got out of bed. Her face was already swollen and her body was sore from Chiya's "lesson." She washed her face in the little ceramic basin in her room and dressed in her soft, gray uniform.

Quitsu sat on her desk and looked at her disapprovingly. "You're just determined to get the two of us killed, aren't you?"

"Not you too," Kai said with a sigh. "All I'm doing is trying to lay low. But trouble keeps finding me."

Quitsu jumped onto the bed beside her. He leaned his furry body against hers, his solid warmth comforting her.

"You will settle in. People are just jealous. They can tell you are special." "How do you know that?" she asked. "All I've done is manage to avoid dying. I can't even moonburn."

He was silent for a moment. "I don't know how I know. Seishen don't even understand the bond fully. All we know is that we wake with a certainty—that we have a soulmate. And when the right time comes, the urge to find that burner overpowers us. But I knew you were special when I first awoke."

"How?"

"Because the goddess sent you me! You must be blessed indeed." He chuffed his cheeks out, laughing at her.

She swatted at him. "Who am I to doubt the wisdom of the great seishen?"

"Speaking of not doubting," Quitsu said, "I found a place I think you should see. Come with me."

Quitsu stopped in front of a stately, three-story tower, its three black-tiled roofs ornately flanking whitewashed walls. It stood across the courtyard from the entrance to the main citadel building.

"Where are we?" Kai asked, gazing up at the stone facade.

Two tall doors loomed above them, with a smaller, person-sized door cut into one of them. The stone awning above the doors was carved with swooping curves and swirls. A menagerie of stone gargoyles sat high above the courtyard, keeping watch.

"You'll see," he said.

They pushed through the door and entered a dark antechamber, lit by the citadel's trademark silver orbs. They walked into the next chamber and Kai couldn't help but gawk. The room was huge, a long rectangle that betrayed the depth of the tower's squat exterior. Its ceiling was vast and vaulted, and tiny silver orbs hung, winking like stars. The room was paneled in dark wood, and fireplaces lined the walls. High windows along the upper walls poured in slanted light from the remnants of the setting sun.

But most of all, she saw the bookshelves. Tall and voluminous, with ladders to reach the upper shelves. She had never seen so many books. Her parents had only five books, and she had read them over and over as a child, even her mother's medical textbook, Herbs and Tinctures of Eastern Kita.

She looked at Quitsu in amazement. How had he known she would love this place?

"Impressive, isn't it," he asked with a smirk. "You could get lost in here." "I'll make sure that doesn't happen," a voice rang out from among the stacks.

"Who's there?" Kai asked.

A small, wizened man appeared out of one of the rows of books and approached them. He was short of stature and walked deliberately, leaning heavily on his cane. His clothes were simple: brown cotton trousers, a collarless white shirt with its ends hanging free, wrapped into an olive green obi belt. He had a shock of white hair that formed a halo from ear to ear, with nothing on top. He wore half-moon spectacles low on his nose, distracting from the sea of wrinkles on his smiling face.

"I'm Kai."

"Master Vita," he said, flourishing a little bow. "And, Quitsu, excellent to see you again."

She looked at Quitsu with a raised eyebrow, but he pointedly ignored her. The fox was full of surprises.

"Would you like to join me for some tea?"

It took Master Vita twice the time it would take Kai to make the tea. She almost offered to help him a dozen times, but bit back her offer. He seemed the proud type. While he worked, she studied him. There was something off about him, but she couldn't quite put her finger on it. Was it something different? His mannerisms?

Finally, he handed her a small teacup, hand-painted with navy phases of the moon.

"Menthe!" She exclaimed as she took her first sip. "It's my favorite."

"Is it?" He remarked, a twinkle in his eye. They sat in two oversized red chairs next to the fireplace.

And then it hit her. What was different about him. "You're a man," she exclaimed.

Master Vita chuckled, a raspy dry laugh.

"She's not the brightest star in the sky, is she?" he said conspiratorially to Quitsu, who chuffed with laughter.

"I'm sorry . . ." she said. "I didn't mean to be rude. But you're the first man I've actually met in Miina. The first who has . . . a position of honor."

There were hardly any men in the citadel. No male teachers, nurses or even queen's guard, from what she had seen. The men she had seen were servants or foot soldiers, relegated to lowly tasks.

"I'm not sure serving as head of the library counts as a 'position of honor,'" he said. "In truth, I am the only one who knows how this place is organized, so they really had no choice but to let me keep the position."

"What do you mean, let you keep it?"

"I can see how coming from Kita, this would all be very foreign to you. The monarchy was not always as . . . distrustful of male Miinans as the current administration. Once, there were many men in positions of power and influence. Of course, the moonburners still ruled, but everyone got along a bit better than now. But after the Flare War, we were no longer trusted. These days, we hardly even have male officers in the army."

"How could you not trust half of your population?" Kai asked.

"It doesn't make a lot of sense to me either, especially as one of those 50 percent," he winked at her. "But is it so different in Kita? Are there women leaders and academics?"

"No," Kai said, furrowing her brow. "The women mostly stay in the home."

"And how is that so different from here?"

"Well, it is natural for a woman to be in the home with her children . . ." Kai said.

"So is it unnatural for a woman to be a master moonburner? A soldier?"

"Well, the king would certainly say so . . ." Kai was getting turned around

now. Her face was growing red.

"I don't know," she admitted. "I need to think more on it. The truth is, I don't know anything about being a man, or a woman, or what is natural and what is not. I'm afraid I've done a poor job of both."

Master Vita peered at her through his half-moon spectacles. He seemed amused by her distress, which she found both frustrating and oddly comforting.

"It sounds like you have a lot of learning to do. Luckily, you've come to the right place." He gestured grandly to the shelves of the library, almost knocking his teacup over.

He walked to one of the nearby bookshelves and made to step onto the closest ladder.

Kai sprang up, moving to intercept him.

"Can I do that for you?" she asked. The last thing she needed was to be back in the hospital ward explaining the librarian's broken leg to the nurse.

"Why, how chivalrous of you." He stepped back, motioning her up the ladder.

She climbed the ladder and examined the books before her. Some of the titles sounded fascinating. *Gods and Goddesses: Societal Implications of the Fracturing; Seishen Zoology; Burner Lineage.*

"What am I looking for?" she called down.

"*Miinan Social History: Abridged,*" he called back. "It's one row further, I think."

She stepped up a few more rungs on the ladder. There it was. She pulled the large dusty tome from the shelf, tucking it under her arm and making her way back down.

"It doesn't look particularly abridged . . ." she noted.

"Well, certainly more abridged than the eight-volume set," he replied.

The first bell rang as she dusted herself off.

"I should go," she said. "Can I come get this after classes, Master Vita?"

"Of course."

"Thanks!" she cried over her shoulder, already heading out the front door towards the dining hall.

Kai's classes that night were blessedly uneventful. She and Pura explored the boundary walls of her moonburning blockage; Mistress Furie lectured about the early Miinan monarchy; they learned the proper care for nighthawks in Zoology; and Nanase put them through their paces on the archery range. Kai knew her way around a bow and arrow, and quickly adjusted to the more compact baliwood bows the moonburners favored.

It had been a good night, almost normal. The novices had given her a wide berth after her defeat of Chiya in the ring, regarding her with a sort of awe.

Nanase had told her to report to the samanera weapons class the next night. Even Quitsu seemed in good spirits, trotting beside her to classes, basking in the whispered exchanges and outright stares.

Kai stopped back by the library to pick up the book she had left with Master Vita and then made her way to the dining hall, famished. The night had been busy, and not even Chiya and silent Tanu could keep her away from food. She heaped her plate with succulent curried axen meat, fried rice, steaming vegetables and two hot honeycakes.

She had loved the gooey honeycakes as a child; they had been her mother's favorite, too. The two of them had mock fights over the last cake, to her father's delight. He would make up competitions for them to determine who took the last cake: running two laps around the garden or finding the biggest spider to bring back to the house for his inspection. Kai had always won. She realized now, wistfully, that her mother had no doubt let her win.

Kai shook off the memory and the pang of sorrow it brought, and joined Maaya and Emi, who were sitting at their usual table.

Maaya flipped a braid over her shoulder and greeted Kai with a wide grin. "We heard you gave Chiya a whooping in your novice class yesterday."

Emi nodded, leaning forward conspiratorially. "I wish I could have been

there to see that cow hit the dirt."

"I didn't exactly get away without a scratch," Kai said, pointing to her swollen eye. "But it was pretty satisfying when she went down."

Emi leaned forward further, lowering her voice. "Some of the students are planning to sneak into town this morning. There is a concert at one of the taverns, and the musicians are friends of one of the samaneras in our class. They wanted me to invite you."

Kai's heart beat faster. Invited to something? She had never even been to a birthday party for the village children in Ushai. Her parents had made her say no to any invitation she got, which were few and far between.

"Sneak out? Would we get in trouble if we get caught?" Kai asked. As eager as she was to go, she was just getting her feet under her, and didn't relish a lecture from Nanase.

"Students do it all the time, it's a rite of passage," Emi assured her. "The teachers look the other way."

"She's right," Maaya said. "Even if we did get caught, it would just be a slap on the wrist. It will be fun."

"You're both going?" Kai asked.

They nodded in unison.

"I'm in."

CHAPTER 13

A quiet knock sounded on her door, and Kai opened it, cringing at the creak the old hinges made.

Maaya and Emi slipped in. Maaya was wearing a soft olive dress wrapped around her, tied with a wide tan belt. She wore matching knee-high leather boots and a brimmed brown cap that mostly covered her silver hair. Emi looked even more stunning than usual, sporting tight red trousers and a fitted long leather coat with a high collar. She wore a black slouched knitted cap and kohl eyeliner around her dark eyes. They both looked at Kai with distaste.

"What?" Kai asked, and then looked down at her novice grays. Her heart sank. "I don't have any other clothes."

"Well, that won't do; you'll stand out like a sore thumb," Maaya said, shaking her head. "Lucky you have us. We thought ahead." She tossed a package at Kai that had been tucked under her arm. Kai unwrapped it and spread the clothes on her bed.

"A leather skirt?" she asked weakly.

"You have to look the part," Emi said, grinning devilishly.

Kai changed into the tight brown leather skirt, soft white collared shirt, and navy vest that buttoned tightly under her bosom. The girls had loaned her leather boots and a knit blue hat to finish the look.

"I look ridiculous," Kai said, panic rising in her. Her legs felt naked. She had never worn clothing so short or tight; she had always dressed loosely to hide her figure.

Maaya and Emi shook their heads, surveying Kai with pride.

"You look gorgeous," Emi said.

"I can't . . . I can't go out like this," Kai said, tugging the skirt down as far as it would go. Which wasn't far.

"Woman up, Kai," Emi said.

Maaya laid a hand on Emi's arm, shooting her a look. "What's wrong?" Maaya asked, gently. "I know it's a little different than what you're used to, but it's not that revealing. Besides, the point of tonight is to be a little daring, to do something different than you normally would."

Kai blew a lock of hair from her eyes, not sure whether to tell them the whole truth.

Quitsu, who had been observing silently from the bed, jumped onto the desk, startling them all. "She is nervous because she's never dressed like a girl before."

"Traitor," she muttered.

Maaya, having already gotten over the surprise of hearing Quitsu speak once, found her tongue more quickly. "What does he mean?"

Kai closed her eyes and leaned back against her desk, trying to force down the memories that were threatening to overwhelm her. Friends she couldn't have, ways she couldn't act, boys she couldn't flirt with, dresses she couldn't wear. All because of her secret.

"My parents knew I was a moonburner from the day I was born. They knew what it would mean in Kita. So, they pretended I was a boy," Kai said. "For seventeen years."

Maaya and Emi's expressions were a matched set—wide eyes and open mouths. Kai couldn't help but chuckle.

"My parents planned to smuggle me to Miina when I was eighteen, so I could join the citadel. But I was exposed. My punishment was to be left in the desert to die. That's how I ended up here. Thanks to Quitsu, anyway." She scratched his ears.

"I can't imagine what you must have gone through," Maaya said.

"Why didn't your parents just move to Miina when you were younger?" Emi asked. Maaya shot her another sidelong glance.

"Er, sorry," Emi said. "It just seems like an easier solution than putting you through all of that."

Kai frowned. Her parents had told her she couldn't start her training until she was eighteen, but the novices here started as young as twelve. Had they lied to her?

"I guess . . ." Kai said, fumbling for something to say, "because of the ranch? We couldn't leave our land? I never thought to ask them. And now . . . it's too late."

Quitsu rubbed his head on her arm, lending his warm strength to her.

"This is getting a little heavy for moonburner day out," Emi said.

"What Emi means," Maaya piped in, "is that we are very sorry for what you went through."

"Yes, that is what I mean." Emi crossed the room and sat on the desk next to her. "Listen, Kai. Maybe a few of the moonburners here had perfect easy childhoods, but most of us didn't. Maaya's older sister was killed in a sunburner raid, and her parents have never been the same."

Kai looked at Maaya, whose jaw was set, her arms crossed. She gave a sharp nod.

Emi continued, "My parents died when I was young from cherry fever. I had the good fortune to live with my aunt who thought she'd pay for my room and board by renting me out to some of the men in the neighborhood."

Kai swallowed, her stomach souring.

"It only took one man bleeding out before she realized that wasn't a particularly lucrative business scheme," Emi said, her eyes flashing like steel.

"I don't mean to make light of what you went through, I'm sure it was horrible. But a lot of us have been through horrible things. But now we're here. We've been given a second chance. We've been given sisters to share our burdens with. And most of all, we've been granted power— power to defend ourselves, to destroy the injustice in this world, to fight for what is right. You're not powerless anymore. We don't have to hide anymore, or be ignored, or be exploited."

"Emi is right," Maaya said. "You are a moonburner. Even as a novice, you're already one of the most powerful women in the world. Don't be afraid to act like it."

"And you've got great legs, so wear the damn skirt," Emi said.

They were both right. It was time to stop being afraid, to stop being the smallest form of herself, to hope that no one noticed her or saw who she really was. She stood up.

"Okay," she said, taking as deep a breath as the tight vest buttons allowed. "Let's go."

The three girls walked out, heads high. Kai's heart was pounding. Quitsu had refused to stay behind, but had agreed to trail behind them once they reached the city, so they wouldn't be immediately recognized as moonburners.

"You know, Emi only gives about one motivational speech per year." Maaya whispered as they made their way through an alley behind Kai's dormitory. "You should be honored."

Kai laughed quietly. "I am, I am."

"Quota is met," Emi said.

"How are we going to get out of the citadel without being seen?" Kai asked, as they turned a corner. The rising morning sun wasn't particularly conducive to sneaking.

"You let us worry about that," Emi said.

Emi led them through a maze of back alleys and deserted squares until they reached a part of the citadel Kai had never visited. It seemed older, or perhaps simply neglected, the whitewashed paint coated with a thin layer of dust.

They peered around a corner into a triangular courtyard. One side of the triangle was bordered by a grassy hill which backed up against the citadel wall. A compact white marble building nestled against the hillside, its entrance marked by a carved marble archway.

"What is this place?"

"The crypt," Emi said, in her best spooky voice, waggling her fingers.

"Very funny," Kai said.

"Seriously. It's the crypt," Emi said. "Let's go."

Before Kai could protest, Maaya and Emi darted across the courtyard, opening the huge wooden door and slipping inside. Kai and Quitsu followed.

"Don't even say it," she said to Quitsu, as disapproval radiated from his furry body.

"I wouldn't dream of it."

The door opened into a cool antechamber, dimly lit by a few orbs.

"One of these days," Kai muttered, "someone is going to explain to me how all these damn orbs got here."

Maaya looked back at Kai as they made their way down the stairs at the back of the antechamber.

"I keep forgetting you didn't grow up here. The orbs have always been here. They say they were one of the first gifts Tsuki gave to the moonburners when they established Kyuden and the citadel. So they would never be without moonlight."

"All that means," Emi said, "is that no one knows how they got here, or how they work." Emi's snort rang off the stone walls. "Tsuki's gift, my foot."

"Do they actually give off moonlight? You can burn from them?" Kai asked in wonder.

"It's weak, but yes, in a pinch. Better to use your moonstone, if you can't get moonlight."

They finally reached the end of the staircase. It had grown much colder and Kai shivered in her thin white shirt. The shadows clung to the walls. A musty, vaguely unpleasant smell permeated her nostrils.

"What are we doing here?" Kai whispered, her voice echoing in the stone room.

Neither of the girls answered her. Emi turned back the cuff of her shirt and lit her moonstone link, so it shone bright white. She held her arm aloft. Kai swallowed her questions. Somehow, it seemed wrong to speak here.

The moonlight shone off the objects near them, but was swallowed by the blackness of the periphery of the room. In the dim light, Kai could see that the room was made entirely of stone, with a low, vaulted ceiling. They walked down an aisle way that passed between rows of crypts. They were the kind favored by the rich—stone sarcophagi with the likeness of the inhabitant within carved on top. A stone sarcophagus one row back caught her eye, the light just reaching it. It was huge, built on a dais with stone arches crossing from corner to corner and meeting in the middle. Kai could just see a woman's likeness was carved on top. The features . . . looked strangely familiar.

"Hey!" she called, drawn to it. "Come here for a second."

She crossed over one aisle and climbed the steps. The light followed as Emi and Maaya met her.

"We're not here on a field trip. Let's go," Emi said.

Even rendered in stone, the woman was young and beautiful, a delicate circlet on her head. Her face reminded Kai of someone, but she couldn't put her finger on it. At her feet lay a lynx with soft tufted ears, its head tucked peacefully on its knees. Her seishen?

Maaya read the inscription. "Azura, beloved daughter and sister." Kai's mind reeled, the Oracle's words flooding back into her mind.

"No, no, no," Emi said, grabbing Kai's hand. "Let's go."

Kai let Emi pull her away back to the main aisle and they continued into the bowels of the crypt.

"Who was she?" Kai asked, heart racing.

"She was the queen's sister," Emi said. "She died. They say it almost drove the queen mad with grief. Somehow I don't think she'd appreciate us lurking around."

Kai's thoughts tumbled as they walked the rest of the way through the dark crypt. *Daughter of Azura.* Those were the Oracle's words. Was it a different Azura she was talking about? How could she be the daughter of a dead woman? Kai had to know more.

CHAPTER 14

Kai came back to herself as they pulled up short in front of a sarcophagus in a corner alcove.

"Felicita," Kai read.

Emi stood up one step, and placed both hands on the stone woman's bosom.

"What are you doing?" Kai asked.

Emi pushed, and a grinding noise followed. A portion of the wall behind the sarcophagus slid to the side, revealing a narrow passageway.

"Seriously?" Kai asked.

"We're pretty sure this passage was designed by a man," Maaya said with a giggle.

They came out of the tunnel into a dark alcove. The alcove led to a covered walkway that opened onto a courtyard. A fountain bubbled, depicting a woman pouring water into the mouth of a man down on one knee.

"If you ever need to get back," Emi said, "just find your way to the square of the thirsty man."

Kai looked back over her shoulder at the fountain, strangely disconcerted.

"We're pretty sure that was designed by a man, too," Maaya said.

It was Kai's first glimpse of Kyuden from the ground. It felt strange to be sneaking about in the daytime, as the sun's first rays fell on the tops of the dingy buildings, turning the formerly white walls a fiery orange. Kai trailed after Emi and Maaya, taking it all in with wide eyes.

The city was a maze of narrow cobblestone and dirt streets, with a mish-mash of stone and brick buildings built so closely together that they resembled strange parasites feeding off one another. Wherever she looked, the white stone walls of the citadel loomed high above them.

The city showed signs of neglect, which only got worse the farther they walked.

Emi must have seen Kai's wrinkled nose, and chuckled. "City living. It's a beautiful thing, isn't it?"

"We're in the old city right now. It backs up against the Citadel and the river," Maaya explained. "These are some of the oldest buildings in the city, which is why the planning leaves . . . something to be desired. The new city is across the river. That is where most of the wealthy and merchants live. It's much nicer than this part."

As they walked, the cobbled streets gave way to mud, which mixed with trash and waste, splashed onto the nearby buildings by wagon wheels and horse hooves. Beggars and wide-eyed orphans gathered in clutches in door frames and alleyways, sorting through garbage for treasures discarded by the more fortunate. It looked as if the abundance enjoyed by the queen and her moonburners did not extend to all of Miinan society.

"Is this still the old city?" Kai asked.

"No," Maaya said. "This is the Meadows. It's the poorest part of the city."

"The Meadows?" Kai asked. Nothing seemed further from the truth.

"I think people started calling it that ironically. The name just sort of stuck," Emi explained.

Kai could tell they made it through the Meadows when the streets returned to cobblestone with deep carved gutters for waste.

"We're almost there," Maaya said. "This neighborhood is called the Coin. It's near the gates to the city walls and the port, which means a lot of the merchants live here."

They crested a hill, and Kai's breath caught in her chest. The sun was fully up now and glistened off the river that snaked below them. Thousands of buildings nestled against the hillside leading down to the river. Their tiled roofs glistened in the sun, like the scales of a great dragon.

"Wow," Kai said.

"I've never been to Kistana," Emi said, referring to the Kitan capital, "but I think it's safe to say we live in the most beautiful city in the world."

They soon reached their destination, a respectable three-story inn called The Fox and Fiddle. Kai glanced up along the tops of the buildings for Quitsu and saw his silver fox form. A good omen perhaps?

The tavern room of The Fox and Fiddle was large and welcoming, flanked by two large stone fireplaces and topped with half-timbered ceilings. The warm wood walls were covered with ancient-looking musical instruments, some that she didn't recognize at all. Well-worn tables were nestled throughout the room, full with customers enjoying steaming hot meals, cold beverages, and good conversation. They wound their way through the patrons and found Emi's friends, two other young women wearing hats, sitting at a high table near the back.

Pleasantries were exchanged, and Kai met Stela and Leilu, two samaneras. Stela had an exotic look to her, with dark almond skin, freckles across her nose, and big silver earrings that jangled when she moved her head. Leilu was tall and lean, with a long oval face and sparkling straight white teeth. Both had big smiles and easy laughs.

"We really wish we could have seen you drop Chiya to the dirt," Stela said. Kai chuckled. "You and about every other samanera in the citadel!"

"We should sell tickets next time," Emi said. "We'd make a fortune."

A wrinkled serving man placed down a chilled blue glass bottle and two ceramic cups on their table.

"Three more cups please," Stela said.

"And an order of the duck dumplings," Leilu called after the man, who was already moving on to serve his other patrons. "And the fried noodles."

Stela cast a pointed look in Leilu's direction. "What?" Leilu said. "I'm hungry."

"You're always hungry," Emi said.

"Exactly," Stela agreed.

The serving man returned with three more cups and Stela filled them with a clear liquid, distributing them.

She held up her cup. "To a much deserved day out."

"And to new friends," Maaya chimed in, casting a warm look at Kai.

"Kampai." The girls said, clinking their glasses together and downing the contents.

Kai followed suit and let the cold drink slide down her throat. The flavor was sour and the liquid burned a trail down her mouth and throat. She coughed.

The others looked at her with amused gazes. "Not a fan of sake?" Emi asked.

"It's terrible," Kai admitted.

The others laughed.

"An acquired taste," Maaya said. "Have you . . . not had it before?"

"I didn't get out much," Kai said. "But you probably already guessed that."

"Pour her another," Leilu said. "She's got lost time to make up for."

The second cup went down easier than the first. The burning nestled in her stomach, turning into a pleasant warmth.

Steaming plates of dumplings and noodles arrived and the girls dove in, chatting about classmates and teachers. They made Kai down another glass of sake, which was already going to her head.

"I wonder," she mused, "if I get drunk, will Quitsu get drunk too?"

"Only one way to find out," Emi said with a devilish grin as she poured another round.

Emi had just flagged down the server to order another bottle when the band stepped onto the makeshift stage in the corner of the tavern room. There were four members: a singer, a biwa mandolin player, a bambu flute player, and a drummer. They all appeared to be in their early twenties and were very good looking. The mandolin player made Ren look like a country farmhand.

"Rox, the singer, and I grew up together," Stela said. "He's like a brother to me."

The other girls were staring at the band with the same fascination Kai hoped was hidden from her own face.

"They're all so . . ." Emi said, lost for words for once.

"Attractive?" Stela said, smirking.

"Yes," Maaya said, eyes glued to the stage.

"It's almost distracting," Emi said.

"Rox left for a few years to study music under some master up in the

Akashi foothills. I think they all met up there."

"They breed them well up there," Leilu said.

"Just wait until you hear them play," Stela said.

The biwa player finished tuning his instrument, and the band started into a lively tune about a man, a woman, and a summer meadow. Kai had never heard such wonderful music before. Rox's voice was silky and soft, with a surprising vocal range.

The melodies of the biwa and the flute floated and wove together, playing off each other like partners in an intricate dance. When the song was over, the silence hung in the tavern room for a moment before the audience erupted into applause.

Stela grinned with pride as if they were her own children on stage. "I told you they were good."

When Rox announced that the band was taking a break, they were swept off the stage by friendly patrons and offers of drinks. Rox and the biwa player extricated themselves from their throng of admirers and made their way to the girls' table.

Stela made the introductions. "Ladies, this is Rox and Atsu."

Rox and Atsu sidled up to their table on either side of Stela. Atsu looked appreciatively at Maaya, one elbow on the table.

"Maaya. That's a beautiful name," he said.

"Thanks," Maaya replied, a giggle escaping her like a hiccup.

Emi rolled her eyes and turned to Rox. "You guys were great. Really. I've never heard anything quite like it."

"Thanks," Rox said. "We have a good thing going. But it's always nice to get some new fans, especially friends of Stela. You all have the most interesting lives." He winked and playfully palmed Stela's hat-covered head.

"It sounds more exciting than it is," Stela said.

"I don't know, looks like you've seen some action lately." Rox said, nodding towards Kai.

Kai started. He was talking to her. Her hand flew to her eye and her cheeks grew hot.

"Just a little training incident," she said.

"You should see the other girl," Maaya said. "Kai dropped the toughest girl in our class."

"We know now to stay on your good side," Rox said, holding up his hands in mock surrender.

"And what about you?" Atsu asked Maaya. "Are you a fighter too?"

"She's more of a lover than a fighter," Emi chimed in before Maaya could

respond.

Maaya shot her a mortified look, but was mollified when Atsu replied: "I like the sound of that."

The musicians were soon summoned back to the stage. After refilling their drinks, they began to play again. Their second set was even better, and when Atsu took the lead on a ballad, with some pointed looks towards Maaya, Kai thought the girl might melt out of her chair.

When they finally took their fingers off their instruments, the applause was even louder.

"We should probably head back," Emi said. "It's getting late."

Kai had forgotten that she was supposed to be sleeping and that she would have to face Pura in just a few hours. Her head was already starting to pound.

"Oh goddess," Kai said. "Class."

"Me too," Leilu said. "Bed is calling."

"I'm going to stick around for their last set," Stela said. "I'll be fine to head home on my own. "

"Are you sure?" Leilu asked. "You'll have to head through the Meadows. It's pretty late."

"I don't mind staying with Stela," Maaya offered. "My night is light tomorrow."

Emi looked at Maaya for a long moment. "Uh-huh," she said. "How kind of you to volunteer."

"I'm a team player," Maaya said, smiling sweetly.

CHAPTER 15

The street was quiet as they left The Fox and Fiddle, afternoon shadows falling over the stone buildings. As they made their way back, Kai caught a glimpse of a flash of silver in a nearby alley. She had totally forgotten about Quitsu. She'd have to ask him if he felt tipsy.

Emi and Leilu set a quick pace, and Kai struggled to keep up, between her heeled boots and her pounding head.

"Don't look back," Emi said, "but we are being followed."

Kai looked over her shoulder instinctively and caught a glimpse of a man in brown before he ducked behind a corner.

"What does he want?" Kai asked. "Probably our money," Leilu said.

"Or our virtue," Emi said.

"Let's hope just our money," Leilu said. "We know you don't have any virtue left to take."

Emi barked a laugh. "Nice one."

"Should we take our hats off; show him we are moonburners?" Kai asked.

"No," Emi and Leilu said together.

"It's daytime," Emi explained. "We can't intimidate them with burning. Plus, there are plenty in the city who would be even happier to take down a moonburner."

Kai opened her mouth to ask why, but before she could, Leilu ducked into a dark alley. Kai quickly followed, despite a growing sense of trepidation. They flattened themselves against the wall behind a pile of garbage.

"I hope we lost him," Leilu whispered.

Two shadows entered the other side of the alley.

Leilu sighed. "Damn. There's more."

Emi and Leilu stepped into the center of the alley and Kai quickly followed suit.

"We don't want any trouble. We don't have any money," Emi called. Her stance was wide but calm. "Let us pass."

Kai turned back the way they had come and saw the man in brown had been joined by a large, dangerous-looking friend.

Emi slowly loosened a dagger from its sheath on her belt and Leilu drew two twin needle-sharp blades. Kai cursed herself for not being more prepared. Had she grown soft in a few weeks at the citadel? A sliver of silver streaked up the alley wall behind the men in front of them, catching Kai's eye.

Quitsu was crouching on the edge of the roof, ready to attack. At least she had him.

"Fine clothes like those, I'se be betting you have something," said one of the men they faced. He took a step forward. He was blocky and stout, with a scar running down the side of his face, pulling his eye down in an expression almost like sorrow.

"And why don hats on this fine summer afternoon?" he looked at his friend in a mock questioning tone. "Very odd indeed."

"If you know who we are, you know who we serve," Leilu said. "Stand aside and let us be."

The other man was skinny, his cutoff sleeves revealing wirey ropes of muscle running up his arms.

"Not everyone is a fan of who you serve, burner," he spit. "My father was a reputable merchant, until your queen stripped him of wealth and his title for the crime of having balls."

The first man looked them up and down.

"Maybe it's time we remind you bitches what having balls is all about. Ain't no moon to help you now."

Kai felt the hairs on the back of her neck rise. The two men behind them were closing in.

She leaned forward and whispered. "Two more behind us."

Emi nodded imperceptibly before leaping at the ringleader, sticking her knife in his eye. Her sudden violence startled Kai. The man's scream echoed through the alley, and he clutched at his face, blood bubbling through his fingers.

Leilu moved on the other one a split second later, slicing at his belly, trying to open up his soft insides. He was too fast, leaping backwards just out of reach of her blade.

Kai spun and dropped to the ground, anticipating an attack from behind. The man in brown stumbled over her, but his friend was still on his feet, clutching a short dagger in his hand. Kai would have to disarm him. She remembered her father's calm voice. "Attack first, when you have the element of surprise. Your opponent will only underestimate you once."

As the man came towards her, she lunged and punched him hard in the throat. He stumbled back, choking, and she kneed him in the groin. He careened sideways onto the ground. She stomped on his hand, grabbing his knife.

A strong arm snaked around her neck and grabbed the wrist of her knife hand, pulling her back against his body. It was the man in brown. He smelled of sweat and dirt; his breath on her cheek reeked of stale onions.

She stomped on his foot and elbowed him in the stomach, but he didn't release her. Kai heard a screech and felt the man lurch forward, screaming. She wrenched herself out of his grip and saw Quitsu crouched on the man's shoulders, claws dug into his flesh. He had the man's ear in his mouth, ripped clean off the man's head.

She turned and saw that Emi and Leilu had dispatched their two attackers as well. The men were on the ground, groaning and bleeding. As she glanced at the two she and Quitsu had dealt with, she saw more figures enter the alley, running towards them. Reinforcements.

"Let's go!" Kai said.

The three girls ran from the alley, Quitsu close on their heels. They entered a market square still dotted with people, despite the late hour.

The market was full of colorful tents and booths, many closed up for the day. The merchants were mostly women, with burly bodyguards standing cross-armed to the side of each booth.

Kai had only paused for a moment to take in the sights, but realized that Emi and Leilu were nowhere to be found. She spun around, searching for their clothing and their hats in the crowd. Where were they?

Two rough-looking men were making their way through the crowd from the alley. She ducked behind a tent and started running across the square, hidden by the bulk of the main tents. She made it to the far side and turned into a narrow, cobbled street between two mismatched buildings.

Kai slowed to a trot, moving through the streets. She had no idea where in the city she was, but she hoped that she could follow glimpses of the citadel, high on its hill, back to the courtyard with the thirsty man. She couldn't see Quitsu, but she was confident that he was following her.

She zigzagged through streets and alleys, hitting dead ends and back-tracking. She loped through the streets for what must have been thirty minutes. She had to be getting close. Based on the smell, she thought she had passed through the Meadows. The sun was low in the sky and would be setting soon. What would Pura do when she didn't show up for moonburning class? Should she try to find someone to ask for directions?

Kai turned right into a narrow street, its buildings lined top to bottom with climbing ivy. She saw a number of people gathered at the end of the alley, and flattened herself against the ivy behind a doorpost, not wanting to attract attention. She peeked through the leaves, trying to gauge whether they were dangerous or not.

The group was clothed in navy blue robes, hoods up. She saw a flash of silver in the air and squinted. She searched for it again and caught sight of it, rippling sinuously in the air. It was a seishen—the queen's seishen.

She peered harder and saw long straight silver hair smoothed down the front of one of the cloaks. She could just see the silhouette of the hard face beneath the hood. Geisa, the queen's general who had attacked Kai's village. There was another figure in a blue cloak that only came up to Geisa's shoulder. That had to be the queen. As Kai leaned further out of her hiding place to see who else she might recognize, the dragon's head flicked in her direction. She flattened back against the wall.

Don't look, don't come over here, nothing to see here! She thought. She glanced back in time to see the group enter a doorway in the side of the alley. The wall of the building rumbled slightly against her back and then the group was gone.

"That was too close," she said, breathing a sigh of relief.

"Agreed," Quitsu said, jumping down from the nearby roof. "I don't get a good feeling from the queen's seishen. There is something off about him."

"Aren't all seishen supposed to get along?" Kai asked.

"Like all humans do?" Quitsu retorted.

She couldn't argue with that.

"Let's check out the door," she said. "Maybe it leads back to the citadel."

Kai stood before the wall where Geisa and the others had disappeared. Nothing. There was no door, no handle, not even an outline of a door. She threaded her hands beneath the ivy and felt the stones, feeling for a latch or seam. Again, nothing.

"Where is the door?"

"I don't know," Quitsu said. " But something tells me that we aren't supposed to know about this."

They looked at each other, the moment stretching between them. What were the queen and Geisa doing in the city, hooded and clandestine?

At breakfast that morning, Kai filled her plate with food, hoping a full belly would make up for the fact that she felt like she had sandpaper for eyelids and a drummer for a brain.

After the dead end in the alley, she and Quitsu had managed to find their way back to the courtyard of the thirsty man. Kai had just enough time to run back to her room, throw her uniform on, and make it to breakfast.

When she sat down at the table, Emi and Leilu fell on Kai with relief, whispering profuse apologies for losing her. Kai was tempted to tell them about the strange scene she and Quitsu had seen in the alley, but something held her back. She didn't want to admit to anyone, even her friends, that she had been spying on the queen.

Maaya and Stela joined them at their table as Kai devoured a plate of eggs. Maaya was positively glowing, as if she had gotten days of extra sleep, rather than missing a night of it. Though she tried to fight it, a smile kept creeping onto her face when her guard was down.

Emi, in typical fashion, called her out. "We can all tell you're in looove," Emi said, exaggerating the word and bobbing her head from side to side in mock dreaminess. She lowered her voice. "But we all know what comes of a moonburner in love. Ten lashes if you're lucky, the headsman's axe if you're not. He's not worth it."

A dark cloud crossed Maaya's face.

"Just for once in your life, can you not be a total bitch?" She picked up her tray and stormed away from the table.

"You're right, Emi," Stela said. "But when it comes to matters of the heart, we have no ears to hear at all. You have to let her make her own mistakes."

"She's not some farm-maid who's going to end up broken-hearted or pregnant. The stakes are too high here," Emi said. "She can't see him. End of discussion."

CHAPTER 16

The days began to flash by as Kai settled into her life at the citadel. The summer faded into a crisp fall, and then into the cool beginning of winter.

Kai took her meals with Emi, Maaya, Leilu and Stela, always hearing the latest gossip and news. The targeted sunburner attacks continued around the city, particularly downriver from the waterfall, below the city's protective walls.

Kai pointedly avoided Chiya and her followers wherever she went, though a few runins were unavoidable. While Chiya and Tanu sent plenty of insults and glares her way, it seemed that Nanase's punishment had been enough to dissuade Chiya from throwing any actual blows.

Kai progressed in her classes, catching up enough to earn even Mistress Furie's approval, though she only showed it with a tight nod of her head. Kai learned to care for the menagerie of unusual creatures that lived in the citadel. She learned to differentiate the koumori from each other, saw that they had different personalities. Her favorite was Peppe, who had first borne her from the Little Tottori Oasis to the citadel. Peppe would click and coo when Kai brought her fruit from the kitchens.

Nanase was true to her promise and moved Kai into the samanera weapons class. Nanase was an excellent teacher, illustrating form and technique while allowing her students to experiment and find their own strengths. After class one day, Kai cornered Nanase as she headed from the courtyard. Nanase's seishen was with her, soaring above them, a silver sliver against the bright moon.

"I was hoping that I could obtain a dagger of some type." Kai said. "Just a small one. To keep with me."

Nanase stopped and turned on her heel, her braids swinging behind her. "Do you not feel safe here in the citadel?"

"No, it's not that," Kai said, backpedaling. "It's just . . . you never can be too careful . . ."

Nanase chuckled. "Only a fool feels safe, and that is because he is too stupid to see his enemies around him. Your request is a wise one, especially until your blockage is dealt with."

Nanase unstrapped a dagger and sheath from her own arm, a short, wicked looking little blade with an intricate carved knot of jade at the pommel.

Nanase handed it to Kai. "Here. The carving means sister. It was a gift to me from someone many years ago."

"I can't accept this," Kai said, trying to hand it back. "Something from the armory is fine, something plain and functional. This . . . is too much."

"I insist," Nanase said. "It has watched over me for many years. Now, I believe it is supposed to be yours. After all, you can't run about dangerous parts of the city during the daytime without a blade."

Nanase turned on her heel, leaving the dagger hanging limply in Kai's hand.

"How does she know everything?" Kai said to herself out loud. Louder than she had thought. Nanase turned back.

"I wasn't always a bureaucrat," Nanase said. "Don't ever forget it."

"Why did you take the job as headmistress, then?" Kai asked, feeling bold.

"A weapon does not choose where to cut," Nanase replied. "The warrior does that."

Kai's least favorite class was Moonburning, although she had nothing but admiration for Pura. She learned all about moonburning theory, weapons techniques, the wanes in power during the phases of the moon and how to store moonlight in a moonstone for use during the day.

Everything a moonburner would need. She learned about scrying, a technique that allowed moonburners to locate someone or something. Pura said there was a way to block a moonburner from scrying you out as well, but the faculty didn't share that with novices.

But still, Kai was blocked. Pura consulted other burners and teachers, but none could recommend a solution to her problem. Pura and Kai linked together, exploring the edges and contours of her blockage, examining it from every angle. Sometimes, she felt like she could almost see seams in the wall, as if it was built by adding one stone to another.

When Kai said as much, Pura paled, growing quiet.

"What?" Kai asked.

"It is nothing," Pura said.

"You know something," Kai insisted. "Tell me. Maybe it could help."

A flurry of emotions passed over Pura's face, before her shoulders sagged. "It's not much," she said. "I have heard . . . in the early days, before the Burning War . . . that moonburning was used in darker ways. Burners would use it not just physically, but against each other's minds. They knew ways to drive each other mad with visions or terrors. They knew how to cut each other off from the moon, sometimes permanently."

"So you think," Kai said, "that someone might have done this to me? You said as much to Nanase."

I do not think so," Pura assured her. "That was very old magic, a dark way that was lost to us. I do not believe that anyone alive today would know how to do this thing."

"But, it is possible," Kai said.

"Yes, " Pura admitted. "It is possible."

Kai and Quitsu spent time with Master Vita too, drinking menthe tea, reading in the big armchairs by the fire and playing Goa with black and white pieces on his ancient carved wood game board. He gave her mountains of books to read, pulling volume after volume until her backlog seemed impossibly long. She almost asked him about the Oracle and her strange prophecy a hundred times, but never did. Somehow, it felt like it had been for her and Quitsu's ears only. Instead, she gently nudged him towards titles that could help her understand her moonburning blockage.

When they took breaks, she would pepper him with questions about moonburners, the queen, the citadel or the city. She was grateful to receive unedited answers from him, unlike some of her professors.

"So not everyone is happy with the queen's leadership?" Kai asked.

"You've been into the city, you must know there is dissatisfaction," Master Vita chided gently. "But yes, there is unhappiness among the nobles and merchant classes, as well. That's what happens when you demonize half your population. There is also discussion about who will succeed the throne, since she has shown no signs of producing an heir."

"An heir?" Kai asked. She hadn't even thought about it. "Do Miinan queens marry?"

"They used to," he said. "But I doubt this queen ever will. I do not think there will be an heir. Let us hope that a strong candidate emerges when the time comes."

Kai turned the new information over in her head, dismayed at how little she still understood of this new world.

Kai didn't know if it was the adjustment from day to night that upset her circadian rhythm, or if it was the Oracle's strange words that floated up, unbidden, when she closed her eyes, but she didn't sleep much. She spent some mornings wandering the citadel's many green spaces, like the garden where she had first met the Oracle.

Her favorite was the herb garden that grew behind the hospital ward. The garden was arranged in neat rows, bordered on one side by a tall wooden wall covered with climbing herbs, and on the other by a serene pond which held aquatic plants.

The nurses and staff had originally tried to shoo her away from the garden, but eventually relented when they realized that she was useful. Kai trimmed branches, pulled weeds, and checked the soil and the plants. When she worked in the garden, it felt like her mother was there. It was as if Kai could hear her careful instruction, teaching Kai the difference between the goatwort, goatweed and sheeproot. She had doused her father's tea with goatwort as a prank, leaving his tongue totally numb for a day. Her mother scolded her half-heartedly, but couldn't stop laughing at her father's slurred speech.

It was one such sleepless night, working in the garden under the light of a weak winter sun, that Kai found herself face to face with Queen Airi. She couldn't hide her surprise. Kai hardly ever ran into anyone else in the garden, besides the few nurses who worked the day shift.

"Your Majesty," Kai said, giving a low bow. "I didn't expect to see you here."

The queen, resplendent in a thick cloak of honey-colored wool with a white fur lining, waved Kai's comment aside. "Every now and then I like to run my own errands. Helps me feel grounded."

"Of course," Kai said. "Can I help you find something?"

"I already found it," the queen nonchalantly waved a bundle of herbs that she had been holding at her side. "But thank you."

Kai stilled her breathing, trying not to appear alarmed. She would recognize that herb anywhere. Nightmark. It was a very powerful sedative. If given in too great a dose, it was lethal. The bundle the queen held in her hand was enough to kill a herd of cattle. Why in Tsuki's name did she need that much?

"Well . . ." Kai continued awkwardly. "I am glad you found what you needed."

"Why are you here?" The queen asked. "Shouldn't you be in bed, resting before your lessons?"

Kai's face colored. "I have a hard time sleeping sometimes. This garden . . . it is soothing. It reminds me of home, of my mother."

"Your mother must be very proud of what you have accomplished," the queen said.

"My mother . . ." Kai said. "She was enslaved to a Kitan official. It's my fault. It happened after I was exposed . . . as a burner."

"Kita is a cruel place," the queen said. "I am sorry to hear about her plight."

A crazy thought struck Kai. "I can't just leave her there, subject to his whims. Once my training is complete, would you allow me to go rescue her?"

The queen was quiet for a moment. "I see this weighs on your soul. I fear this unfinished business will keep you from true devotion to our cause."

Kai opened her mouth to protest, but the queen held up a hand to silence her. "I do not fault you for this. Devotion to one's family is a trait we value here. However, I cannot allow a moonburner to risk herself on a personal mission. You are too valuable."

Kai's heart sank. What did she expect?

"However," the queen said. "We have operatives in Ushai. I will make inquiries into the condition of your mother. Perhaps we can help her situation."

"Thank you!" Kai said. "That would be a great kindness."

"We are hard sometimes, Kai, because we have to be," the queen said. "But we are not animals, like the sunburners. I will see what we can do."

CHAPTER 17

It was a cold winter morning. Quitsu stretched out in front of the hearth like a dog, his dignity tossed aside. Master Vita stoked the fire in one of the big stone fireplaces. He was moving more slowly than usual, his cough angry and deep.

"Are you feeling all right?" Kai asked, examining his coloring as he collapsed into the chair opposite hers. He looked pale.

"Don't you worry."

Kai looked at him skeptically, but decided to let him be. She thumbed through the stack of books on the table next to her. At the very bottom, she saw one she had pulled months ago, *Moonburner Lineage*. She pulled it out and began to flip through the pages. She was disappointed to see only page after page of highly illustrated family trees.

"Are these the Miinan royal family?"

He looked at it through his half-moon spectacles. "Some of them. And the nobility. All the burners should be in here."

The end of the book contained blank pages, no doubt to include the future Miinan royals. The last page with writing showed Queen Airi, as well as her parents and grandparents. There was another name next to Airi's, a name that had been scratched out.

"Did Queen Airi have a sibling?" Kai asked, holding the page out to Master Vita and pointing at the obscured name. Despite the mystery of the Oracle's words and the woman in the crypt dancing through her head on a daily basis, she had not worked up the courage to ask.

He grew still. "Yes. She had an older sister.

"What happened to her?" Kai asked.

Master Vita looked at her for a long moment. "This is not a topic often spoken about around the citadel."

"Please tell me," Kai said. "How can this be my home if there are pieces of it that are hidden from me?"

Master Vita snorted. "That sounds like every home I've ever been in." But he relented. "She died. The queen was heartbroken. Her name and image were wiped from the books and paintings. It was too painful for the queen to hear mention of her."

"When did she die?" Kai asked.

"Well . . . almost twenty years ago now. The whole kingdom was devastated when it happened."

"The whole kingdom?" Kai asked.

Master Vita removed his half-moon spectacles and wiped them with a handkerchief he produced from his vest pocket.

"Azura was like a ray of moonlight. She was the most delightful child, joyful and full of laughter. Everyone in the palace loved her, most of all her mother, the queen. She had every right to be spoiled rotten, but she wasn't. She was kind, generous to a fault. She would spend her free time in the hospital ward or the herb garden, where most children would be climbing trees or getting into trouble. She would have been an excellent queen." He paused, his voice quivering.

"I see why her sister must have loved her," Kai said, trying to give him time to compose himself. The Oracle's prophecy must be wrong. Master Vita confirmed it again. Azura had died almost twenty years ago. There is no way she could have a seventeen-year old daughter.

"Yes," Master Vita said. "Airi. Never were two sisters less alike. Although they had different fathers, so they were only half-sisters. Airi was darkness where Azura was light. She was spoiled, selfish, downright cruel at times. She would play pranks on the servants; she broke the cook's leg by strewing marbles about the kitchen one winter. Although, I doubt she meant to do that," he admitted.

"She played so many mean-spirited pranks on her tutor that he quit and I took Airi on as well. That girl worshipped her sister along with everyone, but you could see jealousy there as well. Always she was in trouble, seeking any attention she could get. When Azura died, Airi lost herself."

"I could see that," Kai remarked, thinking of the queen's ice-cold eyes.

"It wasn't until Geisa showed up and Airi found religion that she seemed to come back to her senses," Master Vita said. "I can't help but wonder if she really has changed, or if she's just a better actress."

"You said Geisa just showed up? Where did she come from?" Kai asked.

"It was rumored that she was a sunburner prisoner, who escaped and pre-sented herself to the queen for refuge. Within days of Geisa's arrival, she and the queen became thick as thieves. There were those who tried to warn the queen that Geisa might have too great of an influence over her, especially with so little known about her past. Their warnings were not . . . well received."

Kai thought about the sunburner's mention of a facility, the ivy-covered door, and the bundle of nightmark in the queen's hand.

"Do you think the queen could be holding sunburners prisoner? Hurting them?" she asked.

"Queen Airi is capable of anything, so long as it furthers her interests." Master Vita leaned forward and locked his eyes with hers. "Curiosity is a gift, and I can see you have much of it. But at the citadel, curiosity is dangerous, especially where Airi is concerned. You must promise me you will abandon any theories of yours and think of it no more."

Kai squirmed, looking away. How could she just ignore the fact that something was going on?

"Promise me," he commanded, with an iron will behind his voice that she had never heard before.

"I promise," she said, sighing.

Kai and Quitsu sat on the front steps of the library in the shadow of the huge overhang. She had stayed long into the day after she and Master Vita had their conversation, staring into the fire and thinking. She couldn't be the daughter of Azura, Azura had died. And besides, her mother's name was Hanae.

"Do you think Master Vita is right about Airi?" Kai asked.

"Yes," Quitsu said. "He has been here a lot longer than we have."

"I hate this," Kai said. "There is something going on, I can feel it. The prophecy, the sunburner attacks. The queen is up to something. But I don't even know what kind of puzzle I'm trying to piece together." Kai sighed and stood up, brushing the dust from her uniform. Her eye caught a silver shape winding through the courtyard across from them. It was the queen's seishen.

She stepped back into the shadows, watching him pass. Geisa strode beside him, a look of permanent unpleasantness on her face.

"Where are they going?" Kai whispered.

"I don't know," replied Quitsu. "But they both make me nervous."

"You know," Kai said. "There is no time like the present."

"For what?" Quitsu asked.

"To start putting together the pieces."

"This is a bad idea," Quitsu whispered as he caught up to her, his paws silent on the stones. "You promised Master Vita you would drop it."

"We're not looking into the queen, just Geisa."

"Somehow I think that violates the spirit of the promise."

"Admit it," Kai whispered. "You're as curious as I am."

"You know what they say about curiosity," Quitsu said. "It killed the seishen."

"No one says that."

Kai and Quitsu stalked Geisa and the seishen, keeping to the shadows of bushes and buildings. They entered the front door of a compact two-story building, an intricately carved square archway above its doors.

"What is this place?" Kai asked.

"Tsuki's temple," Quitsu said.

Kai had never been here.

"You should probably at least pretend to be religious, you know, keep up appearances."

"I'll take that under advisement," Kai said, crouching low. Seeing that the coast was clear, Kai darted across the courtyard and around the side of the temple.

"Let's see if there's another way in," she whispered.

Around the side of the building, Quitsu leaped up into a tree, easily bounding from branch to branch.

"There is a balcony above the chapel," he said. "I see the queen on the ground floor. She's probably just praying. She's known to be very devout."

Kai hesitated. Sneaking into the temple to spy on the queen while she was praying? Suddenly this didn't seem like a very good plan. Kai's excitement began to fade.

"We should go," she said, "before we get into trouble."

"There is another woman present," Quitsu whispered down from the tree. "The Oracle."

The Oracle's words came rushing back to Kai, echoing ominously in her head. She heard them every night in her troubled dreams.

"Daughter of Azura. Daughter of Miina. Hear these truths.

The moon cannot enslave the sun, nor make the day its mistress.

Or victory shall spell defeat, a crimson sky its auspice.

The sun and moon must shine as one, or all will be undone."

The few times Kai had managed to talk to Roweni since that day, she had refused to give any more information about her prophecy. Was the Oracle more direct when she talked with the queen? Maybe Kai could learn something.

Pushing aside her better judgment, Kai scuttled up to the side of the temple, trying to stay out of sight. The building was made of rough-hewn stone and she made her way up easily. She had climbed the few trees around the ranch as a child to avoid the chores her father had assigned her. This wasn't much different.

She reached the stone balcony and grabbed the ornamental railing. It groaned as she hauled herself over the edge, but held. She opened the window, cringing when it squeaked. Quitsu had joined her on the balcony and he slipped inside, checking for signs of other moonburners or servants.

"It's clear," he whispered. She crept inside, dropping off the windowsill onto the floor.

Kai had never been inside Tsuki's temple before. It smelled sickly sweet of incense and candle smoke. She crept from the side room they had entered through a dark wood-paneled hallway to what she hoped was the sanctuary. The temple floor was wide and empty, leaving Kai and Quitsu few places to hide.

The balcony was open as well, but for an ornamental railing of twisting dragons keeping the balcony-goers from plunging to the main floor. Two carved white stone statues of Tsuki flanked either side of the balcony. Kai and Quitsu crept behind one. It was as close as they could get without being clearly visible.

On the main floor of the temple, near the altar, stood the queen, Geisa, and the Oracle. The queen's seishen writhed through the air lazily around the group, nonchalantly defying gravity. The Oracle's tiny seishen sat on her shoulder, its feathers so puffed up that Kai could hardly see the bird beneath.

The queen and the Oracle were two of the smallest but fiercest women she had ever seen, and even from her vantage point, she could see that no love was lost between them. The Oracle's arms were tightly folded before her. The queen's hands were clasped behind her back, a look of disdain on her beautiful face. Geisa stood a strange counterpoint to the taut hostility of the other two women, relaxed and leaning against the tall altar, picking her fingernails with a dagger. Kai had no doubt that she would be ready to strike at a moment's notice.

"I think you are interpreting it wrong. You've been wrong before," Queen Airi said, coldly.

"Yes," the Oracle hesitated. "But, in those instances, there were many paths set before me. In this, I see a night of no moon and a day of no sun."

"A new moon, and an eclipse. My scholars have already interpreted this. It is the perfect chance to strike at the sunburners unaware."

"Yes," the Oracle said. "I do think it means that. But I see more. I see no more moon. And no more sun," she emphasized each word. "If you continue on your current path, I see the end. Of the burners. The sunburners, yes. But the moonburners too."

The queen turned from the Oracle, pacing the floor.

"You must be wrong," Geisa said. "We have prayed to the goddess about our plan and she has assured us of your queen's ultimate victory."

"I fear the queen's ultimate victory will mean our ultimate defeat," the Oracle retorted.

The words reverberated in Kai's head, so alike the words of the prophecy the Oracle had given her months before. Were they related?

"Pardon me if I do not take your hunch over the assurances of the goddess," the queen said.

"Then what do you need me for?" the Oracle snapped.

Geisa stepped forward, leveling a gaze at the Oracle. "I have been asking myself the same question."

The Oracle said nothing, merely glaring at the taller woman. The queen turned, waving Geisa down.

"The fact is, the people trust you, Roweni. They hear your prophecies and it gives them comfort. And so you remain useful. But do not deceive yourself that your gift gives you power. We are all Tsuki's vessels, even myself. And there are ways to make sure you remain . . . cooperative." The queen stepped close to the Oracle and stroked her tiny seishen with one perfect finger.

The Oracle stepped back, grabbing the owl and cradling her in the crook of her arm. "Are we done here?" the Oracle asked stiffly.

"One more time, Roweni. The date of the eclipse? You are certain of it?"

"The day following the spring equinox," the Oracle said.

"Then our path is clear. I will use the day without sun to bring an end to the sunburners once and for all."

The Oracle strode from the temple. Kai held her breath, looking silently for an escape route. She did not think she could extricate herself from her hiding place without being spotted. She would need to wait until the queen and Geisa left.

The queen turned to Geisa, her shoulders sagging. "Why must everyone be so difficult?" she asked.

"People always resent the powerful. She does not understand the weight you carry on your shoulders. She does not have the vision you do."

A small smile flitted across the queen's face. "You always know how to make me feel better."

"It is time, Your Majesty," Geisa said.

Time for what? Kai mouthed to Quitsu.

He shrugged.

Geisa pulled several items from behind the altar and set them on the polished floor. Kai raised her head slightly to try to make out what they were.

"We are so close to everything we have worked for. We must make sure her blessing is behind us in these final days," Geisa said.

"Proceed," the queen said.

Geisa lit the candles in the room with moonlight, causing them to flare around the temple. Geisa handed the queen her dagger and a shiny silver bowl. Geisa picked up a small cage from the floor and pulled a delicate gray koumidi from it. Kai and Quitsu exchanged another look of alarm as the koumidi clicked and cried, struggling weakly in Geisa's strong hand. The queen handed back the knife and Geisa, without ceremony, slit the koumidi's belly, pouring the blood and entrails into the waiting silver bowl.

Geisa began to chant in a language Kai had never heard. The air in the room filled with vibration and a buzz of energy. Kai was frozen where she crouched, heart beating wildly in her throat, eyes locked on the tiny koumidi carcass.

A flash of silver light burned across the room.

Kai squeezed her eyes shut, but still the light burned the inside of her eyelids. The temperature in the temple dropped. She shivered.

When Kai opened her eyes, she could hardly believe what she saw. Standing before the queen and Geisa was a woman, an impossibly tall woman in flowing robes of crimson and gray. She filled the room, her head nearly brushing the ceiling. Her long black hair flowed around her as if a wind danced through the temple, but Kai felt none. The woman's face was blurry, as if looking at it through rain on a window. Her eyes glowed with the light of the full moon.

"My daughters." The woman's voice reverberated through the temple, sounding in several octaves.

The queen and Geisa had fallen to their knees in worship. "Tsuki. You honor us with your presence," Geisa said. "Rise. What news do you have for me?"

"Our opportunity to defeat the sunburners draws near," the queen said. "The spring equinox will bring an eclipse. We will lure them close and then strike when they are defenseless. We will capture as many of them as we can."

"A bold plan," the goddess said. "But capture? You say *capture,* not kill?" "The sunburners do not deserve the sweet ease of death. We have something planned for them much more fitting than death. They deserve to suffer,"

Geisa said, head bowed reverentially.

"Suffering," the woman said, as if her mouth was salivating at the thought. "This pleases me."

"We ask only your blessing for the preparations and battle to come."

"You have it," the goddess said. "But these great deeds will require great sacrifice. Before the spring equinox, you must bring me a true sacrifice. Using that blood, I will craft your victory."

"It will be done," Geisa said.

The huge woman vanished, leaving the air limp and drained like after a rainstorm.

CHAPTER 18

Kai's dreams that night were troubled. The statue of Tsuki in the temple came alive and crushed her beneath its stone foot, wild hair waving in the nonexistent wind. The queen reached into the Oracle's chest and pulled out her heart, putting it into a silver cage while it still beat. Moon and sunburners sat like pieces on a goa board; and she lost piece after piece until only a dark queen remained.

She blinked her eyes in the darkness of the room.

Quitsu had laid down next to her, and she threw her arm over him, pulling his furry warmth to her chest, burying her nose in the soft fur between his ears.

"What the hell was that," she whispered.

"I don't know," he whispered back. "It wasn't what I expected the goddess to be like."

"No," Kai said, leaning up on her elbow. "I thought Tsuki was an extension of the earth. I expected her to be . . ." She searched for the words.

"Peaceful? Gentle? Not a bloodthirsty vision from a nightmare?"

"Right," Kai said. "I feel like it must be some sort of mistake. That what we saw wasn't Tsuki. Maybe she was . . ."

"Tsuki's evil sister?" Quitsu asked.

"Something else," she said. "The blood . . . asking for a true sacrifice?

I've never heard of Tsuki worship that involved killing. Who are they going to sacrifice?"

"I don't know," Quitsu said.

"And why do they want to capture the sunburners? What do they have planned for them?"

"I've never felt bad for a sunburner before," Quitsu remarked. "But there is a first time for everything. We can't let it happen. Can we?"

"How could we stop it?" Kai wondered. "Who would believe us?"

She curled back around Quitsu, her thoughts filling with despair. She was just a novice who couldn't moonburn. What could she do?

Kai dragged herself to the breakfast table, sitting down with a heaviness she felt in both body and spirit. Even Emi looked concerned.

"Are you all right?" Maaya asked.

"Yes," Kai said, forcing herself to down some porridge. "I just haven't been sleeping well."

Quitsu flicked his tail at her.

"Or at all," she muttered.

"I've seen it before," Stela said. "Classic case of studying too hard."

"I wish that was the problem," Kai said. "Do you ever get the feeling that they don't tell us everything that's really going on at the citadel?"

The other four girls looked at Kai for a moment and then burst out laughing. When the peals of laughter subsided, Leilu spoke first.

"Sorry, sorry. You were serious. Of course they don't tell us even half of what is going on."

"Doesn't that bother you?" Kai asked with a hint of annoyance.

"Sometimes," Leilu said.

"Often," Emi chimed in.

"But that's how it works. We're soldiers. Our job is to get our orders and carry them out. We aren't charged with asking questions," Leilu said.

"But what if we were being led down . . . a bad path. A destructive path, that could lead to a lot of death. Wouldn't we have a right to know? To have an opinion?" Kai asked.

"You can't have every soldier second guessing every strategic decision made by the generals. They have to make difficult decisions all the time, even sending burners to their death," Leilu explained.

"I agree with Leilu," Maaya said. "But, I suppose if we were being lied to, that might be another thing. Why are you asking this? Is there something that is bothering you?"

Kai hesitated, trying to imagine explaining all she had heard and seen last night.

"It's nothing," she said. "Don't worry about it."

"It sounds like you are in desperate need of some fun," Stela said. "Lucky for you, there's some fun scheduled for this weekend."

"Another stealthy trip into town?" Kai asked.

"No, the festival," Maaya said.

"The festival?" Kai asked blankly.

"I always forget what a country bumpkin you are," Emi said. "The Longest Night Festival. The winter solstice? The most holy day for moonburners?"

"It's almost the winter solstice?" Kai asked. She had completely lost track of the weeks.

"It's tomorrow," Maaya said. "And every year there is a big party with food and music and dancing."

"And sake," Stela said, raising her eyebrows. "Your favorite."

"I don't have anything to wear . . ." Kai protested, but her friends were already making plans.

While the thought of participating in the moonburner solstice festival for the first time raised Kai's spirits slightly, she couldn't help but think with a pang of regret about her former life. While they could never celebrate a moonburner holiday while living in Kita, her parents had tried to make it special by decorating their house with candles and cooking all of Kai's favorite foods. She remembered falling asleep in front of the fire full of dumplings and honeycakes. She wished her new life didn't mean that those old joys were lost. When had everything gotten so turned around?

☪

Lessons were cancelled the following night on account of the Longest Night Festival. Maaya and Emi filed into Kai's room, tossing a bag of garments on her bed.

"You both look incredible," Kai marveled, taking in the colorful silk dresses and obis they wore.

Emi looked the most striking, as usual, in a black and silver dress that complimented her svelte figure and silver hair. Its scooping neckline exposed her ample bosom. Kai never would have been able to hide as a boy for seventeen years with Emi's figure, she thought ruefully.

Maaya looked stunning as well, in a dress of burgundy. It had a tight-fit-ting bodice that showed off her tiny waist before flowing to a full skirt. Her hair was down around her face, rather than in her usual braids, and she wore a burgundy stain on her lips that matched her dress.

"Maaya you look like a different person," Kai said with admiration.

Maaya grinned, the gap in her teeth bringing back some of her girlish charm. "Thanks. I bought the dress especially for this."

"And what do I look like, boiled cabbage?" Emi said, hands on her hips, feigning injury.

"You always look amazing," Kai said. "And you know it."

"We get tired of looking at you sometimes," Maaya echoed.

"If only there were going to be some eligible men at this party," Emi said.

"If only it mattered," Kai said. "It's not like you could do anything with one if you found him."

Emi flopped on the bed dramatically. "This life of chastity just doesn't suit me. It's a waste."

Kai snorted. Maaya said nothing, her gaze distant for a moment.

"What have you brought me?" Kai asked. "Will anything fit?"

They poured the garments out of the bag onto the bed and pawed through them, discarding a few obvious non-contenders. Kai's eyes kept falling back to a deep purple dress.

"Put it on," Emi ordered.

Kai obliged, and through she had no mirror, she knew that it looked good. It was made of a soft chiffon fabric that she kept wanting to run her hands along. It was gathered at one shoulder, with a long drape of fabric flowing over the shoulder, down to the floor. Emi wrapped a light purple obi decorated with silver herons in flight around Kai's waist. It tightened the dress around her, giving her muscular figure some semblance of femininity.

"Perfect," Maaya breathed. "You look stunning."

Even Quitsu nodded quickly to her from his perch on the desk in the corner of the room. As the dress was sleeveless, Kai couldn't strap her dagger to her arm as she normally did. She examined the dress, trying to figure out a spot to stash the dagger.

"Just leave it," Emi said. "We'll be in the citadel the whole time. And it ruins the look."

Kai hesitated, but left the dagger on the desk.

Next, Emi pinned up Kai's hair, muttering all the while about how desperately Kai needed a haircut. It was true, her short cut had grown out just below her ears and had no semblance of a style. It just hadn't been a priority.

When she was finished, Emi stood back with Maaya, admiring their handiwork.

"Sometimes I surprise even myself," Emi said with approval.

"Doesn't Quitsu get to dress up?" Kai asked as they opened the door to leave.

He hissed, backing into the corner.

"Kidding, kidding," Kai said. "Come on, furball."

Kai marveled at the transformation of the citadel as they made their way to the garden behind the temple, where the festival was held. The courtyards and walkways were strung with lights and bright paper lanterns in twinkling constellations. Flowers had seemingly sprung up from the cobblestones and walls of the whitewashed buildings.

"How do they do this?" Kai asked, taking it all in.

"The staff works for days preparing it all behind the scenes. The food is delicious too."

"This is my favorite day of the year," Maaya said, face upturned, basking in the lantern light.

As they reached the garden where the festival was held, Kai was greeted with even more marvels. There were orbs hanging along the edge of the garden, giving off a warmth that banished the winter chill from the air. Lights were strung everywhere, in the trees, along the paths. There were tiny flashes of light in the sky, so fast Kai almost missed them as she turned her head to catch a glimpse.

"What are those?" she asked.

"Sparkbugs," Maaya said. "Mistress Adiru grows them special and hatches them for the festival every year."

"They are the only bugs I don't find totally creepy," Emi said, as one alighted briefly on her hand and then took off again.

There were tables laden with foods that Kai had never seen before:

grilled fishes, tiny pastry cakes, rice rolls delicately stuffed with fresh fish, vegetables and other delectables.

"These are ma favobite," Emi said, speaking around the two rice rolls she stuffed into her mouth.

And the people. Kai had never seen the moonburners dressed so extravagantly. They were robed in dresses of every color and cut, disguising their deadly military precision under a cloak of femininity. There were many faces she did not recognize, as well, citizens of Kyuden who didn't have the trademark silver hair of a burner, men and women mingling and chatting with the citadel's inhabitants.

Music was drifting from one of the corners of the garden, and Kai recognized the musicians just as Stela and Leilu found them.

"Is Rox's band playing?" Kai asked.

"Yes!" said Stela, looking phenomenal in a chartreuse dress that highlighted her almond skin.

"I told Nanase that I had the perfect band, and she had the staff hire them! It could be a big break for them, there are a lot of important people here."

Leilu, in a flowing rose-colored dress covered in a tiny golden-leaf pattern, pulled a little bottle from the back of her obi.

"Shall we?" She winked.

Kai groaned, but followed the other girls to a less-crowded corner of the courtyard, closer to the band.

Kai took a quick swig of the fiery liquid and passed it to Maaya, who was staring at the band with the intensity of a falcon locked on its next meal.

"Maaya," she said, nudging her.

"Huh?" Maaya said, attention swinging towards Kai. "Oh." She grabbed the bottle and took a sip, eyes still on the band.

Kai and Emi exchanged looks and Emi shook her head, lips pursed. Not good.

The night swirled around them, filled with vibrant colors, laughter, music, and dancing. Kai lost track of time, enjoying the company of friends, and even dancing with a few men who braved entering their circle. While most men went straight for Emi, Kai didn't mind. She had never had such a wonderful time. She hoped the night stretched on forever. The only damper was the disappearance of Maaya and Atsu, to Rox's annoyance and Emi's concern.

As Kai came back breathless from a stretch of dancing, the crowd parted for a tiny figure flanked by a taller one, still in a master moonburner uniform. Kai realized almost a beat too late that it was the queen and Geisa.

Their circle broke into a semicircle facing the queen, bowing respectfully. "Your Majesty," Emi murmured.

"Daughters. It brings me joy to see you having such a wonderful time," the queen said softly. Even among the rich and colorful dresses of the guests, the queen was set apart. Her silver hair was ornately gathered on her head, decorated with tiny silver chains that caught the moonlight. Her dress matched the silver of her hair and shimmered at the cuffs and neck with tiny glittering gems woven into the fabric. She looked like a goddess glowing in the night.

"It is a wonderful celebration," Kai ventured, trying to keep the images of the koumidi entrails flowing into a silver bowl from her mind. "I have never seen anything like it."

"I'm glad you like it. It is important to remember to celebrate. Though we live in hard times, we have much to be grateful for."

The other women murmured their assent.

"Kai," the queen said. "Please stop by the throne room tomorrow. I have news about the . . . inquiry we discussed."

It took Kai a moment to remember that the queen had promised to look into her mother.

"I can speak now," Kai said.

A shadow passed over the queen's face. "I'm not sure this is the time to discuss that, daughter."

"Please," Kai said. "If you know something, please tell me."

"Very well," the queen said, gesturing for Kai to join her.

They paused a few steps past the group and Kai shifted from one foot to another.

"I did have our operatives inquire into your mother's well-being. I am very sorry to report that your mother is dead."

CHAPTER 19

Suddenly, the night air felt very cold. The merrymaking around her seemed alien.

"Dead?" Kai asked, voice cracking.

"I'm sorry. Our operative is quite certain. Your mother tried to escape, but was caught. She fought . . . and was killed."

Kai nodded numbly.

"I'm sorry to be the bearer of such sad news on a night that is supposed to be joyful. But be assured, you have a new family now." The queen took Kai's hands in her tiny ones and squeezed. Then she turned and disappeared back into the crowd.

Kai felt like she couldn't breathe. She made her way towards the entrance to the courtyard.

"Kai!" She heard Emi call, but Kai waved her off. She needed to be alone. She walked through the courtyard, deaf to the world around her. How could her mother be dead? She was so strong, so capable. She could have lasted more than a few months. She wouldn't have tried to escape if she didn't have a solid plan.

As Kai left the courtyard, her mouth felt dry, her skin clammy. The cheerful lights decorating the skies above her suddenly felt harsh and intrusive.

"Kai," Quitsu said, trailing behind her. "Slow down."

"Just give me a few minutes alone," she called back to him, her voice catching in her throat. She didn't want to be around anyone, even Quitsu.

Kai fled, half stumbling, through the lonely space of the citadel, dark and devoid of life. Everyone was back in the main courtyard, enjoying the festival. She slowed in front of the hospital ward, cutting around the side of the building to stop by the herb garden.

She fell to her knees on a soft patch of dirt ground next to the little pond, tears flowing freely. Her borrowed dress would be ruined, but it didn't matter.

Tiny pink flowers sprouted from a cluster of leaves draped down the rocks bordering the pond. Their beauty offended her. What right did they have to live such a lovely carefree existence, content only to bloom and die with no complications? She ripped them out of the ground in a fit of rage, throwing them into the cool night air.

She instantly regretted it. It wasn't the flowers' fault. She looked out at the scene in front of her, just a blurry, tear-streaked vision. It was still achingly beautiful. The stars shone brightly, the constellations standing out in stark relief against the dark sky.

She remembered laying out in the hayloft above the cattle barn back home when she was a child, both her mother and father on either side of her, pointing out their favorite constellations. Her father's favorite was the rearing stallion, Esku, while her mother loved the constellation Koto, the trickster fox. She thought of Quitsu. That was probably her favorite now, too. She shouldn't have left him.

A noise behind Kai drew her back to herself. She stood and turned to face whoever was interloping in her private sorrow.

"Chiya?" Kai asked. The woman was standing just a few yards from her, still wearing her samanera uniform. She must not have gone to the festival. "What do you want?"

Chiya's eyes glittered dangerously in the moonlight.

"When a drowning man is trying to stay afloat, he can't afford to be pulled down by the weight of his possessions. Even his clothing. He has to lose the dead weight."

Kai wiped her face and stood. "I don't expect you to care, but this isn't a good time. Please just leave me alone."

"It's never been a good time for you, has it Kai? You're nothing but a waste of time. You're a moonburner who can't burn. You are dead weight. Pulling us down."

Kai's anger flared. "What did I ever do to you to make you hate me so much? What do you want from me?" she shouted.

"I want you gone!" Chiya lunged forward and pushed her. Kai stumbled backwards, heels striking the rough rocks bordering the pond. Kai's legs went out from under her, and she fell backwards into the water. As Kai came up for air, Chiya vaulted over the stone rim and grasped Kai's neck with one big hand, pushing her under the shallow, brackish water.

Kai kicked and fought, trying to find purchase on her assailant in the dim water. She scratched and clawed and flailed at the hands holding her down, but Chiya's grip was like iron. Kai's lungs burned.

The Gleaming, she thought. It would kick in soon, to save her. Her thoughts were growing fuzzy and dim. Nothing. Where was the goddess? Kai thought of the dark figure in the temple, and with a sinking feeling, realized that no help was coming.

Kai's struggles grew weaker. The soft bottom of the pond pressed beneath her back. She could feel the slimy stems of lily pads brushing against her face and neck. It would be easy to stop struggling, to stop fighting, to stop trying. She was alone. Her mother was gone.

But a part of her wouldn't be quiet, wouldn't let her give in to despair. She wasn't alone. She had Master Vita. Maaya and Emi. She had people who cared for her. And then there was Quitsu, who would die if she died. Who had saved her in the desert. She felt herself growing angry. She had fought off a manga cat. She wasn't just going to let Chiya drown her in a pond.

She opened herself to the moonlight as Pura had taught her, and the light flooded her, filling her with its heat. She pushed at her blockage, trying to force the light through the seams that she knew were there, that she had explored and touched with probing mental fingers again and again. There had to be a weakness. She willed the moonlight to leave her somehow, to fight for her and burn Chiya.

Still, nothing happened. She took in more and more, feeling the water around her growing hot. She could feel the hands holding her down loosening as her skin heated.

She filled herself with more moonlight, straining and pushing at the blockage with all her mental might. She saw a seam appear, a tiny crack down the smooth mortar of the brick walls of her mind. She redoubled her efforts, sending the light into the crack, expanding it, weakening it. The crack grew wider, until, with a final push, the bricks of the wall exploded away from her, tumbling down into nothingness. The power poured from her in an explosion of white light and heat that blew Chiya back from her. Kai dragged herself from the pond, stumbling over the side onto the ground. Her head pounded and her vision was blurry. She tried to fight her nausea as the world spun around her, but it was too much. She succumbed to blackness.

A memory floated to the surface of the blackness, like oil rising to the top of still, dark water. Kai had been eleven, almost twelve. She sat at the little square table in her home in Ushai, the remnants of a meal of stew beef and root vegetables on her plate. A fire in the hearth and candles on the table, a sliver of moonlight shining through the nearby window.

She argued with them. She had been angry about something . . . what? There was someone in town . . . a tinker, a performer . . . Oh yes, a troupe of performers. Her parents had forbidden her from going into town, like they always forbade her from doing anything that brought her too close to the watchful gazes of their neighbors.

She fought, she yelled, she cried, trying every tactic she had in her pre-teen arsenal. But they stood firm. When she realized she had lost, she stood and shouted at them. The candles on the table had flared to an unnatural height, twice the length of the tallow sticks. She had fallen back in fear, partly at what had happened, but mostly at the looks on her parents' faces. First panic, quickly painted over with a look that could only be described as resignation.

She and her mother had set out the next day, provisioned for days with their two swiftest horses under them. Kai opened her mouth to ask her mother questions a hundred times, but the look on Hanae's face silenced her. After two days and a night they reached a wood that she had never seen before. It felt twisted and old and sinister, the trees wearing black bark and suffocating mossy coats. The ground grew soft under their horses' feet and the horses shied from every sound and creak they heard.

"Please, Mother, tell me where we are going," she heard herself beg in her high, youthful voice.

Hanae reigned in her horse and finally turned to face her daughter.

"We are going to see someone who can help us. The candles . . . your moonburning is dawning. Your use of it will be unpredictable, even dangerous. Dangerous for all of us. We are going to see someone who can help us control it."

Kai remembered feeling very small, dwarfed by the dark forest canopy. Small in understanding; trapped in a body that was intent on betraying them.

They continued to pick their way through the darkness for what felt like hours. Eventually they came upon a clearing, a place where the dense canopy yielded its dominion and allowed a patch of moonlight to break through. A dark, squat house sat in the middle of the clearing, smoke curling from its tiny chimney.

A shiver traveled through Kai, within both her twelve-year-old self and her remembering self. A woman met them at the door, not the hideous crone that Kai somehow had been expecting, but a tall, well-built older woman with silver hair pulled back in a loose bun at the nape of her neck. Though she gave off the appearance of age and wisdom, her olive skin was flawless and her gray eyes were sharp. She wore a basic gray wool dress, with a white apron tied around her waist. She ushered them inside.

The woman sat Kai by the fireplace with a piping hot pastry on a plate. Hanae and the woman moved to the other side of the small cabin, the way adults did when they didn't want children to overhear. Young Kai turned her head slightly to maximize her eavesdropping, but then forgot all as she caught sight of the huge silver cat sitting on the chair across from her.

As her younger self gazed in rapt attention at the cat, who Kai now recognized as a seishen, Kai focused on the conversation between Hanae and the woman.

The conversation flickered. Her subconscious had only heard some of it.

"You sure? The procedure can have . . . permanent side effects. She could be stunted."

"I can't give her over to the citadel yet. She's too impressionable. That place . . . it will ruin her."

"This might ruin her."

"But she will be with me. Me and her father. Who love her."

The woman held her hands up. "I can't do anything about her hair changing colors. That is beyond me."

Hanae shook her head. "I will handle that. She will remember nothing of this?"

"Not until the blockage is removed. The memory may come back with the power."

"All right." Hanae sighed deeply.

"I do not know if what you do is brave or foolish," the woman said, a hint of sympathy in her eyes.

"Only time will tell."

Hanae and the woman ushered Kai onto the little low bed in the corner of the room. She lay down and closed her eyes, as instructed.

The woman busied herself, opening the windows to let the moonlight in and placing several moonstones around Kai's body, including one on her chest. She could feel that heaviness, that weight.

Kai marveled at her utter trust in her mother and the woman. But what child suspects their parent of ill intent? She wanted to shout at herself to push the stone from her chest, to flee from the cabin and never turn back.

The woman knelt at the head of the bed and went to work, weaving a spell that would cut Kai off from the moon for the next seven years. Kai's young self screamed and thrashed wildly, held down by the iron grip of her mother. She remembered the suffocating feeling, the wall being built, brick by brick. It felt like it would kill her, bury her, cut her off from all air and light and life. The memory filled with blackness.

INTERLUDE

General Ipan stretched in his chair, massaging a knot in one shoulder with a rough hand. He still wore his armor, burnished gold in the lamplight, with a sunburst on the breastplate.

"I'm getting old, Kuma," he said to his seishen, a great golden bear resting by the tent's little stone brazier.

"You've been saying that for the last twenty years," Kuma remarked.

"Well, it's been true for the last twenty years," he said. "And more besides."

General Ipan was still strong and able, and his men respected him. But he'd be lying to himself if he did not admit that his armor felt heavier at the end of a long day and his axe arm tired faster than it once had. He ran his hand through his thinning golden hair and sighed.

"A man of my age should be bouncing grandchildren on his knee, not riding around the desert on a lion-horse in full armor."

Kuma just blinked. After years of companionship, the bear had no doubt learned that Ipan's comments didn't always warrant a response.

A silver light flashed from the bowl of water standing on the washbasin.

"My, is it that time already?" General Ipan picked the basin up and brought it to his desk, setting it before him. He pulled light from the sunstone set in the pommel of his dagger and traced symbols across the surface of the water. A silver-haired figure appeared before him, wavy and faint. No one knew that this bowl was more than just a regular bowl.

Well, no one except the woman who possessed the bowl's twin.

"Good evening. Or should I say good morning to you. Struck fear into the heart of any young moonburners today?"

"No. But the day is young. And you? Fallen off any golden eagles lately?"

General Ipan blustered. "One time that happened, one time. It was ages ago, and I had hit the sun whiskey a little too hard the night before. Yet I'll never hear the end of it!" He threw his hands up in mock surrender.

The voice on the other end chuckled. "You know I'll keep teasing you about it until you do something even more embarrassing."

"It's only a matter of time," Kuma chimed in, his deep baritone ringing across the tent.

The woman laughed even harder.

"Not you, too," the general said. "Ganging up is completely unsportsmanlike. I cry foul."

The blurry vision seemed to wipe a tear from her eye.

"Okay, okay. I yield. I don't have much time tonight. What news?"

"Trouble brewing, my old friend," General Ipan said. "You know I can't tell you much, but just be on your guard. We continue to escalate here."

The woman sighed. "Yes, here as well. All our years of effort, and for what? The war continues."

"We are but weapons in the hands of our monarchs. We do not choose where to cut."

"I know, I know. I do have something . . . bigger . . . to share. The queen is planning a major offensive. She and General Geisa seem to think it will mean complete victory."

"That is troubling to hear."

"You and I both know Queen Airi ruling both Kita and Miina would be a disaster. I am tempted to share the full breadth of this intelligence with you, so long as you can provide me with some . . . assurances that Miina will be allowed to be free once the queen is dealt with."

"I will see. The prince is tired of this war; I think I could gain some traction there. But we face the same problem as always. If Miina is to remain sovereign, who will take the queen's place? There would be civil war."

"I might . . . have a lead in that regard."

"Really?" The general leaned forward.

"It is too soon to be certain. Find out if you think a deal can be struck, and I will find what I can."

"Agreed."

BOOK THREE

CHAPTER 20

When Kai woke, she felt a heavy pressure on her chest where the moonstone had sat and burned at her years ago. She struggled to take a breath. Her throat felt sore and raw from swallowing water. She opened her eyes and blinked, laboring to move her head.

She pawed at her chest as if to rid herself of the remembered moonstone.

"Hey!" an indignant voice said.

"Quitsu," she croaked. "Get off of me."

He perked up, placing his two front paws on her collarbones. He licked her face once and then stepped to the side of the bed, sitting there and looking at her with his pointed fox face. "I'm glad you're awake."

"How long have I been out?" "Almost a week," he replied.

"A week!" She cried. She tried to sit up and collapsed back on her pillows, head swimming. Her stomach rumbled.

"You burned a lot of moonlight. It lit up the entire sky. At first they thought it was a show for the Longest Night Festival, but they figured out pretty quickly that no one had planned it. The nurses weren't sure if you had burned yourself out, or if you would ever wake up. It's been infuriating."

"Burned myself out?" Kai felt a sense of dread rising in her. She opened her mind to the waves of moonlight as Pura had taught her, drawing in a trickle. She concentrated on sending it into one of the orbs above her bed. It flared brightly, and returned to normal.

Kai and Quitsu sighed simultaneously.

"I can still burn," she said, her relief palpable. "And my blockage is gone."

"That was our hope," a female voice said. Kai scooted up in bed and turned to face her visitor. It was Pura.

"I'm glad you are all right," Pura said, standing by Kai's bedside. She held a package wrapped in cloth in her hands. She looked down, fidgiting with the cloth.

"Me too," Kai said.

Pura handed Kai the package. "Congratulations."

"What?" Kai furrowed her brow and unwrapped the bundle. It was a set of light blue robes, the kind that samanera wear. Nestled on top was a moonstone link like the one that she and Pura had worked with countless times.

"I don't understand."

"You passed your test. You're not a novice anymore."

Kai looked at her, stunned. So almost being killed was . . . a test? Quitsu made a low growling noise, clearly displeased.

"So Chiya trying to kill me . . . that was the test?"

Pura sat down on the side of the bed, as if her energy had left her in a rush. "It doesn't normally happen this way. The novice is placed in a tank that fills with water, but they can extricate themselves using fairly simple burning skills. The test shows that they have mastered the fundamentals and can stay calm under pressure, a trait we need in master moonburners. But with your blockage . . . you weren't ready for that test."

Kai nodded stiffly.

Pura continued. "The queen has ordered that all novices and samenera are tested to move up in rank. The war is escalating and we need all the masters we can get." She was shaking her head as she spoke, clearly not pleased with the shortened timeline.

"You have the capacity to be an extremely powerful moonburner. We need you. We thought that since your talent had manifested itself in near death experiences, that a simulated near-death experience would be enough to motivate you to break the block."

"But in those other moments, I didn't control my moonburning. It just . . . happened," she said weakly, trying to understand.

"Yes, but since you were never actually in danger of death in this situation, we hoped the gleaming effect would not kick in. You'd have to do it yourself. And you did." She squeezed Kai's hand.

Kai pulled her hand back, closing her eyes. "So you weren't going to let Chiya kill me?" Kai asked.

"No, of course not. We're not monsters," Pura said.

"Are you sure?" Kai muttered, under her breath. She couldn't believe that someone trying to drown her was just a simulated experiment, a calculated risk.

Pura's face twisted. "Kai . . . I'm sorry. It isn't right, what we did. I argued against it . . . but it wasn't my call."

Maybe Pura hadn't wanted to test Kai, but she had stood by and let it happen. Didn't that make her just as responsible?

Pura stood up and pulled out a folded piece of paper from her pocket. "Here is your new class schedule. You will continue moonburning training with me. You will also have field medicine, survival training and tactics. It's a little different from the normal samanera curriculum, but all the novices moving up are taking this course load. General Geisa and the queen seem certain that something big is coming."

With that, she turned on her heels and strode from the room. Kai looked at her schedule and swallowed. She thought of the Oracle's words: *A day with no sun and a night with no moon.* They were coming, that was certain.

And soon.

Kai changed into her light blue samanera uniform. She supposed she had earned it, but she didn't find any joy in it. Her mother was dead. Her last link to her old life. Now this uniform, this place, was the only life she had. She wasn't sure she wanted it anymore.

Kai was released from the hospital ward after a fair bit of poking and prodding by the nurse. It was late at night; the sky was just beginning to lighten in the east. As Kai and Quitsu walked to her dormitory, Kai drew in a bit of moonlight. Its warmth comforted her.

"Quitsu . . ." she started, unsure how to apologize.

"I know," he said. "You are forgiven. But let that be a lesson to you.

You're stuck with me."

"I know," she smiled. "But, where . . . were you?" she asked, trying not to sound accusatory. "I was sure that you would come when Chiya started attacking."

"They thought of that. Apparently there is a chemical called lusteric, which keeps you from being able to moonburn. It apparently knocks out seishen, too. Chiya grabbed me and forced me to drink some before she went for you."

"Lusteric," Kai remembered. "That's what the sunburners gave me when they attacked me."

Then Quitsu's words truly sank in. "Wait, you were unconscious? Vulnerable?" A spark of anger flamed to life inside her. It was one thing to attack her, but Quitsu? Seishen were sacred.

"When I awoke, I had been taken to Nanase's office and I was being watched by that damn bird," Quitsu said. "I don't think I was in any danger. You, however . . . that is another story."

Kai's anger fizzled. "I thought I was dead. Part of me just wanted to . . . let go. It would be easier that way, now that my parents are gone. But I felt so guilty that you would die too. I had to try to live."

"I know things are hard right now, especially . . . with your mother," Quitsu said. "But it will get easier. Now you can burn, and truly start your training."

"What's the point?" Kai threw up her hands. "I don't even think I want to be a moonburner anymore."

"You are a moonburner. You were born one, or I wouldn't be here," Quitsu said. "And supposedly, you're going to be very powerful. So if we have any shot at making any difference around the citadel, you need to train and become a master. Then you'll be able to make them listen."

Quitsu was right, as always. Not that she'd ever tell him that. The best strategy right now was to learn everything she could. And wait.

"I don't know what I would do without you," she said.

You'll never have to find out."

They walked for a moment in silence.

"I hate that they were right about my blockage," she said. "But I guess I should just be happy that it's gone."

"I hate it, too," he said. "But they've been doing this a lot longer than we have. They had . . . theories. We had only speculation."

"I know something about it that they don't," Kai said, the dream flashing through her mind. "Someone did create my blockage with dark magic."

"Who?"

"My mother."

The next morning, Kai started moonburning training in earnest.

"Now, in some ways," Pura said, "moonburning is fairly limited. You take the moonlight and turn it into heat in some form. But what you do with it is limited only by your creativity, and the materials around you."

Kai soaked it all in like a sponge, listening to Pura explain how you could use moonburning to boil water, make rocks explode with the heat of the pressure, create wind with currents of high and low pressure, and of course, make fire. All forms of fire. Sparks, flames, fireballs, orbs, even lightning, if your technique was good enough.

"Your burning doesn't have to be dramatic," Pura said. "Subtlety is powerful. You can use it to melt the edge of your opponent's sword, so it won't slice through you. You can cauterize wounds. You can give a person or an animal a nip that will distract them or cause them to move when you want them to." Kai yelped and leaped to her feet, feeling a spark climbing up her spine. A smile tugged on the edge of Pura's mouth.

"You can draw the heat out of things, stop a fire, pull light from a torch or a candle. The best burners aren't always the most powerful, although that helps when you are hurling fireballs at someone. The best are the most creative."

"Moonburning can also be used for evil, throuh," Pura seemed to hesitate before continuing. "In the past, atrocities have been committed with moonburning. People burned alive, their blood boiled from the inside. You can make someone's heart stop by heating it too high. There are many ways to torture someone with moonburning. These methods are forbidden, but always be cautious. The power can be intoxicating. Stand firm in who you are and do not be tempted by a dark path."

As Kai walked into the main courtyard of the citadel the next morning, she saw a gathering of masters, samaneras, and novices on the steps outside the queen's tower.

"What's going on?" Kai murmured.

Kai walked closer to the group and caught sight of Maaya and Emi. She made her way through the crowd and scooted in behind them.

"Morning," she said.

Maaya and Emi were both wearing navy blue master uniforms. Maaya's hair was pulled in one long braid down her back, instead of her characteristic pigtails. They took turns pulling Kai into a tight embrace.

"I'm so glad you are all right!" Maaya said. "We came to visit you in the hospital before we left for our test, but you were unconscious."

"It means a lot that you were there, even if I didn't know it," Kai said.

"I can't believe they let Chiya do that to you. It's horrible," Emi said. "No one should have to go through the test like that, thinking they are going to die."

"I agree," Kai said. "But I guess with my blockage . . . they had to use unconventional tactics." Kai hurried to change the subject. "But look at you both. Master moonburners! Congratulations."

"We can't quite believe it ourselves," Emi said.

They fell silent as the queen walked into the courtyard with her head held high, gliding across the stones. She wore her thin silver circlet and a pale pink dress trimmed with white fur. She looked every inch a royal. The women standing in the courtyard quieted as she stopped before them. Nanase and General Geisa flanked her on either side.

"My daughters. It fills me with pride to see you before me. You are the protectors of this kingdom, women who selflessly sacrifice their own desires and dreams for the good of our people." The queen's voice rang out over the courtyard like a clear bell.

"I do not have to tell you that we live in a dark time. Despite our best efforts, our enemy has grown bolder. He attacks our own country, our own people. He will not be content until Miina is under his thumb and every last moonburner is dead."

"It is in the darkest night that the brightest stars shine. And we have need of you now, you bright stars." She gestured to the woman who now stood next to her. "You all know General Geisa. She has bravely led our moonburners in battle for the last eighteen years. She and an elite group of burners have been taking part in a very special, secret mission. And now we have need of more. The general needs six moonburners to join her mission. No questions asked. We need the bravest and most loyal to enter into the unknown and trust in the righteousness of our cause."

The first to raise her hand was Chiya. Kai breathed a sigh of relief. Chiya on some mysterious mission? Hopefully gone from the citadel? She couldn't have dared hope. Four more hands went up, one at a time and the queen nodded warmly at each. Emi started to raise her hand, and Kai grabbed her arm quickly.

"Don't," she whispered fiercely.

Emi looked at her in alarm. "Why not?"

Kai stalled as she tried to explain, her mind replaying the sight of the koumidi's blood spilling into the bowl and the dark woman speaking of a sacrifice. Emi would never believe her.

"Geisa . . . she attacked my village. She almost killed me and my mother. She slaughtered innocent men, women and children. Is that really the type of special assignment you want to sign up for?"

Emi bit her lip, looking back to the other five women who had joined the queen on the top step. But another hand went up and the moment passed. Emi looked back at Kai crossly. "You should have let me make my own decision."

"Trust me," Kai said. "You didn't want to volunteer."

CHAPTER 21

The days began to fly by as Kai engrossed herself in her new curriculum. She had missed about a week of classes while she was unconscious, but she caught up quickly. Under Pura's tutelage, Kai quickly mastered the basics of moonburning and began to progress to more difficult concepts.

Kai was grateful she didn't have to attend History with Mistress Furie anymore and could concentrate on practical skills. Many of her lessons in field medicine mirrored topics Kai's mother had covered when she was a child. During the class on stitching wounds, Kai wistfully remembered practicing stitching on the skin of an orange, which her father had pretended was a fallen soldier, delivering a moving eulogy before he ate it. She shoved the memory down. She would focus on moving forward, not looking back. It was the only way.

Weeks passed, and then months. Kai still spent some of her free time in the library with Master Vita, but not as much as before. She, Maaya, Emi, Stela and Leilu had grown even closer, and together they would take trips into town, practice their burning, or play goa. Kai relished the distraction that her friends brought. When she was with them, she could almost believe that they were normal students at a normal school.

Yet there were more signs that the war was escalating. Moonburners were going out on more frequent missions and some were not coming back. Kai's friends would be gone for days, coming back hollow-eyed and mute about what they had seen. It was a stark reminder of their true situation.

☽

As spring grew near, the last vestiges of winter clung to the citadel with frosty fingers. Kai, Emi and Maaya sat in the warmth of the dining hall, shoveling food down like starving orphans. Moonburning made you hungry.

"The two armies are stationed right across from each other outside the Churitsu Plain, like they have been for years," Maaya explained. "But the skirmishes into each other's territories are growing worse. The sunburners are bypassing the army and going straight towards the civilians, where they can inflict the most damage."

Maaya and Emi shared an uneasy look.

"And so are we, aren't we?" said Kai. "Is Geisa making you attack civilians?"

They both looked away, Emi at the ground, Maaya studying her fingernails.

"I don't know what's worse," Kai said. "Sitting around wondering if your friends are going to come back from a mission in a coffin, or knowing that they are out there, killing innocent civilians."

"It's the job," Emi said. "And they aren't innocent, they are Kitans. They could be harboring sunburners or assisting the enemy."

"It's strange," Kai said coldly. "Emi's lips are moving, but all I hear are Geisa's words coming out of them. The moonburners attacked my village, and I can tell you for a fact that none of us were harboring sunburners or helping the army. We were just trying to stay alive." She closed her eyes, remembering the flames licking up the buildings, the screams and the smoke. Sora's unconscious body in her arms.

"Kai," Maaya said, ever the peacemaker. "That's not fair. We're soldiers. We're just following orders."

"Maybe we shouldn't be following Geisa's orders," Kai hissed. "When does it end? Are we going to keep killing until there is nothing left alive in Kita?"

Maaya's gaze returned to her fingernails. "It's not our place . . . to question. The queen and the general know what they are doing. They have a plan for a major offensive, one that could turn the tide and end the war."

"Maybe we should question," Kai said. "Because I know a bit about the queen's grand plan. And it's not for peace." The words of the giant goddess echoed in Kai's head. Suffering.

Emi and Maaya sat silently for a moment, pushing food around their plates.

"I'll talk to you later," Kai said, standing up. "Suddenly, I'm not feeling very hungry."

Kai left the dining hall feeling restless.

"Let's go see Master Vita," she said to Quitsu, a little shortly. It had been a week since they had visited him.

"You don't think you were a little hard on them?" Quitsu asked.

"It just drives me crazy sometimes," Kai said.

"What?"

"That I'm the only one who questions anything," Kai said. "Everyone else takes this life at face value, like there could be no other way."

"Maaya and Emi grew up here. They don't know any other way. You do. You have the benefit of a different perspective."

"I guess you're right," Kai admitted.

"And you have me," Quitsu said, smirking. "To tell you when you're being an unreasonable idiot."

"Lucky me," Kai grumbled.

"What is going on with you?" Quitsu asked. "That was a good joke."

Kai sighed. Why did she ever think she could keep anything from him? "Today is my birthday."

"Ah," Quitsu said. "It's all becoming clear."

"It's no big deal," Kai said. "I don't want any fuss. It's just . . . the day when my parents and I were supposed to start our journey to Miina. If things had gone differently."

"I'm sorry, Kai," he said. "And happy birthday."

"Thanks, furball."

"You know, if it's your birthday, then it's my birthday too. You didn't get me anything, and you don't see me sulking."

"You are the worst!" Kai said, flicking moonlight at him.

He started running across the courtyard, looking back at her with his pink tongue sticking out of his mouth.

She laughed and followed.

"Master Vita," Kai called as she walked through the front door of the main room of the library. Master Vita sat in one of the large armchairs by the fire, book in hand.

"Kai," he said. "Be a dear and put another log on the fire, will you?"

Kai obliged, picking a big log of crisp, dry wood from the stack beside the fireplace. As she went to put the log into the hearth, she noticed that another figure sat in the chair with its back to the entryway.

"Nanase?" Kai said with surprise. "What are you doing here?"

"I wasn't aware I had to explain my comings and goings to a samanera," Nanase said, with a hint of a smile.

Kai blushed. "I apologize. Your presence surprised me."

Nanase stood. "I find there is knowledge to be had here that I cannot find elsewhere."

"That is the nature of libraries," Master Vita said, leaning on his cane and coming to a shaky stand.

"Indeed," Nanase said. "Thank you, Master Vita. Our talk has been most enlightening."

Kai watched Nanase leave, and then turned to Master Vita with eyebrows raised.

"What was that about?"

"Nothing interesting," Master Vita waved her off. "She was inquiring about the familial line of one of the students."

"Uh-huh." Kai sensed there was something he wasn't telling her.

"Would you make some tea, dear?" Master Vita asked, changing the subject.

"Of course." Kai filled the teapot with water from the little spigot near the library's back door. As she returned to the fire, she saw Master Vita trying to move the big armchair closer to the fire.

"Are you cold? Do you want your sweater?" She asked, hanging the kettle on its hook above the fireplace.

"That would be lovely. It's hard to believe we are nearing the first day of spring," he said.

Kai fetched his sweater from his little bedroom in the back of the library and brought it to him.

"Quitsu tells me it's his birthday," Master Vita said. "So I can only assume that it is your birthday as well."

Kai shot Quitsu a stern look.

"What?" he asked. "I didn't tell him it was yours."

She rolled her eyes. "Yes, today is my birthday. But it is just another day."

"Nonsense! It is a most special day! And no one should go without a gift on their birthday. Lucky you that I have just the thing. You sit here by the fire while I get it."

"You really don't need to," Kai protested, but he was already out of his chair, shuffling towards the back of the library.

Master Vita returned and sat in the chair beside her. He held out a small package, wrapped in soft green cloth.

She unwrapped it slowly, revealing a silver necklace. The pendant was a round black matte stone, unremarkable on its own. It was held to the silver chain by a cage of ornately wrapped wire, looping and circling the stone.

"It's beautiful," Kai breathed, throat tightening. She had never gotten a gift like this, something so beautiful . . . so feminine.

She threw her arms about Master Vita, who patted her back the way old men do.

"Now, dear, nothing to get all worked up about."

She pulled from the hug, blushing.

"I haven't even told you the best part," Master Vita said. "What do you mean?"

"That is more than just a pretty piece of jewelry, my dear. The stone is special, very rare. It grows hot when someone tells a lie in your presence. Only you will be able to tell."

Kai looked at the stone with newfound admiration. "That's amazing. How does it do it?"

Master Vita made a dismissive gesture. "Even I don't know everything. But I figured in this place, it will be useful to be able to tell truth from deception."

Kai's elation dimmed, as she thought about her future as a moonburner—as one of Queen Airi's weapons. It was true, she wouldn't be able to trust everyone.

She hesitated, holding the necklace out to him. "This is a precious gift—one of a kind. I can't accept it."

Master Vita put his hands on hers and pushed the necklace back into her lap.

"I don't have any children, and I won't live forever. It is better that the necklace go to someone who can use it, instead of going into a storage room somewhere after I die, forgotten."

She saw the logic in that and clasped the necklace behind her neck. Quitsu, sitting on the arm of her chair, sniffed at the necklace, taking a closer look.

"Tell me a lie, Quitsu," she said, smiling. "Let's test it out." Quitsu cast her a mischievous look.

"Your hair is growing out nicely," he said. Master Vita snickered.

The pendant grew warm at her neck as one hand flew up to meet it, the other to her hair, which was most certainly rebelling in the transition from close-cropped to shoulder-length.

"Wow!" she said in mock injury. "With friends like you, who needs enemies."

"What about you, Master Vita, a lie?" She asked.

Before he could respond, a deep boom sounded outside and the library shook slightly. They sat still for a minute, listening. Then, another boom, closer.

"Stay here," Kai instructed as she ran for the door to the courtyard, Quitsu at her side.

CHAPTER 22

It was about half an hour past dawn, and morning rays were peeking over the buildings into the courtyard. Kai's dormitory building was on fire, black smoke beginning to billow skyward.

A shadow swept across the stones, and she followed it with her gaze, hand to her face to shield her eyes from the sun. A huge golden eagle banked left as its rider, a large man with curly golden hair, hurled a pure bolt of electricity at the practice ring. The bolt exploded with a force that almost knocked Kai off her feet.

"Look out!" Quitsu cried, as another eagle and rider swept between the buildings, eyes on them. Kai and Quitsu dove into the shelter of the library doors as a shower of rock and mortar rained down on them. Other moonburners were running into the courtyard, drawn by the commotion, but they were just target practice for the sunburners.

Kai rose from the rubble and ran towards the koumori rookery, skirting the outside of the courtyard. They were sitting ducks on the ground, but in the air, at least they stood a chance. She saw on the other side of the courtyard that the moonburners and citadel guards had formed ranks with baliwood bows, shooting volleys at the intruders.

"I've only seen two eagles," Kai said to Quitsu, as they paused behind a column. "I think it's more of a raid than an all out attack. "

"I hope you're right," Quitsu said.

Two more winged shapes swooped over the citadel . . . bringing the total to four.

"Damn. " She'd jinxed it.

They made a final run for it and reached the rookery. "I'll watch for riders," Quitsu said. "You get a koumori tacked up. "

The koumori shuffled nervously from foot to foot on the ceiling of the rookery. Kai whistled at Peppe, who dropped from the ceiling, twisting to land on her feet. She approached Kai with anxious clicks.

Kai grabbed Peppe's tack and began pulling the straps tight.

"I know you don't like being out in the daytime," Kai said in a soothing tone. "But I need you to be brave. "

When Peppe's harness was secure, Kai looked around the rookery for a weapon.

Nothing laying around was even sharp. Kai had her jade-pommeled knife strapped to her arm, but that wouldn't help her much in an air battle.

"Damn it, Mistress Adiru," Kai cursed. "Why are you such a neat freak?"

She ran into the adjoining equipment room where she had located Peppe's tack and found two long bladed-knives that she tucked into her belt, an axe used for chopping wood and a koumori goad, a rod infused with moonlight that gave an electric shock to whatever it touched. She hated using them on the koumori, but she wouldn't have the same qualms about a sunburner. Quitsu bounded into the room and surveyed her makeshift weapons with dismay.

"The trees and koumori will be terrified," he said.

She rolled her eyes. "Never an off moment for you, is there?"

He jumped into her arms, burying his face in her neck for a moment, his cold nose pressed to her skin. "I tease because I care," he said, and then leaped to the ground, bounding ahead to scout the skies for her.

She led Peppe by her reins to the edge of the rookery and mounted. Both she and Peppe shifted nervously while waiting for Quitsu's instructions.

"Hold," he called back, and she saw a shadow pass by. "It should be clear now," he said. "Be careful."

"You too," she said, as she and Peppe took to the skies, bursting from the doors of the rookery.

The golden eagles that the sunburners rode were bigger than

koumori. Koumori were largely gentle creatures, without much fighting ability. If she went head to head with one of the eagles, she and Peppe would be ripped to shreds.

She directed Peppe to land on a pitch of the library roof, half shadowed by another peak nearby. The rising sunlight was streaming into the courtyard behind them, and she hoped that she was nearly invisible in the shadows. She watched the invaders swoop over the citadel, bringing more destruction with each deadly pass.

Her anger flared, growing stronger within her like a cauldron coming to boil. There were defenseless citizens here, servants, children. What did they hope to accomplish with this attack? An eagle passed in front of her, close to her hiding spot. She recognized the rider, his face twisted into a mask of cruelty and arrogance. Daarco!

She braced her legs on her koumori as she pulled the axe from one of the koumori harness straps, a grim smile on her face. She had never thrown an axe at a moving target before, but the knives wouldn't have enough force and the goad would be useless. She'd have to make it work.

Daarco's eagle was coming back around for another pass. He was distracted, sending a stream of lightning towards some women running across the courtyard. Kai lifted the axe, said a prayer, and hurled it with all her strength. It soared strong and true, circling through the air towards him. His eagle began to bank as it approached, and the axe buried itself in the flesh of his back, not his chest or head.

Damn!

The force of the blow threw Daarco off balance, causing him to lean precariously off his eagle. The bird—sensing its rider's distress—compensated, and Daarco righted himself. The eagle began to swing around.

"Time to go," she said. "Appu."

Peppe launched herself off the roof with such force that Kai slipped sideways over her wing, grabbing the straps of the harness just in time. The library roof exploded behind them, spraying tile and mortar. Kai blinked to clear her eyes and looked behind her. Another rider was gaining fast.

She ducked as a lightning bolt flew at her, its deadly energy causing her hair to rise on end. Another bolt streaked towards them, and Peppe dodged, knowing instinctively what to do. Kai gave her the reins, hanging on to the straps for dear life. *Just hop on a koumori and fight an air battle,* she thought. *Smart idea, Kai.*

They dodged another lightning strike, even closer this time. The rider was gaining on her. It wasn't Daarco. He was wearing a golden helmet in the shape of a lion's snarling face. The golden accents on his leather armor made him sparkle in the sun. She drew moonlight from her moonstone bracelet and threw a lightning bolt back at him. He ducked, and it missed him, streaking past his head.

Great, now her link was empty. She had poured too much moonlight into her strike. As the rider streaked after her over the tops off the Kyuden roofs, she directed Peppe across the city. As long as he was chasing her, he couldn't destroy the citadel.

They flew over the rooftops of the city, passing the ramshackle quilt of the Meadows and the stately manors in the finer parts of town. Kai didn't know how long they could keep up the chase. Peppe already showed signs of tiring; koumori were used for distance flying, not speed. Kai sensed heat and ducked, a bolt of lightning flying over her head.

The sunburner was coming up behind her on her right side. If he gained on her, she wouldn't be able to avoid his attacks at point blank range. Kai loosened the koumori goad from where she had tucked it into the harness, gripping it in one hand.

"We have to be brave," she whispered, not sure if she was encouraging Peppe or herself. She threw one more glance over her shoulder and saw that the rider had gained.

"Da!" she shouted, pulling back on the reins. Peppe obeyed instantly, dropping down and slowing. The eagle shot by them, and Kai spurred Peppe forward, stabbing the goad into the soft feathers of the eagle's side. The goad buzzed in her hand and the bird screamed and flailed, knocking Kai and Peppe with its outstretched wing. Its talons locked onto Peppe's harness and flesh, and she screamed too. Kai and the other rider were powerless as the two locked creatures began spiraling towards the earth.

Kai grew disoriented as the ground spun up to meet them. At the last moment, the eagle pulled up with a scream, and they crashed into a stand of dense bushes, a spinning and tumbling jumble of legs, feathers and skin.

The force of the impact threw Kai from the saddle and tumbled her a dozen feet from Peppe. She stared up at the blue sky, dazed, head ringing. She was alive. She tried to move and found she could. It was painful, but she didn't think she had suffered any permanent damage. She got to her hands and knees and looked around, disoriented. They had flown past the city limits and were on the outskirts of Kyuden.

The other rider! She scrambled to her feet and looked around the tangle of bushes. She saw him still on the ground, helmet thrown from him. He rolled to the side, holding his head. His mount was alive, but struggling to get to its feet. She ran over to him, feeling as if she was moving through stiff molasses. Her head still spun. She had lost the daggers in her belt in the crash, but she pulled the jade-pommeled knife from its holder on her arm. She threw herself onto him, knees pinning his arms down, knife pressed hard into his throat.

She looked into his face and her eyes widened.

His widened too. "We have to stop meeting like this," he said with a crooked grin.

Despite herself and the severity of the situation, she grinned back. It was the man with the long golden hair, who had spared her on her way to the citadel.

She bit her lip. She should have already killed him. It was bright morning now—he could burn, she could not. Even with her knife to his throat, he could kill her at any moment. But he wasn't. And he hadn't.

She looked into his startling green eyes and her eyes traced his strong jaw, fine nose and full lips. She couldn't do it. Not because he was the most handsome man she had ever seen. But because she wasn't a killer. Not like this.

She stood quickly, not knowing if she could trust her decision.

"You spared my life once. My debt is paid. " She hesitated. "Don't make me regret this kindness."

"We all have regrets," he called after her, as she strode towards Peppe, who seemed, miraculously, to still be in one piece. "But that will not be one of yours."

It was only later that she realized that her necklace had stayed cool against her chest as he said it. He had spoken the truth.

CHAPTER 23

Kai and Peppe approached the citadel cautiously, but it appeared that the fighting was over. Kai surveyed the citadel in dismay as they swept down out of the smoky air. The dormitory buildings were still burning hotly, and the temple building had been hit too. Flames licked the sides of the buildings as the citizens did their best to keep the fire from spreading. Come nightfall, even the most basic burner could suck the heat from those fires in an instant, but until then, they were limited to fighting the fires with buckets and hoses.

She landed outside the rookery and dismounted a bit unsteadily. She needed to find Quitsu—and then make sure Master Vita was all right.

As she walked out of the rookery, Kai saw the body of a golden eagle and its rider, mangled on the cobblestones. She approached, curiosity drawing her to it.

"It won't be the last," Nanase's voice sounded behind her like a whip. "The queen will be on the warpath after this."

Kai just nodded, unable to draw her eyes away from the ghastly sight of the dead rider, his neck twisted unnaturally.

"Where have you been?" Nanase asked. Apparently, she wasn't actually looking for an answer, because she continued. "We need your help here. Head to the hospital ward."

Kai nodded, suppressing the images coming to mind of her straddling the handsome sunburner with a knife to his throat. She shook away the memory, jogging towards the hospital ward. No one could ever know that she had spared him.

As Kai entered the hospital ward, the smells and sights threatened to overwhelm her. Women filled the beds and others lay on makeshift cots or on the floor. She saw a silver fox sitting on one of the beds and ran to him.

"Quitsu," she said, relief filling her. He rubbed his head against the underside of her chin.

"I was worried," he replied. She nodded, but he was forgotten as she realized who was in the bed.

"Emi," she said softly, eyes tracing her friend's injured form. Emi lay unconscious, with angry burns on one side of her beautiful face, singeing off part of one ear and her silver hair and eyebrow. Her arm on that side appeared to be broken and was set in a sling.

"She has internal injuries," Quitsu said. "They don't know if she will make it."

"What happened?" Kai asked.

"She was fighting the fire in the dormitory building, and a beam collapsed on her. One of the other moonburners dragged her out."

"No time for sorrow, Kai." The nurse she had seen so many times put a hand on her shoulder. "She is stabilized. There are others that could use your help."

And so Kai went to work. Her mind quieted in the bustle of fetching towels, blankets and medicine, boiling water and cleaning wounds. It wasn't until the sun set and all the women breathed a collective sigh of relief that she realized how quickly the day had passed. The healing work picked up with the assistance of moonburning; the fires were quickly doused outside. Halfway through the night, the nurse told Kai to get some sleep. She didn't argue.

Kai and Quitsu walked out of the hospital ward to head towards her room, but she stopped in her tracks.

"Our room is probably completely burned," she said.

"They've set up a makeshift dormitory in the glass classroom," Quitsu said.

She looked around the courtyard and headed towards the library. The big chair by the fire would be more comfortable than a cot in a classroom.

"Let's make sure Master Vita is all right."

"Master Vita," Kai called as she entered the library. The windows had been blown out and several large chunks of rock lay in piles of rubble on the floor near the doorway. There was no response. Kai called out again, trepidation filling her.

"Quitsu, can you find him?"

Quitsu ran ahead of her into the cavernous library as she continued looking around each corner. "Over here!" Quitsu's voice cried from the back of the library.

Kai ran to him and fell on her knees when she saw Master Vita's unconscious form, trapped under some loose wood. Part of the exterior wall had crumbled, and it looked like a beam from the window frame had landed on him.

Kai felt for a pulse and was relieved to find one. She and Quitsu cleared the rubble, and she strained to lift the beam. She heaved and managed to move it just enough to drop it to the ground by Master Vita's feet. Kai gathered his frail form into her arms and stood, bearing him into the small bedroom she saw through an open door. She laid him softly on the bed. His breathing was labored.

"Is he all right?" Quitsu asked, as she checked him over in the way she had been taught.

"I think so." Kai breathed a sigh of relief. "It seems like he is mostly unharmed, save bruising around his legs and a bump on his head where he must have hit it as he fell."

Kai collapsed into a chair next to his bed, her fatigue washing over her.

The next thing she realized, Quitsu was nosing her awake. "He's waking up," Quitsu said.

It took Kai a moment in her disoriented state to realize who "he" was and remember where she was. She drew her chair closer to the bed, rubbing her scratchy, dry eyes.

"Master Vita? Are you all right?"

Master Vita opened his eyes and started coughing, such a fitful cough that Kai stood up, alarmed. She looked at Quitsu.

"He's been coughing in his sleep. It sounds bad," Quitsu said.

Master Vita opened his eyes, tears leaking out of the corners. He held out a shaky hand, pointing towards a dresser at the far side of the room.

"Bottle," he croaked between coughs.

Kai quickly looked through the items on top of the dresser, but didn't find any bottles. She began rifling through the drawers full of clothing and books. The top drawer, the smallest, contained journals, an inkwell and nibs and several bottles. She pulled them all out and brought them to Master Vita's bedside. She held them up to him, one at a time.

"Which one? The blue one?"

He shook his head imperceptibly.

"The green?" She held up a small green bottle with a rubber stopper.

He nodded, but before she could give him any of the liquid inside, he was wracked with another fit of coughing, his frail body thrashing. She waited with the bottle held aloft for what seemed like an eternity, until the coughing subsided enough for him to lay back on his pillow, limp and drained.

"Let me," he said, taking the bottle and putting a few drops under his tongue. He instantly relaxed, his breathing becoming deeper and more regular.

"Master Vita," she said, her concern growing. "What is wrong?" She looked at the bottle, which was now empty.

"Rainier Apothecary" was all the label said, it held no clue to its contents. He took her hand and squeezed it.

"I will explain it all, but not now. I am so tired." He was already falling back asleep.

She took his shoulders and shook him gently, holding the bottle before him.

"Do you need more?" His eyes fluttered open.

"Yes," he said. "In town. The market. Apothecary." He slipped into unconsciousness.

"I don't like this," Kai said, finding it hard to tear her eyes from Master Vita's form. First Emi, now Master Vita. Terrible things were happening to people she cared about.

Kai stood and strode to the door, bottle in hand.

Quitsu called after her. "Your clothes," he said.

She stopped in her tracks and looked down at her pale blue uniform. It was badly torn and blackened from her flight and time in the hospital.

"You can't wear those into town," he said. "We don't want to draw attention to ourselves. At least any more than we have to.'"

"You're right," she admitted, turning. She couldn't think straight. Her body wanted to propel her forward, to take some action that would distract her from her worry over her friends.

Kai rummaged through the drawers of Master Vita's dresser, looking for something that would fit her. She didn't mind dressing in men's clothing. In some ways, she was still more comfortable with it. She found a pair of green trousers, a white linen shirt and a brown belt. Topped with Master Vita's hooded cloak, Kai should be able to blend in.

She began stuffing the other clothing she had pulled out back into the bottom dresser drawer when her finger hit a hard corner.

"Ow," she complained, pulling her hand out and sucking on her cuticle. She moved the clothes aside and found a small oil-painted cameo portrait. The detail was exquisite; she couldn't help marveling over its craftsmanship.

"Look at this," she said.

Quitsu jumped onto the dresser, examining the cameo with his sharp eyes.

"It's Master Vita," he said.

"What?" She looked closer. She drew in a breath.

"It is!" It was a younger version of him, but it had his same earnest expression, the unmistakable wrinkles by his eyes.

"He was handsome," Kai smiled, taking in the sight of Master Vita in a happier time.

"The girl is beautiful too," Quitsu said, examining the other figure in the work of art. "I wonder if it was his daughter?"

The girl looked to be in her mid-teens. She looked . . . familiar. The young woman had a round, delicate face, twinkling gray eyes and a petite nose. Her silver hair was drawn back, and her ears stuck out in a way that would be unattractive on another woman, but somehow only seemed endearing on her. Kai scrutinized the painting and drew in a breath. There was no mistaking those ears. But how could it be?

Kai fingered the oil of the cameo. "It's my mother," Kai said, finally. Quitsu stood on the dresser, hackles up. "What?"

"It's her," Kai said firmly. "Her ears . . . they're the same. I see her so clearly."

Quitsu jumped from the dresser and they both looked at Master Vita, who was still unconscious.

"How is that possible?" Quitsu asked. "Your mother is from Kita, isn't she?"

"I always thought so," she said. "But I never really asked. We didn't talk about things like pasts or futures. It was always about surviving the moment." Kai turned the picture over and saw a small silver engraving on the back. "Vita and Azura."

She and Quitsu looked at each other, eyes wide, mouths open. "Like the Oracle said. Daughter of Azura," Kai breathed.

"So, your mother was the princess of Miina?" Quitsu said. "Doesn't that make you . . . a princess of Miina?"

Kai's mind raced. "I . . . don't know. No one knows she is alive. Was . . . alive. No one knows she had children."

"We need to find out why everyone thought your mother died. And how she ended up in Kita."

"But who would know? My mother and father are dead," Kai said. They both looked at Master Vita.

Kai sat back down on Master Vita's bed. She shook his shoulders gently, and then more firmly.

"Master Vita," she said. "Master Vita!"

He moaned and moved his head, but fell back into sleep.

Kai let out her breath in a frustrated hiss. "Let's go get the medicine," she said. "Hopefully he'll wake up by the time we get back. He owes us some answers."

CHAPTER 24

Kai and Quitsu had no problem slipping out of the citadel gates. Between the chaos of the attack and the continued rescue efforts, no one seemed to pay much attention to a cloaked figure dressed in street clothes. Just to be cautious, Kai used her link to moonburn slightly, pulling the light from her, angling it so that she and Quitsu were cloaked in shadows. Burning rejuvenated her, making her feel more awake and alert than she had any right to be after fighting in a battle, crashing a koumori, and bandaging wounded for a day.

Kai followed the sporadic signs and the general press of people towards the market area closest to the citadel. She had to ask for directions a few times, but slowly made her way to the right street. The entrance to Rainier Apothecary sat in a narrow alley off a quiet market square. The building was old but tidy.

A man bustled out of the back of the store, wiping his hands on a towel. He was painfully tall and thin, but moved quickly and efficiently. He hooked spectacles over his ears and smoothed his white, somewhat stained apron before him.

"Hello, miss," he said, despite Kai's men's clothing. "How can I help you?"

"Hello," she replied, not sure exactly what to ask for. "I am a friend of Master Vita's."

At the mention of the name, the apothecary brightened visibly.

"He has some medicine from your shop, in a green stopper bottle. The medicine has run out, and he seems to need more. I told him I would try to get it."

"Ah, Master Vita! An old friend, an old friend indeed. It's such a pity about his illness. I am just doing my best to make him comfortable. There is nothing I can do, of course."

Kai recoiled slightly, taken aback by this news. "What do you mean?"

The man leaned back, examining her. She couldn't help but squirm under his intense gaze.

"You can't be a very good friend of Master Vita if you didn't even know he was sick," the apothecary said, arching an eyebrow over his spectacles.

Guilt stabbed at her. Kai hadn't visited Master Vita very often over the past few months. But she had been distracted with her lessons and trying to unravel the citadel's secrets. But still, it grated on her to have this man judging her. She had never seen him visit Master Vita.

"Master Vita is very private. He would never share that something was wrong unless he had no choice," Kai said. "I want to help him, and I can't do that unless you tell me what is wrong with him."

"Master Vita has consumption. It's fairly advanced. He won't last the year."

Kai's heart sank as she imagined the world without Master Vita's cheerful smile and barking laugh, his shock of white hair and his half-moon spectacles.

"There must be something that can be done. The medicine you give him . . ."

"The medicine just provides comfort, to ease the symptoms. It is not a cure. The only ones who had a prayer of curing him were those blasted moonburners at the citadel, but they refused to help him. It is too far advanced now."

Kai opened and closed her mouth, working through her confusion. "The moonburners refused to help him? But . . . he works at the citadel. He keeps the archives . . . he is so important."

"He didn't want to talk about it, but I worked it out of him. He went to them for help, and they said they couldn't help him. That was a lie though; I'm certain of it. I know the kind of healing powers moonburners have. Make no mistake. No man is important to the citadel. No man is worth their concern, or, apparently, medical care.

Even if they abided by him continuing to work there."

Kai wished she could protest. But it was true, the moonburners had a blind spot when it came to men. How could a society operate when it didn't think half of the population was worth the space they took up?

As the apothecary continued his tirade against the moonburners, Kai became lost in thought, the words washing over her. A name jarred her back to reality.

"If Azura had become queen, instead of her viper sister, things could have been different."

"Master Vita had something of hers. Azura's," Kai said eagerly. "Did he know her? What can you tell me about her?"

The apothecary's face became a still mask, as if she had just hit on a very troubling subject.

"Please . . ." Kai said. "I didn't grow up in Miina, I don't know what happened. I just hear whispers."

He hesitated, but relented. "It was about twenty years ago. Princess Azura, Airi's older sister, was heir to the throne. I didn't live in Kyuden then, but there were many in the countryside that hoped that she would be the one to end the war."

"A peace delegation came from Kita near the spring of that year. Everything was going well; like I said, things looked hopeful. The new Kitan king, Ozora, seemed forward thinking and even-tempered."

Kai snorted. The apothecary held up a hand, apparently getting into his story now.

"But a few weeks into the visit, one of King Ozora's sunburners, an up and coming captain, was found in a compromising position with one of the queen's daughters."

"Azura?" Kai asked, wondering if she knew the rest of the story.

"Airi. He swore that she had come on to him and he was trying to fight her off, but none of the moonburners believed him. The queen demanded his head. The fragile peace that had been forming began to crumble. It was Azura who suggested a middle ground. She suggested that he be exiled to the Tottori Desert, to let the gods determine whether he was guilty or innocent. The sides relented, and it seemed things would be all right."

"But two days later, Azura was found dead in her room. Battle broke out, and one of the sunburners was killed. The queen was convinced the king had killed Azura for her suggestion, and Ozora was convinced it was all a conspiracy to avoid peace and destroy them. Ozora and his remaining sunburners fled, vowing revenge."

"How did Azura die?" Kai asked, the pieces of something beginning to coalesce in her mind.

"Poison," the apothecary said, shaking his head. "Gives a bad name to the business I'm in when people die of things like that. Master Vita found her, actually. He was heartbroken."

I bet he was, Kai thought.

The apothecary chatted on, clearly grateful to have someone to talk to, even about a forbidden subject. "They say the Gleaming and the exile of the Kitan moonburners to the desert started with the exile of that captain. King Ozora was so bitter to have lost his close friend that he started the testing. He swore to never trust another moonburner."

"Seems like a bit of an overreaction," Kai muttered. "Did they ever find the sunburner who was left in the desert? Did he die?"

At that moment, Quitsu jumped onto the countertop next to where Kai leaned.

The apothecary started, the color draining from his face as he looked from Kai to Quitsu.

"It's all right," she said, holding her hands up. "We're friends of Master Vita. We're not here to get you in trouble. Did they find the sunburner's body?"

"No," the apothecary said, voice wavering. "They never found his body. They assumed he must have been devoured by the desert creatures."

She looked crossly at Quitsu.

"Now please," the man said, shoving a green bottle into her hand. "Take the medicine and go."

Kai and Quitsu strode back towards the citadel. Kai's mind raced as she tried to process the new information she had acquired over the last few hours. She suddenly felt dizzy, like her world was lurching sideways.

"I need a minute," Kai said, unsteadily. She collapsed into a chair in front of a nearby restaurant. She ran her hands through her hair and took a few shaky breaths. Her mother really had been heir to the moonburner throne.

"Are you all right?" Quitsu asked.

A woman bustled out of the restaurant, handing them a folded paper menu.

"Can I get you anything to drink?" she asked cheerfully.

"We aren't staying," Kai said, dragging herself to her feet. "I just needed to sit down for a moment."

"Let me know if you change your mind," the woman said, leaving the menu.

"When is the last time you ate?" Quitsu asked Kai as she straightened up. She paused, trying to remember. She wasn't sure.

"Sit down," Quitsu said. "We're staying."

"But Master Vita . . ." Kai protested weakly. Her stomach did feel cavernously empty, now that she thought about it.

"You won't be able to help him if you pass out on the way back to the citadel."

Kai sheepishly informed the woman that they would, in fact, be staying, and ordered a bowl of hot soup and buns stuffed with spiced meats. She nearly wept with happiness as they arrived.

Quitsu pondered their new information while she stuffed her face. "What do we know?" Quitsu said. "Princess Azura is your mother. Which means she is not dead, like everyone thinks."

"Or was not dead," Kai corrected. "Originally."

"Master Vita might have helped her. He was her tutor, which means that they spent a lot of time together. He found her body."

"He could have given her something to make her seem dead. Then, she would be placed in the crypt," Kai said.

"And we know the crypt has a tunnel into the city. It would have been easy for her to escape," Quitsu said.

"That seems awfully risky," Kai said. "What if she couldn't get out of the crypt? She would have been buried alive."

"Escaping the citadel must have been important enough to risk her life for," Quitsu said.

"But why? What was going on here that she needed to flee?"

"We know she intervened to stop the sunburner captain from being killed."

"Right . . . to prevent an all out war. But it ended up happening anyway."

"I don't know," Quitsu said.

"I don't either," Kai admitted, licking her fingers to get every last bit of dough. "We need more information."

"But I bet there is someone who can tell us." "Master Vita," they said at the same time.

Fortified with a hot meal, they resumed their journey through the city's winding streets back to the citadel. What had been so important that her mother had left the citadel and everything she knew? And how could her dark-haired mother be the silver-haired moonburner from the photo? Kai turned these questions over in her mind, but always reached the same conclusion. She needed more information.

Kai pulled up short, looking around the square they had just entered. "Where are we?" she asked, looking around for landmarks. She had been so engrossed in her thoughts that she hadn't been paying attention to their route.

Quitsu jumped onto the counter of a buttoned up stall for a better view. The sun was setting, and the square was deserted. A cold breeze blew, and Kai pulled Master Vita's cloak tightly about her, thankful for its warmth.

"It looks familiar," Kai said, walking forward a few paces. She looked to her left and her eyes widened as she recognized the narrow, ivy-lined alleyway she had once seen the queen and General Geisa disappear into.

"Quitsu," Kai whispered, suddenly feeling like they were being watched. She crept into the alley and stood before the brick wall that had confounded her last time.

"The invisible door," Quitsu said. "Our old nemesis. We meet again."

"Do you think I can open it now that I can moonburn? It probably leads back to the citadel," Kai mused.

She drew in light from her moonstone and sent a tendril of moonlight against the wall, trying to caress it to reveal its secrets. The outline of a door appeared with hinges and a latch.

"Look!" Quitsu said, excitedly.

"I can't believe that worked," Kai said. "It's not very secure."

"They probably don't expect anyone to know there is a door here. People don't generally go about burning moonlight at random brick walls."

Kai rolled her eyes. She lifted the latch, but it was locked. Quitsu snickered.

She shot him a look. She tried teasing the lock with moonlight, but it didn't work.

"I spoke too soon," she admitted to Quitsu, who was pacing back and forth before the door. "Any ideas?"

"Unfortunately, no."

"Stand back," she said. "I am going to try something."

"Kai . . . is this a good idea . . ." Quitsu asked, but it was too late. She had already pulled in moonlight, draining her moonstone link. She sent a jet of fire into the latch, melting it.

Quitsu ducked behind her, shielding his eyes from the light.

She took her knife and carefully laid it into the edge of the still-smoking door, just above the twisted metal of the latch. The door groaned and swung open.

"Subtle," Quitsu said.

But Kai had a smile on her face.

"Stop worrying. If we get caught, we'll tell them we were looking for a shortcut back to the citadel. What's the worst that could happen?"

CHAPTER 25

They stepped onto a landing before a twisting staircase that led down into darkness. Kai grabbed an unlit torch set on a hook on the wall and lit it with a match that rested in a nearby recess.

No moon orbs here. Odd.

Kai pulled the door shut behind them. She and Quitsu started down the staircase, the stone walls on either side cold and wet with damp. It grew colder the further they descended.

"I'm beginning to think this wasn't such a good idea," Quitsu whispered.

"You and me both," she said, swallowing thickly. Her elation at successfully opening the door was quickly turning to trepidation. Her hand was sweaty on the torch, and the hair stood up on the back of her neck. Where were they going?

The stairway came to an end, and they found themselves in a wide hallway. Ahead of them, the hallway was lit with torches.

"Put your torch out," Quitsu urged.

She complied, and they crept forward, keeping to the shadows on the right side of the corridor. They turned a corner, and she drew her breath in sharply. There were bars lining the left side of the hallway.

"A dungeon?" Kai whispered, her voice hardly perceptible.

"The citadel has a dungeon above ground," Quitsu said uneasily.

"Why does it need a secret dungeon?"

They inched forward, sticking to the shadows cast by the flickering torches. She looked into the first cell she could see and clasped her hand over her mouth to keep from exclaiming. There was a man inside, dirty and foul-smelling. He had a long scraggly beard and wore stained, tattered pants. His chest was crisscrossed with lines and bruises from what she could only imagine to be daily beatings and flogging. But despite all of this, what drew her eyes most was his hair. His hair was not blonde, but golden, like wheat flax in summertime. Though greasy and unkempt, it shimmered in the firelight. A sunburner!

The sunburner raised his head and peered through the bars of his cell. "Who's there?" he asked, eyes trying to penetrate the clinging darkness.

Kai pressed herself to the wall, Quitsu behind her, eyes closed, willing him to look away.

He lost interest, letting his head droop back down towards his chest in defeat.

She breathed out a shaky breath, and they continued their slow, silent walk through the hallway, her sense of dread growing the farther they walked. She counted six sunburners in the cells they had passed so far.

"The sunburner who attacked us was right," Kai said, understanding dawning. "They are capturing sunburners."

"Why?" Quitsu whispered. Kai just shook her head.

They reached the end of the hallway, and it opened into a bigger room, well-lit with oil lanterns. The room housed more cells, though they were cleaner and more spacious than those housing the sunburners. The open area in the middle held a table and what appeared to be medical instruments. She and Quitsu exchanged a questioning look. Both of the walls were lined with cells, so there would be no clinging to one side to avoid detection.

"Let's just walk through," Kai whispered. "Quickly, like we belong."

Quitsu shot her a look of disbelief, but nodded.

She stood, straightened, and began striding into the main room. She pasted a look of disdain on her face and looked straight ahead. She had passed through most of the room without incident when she caught sight of the prisoner in the final cell to the right. She stumbled, stunned, against the wall of the hallway on the other side. She couldn't look away.

"Quitsu," she hissed, motioning with her head. "It's Chiya."

Quitsu's mouth dropped open, an expression she would have laughed at in less serious circumstances.

The moonburner was lying on a stone bed with a thin mattress, covered with a blanket, eyes closed. A silver seishen body was lying motionless beside her. When Kai said her name, however, her eyes flew open.

Kai turned to flee, but stopped when she heard one anguished word. "Help. "

She turned back to Chiya, and their eyes met.

Chiya's blazed with recognition and she flew to the door of her cell, gripping the bars. "Kai. What are you doing here?" she said, her eyes fierce, but her voice low.

Kai drew closer. "We . . . found a passage. We didn't know where it led. What is this place?"

As she neared the cell bars, she got a better glimpse at Chiya, standing in thin white pants and a form-fitting white top. She had a distinct bump on her abdomen that while still small, seemed remarkably out of place against her muscled form.

"Are you . . . are you . . . pregnant?" Kai asked in disbelief. "I thought you went on the special mission?"

Chiya's face twisted bitterly.

"This is the special mission," she hissed. "Our ultimate sacrifice for the good of the moonburners and the citadel."

"I don't understand," Kai said.

"Neither did I. I thought I was volunteering for battle and glory. But I was volunteering to be a laboratory rat. To be impregnated by those disgusting sunburners and bear perfect moonburner children who can be trained for the queen's army."

"I don't understand," Kai said again.

"It takes the mating of a sunburner and moonburner to beget a child who has burner powers," Chiya said. "Hence, turning us into brood mares."

"That can't be true. Neither of my parents were burners. They were just normal people. My father was a rancher." As soon as Kai said the words, she realized the falsehood. Her mother wasn't just a normal person. And apparently, her father wasn't either.

"Things aren't always as they seem. Maybe you never knew it, but they were burners. I've seen the evidence."

Kai opened and closed her mouth, dumbfounded. Her father was a sunburner? "I can't believe it," she said softly.

Chiya misinterpreted her words. "Do you think they would go to all this trouble if it wasn't true?" Chiya motioned to the intricate cells and machinery. "The burners hold many closely-guarded secrets. This is one."

Kai's mind whirled. "But . . . sunburners and moonburners are raised to hate each other. With the division of the countries, how can there be any burner children left?"

"Very astute. There are fewer and fewer children born with burner abilities. Didn't you ever wonder why the dormitories are so empty? The classes are so small? If the war doesn't end soon, the moonburners will go extinct."

"Does the queen really hate the sunburners so much that she would prefer this over peace?" Kai said, horrified. "I can't believe she would do this to her own people . . ."

Chiya let out a harsh laugh. "Believe it." Her voice was tinged with hysteria. "She stood outside my cell and watched as I was raped by a sunburner." Chiya's voice cracked and the ferocity drained from her. It was as if she collapsed into herself, becoming small and fragile. A tear leaked down one cheek.

"Please," Chiya said. "Get us out of here. No one knows where we are. They drug us with lusteric so we can't moonburn. Tanu just lies there, drugged up, all day. Please. Think of something."

"I'll try. But won't they let you out when you have your baby?"

Chiya shook her head, tears flowing freely now. "No. I overheard General Geisa say that they are going to breed us again and again until we are all used up. And then I'm sure they will kill us."

Kai shook her head back and forth, the shock and the horror of it washing over her.

"Please, Kai." Chiya gripped her hand through the bars. "I know I was cruel to you, but this is bigger than you and me. This is about the future of the moonburners." She stopped, choking on her tears. "I'm a warrior. I can't . . . I can't live like this. I'd rather die. Either get me out, or get me a weapon, and I'll end it myself."

Kai squeezed the other woman's hand, the bitterness Kai had once felt towards her falling away.

"I promise," she said.

Kai and Quitsu made their way up the staircase on the other side without encountering anyone. When they reached the door at the top of the stairs, Kai said a prayer and poked her head out. If the queen or General Geisa found out what she knew, she would end up in one of those cells next to Chiya.

"It's the throne room," Kai said, opening the door and creeping out. The door was set behind the raised dais that housed the throne. It was a good place for a secret passage; no one but the queen and Geisa ventured onto the dais. The room was silent and dark.

Kai slipped out the front door of the building into the dusky courtyard, closing the huge door softly once Quitsu made it through. She looked around for a moment, unable to form a course of action amongst the cacophony of thoughts racing through her head.

"Geisa," Quitsu hissed, and Kai saw the woman rounding the far corner to enter the courtyard in front of the throne room. Kai launched into action, dashing away from Geisa towards a stand of ornamental trees and tall grasses nestled against the building. She dove behind the largest tree trunk, wriggling in between the grasses into the dark loamy soil. She prayed the grasses were tall enough to cover her.

Quitsu, who was crouched next to her, crept onto her back to peer out of the grass.

"The queen has joined her," he whispered, his words so soft to be almost indecipherable. "They are talking. The queen seems upset."

Oh, goddess, Kai thought. What if they had some sort of secret alarm on their dungeon? What if they knew she had been there?

"They are walking away," Quitsu said. "Towards the main courtyard."

Kai deflated as the surge of adrenaline left her. Quitsu jumped from her, and she rolled onto her back, looking into the starry sky, partially blocked by the lacy foliage of the trees above her.

"How could she do that to her own people?" Kai wondered. "How could she hate sunburners so much that this is a better solution than peace? Imprisoning her own subjects?"

"I don't know," Quitsu replied.

"All my life I wanted to be a part of the moonburners. I thought I would use my magic to help people, to free people from the tyranny of King Ozora's rule. But maybe the sunburners have it right after all. Maybe we should just let them kill us all. It would be better than living in a cage like Chiya."

"Don't say that," Quitsu chided. "There is good here."

"Like what? Tsuki with her blood sacrifices? Slaughtering civilians on nightly raids? Nothing is like I thought it would be."

"No. Like your friends—Nanase and Pura. There are people here who are trying to do good. You can't give up. Obviously everyone isn't in on the queen's plan, or she wouldn't have to keep it secret. She must expect opposition."

Kai looked at the moon, just visible, sitting low in the sky. Most nights, the moon was a welcome companion, a guiding light and a steady comfort. Tonight it felt distant and aloof. Why would it care about the lives or deaths of mere mortals like her? This was all too big for her.

"I promised I would free her. Why did I promise that? How in the world will I ever free her?" Kai lamented.

"Because you couldn't leave her," Quitsu said. "We'll come up with something. You're not in this alone."

She scratched Quitsu's soft chin, taking comfort in his warmth. She wasn't alone. They'd come up with something.

Loud voices from across the courtyard broke the silence of the night, and Kai sat up amongst the grasses, wearily.

"What's going on?" she asked.

"Let's find out."

A large group of women were gathered in front of the burnt dormitories. Kai crossed the courtyard and pushed through the tightly-packed crowd to the front, Quitsu at her heels. She drew a sharp breath.

A moonburner was curled on the ground, silver hair disheveled and face tear-stained. Next to her lay a man. He was bloodied and beaten. As another woman delivered a kick to his ribs, she saw his face. Atsu! The handsome biwa player from Rox's band. The one who flirted so shamelessly with Maaya and had her blushing up to her eyebrows.

Kai's heart sank as she realized what had happened. Maaya and Atsu had been found together. The moonburner on the ground was Maaya.

"They'll kill her," Kai said to no one at all, insides twisting. She caught sight of Leilu and Stela. Leilu's face was a mask of grief, Stela's one of fury.

The crowd across the circle parted as the queen stepped forward.

The queen held up her hands and the crowd quieted, drawing back from the two on the ground. The queen's doll-like face was the perfect mix of sorrow and anger, a mother wronged and disappointed.

"In this time of war, one of our own has betrayed us. What words do you have in your defense, Maaya, daughter of the moon?"

Maaya climbed onto her knees and looked up at the queen, trying to muster what was left of her dignity.

"I . . . I did not lay with him, Queen Airi. He just kissed me. It was . . . just a kiss," she broke off, numbly falling back onto her haunches.

"Is this true?" Queen Airi demanded of two moonburners, who apparently had found Maaya and Atsu in the act.

"We only saw them kissing, Your Majesty. But we do not know what might have happened on other occasions," one woman said, looking at Maaya with disgust.

The queen looked thoughtful. "Does anyone have testimony to offer in this matter?"

The women in the circle were silent, shuffling from one foot to another, avoiding eye contact.

"If we have no proof that this moonburner has lain with a man, then we shall not punish her for it," the queen said. Maaya looked up, hopeful.

"However, she has still broken our laws. She will be given ten lashes and stripped of her title as moonburner. She shall serve in the citadel. Let her be a reminder to those who chafe under the burden of their duty. We never promised you an easy life. But there will be glory and honor, serving your goddess and your queen."

The ranks of the moonburners swelled with pride as the queen continued her patriotic speech. Kai couldn't hear the words through the angry beating of her heart. All she could see was how this place destroyed good people. Sweet, devoted Maaya, bloody and weeping on the stones. Emi, burned and disfigured in her hospital bed. Master Vita, who had devoted his life to the pursuit of knowledge, left to die alone in the library. And Chiya. Chiya, whom she had hated and feared even an hour ago.

She suddenly understood why her mother had kept her from the citadel as long as possible. Her whole life, she had thought the citadel would be her refuge. But how could it be? Not when Queen Airi, who was so perfect on the outside, was rotten to the core. Her poison had spread, and no corner of the citadel was untouched. There was nowhere

Kai or her friends could be safe.

Kai curled her hands into fists and began to step forward. She didn't know what she was going to do, but she had to do something.

Quitsu dug his claws into her shin. "Don't. This is not the time. Forging forward with no plan will only get you killed. Or worse . . ." he motioned his head towards the throne room.

Quitsu's warning rang true, and she stepped back, swallowing. The moment had passed, the queen was already leaving the circle, her attendants at her side. She turned back.

"Oh, and the man will be executed," she called over her shoulder, as if she were waving a flippant goodbye to a friend.

"No!" Maaya screamed. She threw herself across Atsu's unconscious form, sobbing. The moonburners in the circle tore Maaya from him, hauling her bodily towards a post near the rookery. Kai had never known what it was for until now. She swallowed as she saw Maaya being chained to it.

"My queen," Stela said, stepping forward. The queen turned back.

"This man is a friend, a good man. He did not understand the rules. He doesn't deserve death. Please, I beg you. Spare him."

"No man is a good man," the queen said, "and ignorance of the law is no excuse. This man is a criminal and will be punished accordingly." She motioned with her head and two moonburners hefted Atsu's unconscious body, carrying him towards the dungeons.

"As for you, daughter, report to General Geisa in one hour. She has a special lesson on loyalty that I believe you should hear."

General Geisa nodded at Stela with a grim smile, before rolling up her sleeves and heading towards the whipping post.

Kai began to walk stiffly towards Stela, who stood with her head down and fists balled. She felt a hand on her shoulder. It was Pura. Her face was kind. Kai turned to her, emotions flowing over her like a tide.

"This is wrong," she said, choking on the words.

"I'm sorry. I know they are your friends. But this world we live in . . ." Pura hesitated. "Sometimes it is cruel."

Kai turned back towards Maaya and Geisa, who had been handed a long whip. The least she could do was be there for her friend. The least she could do was watch.

"Kai," Pura said more insistently. "I need you to come with me."

"No. I need to be there . . . for Maaya. And Stela. To be with them."

"I know you want to. But I've been instructed to collect you, immediately."

Her eyes widened and panic stabbed at her. The door she had burned out. Someone had connected her to the break-in at the facility! Now Pura was going to get rid of her for good.

"Why?" Kai asked with a calmness she didn't feel.

"With the recent attack, and the losses we suffered, we need all the masters we can get. You and some of the other samaneras are headed to the Akashi Mountains for your final test."

"A test? In a time like this?"

Pura shook her head and shrugged. "I know it seems silly, but its a tradition that goes back many generations. The test is a part of us."

Kai turned to look at Maaya one last time before allowing Pura to lead her away. She knew she was being a coward, but a part of her was relieved to have this excuse not to watch. She would pass her test, become a master moonburner, and come back to do everything in her power to help her friends.

Master Vita! She had forgotten all about his medicine.

"Pura, can we please stop by to see Master Vita before we leave? In the library?"

Pura shook her head. "No time. They are already saddling the koumori."

"Then, would you give him something for me?"

Pura raised an eyebrow at her.

"He's sick. It's medicine. He needs it." She pulled the green bottle out of her pocket and handed it to Pura. "Please."

CHAPTER 26

K ai and five other samanera rode in a loose formation behind Nanase on their way to the Akashi Mountains. Kita and Miina nestled up against the mountain range, which formed a forbidding wall of dark rock and snow. Kai didn't know what lay on the other side of the mountains. Maybe no one did. They were said to be impassable.

The green land of Miina stretched across below her, bleeding into the emerald green of the Misty Forest. It would normally inspire her, but all she felt was an aching sorrow. Poor Maaya. She didn't deserve this fate.

The temperature dropped as they grew closer to the mountains, as if the peaks sucked the heat from the world. The cold air numbed her body, matching the numbness of her mind. She couldn't even think about all that had happened in the last few days. It was too much.

Despite Pura's insistence on speed, it had taken hours to ready their group for departure, and the day had dawned with bright and harsh light while they flew.

The samanera issued a collective sigh of relief when they landed. The sunburner attack on the citadel was fresh in everyone's mind and flying during daytime left them feeling particularly exposed. They landed in a clearing near an alpine lake, filled with tall green trees, blue thrush grass, and yellow moss. It was a landscape unlike any she had ever seen.

Nanase dismounted her koumori and walked a little way into the clearing. Her eagle seishen, which had been flying in formation with them, landed on a high branch behind her. The samanera, exchanging glances and shrugs, followed her like a herd of ducklings. Nanase turned to address them.

"These mountains represent the edge of the known world. But as moonburners, you are asked to go beyond the known, into the unknown. Without question and without reservation. And sometimes you are asked to do it alone. With no support, with no resources. Today is one of those days. Each of you will be given one vial." Nanase pulled six small vials out of a pouch at her belt. "You will travel into the mountains. You will find the spring that flows with purple water. Fill your vial and return here to camp. If you do so, you will pass the test."

"Purple water?" Kai murmured. "Is that a metaphor?"

"Nanase doesn't seem to think so," Quitsu whispered back.

"Kai?" Nanase's sharp voice rang across the clearing. "Questions?"

"Um, yes," Kai said, her cheeks flushing, her mind scrambling for a question. "Is the spring water potable?"

"So sure of your success already, are we?" Nanase said. "Yes. You may drink from the spring. In fact, legend says that only the worthy will find the spring and that those who drink from it will be granted what they wish for most in life."

That would be nice. Maybe she could wish that Queen Airi had never been born. Kai wondered if Emi and Maaya had drank from the spring. Or Chiya. It didn't seem like they had been granted their deepest desires.

"The stream is a two-day hike from here, if you were hiking straight to it. You will leave camp several hours apart. This is meant to be a solitary endeavor. Usually we only bring one samanera at a time to be tested, but due to . . . recent events, we've brought you all. If you come across each other, pass by and keep moving. Do not speak to one another."

One of the samanera spoke up, the freckle-faced girl that had seemed to dislike Kai from her first History class. "If this is a solitary endeavor, Kai should have to leave her seishen behind. Otherwise, she has an unfair advantage."

Quitsu hissed. Kai raised an eyebrow. *Thanks for throwing me under the cart-horse,* she thought.

"A seishen is an extension of their moonburner companion," Nanase said coldly, briefly eying her seishen above her. "Kai can no more leave Quitsu than she can leave her arm or her leg. Would you like to attempt the test without a leg?"

"No, Headmistress," the girl muttered.

"Very good. Since you are so eager to excel beyond your compatriots, why don't you set off first."

The girl opened her mouth to ask another question, but was silenced by Nanase.

"Lastly, you will receive no supplies or provisions. You have been trained to survive in the wild. Good luck." Nanase handed the freckle-faced girl a vial. The girl straightened her uniform, gave a final glare to Kai, and strode off into the woods.

Kai was fourth to depart from the clearing. She and Quitsu settled into a comfortable pace. The long rays of afternoon light fell across the mountains, setting the chiseled peaks and snowy patches on fire with color.

"This is stupid," Kai grumbled. "We should be back in the citadel, helping our friends, not out here in the middle of nowhere, jumping through pointless moonburner hoops."

"The faster you pass the test, the faster you can get back to the citadel and execute your brilliant, foolproof plan to rescue Chiya and overthrow the queen."

"I don't have a brilliant, foolproof plan to rescue Chiya and overthrow the queen," Kai said.

"Exactly. Maybe we should take these few days to try to form such a plan?" Quitsu said.

Kai took a deep breath and let it out slowly. "All right. First things first. How do we find a purple spring in the middle of a mountain range?"

"Scrying?" Quitsu said.

"That's the only thing I can think of," Kai agreed. "So first we need to find a pool of water. How to find a pool of water in the middle of a mountain range?"

"Ask around," Quitsu said. Before Kai could reply, Quitsu darted off into the trees.

Kai continued on her path, swatting an occasional bug. As the sun set, the air grew colder, and she shivered in her thin, light blue uniform. Kai pulled in moonlight and wrapped heat around herself in a protective bubble.

"Perfect," she said, now toasty warm.

Quitsu bounded back out of the trees, pine needles sticking out of his fur, a twig caught in his tail. Kai suppressed a smile. Quitsu had become accustomed to the citadel as well, it seemed. A city fox.

"Some raccoon dogs said there is a pond a ways up and to the east," he said.

"Raccoon dogs?" She asked. "They told you this?"

"Yes," he said, impatiently. "Come on."

She followed, shaking her head. "Since when do you talk to regular animals?"

"Since always," he said over his shoulder. "You just never asked!"

They found the lake, a cool oval mirror reflecting the light of the moon and stars over the silent tree tops. She knelt next to it, drinking her fill.

Kai performed the scrying ritual Pura had taught her, drawing symbols with moonlight across the surface of the water and asking the water to locate her target. Pura had said that scrying had to do with a moonburner's inherent connection to the earth. Even knowing this, it still seemed miraculous when a faint picture of a spring appeared on the water, illuminated by the moonlight. It looked like the spring was partially within a cave, surrounded by crystals that gave off a pale purple glow in the silver light.

"That makes more sense," Kai said.

Quitsu peered at the image from beside her. "See if you can move it out."

She did as Pura had taught her, willing the image to pull out further, pushing the moonlight into it. The image of the cave blurred into an image of a ravine, sparkling slightly with some sort of mineral.

"Ravine. Check," she said, running the image along its length. The bottom flattened out into an expanse of trees that could be anywhere in the forest.

"Trees. That narrows it down," Quitsu said.

Kai moved the image to the left, what she hoped was the west, looking for any landmarks. Nothing. Then to the east.

"There," Quitsu said. "That rock. It has to be something we can find."

She studied the landmark, a smooth double humped dome of gray rock. "It'll have to do," she said, standing up and stretching her legs. The strain of the scrying had tired her. She shook her head.

"Do you want to see if your new raccoon dog friends can help us find the big rock?" she asked.

"On it!" he cried, running from the lake's edge like a silver blur.

With the help of the forest creatures Quitsu had befriended, they made it to the strange rock formation by sunrise.

"It's harder during the day," he said. "It's easier for me to communicate with nocturnal animals. Closer affinity, I suppose."

Kai could tell that the morning was cold and crisp from the frost on the grass. She burned moonlight from her moonstone link to reinforce the blanket of warm air around her. She hoped it would last until the sun reached this side of the mountains.

"Should we rest, push forward, or look for food?" Kai wondered out loud. She wasn't feeling too tired yet, but the area around the rock formation provided better shelter than the exposed rocky ravine leading up to the spring.

"You're the boss," Quitsu said.

"Let's rest and refuel. We'll set out tonight."

Kai set a few snares in the forest on the other side of the rock, like her father had taught her. She remembered his careful hands guiding her clumsy ones with the knots, showing her how to tie a snare in the most humane way possible. She looked around, taking in the view of Miina through the sparse trees. He would have loved this place.

She gathered a few nuts that she recognized from her survival training class, and Quitsu came back with two eggs he had stolen from some unfortunate bird's nest. They gathered firewood, took a nap, and by the time she checked her snare that afternoon, it was filled with a lean alpine rabbit.

Kai hummed as she cleaned and dressed the rabbit, setting it to cook. For the first time in a long time, Kai felt a moment of peace.

"You seem almost cheerful," Quitsu remarked.

As soon as he said the words, Kai felt a stab of guilt. "I don't have the right to be, with everything going on at the citadel. But . . . I miss being outside. I feel like I can finally breathe again. Maybe we just . . .

shouldn't go back," Kai suggested. "We could just live out here in the wilderness." The idea of it captivated her for a moment. To wash her hands of politics of the citadel, the impossible task that waited for her . . . it had appeal. She thought about the woman her mother had taken her to, deep in the Kitan swamp. She had done it.

"Could you live with that choice?" Quitsu asked.

Kai shook her head. "It's tempting. But I have to go back. I can't abandon Chiya and the others."

Appetites satisfied, they bid the clearing farewell and began their hike towards the spring. The ravine was steep and treacherous, with huge boulders to scramble over. No wonder the spring was difficult to find. No one would come this way by choice.

A huge half moon had risen over the mountain peaks, and now lit their way. The rocks and ground glistened faintly with a purple mineral that caught the light. As they neared the top, the boulders became slick with water. The mineral deposits grew, and small purple crystals began to poke from the ground in clusters, clinging to the rocks they climbed.

"These things are beautiful, but a nightmare to climb over," Kai said, resting for a moment and examining her scraped and bloodied palms. The knees of her leggings were torn, exposing her battered knees beneath.

"We've got to almost be there," Quitsu said, showing no signs of being the worse for wear.

Quitsu was right. They climbed for another twenty minutes before Kai pulled herself up on a wide rock ledge. Water flowed off the ledge to her right in a trickling waterfall. She put her hands on her knees, catching her breath. When she stood, her eyes widened.

The scene in front of them was like a foreign landscape. Back from the ledge yawned a cave mouth, made out of dark rock. Its floor was carpeted with purple crystals. Some were tiny, forming a miniature forest, while others stood as high as her waist and as big as her thigh, sticking out at odd angles.

Through the crystals wove a gentle stream, flowing over the side of the ledge and forming the waterfall she'd seen. As soon as she set her foot on the ledge, an inhuman scream sounded, coming from the cave.

"What was that?" Kai said, realizing with a sinking feeling that their route so far had been too easy.

"Part two of the test?" Quitsu said.

Kai drew her dagger and advanced.

They crept into the cave, picking their footing carefully. Kai burned and cast a silver light above them. When the mouth of the cave was just out of sight, they found the spring pouring from a low table of rock on the side of the cave wall. Crystals veritably exploded from the source, crowding around it like eager children.

"The water must make the crystals," Kai said.

Quitsu let her take in the sight for a moment and then approached the fountain.

"Let's fill that vial and get out of here," he said. "Before we meet whatever screamed earlier."

She knelt down, careful not to cut her already bruised knees on the crystals that clustered around the spring. The vial filled in an instant, and she held it up to the light at the cave mouth. Floating flecks glistened purple in the clear water. She stoppered the vial and put it in her pocket.

"Should I drink some?" Kai asked, half to Quitsu and half to herself. "We didn't come across any water since the lake last night. It's a long way back."

"Let's cut to the chase, shall we?" Quitsu asked. "You could make it back to the lake. You know the way. You're thinking about what Nanase said. About your fondest wish being granted."

"Sometimes it's annoying that you know me so well," Kai said.

"You should drink it," Quitsu said. "We could use a little wish-granting right about now."

She dipped her hands into the cool water and lifted it to her lips. It carried a hint of sweetness.

"It's good," she said, drinking her fill.

"Hope you don't grow purple crystals out of your ears," Quitsu said.

"Great," Kai said, throwing her hands in the air. "That would have been the type of thing to add to the pro and con list before I drank the water." Quitsu just grinned his foxy grin.

Kai turned to leave and found herself looking into two glowing eyes. "Quitsu . . ." Kai said, slowly backing away from the unblinking eyes.

"What is it?"

As if it had heard her question, the dark silhouette of a huge head reared back, and a pillar of violet flame jetted towards them.

CHAPTER 27

Kai dove out of the way behind one of the pillars, landing hard on the craggy crystalline ground. A large crystal drove into her ribs—the sudden pain stunning her.

That's going to leave a bruise, she thought.

The only physical weapon she had was her jade-pommeled knife, but it was nighttime and the half moonlight streaming from the cave entrance was all the weapon she needed. She burned moonlight, letting it fill her with its energy. She felt alive, as if her soul was on fire.

"Come on then!" she yelled, getting to her feet. She cast a moonlit orb into the heights of the cave, disturbing a flock of bearbats clinging to the ceiling above. She ducked as they dropped from the ceiling, making for the cave entrance. And then she truly saw her opponent.

"Crap."

It had to be at least ten feet tall at the withers and thirty feet long. A dragon. A real, live dragon. It spread its wings and reared on its haunches, letting out the unearthly scream they had heard before entering the cave. Its violet scales glimmered in the light of her orb, and its bright white teeth flashed dangerously.

"It couldn't have been just a journey of self discovery, could it?" Quitsu said, reappearing at her side, his hackles raised in a mohawk down his back.

"Nothing is ever easy," Kai said. As adrenaline coursed through her veins, she found herself strangely calm. This was a fight she understood.

The dragon had apparently allowed her enough time for self reflection. It blasted another shot of fire at them.

Kai remembered her training, drawing the heat from the fire and channeling it into the rock walls of the cave. The dragon's fire felt strangely familiar as she handled it. Like moonlight.

Her opponent didn't give her much time to ponder this oddity as it surged forward, jaws bared. She threw up a shield of intense heat in front of them, causing the dragon to shy back.

Kai took advantage of the dragon's temporary withdrawal and threw lightning bolts at it—one, two, three, in rapid succession. The bolts seemed to go right through it, making it stronger. It lashed out with its huge serpentine neck, and she and Quitsu dove to the ground again. Its jaws just missed them.

She threw a fireball at the dragon's head and landed a direct hit, but the beast hardly even flinched.

"It's like the moonlight is feeding it," Quitsu cried, echoing her very thought.

What was going on?

She pulled her knife from its sheath and tossed another lightning bolt at the dragon. She was tiring now. She wasn't used to burning this much moonlight at one time.

"Quitsu, distract him," Kai said. "I have an idea."

"I don't want to be the bait," he said, but jumped on a tall crystal.

Kai crawled to the side of the spring and clothed herself in shadows, crouching.

"Hey, dragon, over here!" Quitsu yelled at the dragon. "Fox appetizer! Want a piece?"

The dragon reared back and struck in the same manner it had before. But this time, Kai was ready.

Quitsu dove from the crystal, Kai leaped from her crouch and stabbed her knife straight into its violet eye.

But it was gone.

As soon as her knife touched where the dragon should have been, it vanished. Kai stood up, gripping her dagger with white-knuckled fingers.

"What the hell?"

The sound of slow clap sounded from the cave entrance.

"Impressive," a female voice said.

Kai walked towards the entrance and into the moonlit night. The voice belonged to a moonburner, one whom Kai had seen around the citadel, but had never spoken to.

"I don't understand," Kai said.

"You don't think we can afford a real dragon for every moonburner exam, do you?"

"It . . . wasn't real? Then what?"

"An illusion powered by moonburning and a very old relic." The moonburner opened her hand to reveal a delicate violet crystal, carved into the shape of an intricate dragon. "It's been in the citadel's possession for years. Quite an impressive piece of magic. I think it used to guard something important."

Kai said nothing. Perhaps she should be fascinated by how the relic worked, but she just felt tired. Tired of games. Tired of falsehood. Tired of the citadel staging life-threatening encounters to test her.

"You passed," the woman continued. "Return to base camp and find Nanase. Congratulations, master moonburner."

Making their way back down the ravine was even harder than coming up it. Kai's arms and legs were fatigued from the journey up, and the boulders were slick with dew and frost from the cold night air. At least they had found the spring quickly. Surely they had been faster than the other samanera. It had taken them hardly two days.

Kai and Quitsu reached the clearing with the strange rock as the sun was beginning to rise. They decided to rest for the day and make their way back to Nanase's camp in the evening. Despite the hard ground beneath her, her fatigue from the day pulled Kai into a deep sleep.

She awoke with a start. It was nighttime. Had they slept so long? Quitsu was still sleeping beside her peacefully. She peered into the trees around them, listening and looking for what might have disturbed her. Her eyes scanned past a break in the trees and then flew back. There was a figure standing there.

Kai stood, suddenly alert. She eased the knife out its sheath strapped to her arm. Hopefully it was just one of the other samanera.

"Who goes there," she asked loudly, watching the figure.

"I don't . . ." a female voice said. "I don't know where I am."

"Are you lost?" Kai said, taking a few steps towards the figure. "Come into the clearing; maybe I can help you."

The woman walked forward slowly, head swiveling back and forth to take in the immense mountains behind her. The peaks looked especially majestic, their snowy caps illuminated in the silvery light of the full moon.

Wait. Full moon?

Kai looked up, gazing in disbelief at the huge round moon above them. Last night was a half moon; she was sure of it. What was going on?

The figure drew closer to her. The woman was wearing a light white shift cut above her knees. She was barefoot. Not one of the other samanera. What was she doing out here dressed like that?

The woman stopped, an arm's length beyond her. "Kai?"

The woman's face came into the light and Kai's heart dropped from her chest.

"Mother?" Kai asked, shocked. "Are you . . . a ghost?" She couldn't believe it. It was her mother. She looked thinner and had dark shadows under her eyes, but it was undeniably her mother standing before her.

"No, I'm not a ghost," Hanae said. "But I don't know how I got here."

"But you're dead," Kai said, her voice twisting. "You have to be a ghost. Or . . . a hallucination."

"I most certainly am not dead," Hanae stepped forward, taking Kai's hand. She felt solid and real. "Why would you think that?"

"Because Queen Airi told me that . . . she sent moonburners to look for you . . . and you had died."

"She lied," her mother said. "You can't trust her."

"But why would she lie?" Kai asked weakly. After what she had seen in the facility, she should have suspected that the queen would lie about something like this. Did Kai dare hope that she wasn't arguing with a figment of her imagination?

"She only cares about herself," Hanae continued. "She wouldn't want you distracted by thoughts of home. It was probably just cleaner for you to think I was dead."

Kai closed her eyes and gripped her mother's firm hands, palpable relief filling her. She wasn't alone in this world. Her mother wasn't dead!

But then, just as quickly, her relief mingled with an anger she hadn't realized she had been suppressing.

"You lied to me too," Kai said. "I could have gone to the citadel when I was younger! None of this would have happened. And you put a block on me so I couldn't moonburn. The first time I burned, it put me in the hospital."

"You have a right to be angry with me," Hanae said, raising her hands. "But you have to understand. What I did, I did to protect you. If you burned while we still lived in Kita, it would have meant death for all of us."

"You could have at least warned me. Told me what you had done. I would have understood."

"You were a lonely girl in the middle of nowhere living a lie. How could I tell you that I was taking from you the only magical thing in your world? You would have been miserable."

"So instead, I thought I was broken? You didn't have the right to make that choice for me. Not when I had to live with the consequences," Kai said, blowing her hair from her forehead in frustration. "But that's what you do, don't you, Azura." Kai enunciated the syllables of the name, drawing each out like a piece of taffy. "You made your choice to leave, and Miina had to suffer the consequences."

Her mother grew very still. Her voice was quiet. "You speak of things you cannot know."

"I've figured it out," Kai said. "But what I can't understand is why. Why you abandoned your country. If you think Airi is such a terrible ruler, why did you leave Miina in her hands?"

"It's complicated," Hanae said.

"Enlighten me."

"It would take more time than we have here tonight," Hanae said. As if her words were a prophecy, Hanae flickered briefly.

"What . . . what was that?" Kai said, looking around wildly.

"I think I know where we are," her mother said, drawing Kai into the middle of the clearing. She opened her mouth to say something, but the jade-pommeled dagger sheathed on the inside of Kai's forearm caught her attention.

"Where did you get that?"

"Nanase gave it to me. Why?"

Hanae smiled. "She was always too clever for her own good."

"What are you talking about?" Kai said.

"I gave her that knife. She was like a sister to me, growing up. If she has given it to you . . . she must at least suspect your true identity."

Nanase knew who she was before Kai did? That was disconcerting. Her mother flickered again, bringing Kai back to the moment. "You said you know where we are?" Kai asked.

"We are in the spirit world. Occasionally moonburners travel here by mistake or in dreams, but usually it is reserved for creatures of the spirit, like seishen."

"The spring," Kai said, realization dawning on her. "I drank from the purple water of the spring. It is said to grant a wish, or your deepest desire. I guess . . . mine was to see you again."

Kai's anger broke and tears welled in her eyes. She bit her lip, looking away from her mother's concerned face.

"I don't know how much more time we have. Are you all right?" Hanae asked. "Are they mistreating you?"

"No," she said. "But everything is spinning out of control and I don't know what to do. The war is escalating. Geisa is planning a major offensive, but the Oracle says it will be the end of us all. And the queen is keeping moonburners in cages and breeding them with captive sunburners."

All her fears and worries poured out, faster and faster. "One of my friends is in a hospital bed, and the other was beaten and stripped of her title as a master. And Master Vita is dying."

"Master Vita is dying?" Hanae asked.

"Yes. He has consumption. He could already be dead. And you . . ." Kai said, a desperate plan beginning to form in her mind. "You could stop it all. I will come for you. I will rescue you and bring you back to Miina and you can help me fix this mess."

"I will never go back, Kai. I cannot."

"You can. I can't do this alone." The hot tears trickled down her cheeks in rivulets.

"You have always been the strongest person I know," Hanae said. "Strongest willed, too. But strong. You will find a way."

"But you're Azura. Heir to the throne. Everyone loved you. I'm no one."

"You are my daughter," she said, taking Kai's face in her hands, tears in her own eyes. "Everything good in me is in you. But you are twice as smart, twice as strong, and twice as brave, because you are the best of your father as well."

"Father?" Kai asked, her voice coming out very small.

Hanae shook her head. "Youkai executed him shortly after you were exiled. He died well."

Kai drew a shuddering breath and tried to push aside the grief crashing over her.

Hanae flickered again.

"Wait," Kai said. Hanae was growing fainter. "You are still in Ushai? With Youkai?"

Her mother nodded. Kai threw her arms around her mother and was met by the odd sensation of someone who was both there and not there. "I love you."

"I love you too."

Kai awoke as evening dawned. The true evening, not the evening in the spirit world. She stared at the spot where her mother had stood. The moon was back in its half-moon form, rising cheerfully in the sky.

"What's wrong?" Quitsu asked.

"Let's get moving. I'll tell you on the way."

She recounted everything to Quitsu as they made their way back down the mountainside. Quitsu took it in stride, as he did with everything.

"Your mother said that seishen come from the spirit world?" Quitsu said. "That would make sense. We aren't born really. We just . . . come into being, out of the mist. The seishen elder never really explained it to us."

"You don't remember it?" Kai asked. "The spirit world?"

"No. The first thing I remember is being in the Misty Forest, with the other seishen. But it was fuzzy. We come out of the mist when our burner is born. We are fully formed . . . but mentally, we mirror our burner. The seishen elder cares for us. But as the burner grows, we too grow in intellect and understanding. I was there a long time. Years longer than most. But I knew you were out there, somewhere. It was faint."

"Probably because of the blockage. I couldn't burn," she said.

194

"That's what I assumed," he said. "Most of the seishen—and there were only a few of us at a time—would leave after perhaps a dozen years in the forest."

"When your burner starts to burn, you are called," she mused. "I think so."

"How did you find me in the desert?"

"The seishen elder told me to go and where to find you. He knew something was wrong. I don't know how."

"However he did it, I'm glad he did. Maybe we can go ask him someday."

Quitsu looked down the mountain, to where the Misty Forest lay, nestled in darkness. "Maybe."

They reached the lake where she had scryed before, seeking the purple spring.

"Let's stop." She drank from the cool water at the lake's edge. She was about to rise from her knees, but paused. She began performing the scrying ritual, tracing the symbols on the water.

"What are you doing?" Quitsu asked.

She drew faster, pulling the moonlight into her, warm and urgent. When she finished, an image appeared on the water, as before. But this time, it was of Ushai, of Youkai's sitting room. The room was partially rebuilt from the state it had been in after the moonburner attack and fires, with signs of painting and carpentry in progress. The room had been filled with new opulent furniture, a thick rug and a silver tea set. There was a woman in a white robe and obi pouring tea. Her mother.

"It was real," she said. "I can't believe it."

"Is that her?" Quitsu asked.

"Yes. And she's still a slave. I have to rescue her."

"How?"

She ran her hand along the surface of the water, banishing the image. "That's a good question. Any ideas?"

"No," Quitsu admitted.

"Me either," Kai said, standing and brushing the dirt from the torn knees of her leggings. "We'll think of something."

CHAPTER 28

K ai and Quitsu were the first to arrive back at Nanase's camp.

"Congratulations," Nanase said, taking Kai's vial and holding it up to the firelight. "I never had a doubt."

"Thank you," Kai said quietly.

Nanase cocked her head, studying her. In that moment, she looked like her seishen.

"You drank from the spring."

"How did you know?" Kai asked.

"That's the funny thing about getting what you want most in the world. It's never what you thought it would be. Now, kneel," Nanase said, rolling up her sleeves.

"Why?" Kai asked nervously.

"It's time to give you the moonburner sigil," Nanase said. "To truly make you one of us."

"What?" Kai asked.

"We each wear it." Nanase said, turning around and folding down the high collar of her uniform. She bore a mark below the base of her neck, a circle with two crescent moons inside it, back to back. "It marks us as master moonburners. Wear it with pride."

Kai nodded, pushing down the feeling of unease growing within her, as she recalled helping her father hold down squealing calves to brand them with their ranch's symbol. She knelt.

Nanase folded down the neck of Kai's light blue uniform. She placed one hand firmly on Kai's left shoulder and the thumb of her other hand at the base of Kai's neck.

Kai felt a warm sensation that grew hotter. She hissed through her teeth as the pain flared, but then it was gone.

"Well done," Nanase held out her hand and they locked wrists in a shake. "You are a master moonburner now."

As the dawn approached, Kai found herself and Quitsu sitting across the fire from Nanase in uncomfortable silence. Nanase had flatly refused Kai's request to return to the citadel before the other moonburners returned from the test. It was "too dangerous" for Kai to travel alone.

Kai fingered the jade-pommeled knife, her mind running in circles. "When you gave me this knife," Kai said, "you said it was a gift from someone who was like a sister to you. Will you tell me about her?" Kai wasn't sure if Nanase knew that her mother lived. She needed to tread carefully.

"We grew up together in the citadel," Nanase said. "We played together when we were young. She came . . . from an important family. I didn't. My mother was a kitchen maid. My friend insisted that I come to all her lessons with her; she was so adamant that her mother relented. I owe my education, my position . . . everything to her."

"She sounds like a good friend," Kai said carefully.

"She was," Nanase said.

"Was?"

"Yes. She died when she was young."

"I'm sorry," Kai said. Maybe Nanase didn't know Azura was still alive.

"I often think that things would be different today if she had not died."

"Did she have any children?" Kai asked. Quitsu's tail flicked her ankle.

"What a strange question," Nanase said, examining Kai across the fire with her hawklike gaze.

Kai met her eyes, willing her to talk first. *Did you give me this knife because you know I am her daughter?* Kai wanted to shout.

"But no. She died too young," Nanase said. "Though I do not doubt that if she had, her child would play an important part in things to come."

"What things?"

Nanase sighed, "War."

☾

It was two more days before the other girls straggled in. The sigil on Kai's neck itched, though she wasn't sure if it was just in her head.

Her father had borne a similar marking on the inside of his left forearm. He had worn leather wraps around his forearms that she had assumed were functional, but now she saw them for what they were. A disguise. She remembered asking him about it. They had just delivered a calf that had been twisted in his mother's belly. Her father had reached up into the cow to turn the calf and allow it to be born safely. As they washed off in the large trough, she asked him.

"Father, what is that marking?" It was outlined in white on his tanned skin, a circle and an upside down triangle, overlapping each other. He continued washing for a moment before he answered.

"Never let your brother get near you with a cattle brand," he said, tweaking her nose.

Her eyes widened. "Your brother did that to you?" she asked.

"Just be glad you are an only child, my little fox," he said. "It's much safer that way."

She had been so young. She had never made the connection between the symbol on his arm and the symbol borne on Kita's flag. A circle and a triangle, the golden sun. The symbol that must be borne by all sunburners. Her father was a sunburner. She was certain. It explained so many things. She had to get to her mother. She needed answers.

Nanase packed her camp and gathered the new moonburners together. She addressed them.

"Welcome to the ranks of the moonburners. With your test to advance to samanera, you showed us your moonburning skills. With the ordeal of the last few days, you have proven your mental strength, dedication and ingenuity. Well done, sisters."

There were a few whoops and claps.

She raised her hands to quiet them. "Unfortunately, there is no time for celebration. We are at war. We have word that a group of sunburners is stationed close to the border of the Tottori. They are being sheltered in a Kitan town, hiding themselves among the inhabitants. Our mission is to infiltrate and attack. We will be joining an additional force of moonburners by air and will execute the attack together."

Nanase continued. "Make no mistake, this will be a difficult mission. There will be civilians present. But remember that the sunburners did not have mercy against the innocents at the citadel. Their attack was ruthless and many were lost. If they choose to use their civilians as a shield, we have no choice but to break through them."

Nanase went on to lay out the details of their mission. It would be a quick airborne attack, with the hope that they would take the sunburners by surprise.

Before long, Kai found herself mounted on a koumori, Quitsu strapped in front of her. Their formation flew across the foothills of the Akashi Mountains and the Misty Forest, silent black shadows in the moonlight.

As they reached the borderlands, their koumori were joined by a squad of six other koumori and riders. The groups blended silently. Kai's fingers ached from gripping the reins, and her backside was numb. Koumori riding was not the most comfortable means of transportation.

Quitsu's eyes were closed, he was either asleep or terrified at the flight. As they finally slowed and began to descend, Kai got her first glimpse of their target. The moon illuminated the humble buildings below them. The town had a rudimentary wall, similar to the wall around her village in Ushai.

Nanase threw the first fireball, a look of grim determination on her face. There might not even be sunburners here; Nanase had admitted their intelligence was weeks old. But the lives of a few hundred Kitan villagers were a price the general was willing to pay.

The other moonburners followed Nanase's lead, throwing fire and sweeping to the left and right to regroup, as they had been taught. Kai took her shot, purposely throwing wide and missing any buildings. The fires thrown by the others were spreading. Screams punctuated the night air as townsfolk ran out of their homes, driven into the open by the flames. As the fire lit the village, Kai's eyes widened.

"I know this place," she said to Quitsu, recognition flooding her mind with memories. The gates of the city were decorated with a phoenix in flight, one of the signs of the Kitan monarchy.

"How?" he asked from his perch before her, in a somewhat strangled voice.

"I came here many times with my father, to sell our cattle. This village is less than an hour's ride from my hometown."

A plan coalesced in Kai's mind. She took another shot at the village and circled near Nanase. She shouted at the other woman. "No sunburners have come out to defend the village! If they were here, they would have showed themselves by now!"

Nanase surveyed the scene. "We pull back!" she yelled at the other burners.

The leader of the six from the citadel circled closer to Nanase. "Our orders are to keep attacking until the town is destroyed," she said.

"You have new orders," Nanase said. "Fall back and regroup."

The moonburner grimaced but obeyed, shooting a white light into the air that signaled the burners to regroup and head back to Kyuden.

Kai reigned her koumori back a bit, circling once, so the other women fell in ahead of her behind Nanase. As they headed back towards the Tottori Desert, Kai silently directed her koumori to the west, away from the others.

"Where are we going?" Quitsu asked.

"To get my mother."

Kai set her koumori down outside the walls of Ushai, by the sun gate. The village looked much as it had when she had left. Signs of rebuilding dotted the town—scaffolding, new construction and piles of building materials. They still had a long way to go.

Kai and Quitsu crept into the town, sticking to the shadows. It was after midnight and most townspeople were in bed. Kai realized, wryly, that she had truly grown used to sleeping during the day and being awake at night. The silence of these streets felt wrong.

They made their way into the center of town, Kai remembering each turn. She led them to the servant's entrance of the town hall, at the back of the building.

"I think we should try Youkai's room first. If my mother is not there, we try the servant's quarters, or last, the dungeons."

"And if she's not in any of those places?" Quitsu voiced the question she had been pointedly ignoring.

"We figure out a new plan," Kai said.

Kai moonburned, wrapping them both in shadow. She opened the door into the town hall. It let out a loud creak and they both cringed. She waited for shouting voices or guards to be called, but there was no response.

They crept into the building. As they rounded the corner that opened up to the hallway in front of his room, Kai sighed with relief to see there was no guard posted. There must be a rotating guard throughout the building. They crossed the hallway on tiptoe, and Kai gently turned the doorknob. It was locked.

She stepped back and burned light into the lock. It began smoking. She moonburned a thin line of heat, severing the threads of the bottom portion of her tunic. She ripped it off, and wrapped her hand in it. She pulled the door open, the bolt of the lock melted.

She crouched outside the door and motioned for Quitsu to go in and examine the situation. He padded silently into the room and quickly returned.

"Youkai is asleep in the bed. Your mother is sleeping on a mat on the floor. Her ankle is chained."

She entered the room, crouching on her hands and knees, pulling the door mostly shut behind her. She could see her mother's prone form on the far side of the room. Youkai's snores were loud and constant. Her blood began to boil as she thought of her mother chained in that man's bedroom.

She reached her mother's side and put a hand over her mouth, shaking her slightly. Hanae awoke with a start and began to cry out, but Kai looked intently in her eyes, putting a finger to her lips. Hanae's eyes widened in recognition and she nodded slightly.

Kai removed her hand from her mother's mouth and listened for the snores. Still even.

"Kai?" her mother whispered. "What are you doing here?"

Kai found herself grinning. "I was in the area. I figured I may not have a better chance to rescue you."

Kai took the piece of cloth from her tunic and wrapped it around her mother's ankle, inside her shackle. She moonburned heat into the hinge of the shackle and waited. She touched it experimentally, and when she found it cool enough to touch, she pulled, ripping the two sides apart.

Hanae pulled her into a fierce embrace, and for a moment, Kai almost let her guard down, almost let the madness of the past year wash over her. But she pushed those emotions down and pulled away. There would be time for sharing and mourning, later. When they were safe.

Quitsu was already at the door, waiting for them to follow. As they approached the door, Hanae turned, surveying the room. Before Kai could even register what she was doing, she grabbed the knife from Kai's forearm sheath, leaped onto the bed where Youkai slept and slit his throat.

Kai was so shocked that she couldn't help a small cry escaping from her lips. She had been prepared to face Youkai if she had to, but to kill him in cold blood was another thing altogether.

Hanae wiped the blade on the bed cover and returned it to Kai. "Now I'm ready to go," she whispered.

Kai, mouth still hanging open, shook her head to clear it. They would talk later. She peered out the door and found the hallway empty. She wrapped the three of them in shadows as they made their way back to the servant's entrance, but it wasn't necessary. They didn't encounter a living soul.

As they reached the sun gate, Kai breathed a sigh of relief. Her koumori was just around the corner, waiting in the dark shadow of the town wall. She wasn't sure if he could carry three of them, but they would figure something out. She couldn't believe they had done it.

Kai turned back to her mother and saw a flash of metal in the moonlight. The world went dark.

CHAPTER 29

K ai came to in a rush. Her head was pounding, and the skin on her face felt stretched, as if covered in dried blood.

She was chained to a pole in the middle of a tent, her hands behind her back. The tent was large and well-lit with lanterns. A rich rug carpeted the floor beneath her, flanked by a simple sturdy desk and what appeared to be a bedroll. A washbasin with a bowl and pitcher stood by the entrance flap. As she craned her head around behind her to get a view of the rest of the tent, she froze. A suit of golden armor stood against the back wall like a hollow metal man. It was polished to a shine and had ornate sunbursts across the chest. The helmet was styled like a lion. She knew that armor.

The tent flap opened and Kai met the narrowed eyes of the man who stood in the doorway. It was as if all the malevolence and hatred of hundreds of years of war had been funneled into those eyes.

"Daarco," she said, willing her voice to be strong and sure. "To what do I owe this pleasure?"

A look of startled confusion passed over his face, and for a second, he was just a man.

A deep, throaty laugh sounded behind him and Daarco stepped to the side. The man with the golden ponytail stepped into the room, clapping Daarco on the shoulder.

"I told you this one had spirit."

Behind the man came a golden lion, huge and muscled and menacing. Kai gaped at it. She could tell by the uniformity and brightness of its golden hair that it was a seishen. It was magnificent.

Daarco took up a place by the door, scowling and stiff, arms crossed over his chest. The seishen took up a post on the other side of the door, sitting on its haunches and licking one giant paw.

The other man pulled up a stool before her and sat. Kai's heart fluttered. She mentally shook herself. She was probably going to die here, and it likely wouldn't be pleasant. Was she such a foolhardy girl that the thought of being close to this man outweighed those truths? In the end, it didn't matter if she was tortured and killed by an attractive man or an ugly one. She would be just as dead.

"I'm sorry about the manner in which we brought you here. I had my physician look you over, and he assured me you are unharmed." His words were fine and educated, his voice rich. She could tell he was trying to put her at ease, which only made her more nervous.

"Where is my seishen?" she asked. "Is he all right? And the woman with me?"

"Your seishen is fine," he said. "Fought like a little devil after you went down, but we were able to subdue him without hurting him too badly."

"May I see him?"

"Later, if you cooperate and tell us what we want to know."

"And the woman?"

The ponytailed man and Daarco exchanged a glance. "She is in our holding cells. She was not cooperative. And it became known to us that the prefect of the town we found you in was recently discovered dead in his bed, his throat slit. His slave woman was missing. She is the likely suspect."

Kai kept her face impassive. "I don't know about that, but that woman is much more than a simple slave. Do not mistreat her."

The man inclined his head, as if he would consider her suggestion. Kai knew she didn't have a lot of bargaining power, but what she did have would be well spent protecting her mother.

"May I ask you a question?" Kai asked.

The man chuckled. "Technically, I'm supposed to be the one asking the questions. I don't think Daarco would let me hear the end of it if things didn't go that way. But, before we begin, go ahead."

"Who are you?" She had a sneaking suspicion, but needed it confirmed.

"My name is Hiro," he said simply.

Now it was Daarco's turn to chuckle. "Make no mistake, moonburner whore."

Hiro shot him a look, but Daarco forged ahead. "You are speaking to the crown prince of Kita."

If Daarco was hoping for a reaction, she didn't give him the satisfaction. But inside, her mind was whirling. She had direct access to the crown prince of Kita. And, if she wasn't mistaken, he seemed . . . sympathetic. Even friendly. He had spared her once, and she had spared him as well. By her account, that left them even. He didn't owe her anything. But maybe . . .

Kai wished she had a better head for political intrigue. She hadn't paid close attention in History class, so she didn't know much about King Ozora's background and lineage. It had been enough that his decree had condemned her to die in the desert. Maybe she should have paid more attention.

"It is a pleasure to officially meet you, Prince Hiro," Kai said. She could have ended the royal line of Kita with a flick of her wrist just a few days before. And hadn't. If anyone ever found out . . . the queen would have her flogged, then killed, and probably flogged again for good measure.

"And who are you?" he asked.

"My name is Kai. I am a moonburner. But I grew up in Kita."

"Thank you for your honesty."

"What do you want with me?"

Hiro leaned forward, putting his well-muscled forearms on his knees. "Information."

Hiro didn't seem like the type to mistreat her for information if it wasn't necessary, but she couldn't say the same for Daarco, who watched the whole interaction with a predatory interest.

"I'll tell you whatever you want to know, on two conditions."

"A little presumptuous of you to think you can make conditions, but go ahead."

"I'll tell you whatever you want to know. But just you." She inclined her head towards Daarco. "No audience."

"Second?"

"Bring my seishen here with me."

The prince looked at her as if weighing his options. "Agreed."

"Hiro!" Daarco sputtered. "She wants to be alone with you to work her feminine tricks . . ."

Hiro looked sternly at Daarco, who fell silent. "I've made my decision. Bring her seishen."

Daarco glowered at her, but obeyed, ducking out of the tent.

They stared at each other, eyes searching, probing, evaluating. His eyes were the green of a pool of water in the forest, reflecting the sunlight. A hint of yellow or gold . . .

She finally looked away, and much to her dismay, found herself blushing.

Pull it together.

"I must admit," Hiro said, "that I did not expect we would meet again, especially so soon. But it seems Taiyo is not done with us yet."

She nodded, not trusting herself to speak.

Daarco returned a short while later leading Quitsu on a thick chain. He was limping and had a gash over one eye, but he was in one piece. Daarco chained Quitsu to the side of the tent opposite Kai and stormed out. His deliberate cruelty of placing Quitsu out of reach grated on her, but she ignored it. Quitsu was here, and he was safe.

Quitsu was clearly having the same reaction, straining against the chain to reach her. Finally, he settled down, sitting down at the end of his chain in obvious distress. Hiro's golden lion seishen rose from its near statue-like seat by the door and padded to Quitsu's side.

Hiro rose, alarmed. "Ryu," he said, with a tone of warning.

The seishen gave Hiro a condescending look and sniffed Quitsu. He licked Quitsu's wound twice, his huge tongue dwarfing Quitsu's delicate face.

"Be at peace, brother," the lion said with a deep throaty growl.

Kai and Hiro looked at each other in astonishment, for a moment forgetting that they were mortal enemies. The seishen were such an integral part of their lives, it was easy to forget that they were not just extensions of their burner partners. There was clearly a shared respect between creatures that Kai had never witnessed.

Hiro's seishen, Ryu, lay down next to Quitsu and they both placed their heads on their paws.

Hiro shook his head as if to clear it from the surprise. He sat back down on the stool before Kai.

A rough plan had begun to form in Kai's mind during the time she had been awake. A plan that involved treason and most likely, a painful death. A plan that involved trusting this man and his intentions, despite knowing so little of him.

Hiro opened his mouth to speak, but Kai spoke first.

"I want to help you," Kai said.

He blinked in surprise.

"But my aid depends on one thing."

"Another condition?" Hiro asked. A smile quirked the corner of his finely wrought mouth.

Oh, Tsuki, why was she staring at his mouth? She forced her eyes to meet his.

"It depends on what type of man you are. I suspect the answer, but I must ask. Are you the kind of man who lives for war or longs for peace?"

His smile turned sad. "I am a man who lives in the world he was born into. To the duty he was born for."

"I don't believe that," she said. "You didn't kill me when you could have. Why?"

"You know me so well to make that judgment, moonburner?"

"I don't claim to know you. But I think I saw the real you in that moment. And you saw the real me. When there was no one to force our hand, to make us killers. And so I ask you again. Do you live for this war or long for peace?"

"I want peace," he admitted. "I am tired of the war; I see the effect it has on my people. We don't even remember why we are fighting anymore."

Her pendant lay cool against her chest. Truth.

"But," he went on, "I don't see an end to it, short of the total annihilation of the moonburners and the death of Queen Airi. My predecessors have not been able to accomplish this task, and it's a task I am not sure I could stomach, even if I could accomplish it." He put his head in his hands, smoothing back his golden hair. He didn't look at her for a long time.

"I believe you," she said. "I want to help you."

He sat up, blinking in surprise. "Want to help me end the moonburners and kill Queen Airi?"

"The second. Not the first." "I'm listening."

CHAPTER 30

So Kai told him. She poured out her story, as she never had before. She told him about the Gleaming and being raised as a boy. She told him about being exposed and left in the desert to die. She left out the part about her mother being a slave to Youkai. That fact, together with his death, was a complication she hadn't figured out how to deal with. She shared her rescue by Quitsu, training in the citadel, and her testing. She shared the part she knew he wanted to hear.

"There is a facility underneath the citadel. But its not what you think. It's not a place to torture sunburners. Well, not only. It's a breeding facility."

Hiro's jaw dropped open. "What?"

"Hasn't the king noticed that the number of sunburners in each generation is declining?"

"Yes." He frowned. "We have to scour the country for those with sunburning talent."

"It's the same in Miina. There are only a few dozen burners in my class at the citadel. The queen figured out why. Only a moonburner mother and sunburner father mating produces a burner child. Because of the escalation of the war between us and your father's brilliant plan to kill all moonburner children, we are going extinct."

Hiro started to laugh, a rich chuckle that warmed her to the core.

"It's so simple. Our hatred of the moonburners made us blind to the thought that they could have any utility at all." He grew quiet. "Maybe we deserve to go extinct."

"Maybe we do," Kai said. "But I think our gifts are miraculous, and if turned to uses other than war, we could do good in this world. The queen is is only concerned about making more moonburners. The sunburners in the facility are being used to impregnate moonburners, to build the next generation of the queen's army. In a laboratory."

Hiro's face twisted. His seishen let out a low growl.

"The queen would use her own people to grow more moonburners?" Hiro asked.

"Yes," Kai said grimly. "They were not given a choice in the matter. This is why I want to help you. But only if your goal is to end this war and bring peace between our people. It is the only way we will survive."

He nodded, standing. "Thank you for your honesty, Kai. You are a remarkable woman. You have given me much to think on."

She felt her face redden again. Her necklace hadn't grown warm with his compliment. Either she was a remarkable woman, or he truly believed it. Either way, she could live with it.

"I will see that someone brings you food and water," he said.

Hiro was true to his word. A tall serving man came in and escorted her to the facilities. When they returned to the tent, he chained only her foot back to the pillar. He gave her water and a simple meal of rice, pickled vegetables and salted meat.

Kai ate voraciously. Her chain was now long enough to allow her to reach Quitsu. The seishen sat in her lap and let her pet him as she shared her plan.

By the time Hiro returned, Kai had fallen asleep on the hard ground. She hastily tried to fix her hair and wipe the drool from her face.

Hiro, as ever, looked painfully handsome. Behind him came a huge man with a mane of golden hair and a ruddy glow to his weathered face, together with a massive golden bear, padding delicately on four huge paws. Hiro's serving man entered after, leading a woman in a torn white dress. Her mother. She looked unharmed.

Hiro motioned to the serving man, who unchained Kai and her mother.

Hiro set four chairs together and motioned them to sit. Both women did, eyeing the two men across from them like wary animals. Quitsu padded to the side of the tent to join the golden bear and lion, slightly out of the way of the conversation. Suddenly, the tent felt very crowded.

"I have stationed guards outside," Hiro said. "And we have laced your food with lusteric. It inhibits moonburning. I'm choosing to treat you both as guests, but I cannot act entirely without precautions. I hope that my trust in you is not misplaced. This is General Ipan," Hiro said. "He leads the sunburner armies and is interested in hearing your offer for himself."

"It is not every day I get to enjoy the company of two lovely ladies," General Ipan said, winking at Kai.

She looked down at her tattered uniform and her mother's dirty, torn shift and let out a gentle snort. "You flatter us, General," Kai said, but softened her words with a smile.

"Why can women never take a compliment?" he asked, throwing his hands in the air. "That's your problem, you know. Always looking for hidden meaning behind the words. Sometimes words are just words."

"Have you ever lived with hundreds of other women, General?" Kai asked. "Words are never just words."

General Ipan erupted in a deep belly laugh, slapping his knee with his huge hand. "I suspect that if I lived with hundreds of women, words would be the least of my problems."

Kai couldn't help but like this general.

"I suspect that you two are not entirely what you seem," Hiro said. "You seem to be a soldier of my mortal enemy and a runaway slave who has murdered her master. I am interested to hear why I should not treat you as such."

Kai opened her mouth to speak, but her mother threw her a warning glance. Kai didn't know which of her mother's many secrets she was urging her not to share, but Kai was out of options. She couldn't do this on her own and she couldn't do nothing. She thought she could trust Hiro. She wanted to trust him.

"As I said, we can help you overthrow Queen Airi and end the war. But only if you and your father give us certain . . . assurances."

"How do you propose to do that?" Hiro asked.

"We will get you into the city during the day. You will free your countrymen and ours. You will take the city, as peacefully as possible. You will demonstrate to the world the madness that Queen Airi has fallen into. You will install a regent until the next queen can be crowned and establish terms of peace. And then you will leave," Kai said.

Gods this feels foolish. She was betting the future of Kyuden, the citadel, her very race on this man's character.

Hiro laughed. "Is it that simple? I'm not sure why I didn't think of it before. And presuming we can accomplish all of these things with minimal bloodshed, who do you propose we install as queen? You?"

It was Kai's turn to laugh. "Not me. Her." She motioned to her mother with her head.

Hanae's jaw was set, her face unreadable. Kai felt a pang of sorrow for drawing her mother back into something she had clearly done everything in her power to flee. But Miina needed her. There was no one else.

"And not to be rude, but what, my lady, is your claim to the Miinan throne?" Hiro asked Hanae.

Hanae sighed deeply and looked at Kai, a pained look on her face. "You might as well tell him, since the seishen's out of the bag."

"She is Princess Azura, rightful heir to the throne. "

The silence in the tent was palpable. General Ipan's seishen stood up and walked in front of Hanae. Or Azura. Kai still didn't know quite what to call her. They looked into each other's eyes, silently evaluating each other. Hanae didn't wither under the intense golden gaze.

The bear spoke in a low rumble. "She is Azura. The vessel has changed, but she has the same qi within her."

General Ipan scrutinized Hanae, his face thoughtful. "I met Azura when she was a teenager, before she so tragically died. I admit, you share some of her features. And Kuma certainly would be able to tell these things, if anyone. I have one question for you though. The answer is one only Azura would know."

Hanae didn't even wait for the question. "We ran into each other in the kitchens. I was stealing honeycakes, you were stealing ale. We both swore we would take our secret to the grave. But, since I have come back from the dead, I believe I am released from my oath."

General Ipan leaned back in his chair, which creaked beneath him. "It really is you. You must have some story to tell."

"She may be Azura, but she is not a moonburner any longer," Hiro's lion Ryu said, standing and joining the circle. "Miinan law requires the queen to be a moonburner."

"How do you know what Miinan law says?" General Ipan said. "All these years, you seishen never cease to amaze me."

Ryu grinned, bearing bright white fangs.

Kai frowned. She hadn't quite figured out the part where her mother was both Azura, the silver-haired girl in the painting with Master Vita, and her ebony-haired self. Kai had never seen her mother moonburn or dye her hair or do anything else indicating she was a burner. And she hadn't known the queen had to be a burner. She felt the threads of her shaky plan begin to unravel.

Her mother came to her rescue. "I burned myself out," she said, matter-of-factly. "I can no longer burn. And what Ryu says is correct." Hanae looked at Kai with a silent apology. "I cannot take the crown, even if I wanted to. Which I don't. But I could . . . I could act as regent until a new queen is crowned."

"And who do you propose?" Hiro asked. "My daughter, Kailani Shigetsu."

Kai's head whipped around to look at her mother.

"She is the current heir to the throne, as Airi has produced no heir."

"Oh no," Kai said. "I can hardly even keep the royal houses straight. I was raised as a boy running cattle!"

The sunburners seemed to accept Hanae's proposition, though, as they were accepting all they proposed in that strange treasonous meeting.

"You would serve in this capacity?" Hiro asked. "Announce who you are and pave the way for your daughter?"

"No," Kai said. "Absolutely not."

They all ignored her.

Hanae nodded. "I ran from Miina and the war to save the man I loved. In the end, it killed him anyway. If I can help end it, I will serve. I owe Miina that much."

CHAPTER 31

They sat together late into the evening and talked about details, terms, and assurances. Hiro's father would need to meet them both and evaluate their trustworthiness for himself. He was a week's ride from them and headed their way.

Kai, Hanae, and Quitsu were escorted to their own tent, which was guarded by two men. Kai had been forced to drink more of the lusteric, and it felt odd to not be able to access the moon's light. It was like the early days at the citadel, when her blockage kept her from her powers.

As the flap closed behind Hiro's manservant, Kai and Hanae were finally alone. Kai didn't know what to expect from her mother, knowing she had exposed a secret her mother had fought long and hard to keep hidden, dragging her back into a world she had fled. And part of Kai still felt a low-burning anger about the lies her parents had told her entire life.

But all of that seemed inconsequential as the two women truly faced each other for the first time in months. Hanae wrapped her arms around Kai, gripping her tightly, tears leaking down her face. Kai felt her own emotional dam break as the stress and fear of the last months poured over her. Her tears joined her mother's, and they clung together, crying and hugging.

After a long while, they pulled apart, wiping their eyes.

"Wow," Quitsu said. "Warn me next time and I'll get my rain slicker out."

The thought of Quitsu in a shiny rain slicker was so absurd that Kai started laughing in great hiccuping peals. She pulled Quitsu up into her arms and hugged him tightly, smearing his silky fur with the salt from her tears. "What would I do without you, furball?" she said, setting him down.

There were two sleeping pallets in the tent, side by side. Kai and her mother sat down, cross-legged, across from each other.

Quitsu curled into Kai's lap, relaxing into her as she stroked his ears.

"Thank you for coming for me," Hanae said softly.

"I may be mad at you, but you are still my mother. Once I knew you were alive, I couldn't leave you."

"I didn't think I would ever see you again. I thought our meeting in the spirit world was a cruel dream. I should have known the desert wouldn't beat you."

"It almost did," Kai replied. "If it wasn't for Quitsu, I wouldn't have made it."

"Thank you, Quitsu," Hanae said, inclining her head slightly.

Quitsu nodded. "My lady, a question for you. You said you burned yourself out. You had a seishen, didn't you?" The unspoken question hung before them.

Hanae's face turned grave and for a moment she looked very old.

"When I burned out . . . I didn't know. I didn't know it would kill her. It is one of the greatest regrets of my life."

Understanding dawned on Kai, and she reached forward to squeeze her mother's hand. "What was her name?"

"Lyra," Hanae said. "She was a lynx. She had the most beautiful silver variegated markings and white tufted ears. She was my best friend. It was her idea, you know."

"What?" Kai asked.

"Your father and I burning ourselves out. It was their idea. We didn't even know it could be done."

Kai crinkled her brow in confusion. "Maybe you should start at the beginning."

Hanae did.

"My sister Airi and I were close as children. Our mother was the queen, obviously, and our fathers were her royal consorts. We never knew their identities, though we knew we didn't share the same father. Our mother had admitted as much to us. We were raised by our tutors, the citadel teachers, the cooks, the moonburner officers. The citadel was our playground, and we thrived. As we grew older, into our teenage years, it became clear that we were more different than we first realized. My mother forced me into classes and special training to be queen. I hated it, although I loved my tutor, Master Vita. He was the only reason I didn't rebel all together. Airi grew jealous of the special training I was getting. She realized, I think, that while she would stay a princess, I was going to be queen. She began rebelling in petty ways, with little cruelties. But still she was a good girl at heart."

Kai snorted. She couldn't help herself.

Her mother shot her a look. "I understand that is not the case now. As I neared the age of eighteen, I was, on the surface, doing everything I needed to be a doting daughter and make my mother proud. But in private, I would flee the city as often as I could. My obligations felt suffocating. Lyra and I would ride across the grasslands outside the city, escaping whenever I could. Master Vita would cover for me, but I know he fretted every time I disappeared."

"On one of those outings, I came across a man riding a golden stallion. He was tall and handsome and had the most brilliant golden hair and deep chocolate brown eyes. His smile could light up a room. I fell for him the moment I saw him, as if the sun shone that day for the first time. I was completely undefended, out in the middle of the day with just a knife to protect me. He could have killed me, but I wasn't afraid. I was already so foolishly in love," Hanae said, eyes caught in a faraway place.

"Luckily, he was friendly, and did not harm me. He was scouting for a peace delegation that was on its way to the citadel from Kita. I knew that there was no future for us, just as quickly as I fell in love with him. The delegation was there to discuss peace, as well as an arranged marriage between me and Ozora. My marriage, if I had one, would serve Miina.

"But there is something about a handsome man that tramples your common sense completely. While my mother was arranging a marriage to Ozora, we were sneaking off to be together. I showed him all of the hidden places at the citadel, and we would disguise ourselves and escape into the city to stroll through the market or watch a fiddler play in a bar. It was all foolish and dangerous, of course, as we were incredibly conspicuous, even with our hats on or hoods up.

"As much as I tried to hide it, Airi noticed his affection for me and grew jealous. You see, your father was so handsome and charming that he had caught my sister's eye as well. One night, she snuck into his rooms and threw herself at him, trying to seduce him. At first, he thought it was me and began to reciprocate. But before long, he realized who she was and rebuffed her advances as kindly as he could. She grew furious. She tore her gown and ran from him, calling out that he had forced himself on her. She was only sixteen.

"I vouched for him as best I could, but I couldn't reveal our love. If the man had seduced one princess, who was to say he wasn't aiming for two? The peace threatened to unravel and something needed to be done to save it. I cried rivers on Master Vita's shoulder until, appalled to see me so distressed, he tried to find a solution. He and Lyra told me an ancient secret. A way to give up your burning. If we could fake my death and commute your father's sentence to exile, we could both burn ourselves out and vanish into the world, to live life as a normal man and woman. No one would ever find us. And so we did it. At the time, though, we didn't realize the cost."

"Your seishen?" Kai breathed.

"Yes, I lost Lyra and your father lost his seishen, Bako. He was a beautiful stallion; the only equine seishen I've ever seen. He encouraged the plan as well. I don't know if Lyra and Bako knew what would come, but I suspect they did. They sacrificed themselves for us, for our love. The pain of losing her still cuts like a knife. It is like losing an arm and yet feeling its silent sensations. It was a long time before your father and I began to forgive ourselves and each other for what we had done."

"How did you?" Kai asked. She couldn't imagine losing Quitsu.

"It wasn't until we had you. Life became worth living again." Hanae stroked Kai's cheek.

"But now I feel a different type of sorrow," Hanae said. "Airi. I had hoped that without me, she could grow into the woman I knew she could be. But she has become twisted and cruel. Shortly after we disappeared, our mother died as well. Airi was alone at sixteen with a country to rule and a war to fight. She blamed the sunburners for my death and I suspect our mother's. And near this time, Geisa appeared as well. She is a fanatical worshipper of Tsuki who quickly gained power and my sister's ear."

"Geisa's hatred of the sunburners runs even deeper than Airi's. I fear Geisa had a role to play in twisting my sister into who she is today. And Ozora isn't much better. He was so angry about how the moonburners treated him and his favorite captain that when he returned home, he vowed to destroy them all."

"Hence the Gleaming," Kai said.

"Yes. He was young and hotheaded. I suspect that he has lost the taste for war over the last twenty years, from what his son tells us."

"Airi is even worse than you realize," Kai said. She poured out the details of the horrors she had outlined when they met in the spirit world. The testing that almost killed her. Emi's injuries. Maaya's beating. Tsuki's appearance in the temple. The facility. The Oracle's prophecy. The eclipse.

Her mother grew paler and paler.

"If I had known what my selfishness would bring, I never would have left," Hanae said. "But I thought Miina would be safe in my sister's hands. And I just couldn't face losing your father."

"It's not your fault," Kai said, some of the anger she had felt at her mother fading away.

"It is," Hanae said. "But it is kind of you to say otherwise."

CHAPTER 32

The next morning, Hiro's manservant, Zeshi, unchained them and indicated that they should follow him. He led them to a small bathing tent where water was heated in big kettles over hot fires. They washed themselves and put on fresh clothes that had been laid out for them—a simple green dress for Hanae and one of aqua blue for Kai.

Kai's heart missed a beat as she ducked inside their tent and found Hiro waiting there. He had no right to be so handsome.

"Can I show you around the camp?" he asked. "Consider it part of your initiation as 'guest' instead of prisoner."

"That would be lovely," Kai said, immediately kicking herself. Lovely? She sounded like a fluttery-eyed schoolgirl.

"I am feeling a little tired," Hanae said. "I'd rather lie down. But you should take Kai and Quitsu."

"Very well," Hiro said. "Let Zeshi know if you need anything else." As he turned to open the tent flap for Kai to exit, Hanae gave Kai a wink and a mischievous smile. Apparently Kai wasn't hiding her feelings for Hiro as well as she thought. But the realization couldn't dampen her spirits. She had one-on-one time with Hiro to enjoy.

Zeshi had given Kai a hat to help her avoid the attention her silver hair naturally brought. Despite this effort, the entire sunburner camp clearly knew who she was. She drew looks wherever she went, from curious glances to downright hostile glares.

The camp was clean and well organized. The soldiers and their followers looked well taken care of, sitting around tidy cookfires interspersed among the neat rows of white tents. The sunburners were consolidated in a large group of fancier tents in the center of camp. They had direct access to the camp's horses and golden eagle rookery, which were on opposite sides in order to keep the horses from growing nervous.

As Kai and Hiro walked through the camp, the tradespeople and soldiers stood and saluted Hiro. He stopped at various fires, saying a few words and introducing Kai as his guest.

"Shira, did the soldiers deliver that new bolt of cloth you needed for the cloaks?" He asked an older lady sitting and mending uniforms.

"Oh yes, m'lord. Thank you."

"Is Mika feeling any better with that new delivery of medicine?" He asked a young woman, introducing her to Kai, and explaining that her young son had fallen ill with a cough.

"Yes, m'lord. Thank you so much for seeing to him."

"Do you know the names of everyone in your camp?" Kai asked, as they neared the pen where the horses were kept.

"Most of them," he said. "They gave up their normal lives to be here and follow us. The least I can do is ensure they are well cared for."

"Not everyone would see it that way," Kai murmured.

Kai paused, resting her arms over a large fence surrounding the camp's horses. The horses were sleek, impressive steeds, large enough to bear a sunburner in full armor. Nothing like the nimble ranch horses she had grown up with. She wondered what had become of Jaimo and Archer after her father had been killed. They probably belonged to Youkai now.

"You seem far away," Hiro said, leaning on the railing beside her.

"Just thinking of home," she said. "I grew up on a ranch. I miss our horses."

"We could go for a ride if you'd like," Hiro said. "Really?" Kai said, her eyes wide and bright.

Hiro laughed. "Wow, you'd think I just offered you the moon."

"The moon isn't yours to give," Kai said.

"Bad example," he said. "We can't stray far, but let's go for a ride."

A groom tacked up two horses; a big chestnut that was Hiro's preferred mount, and a fine, dappled gray mare for Kai.

"She matches your hair," Hiro remarked, as they passed the gates through camp.

Kai pulled off her hat and ruffled her hair so it would lie down. "I have never been one to match my mount to my wardrobe."

"No, you don't seem the type."

Signs of spring decorated the countryside. A warm breeze blew cherry blossoms across their path. Quitsu and Ryu trailed after them, jumping and bounding through the tall grass bordering the road like a pair of kittens. Kai breathed deeply and closed her eyes, savoring the moment.

When she opened them, Hiro was looking at her with an intensity that made her blush. He averted his eyes, like a schoolboy whose hand had been caught in the candy jar.

"It's been a long time since I've ridden for pleasure," Kai admitted.

"Me too," Hiro said. "Brings simpler times to mind."

"My father always said you could trust animals far more than people," Kai said.

"Your father was a rancher, you said?" Hiro asked.

"Yes. But he was also a veterinarian of sorts, the only one our town had. He could nurse just about anything back to health. We always had stray animals running around. It drove my mother crazy, but I loved it."

"He sounds like a kind-hearted man." Somehow, the way Hiro said it made it sound like a trait he respected.

"He was. But he was hard too, when he had to be. Even scary. He taught me to fight. One time, we went on a call to the farm of a man outside of town who had a sick horse. When we arrived, we could tell the horses were terribly mistreated and malnourished. My father beat that man into a bloody mess and told him he would come back every month and make sure he suffered as much as his horses until he treated them right. I've never been so terrified in my life. We went back a month later and those horses looked much healthier, and didn't show any signs of abuse. We went back every month for years. 'House call.' My father would call it. No animal was ever mistreated in that house again."

"That is an honorable thing, looking out for the well-being of others."

"He thought it was his responsibility to look after those who couldn't look after themselves. He said it was what the sunburners used to stand for, before they lost their way."

"A bit of an odd thing for a rancher to say," Hiro remarked, "though I suppose he is entitled to his opinion."

"He wasn't just a rancher. He was a sunburner," Kai said, pointing to the tattoo on Hiro's muscled forearm. "He was your father's best friend and favorite captain."

"Where is your father now?" Hiro asked, eyebrows raised.

"Executed," Kai said. "Because he had the audacity to defy your father and refuse to turn his infant daughter over to be slaughtered." She had been working up to this, she realized.

She and Hiro looked at each other for a long moment. The horses had stopped walking. A cricket sounded in the meadow.

"I'm sorry about your father," Hiro said. "I believe I am familiar with his story. My father was devastated to lose his friend." He raised his hands as Kai opened her mouth to speak. "I'm not saying that is an excuse for what has happened to you and your family. I can't undo everything my father has done. But I will try to be different when I'm king. Better."

Kai's necklace lay cool against her chest. She softened. "I believe you."

The next day, Hiro and Kai walked through camp again. Her mother had pleaded out again on account of a "headache." Kai could kiss her for it.

As they passed the sparring ring, they paused to watch two sunburners spar with sharp ono axes.

"The taller man is better," Kai remarked. "Look how he is toying with the other. He sees his move coming and counters easily. He could take him down quickly if he put his mind to it."

Hiro glanced at Kai sideways, eyebrows raised. "The taller is Wuu, one of our captains and armsmasters. He is one of our best trainers."

"His technique is good," Kai admitted.

"You said your father taught you to fight?" Hiro said.

"Yes."

"What weapons?"

"If it had a blade, blunt or string, he taught it to me. I think it was how he kept himself sharp."

"Want to have a go?" Hiro asked. The two men in the ring were re-racking their weapons and wiping the sweat from their faces.

"Is that a good idea?" Kai asked. "Me in the ring with the crown prince?"

"You scared?" Hiro said, poking Kai's shoulder with a finger.

"No," she said, exasperated. "But won't your people worry about you being wounded at the hand of an evil moonburner?"

"Maybe," he admitted with a shrug. "But if we are to work together, my people have to start trusting you as I do. We'll use staves. No blades. They can't object to that."

He climbed under the rope encircling the ring and held it for her. "Besides, if I can't handle one drugged moonburner in the middle of the day, I'm not fit to be king."

Kai shook her head, but couldn't turn down the playful expression on his face. She climbed into the ring.

"Five silvers on Kai," Ryu said in his deep rumble.

Quitsu chuffed with laughter, jumping gracefully onto one of the fenceposts for a better vantage point. "No bet."

Kai grabbed two staffs from those piled neatly on the ground and turned to find Hiro with his back to her, taking his shirt off. She snapped him in the small of the back with one of the staffs, just hard enough to sting.

"Ow," he said, whirling around.

"Never turn your back on your opponent," Kai said, tossing his staff to him.

He smiled, rubbing his back. "That's the only free blow you'll get."

"Should I take my shirt off too, before we start?" she asked, with mock innocence.

"I believe that is what we would call an unfair distraction." But Kai thought it might even things up. She was having a hard time pulling her eyes from his firm chest, flat stomach, and strong arms. Merciful Taiyo, the man was muscled like a god. Kai came back to herself just in time to throw up her staff and block his overhead blow.

They were fairly matched, trying out tentative test blows at first, exploring each other's styles and weaknesses. The tenor of the fight began to grow as they attacked, sparred and fell back, the sound of their clacking staves echoing through the campground. They were drawing a large crowd, a crowd that she knew was not rooting for her.

She blocked and attacked, her staff whirling in her hands. Sweat poured off of her. She was tiring. Hiro was, too. She could see his chest heaving and his movements were growing sluggish. She thought she still had the better on him in speed. There! His foot caught on a rock and he stumbled a step, lowering his staff to catch his balance. She almost went for the "kill," but held back. She couldn't win this fight. Hiro righted himself and attacked with fury, no doubt angry at himself for opening himself up. She allowed herself to stumble backwards and fall to the ground, with the end of his staff pointed at her eyes.

"I yield," she said.

Hiro stood breathing hard for a moment with his staff at his side before he extended a hand to her and pulled her up.

"Good fight," he said loudly, clapping her on the shoulder.

"The woman can fight, can't she!" he said to the crowd as he grabbed his shirt and held the rope for her.

Kai heard a few mutters and the crowd began to disperse. She saw Daarco towards the edge of the clearing, arms crossed in fury. She looked away as they began walking back to her tent. "Friendly bunch, aren't they?"

"They'll come around," Hiro said.

"I really wish I taken that bet," Quitsu said.

The evenings were quickly becoming Kai's favorite part of the day. Hiro had taken to inviting her to eat with him. Her mother and his staff and retainers joined them, but then would trail off one by one, leaving the two of them alone.

Kai and Hiro talked until the candles burned low, trading stories of childhood, learning to burn and military life. Hiro loved hearing stories of her near misses with being revealed as a girl.

She couldn't help laughing herself as she recounted them, despite how life-threatening it had been at the time.

"As you know, at age fourteen all Kitan males need to be evaluated for service in the army. The recruiter came to town, and we were all supposed to strip down to our underwear to be evaluated by the physician. My parents and I fretted and agonized over how to get me out of it. Finally, my mother gave me a powder to swallow right before that part of the evaluation. I started vomiting and bleeding out of my eyes and ears so bad that they called my mother immediately. The army didn't want to touch me with a ten-foot pole after that!"

Hiro laughed his deep barrel laugh that resounded through Kai's body and warmed her to the core.

"I was throwing up for a week after that. I still don't like the taste of cinnamon."

They were sitting across from each other on two stools, a small table between them at an angle. He leaned forward and put his hand on her knee. Her senses buzzed, as if her body and mind were electrified by his touch.

"There is something I need to ask you. Something serious," he said.

"All right," she said softly, heart pounding.

He looked into her eyes. His golden hair glistened in the candlelight and his green eyes danced with the reflection of the flame between them.

"You threw that fight, didn't you?"

Kai laughed, playfully swatting at him. "I thought you were going to ask me something serious."

"That is serious," Hiro said with mock offense. "A woman beating the crown prince of Kita in a duel? It's a scandal!"

"Not just any woman," Kai said, smiling.

"No, that's exactly right. Not just any woman." He put his hands back on her knees. "I knew it from the moment I knocked you out of the sky. I couldn't have killed you as sure as I couldn't cut off my own arm. There is something about you that speaks to me."

"I . . . feel the same way," she said, embarrassed to find her voice breathless.

"My men warn me that you are a sorceress, manipulating my mind."

"Daarco?" she asked, already knowing it was so.

"Yes. And others. I know I should heed their advice and be wary. But every time I try, I am pulled back in."

He had slid his hands up her legs slightly, so they now rested on her mid-thighs. His face was close to hers, his mouth full and fine. Her excitement was laced with a thread of panic. Was he going to kiss her? He leaned forward and she closed her eyes, sucking in her breath.

Then he did. His lips were gentle but firm, and he tasted both salty and sweet. Her universe narrowed to nothing but the feel and taste of him, the heat of her body and the sound of her heartbeat raging in her ears.

"Sir," a throat was cleared towards the tent door.

As Hiro pulled away, she opened an eye, glaring at the unwelcome intruder. It was Hiro's servant.

"You are wanted in the command tent. There is word from the front."

"I'll be there in a moment," Hiro replied.

The servant vanished.

Hiro looked back at Kai and reached out, tracing her cheek with the rough side of his thumb. "Zeshi always had an impeccable sense of timing," he said. "We'll have to finish this later."

"I'll hold you to that."

She walked back to her tent on the other side of camp slowly, as if in a dream. She had heard the phrase walking on air before, but she had never felt it herself. Tonight, she understood. This thing with Hiro, whatever it was, felt right.

And then someone grabbed her from behind, pulling her back while strong hands shoved something in her mouth. Before she could catch a glimpse of her attacker, he threw a hood over her head, blackening her view. Kai schooled herself to still the panic rising inside her. Her breath came quickly, turning the air inside the hood stale and sickly warm. Her hands were roughly tied behind her back and she was hoisted over someone's shoulder. Though she struggled and tried to scream, she could hardly make a sound.

CHAPTER 33

After a few minutes that felt to Kai like an eternity, her assailant reached his destination. He unceremoniously dumped her on the ground. Her stomach ached from bouncing against the hard shoulder of the man carrying her, and her hands were still painfully tied behind her back. She could see thin points of light through the fabric of the hood and could hear low male voices talking nearby.

Who had taken her? How could she plan when she had no idea what kind of trouble she was in? She wished he would remove the damn hood.

Her wish was granted, and the hood was snatched off her head. What she saw made her heart sink. It was even worse than she had feared. Daarco stood in front of her, a twisted grin on his face.

"Your precious prince isn't here to protect you now, sorceress," he spat the word as if a curse. He pulled the gag from her mouth slowly.

She looked at him coldly, praying that her face displayed calm and defiance, rather than the fear that was curling up her insides. "My precious prince, as you so eloquently put it, is also your commanding officer. And I'm quite sure that you are disobeying a direct order by kidnapping me and subjecting me to this mistreatment."

"Mistreatment?" He said the word as if considering it from every angle. "You haven't seen anything yet, moonburner." He pulled up a stool and sat in front of her. The movement reminded her of one by Hiro just days before, before everything had changed. The movement, the situation, was so similar, and yet it was so deadly different.

She looked around the room, surveying the scene. They were in a small tent, similar to those in the camp. The only furniture present was the stool Daarco sat on and a small table which held a lantern and, to her dismay, an array of sharp, deadly-looking knives and objects. She couldn't even imagine what some of them were for. Torture, no doubt, but what form, her mind was not creative enough to comprehend.

"You see, moonburner, unlike in Miina, we sunburners aren't all just mindless beasts who follow every word of our bitch queen. We are taught to think for ourselves. To think critically." He leaned closer to her.

"Think critically? I'm surprised you even know those words, let alone how to do it," she snapped at him, knowing even as she said it that it was not a good idea to antagonize him.

He backhanded her across the face, snapping her head to the side. Her vision blurred with stars. She tasted the metallic sting of blood in her mouth.

She glowered at him.

He went on. "I have been thinking . . . critically . . . about what could make my prince do a complete about face and make a deal with the enemy. What could make him abandon his men and spend all his time with a burner bitch? Why is he protecting you?" He leaned even closer. "I could only come up with one reason why."

Due to your inferior intellect . . . Kai thought, but held her tongue.

"You have bewitched him. This is all part of a moonburner plot to destroy us from the inside. It's really very clever. You would almost have to admire the plot, if it wasn't a coward's way to wage war. A woman's way."

Kai bristled. "I suppose leaving defenseless infants in the desert to die is the pinnacle of bravery? The very height of manhood?"

"That is politics. I am a soldier. I'm talking about war."

"A convenient distinction. I don't suppose you'll believe me, but I am not a spy, and I have not been bewitching Hiro. I have been drinking lusteric, for Taiyo's sake!"

"You're right, I don't believe you. All moonburners are liars and whores! You try to take everything from us. You took my father from me, and now you try to take Hiro, who is like my brother?" He grabbed a thin knife off the table and knelt in front of her. "I won't allow it,"

Daarco said. He leveled the point of the knife to her throat where she felt its razor-sharp edge begin to bite into her skin. "This is for Hiro."

Kai squeezed her eyes closed, trying to push aside her panic.

"Daarco!" a furious voice barked from the door.

It was Hiro. Behind him stood his tall, silent manservant, Zeshi.

Kai sagged in relief. He really did have an impeccable sense of timing. Hiro's face was hard and his eyes flashed like lightning in a storm.

"How dare you disobey a direct order? She is a guest here. I will have you stripped of rank and sent to clean the latrines for the rest of your career for this insubordination."

Daarco stood up, gripping the thin knife tight in his fist. "She has bewitched you—corrupted you. Don't you see? She has put a spell on you. She is the enemy. She must be killed to break her hold on you."

"I am under no spell," Hiro said. "You do not know everything. She could have killed me and she did not. I trust her. More than I trust you in this moment."

"It was part of her plan! To gain your trust. Don't you see? She must die!" Daarco lunged at Kai with the knife.

Hiro was quicker. He grabbed the other man and heaved him back from Kai, tossing him to the ground. The knife went skidding across the dirt floor. Hiro scrambled on top of Daarco and punched him viciously in the face, knocking him back.

Kai watched the scuffle in shock, but began to register sounds outside the tent. Shouting, the sound of metal on metal.

Zeshi disappeared out the tent flap to investigate. She strained at her ropes and looked around. She couldn't see outside the tent, but there! It sounded like an explosion. Daarco and Hiro were still lost in the rush of their personal battle, pummeling each other and rolling over in the dirt.

A flash lit the tent, a white so bright that Kai's eyes burned with the image of it. Daarco and Hiro lay on the ground, both smoking slightly. Were they dead? A moment later, Hiro began to move, groaning and trying to sit up. Kai breathed out in relief.

Until the tent flap opened. It was General Geisa.

A moonburner cut Kai free from her bonds, and she walked outside the tent, rubbing her sore wrists. Daarco, Hiro, and the two guards Daarco had brought were on their knees in front of the moonburners, wrists tied behind their backs. Ryu had been brought down with a bolt of electricity, it appeared, and his paws were bound. Steam rose from his prone body, but his chest heaved in labored breaths. He was still alive.

Kai couldn't believe how quickly things had changed. Days ago even, she might have welcomed being rescued by her sisters, but now, Kai could only see malice and calculation on General Geisa's otherwise pretty face. The moonburners' presence filled her with dread. Her plan was falling apart and she didn't know if she was savvy enough to piece it back together. It had been such a long shot in the first place.

Geisa strode to stand before the four men, hands on her hips. "My my. What do we have here?" She looked at Daarco, who was practically growling with hatred of the women before him.

"A dog . . . two rats . . ." She went to stand in front of Hiro, bending slightly to look into his face. "And something more. Queen Airi will be pleased with the gifts we bring her."

She straightened and looked at Kai, who was trying to stand to the side, out of her notice.

"You did well, little daughter. Led us right to them."

Kai's mouth opened slightly in shock, before she clamped her jaw shut.

Hiro's head swiveled and his gaze met hers. No more did it hold esteem or compassion. Now it was hard and filled with hatred.

She wanted to run to him, to cry out that it wasn't true, that she had nothing to do with the moonburners finding the camp. But she knew she couldn't say any of those things in front of Geisa. So she only stared at him, willing him to see the truth in her eyes.

"Load up the prisoners," Geisa barked. "We need to get back to Miina by daybreak. Torch the rest of the camp before you go."

"What of my seishen," Hiro said. "Should he not be taken with me, if I am to be a prisoner of war?"

Geisa's laugh was chilling. "You wish you were to be a prisoner of war. But no. You are to be . . . bait. And then, when your job is complete, we will use you until you are worthless and empty, and then you will die alone in the dark, with not even your seishen to mourn you."

Hiro paled. "Those words . . . you were my father's prisoner, weren't you."

"You remember me?" Geisa put her hands to her chest in mocking. "I'm flattered." She leaned down, until her face was level with Hiro's.

"Every mercy your father denied me, I will repay to you threefold. And since I was not able to say goodbye to my seishen, neither will you."

She turned to Kai. "You. Finish the seishen and follow. Prove your mettle, little burner. Bring me its claw for a necklace."

"No!" Hiro jumped to his feet and went berserk. He thrashed and ran towards Ryu, bashing one moonburner's nose bloody with his head. But then he staggered, falling to his knees, his eyes bulging. Geisa stalked towards him. She grabbed him by the hair and pulled him up to his knees.

"It's uncomfortable, isn't it. When your blood temperature starts to rise, to boil? Just another degree and you'll be dead. I'd calm down if I were you. "

She knocked him over the head with the flat of her blade and he fell to the side, unconscious.

Kai watched numbly as they loaded the men onto the koumori, strapping them down. Two women rode double, leaving Kai a koumori of her own. Geisa yelled to her as her koumori took off, laboring under the weight of two bodies.

"Prove your loyalty and finish that seishen, moonburner."

Kai approached Ryu, who snarled at her, snapping his huge jaws. She whispered to him as best she could while keeping her distance. She didn't know how long his bonds would hold.

"I did not betray Hiro. I'm on his side. I am going to free you and you should come to Miina. South of the city, there is a waterfall. Hide there and when Hiro is free, I will send him to you."

Ryu eyed her suspiciously, but seemed placated. She took a deep breath. This next part wouldn't go well.

"I need to take a claw, to prove to Geisa that I followed her orders."

Ryu thrashed in his ropes. "Absolutely not," he growled.

"Please," she said. "For Hiro. I'll only take one. Which one is the least important?"

"All of them are important!" Ryu snarled.

"It's the only way," she said. "Please."

Ryu calmed and pushed out one of his back feet. "The little one."

She didn't have the knife that was usually strapped to her forearm, it had been taken from her when she was captured. She grasped at the moonlight, trying to draw it through the haze of lusteric. She hadn't been

231

dosed sincebreakfast, and it was starting to wear off. She could feel the moonlight pulsing just out of reach. She grunted in frustration. It was too soon.

She ran inside the tent and picked up the most wicked looking knife from the table of implements Daarco had gathered for her. She ran her thumb along the blade to test its sharpness, and yelped as a drop of crimson blood welled from her finger. It would do.

She knelt down, grasped Ryu's foot, and cut clean through the claw. Ryu cried out in pain, but it was over quickly. He mewed softly, relaxing against the ground.

Kai had tears in her eyes.

"I'm sorry, Ryu. I'll do everything in my power to make this right."

She stroked his soft side once before slicing through his bonds. She ran to her koumori, the precious claw in hand. She leaped onto the koumori and lifted off, directing her towards the main circle of tents.

The camp was already in chaos, fires burning and people running, screaming. Kai jumped off her koumori before it hit the ground and ran towards the tent she shared with her mother.

"Quitsu!" she screamed, running through the front flap. "Mother!" The tent was ablaze. They weren't there. As she headed back towards the door, part of the tent roof collapsed in a shower of sparks and flame. She whirled around, looking for an exit. The smoke was stinging her eyes and filling her lungs. Images of the burning house in Ushai filled her mind once again, Sora clutched in her arms, nowhere to go but through flame. Why was there always flame?

As panic began to fill her, she tried again, desperately, to pull moonlight into herself. There! It was only a trickle, but it was enough. She pulled the moonlight into her qi and pushed it out, using its power to dampen the flames.

Kai stepped outside and the scene before her twisted her heart. Men, women and children were running, screaming, trying in vain to bring enough water to douse the hungry flames. She was tired of destruction. She pulled in as much moonlight as she could and burned it, pulling the heat from the flames, sending it dissipating into the air. She was still weak from the lusteric. She could not burn enough to completely put out the fires, but the temporary reprieve seemed to hearten the people and their efforts to put out the rest of the flames doubled.

Kai turned to walk back towards her koumori when her mother ran up to her, enfolding Kai in her arms. Quitsu was close on her heels and jumped into Kai's arms as soon as her mother released her. She squeezed him tightly.

"Come on," Kai said. "I got us a ride."

INTERLUDE

"Geisa, I tire of this."

The man hung from a set of shackles in the center of the cell, blood mingling with sweat and running in rivulets down his bare chest. His golden hair glinted in the light of the torches, refusing to dull.

"My Queen, you know this is important work," Geisa said, selecting another sharp implement from the tall table next to the man.

"I know, I know," Airi said. "But your methods aren't proving effective."

"This one thinks he is better than the dog he is," Geisa said, tapping the flat of the wicked knife to her palm, as if considering her next goa move. "He refuses to mate with the moonburners."

"I'm not a rapist," the man said in a gravelly voice.

"It's not rape," Geisa said with a scoff. "They are offering themselves to you. They serve the goddess."

"I've been with many a willing woman, and the girls in those cages are far from it."

"It's their destiny," Geisa said. "And if you don't feel like using your male parts, maybe we should rid you of them. They're doing you no good." She ran the knife up his inner thigh, letting it linger.

The man ignored Geisa's threat. "Queen Airi," the sunburner coughed, blood flecking his lips.

Airi curled her lip in distaste. She hated that they needed these creatures. They should all be put down like the plague to this land that

234

they were.

"You are not fit to speak to her," Geisa said, smacking him across the face in a vicious backhand. A fleck of blood and spittle landed on Airi's light gray silken dress.

She sighed. Now she would have to throw it out. She was fond of this dress. "Enough, Geisa. I think it's time we try another tactic." She pulled up a small stool and sat just out of arm's reach of the man.

"Give him some water," the queen instructed.

Geisa complied, grudgingly.

"Loosen his shackles."

Geisa did so and the man slouched to the floor gratefully.

"Do you know why we do what we do here?" The queen asked the man, crossing her legs and resting her hands on her knee.

"No," the prisoner said warily.

"We are trying to prevent the extinction of the moonburner race. Only by mating a sunburner and a moonburner will a moonburner child be born."

"No . . . that can't be true."

"I assure you, it is quite true. And as your king is set upon destroying us, I fear this facility is the only way to ensure our continued survival."

The man was silent, contemplating.

"Now, will you help us? The task we ask of you is not unpleasant."

"No," he said.

Geisa moved to hit him again, but the queen held up a hand, staying her. "Why?"

The man sighed, shoulders slumped. "I love my wife."

The queen's face softened. "A family man? I would not have thought. You would truly endure this torture to remain true to her? Would she ask this of you? I think not."

"I don't know," he admitted. "But there was never a question for me."

"What is her name?" the queen asked.

"Varya," he said.

"A lovely name. Tell me how you wooed her? I do appreciate a good love story."

He hesitated for a moment. "Her father was a blacksmith. We were camped for a few days outside of her village and my horse threw a shoe. I took it in, and when I saw her . . . I knew. I sabotaged the shoes on three other horses before I worked up the nerve to ask her father for her hand. We married that day, and she rode with me when we broke camp." He recited the story with a wistful smile.

"She gave up her whole life for you, just like that?" The queen asked.

"Yes," he said. "She likes living in Kistana well enough, but I worry about her and the children, since I've been gone so long."

"Children too?" The queen asked.

"Yes. Two little girls, five and three."

"Delightful ages."

"They are a handful," he chuckled.

"You have given me much to think on . . . what is your name?"

"Thorin."

"Thorin. I can tell that your family means a great deal to you. So here is what I am going to do."

He leaned forward eagerly.

"I am going to send my most capable women to Kistana, where they will locate Thorin's lovely wife Varya and his two darling daughters. They are going to bring them back here, and for every moonburner you refuse to mate with, I will let ten of my soldiers have their way with your wife."

"You bitch!" he said, exploding to his feet. "You tricked me!"

The queen held up her hand, using moonlight to thread currents of burning air around him as tight as ropes. "And if you still refuse to cooperate, I will let my soldiers have their way with your daughters, while you and Varya watch."

He struggled furiously, eyes bulging, face purple with rage.

The queen stepped before him, looking calmly into his livid eyes. "I will have your cooperation. It is up to you whether we do this the easy way or the hard way."

He glared at her, body taught and quivering, before finally sagging in defeat. He nodded.

"Excellent!" Queen Airi said, clapping her hands.

She turned on her heel, pausing in the doorway where Geisa stood. "And that is how it is done."

BOOK FOUR

CHAPTER 34

K ai dropped her mother off in the forest outside of Kyuden, by the waterfall. It wasn't safe for her in the city or in the citadel. Someone might recognize her.

When Quitsu and Kai landed in the rookery, they were greeted by Nanase striding across the courtyard.

"You look like hell," Nanase said.

"Nice to see you, too," Kai said. She looked down at her dirt and ash stained clothes. She did look like hell.

"The queen has requested your presence. Immediately." Nanase didn't wait for Kai's answer, but turned and began walking towards the throne room.

Kai swallowed hard, shooting a glance sideways at Quitsu. *Here goes nothing.*

The throne room was much as it had been when she had entered it that first night at the citadel. But how things had changed. Queen Airi was seated on the throne, with her doll's face and perfect beauty. She wore a low-necked gown of pale blue trimmed with white fur and embroidered with tiny silver fishes. Kai knew now what ugliness lay beneath that perfect picture. As always, Geisa stood by her side.

The queen motioned her forward, but did not rise from her throne. "I am glad to have you home safely, daughter. I will leave to Nanase the duty of questioning how you were captured by the sunburners. I need to speak to you of more pressing matters." She leaned forward, fixing her sharp eyes on Kai. "You know who we hold in our dungeons?"

"I think so, my Queen," Kai said carefully. The official dungeons, or the secret ones?

"Who is he?"

"Prince Hiro. Heir to the Kitan throne."

The queen laughed brightly, and the sound reverberated through the room. "Quite right, quite right. We owe you many thanks for leading us right to this little gift. Here we thought we were tracking an errant moonburner and we find ourselves upon the sunburner's forward camp. A great turn of fortune."

Kai couldn't help herself. "Tracking me?"

"I never thought you had deserted," the queen said, quickly. "I knew something must be wrong. But you must understand, master moonburners are far too precious for one to go . . . missing. We have the means of locating each moonburner if necessary."

Kai's body felt cold, but the brand on her neck burned. Was that it? If it was, she could never be free of the citadel.

The queen stood, descending the stairs towards Kai. "I asked you here because it is imperative that you keep quiet about our royal guest, at least for the time being." She stopped one step in front of Kai and looked her in the eyes. "We have very special plans for him."

"What are you going to do with him?" Kai asked, knowing she shouldn't.

The queen laughed again and looked back at Geisa, who grinned. "No one could blame you for being curious. You did deliver a valuable commodity to me, so I suppose I can share our secret. The Oracle has discovered that in a few week's time, there will be a complete solar eclipse. The sun's power will be weakened for hours. Prince Hiro is bait, you see. We lure the sunburners here, and just when they think it is safe to attack . . . we will crush them." The queen's voice had grown low and hard.

Kai stepped back involuntarily.

And then, just as quickly, the dark cloud passed from the queen's face. She brightened again, and clasped her hands together. "You understand what this means, don't you? We will end this war. Once and for all. And we have you to thank. Well done, Kai." The queen grasped Kai's hands and squeezed.

"Yes, my Queen," Kai mumbled, her stomach a hard pit.

"Now get cleaned up, get some rest, and report to Nanase for further orders." The queen began to walk back up the steps, but turned.

"One last thing. Geisa told me you have a little memento from Prince Hiro's seishen. I'm sure he will be so comforted to have a piece of him." She held out her hand.

Kai fished into her pocket and pulled out the golden claw, which seemed out of place glistening warmly in the sterile white light. She dropped it in the queen's hand and bowed.

"Aren't we supposed to report to Nanase?" Quitsu asked, as they walked past the building that housed the faculty offices.

"I don't care," Kai said. "I need to see if our friends are ok."

When they had left, Master Vita had been unconscious, Emi was in the hospital and Maaya had been whipped bloody. She prayed they were all right. She couldn't do this with just Quitsu. She needed help.

Kai hurried through the front doors of the library, through the stacks and into Master Vita's bedroom. The bed was empty, the blanket neatly folded on top. Other items were in the process of being packed away; with some of the dresser drawers standing open and empty. Kai's heart sank.

"We're too late." She sat down on the bed slowly, fingering the pair of half-moon spectacles on the bed table.

Emotions washed over her. Master Vita had been her lifeline, her hope. He knew everything, he would have been able to help her find an answer. And now she was alone again.

"Too late for what?" A raspy voice came from the doorway.

She looked up, eyes wide, and rushed to wrap the old man in a crushing embrace. "Master Vita!" she cried. " I thought the worst."

He coughed and waved her back. "No need to crush me to death, the consumption is doing just fine at that without your help."

Her cheeks reddened, and she led him to sit down on the bed.

"Are you all right?" she asked, looking him over carefully. He looked smaller and more frail, but much of his color had returned.

"I'm fine, thank you. That nice moonburner Pura came with the medicine you acquired for me. She was kind enough to come check on me a few times, and has ordered me moved to a room in the hospital ward. Apparently, even a man can get care here if he knows the right people." He winked.

Kai silently thanked Pura for her compassion, sitting down heavily in the chair by the bed. Master Vita looked at Kai quizzically, taking in her torn and ash-covered dress.

"I suspect that you have some story to tell. You get the fire going, and I'll make us some tea."

Master Vita made tea and they took seats by the fire in the main room. Weariness entered her as soon as she sat down. Quitsu jumped onto the arm of her chair and leaned against her shoulder.

"To start," she said. "I know my mother is Azura. I know you helped her fake her death. And she is alive."

"Oh my," Master Vita said, taking off his spectacles to clean them with his white cloth. He held them up to the light and put them back on. "I see we do have a lot to talk about."

Kai shared the events of the last days, explaining about the purple fountain, the spirit world, how she had seen the tiny cameo and discovered her mother was Azura. She described how she had rescued her mother and been kidnapped by Hiro only to be freed by Geisa. She told him about her discovery of the facility. Master Vita listened to it all in rapt attention.

"That is a busy few days. I don't feel so bad that you didn't come visit me," he teased.

"I wish I could have been here," Kai said, taking the bait, despite his jest. She put her elbows on her knees and ran her hands through her hair. "I don't know what to do now. I have to get Hiro out. He is a good man and I think he stands a chance of convincing his father to declare a ceasefire. If I don't . . . Queen Airi will use him as bait to capture the sunburners for her breeding program."

Master Vita frowned. "How many burners are in the facility?"

"Six sunburners and six moonburners. I think. I didn't have time to do a thorough census."

"One female to one male. With most animal breeding programs . . ." Master Vita hesitated.

"I know," Kai lamented. "I've been thinking the same thing. You only need one bull for every 20 to 30 cows."

"And if Airi is planning on capturing more sunburners . . ."

"She is going to need a lot more moonburners, too," Kai finished. "How many?" he asked.

"All of them," she replied.

"This is a predicament." Master Vita said. "But are you sure you can trust Prince Hiro? That allying yourself with him is the right choice?"

"Yes," Kai said. "I trust him."

Master Vita hesitated.

"What's wrong?" Kai pleaded. "You have to help me."

"The last time I meddled in affairs of the state, it didn't end how any of us expected," Master Vita said. "We ended up with Airi as queen. If I had never helped your mother, she would be queen now, and none of this would be happening."

"You don't know that," Kai said. "Maybe things would have gone even worse if you hadn't helped. But you tried, that's the important thing. You did what you thought was right. And if you have regrets, this is your chance to make it right. My mother has agreed to be queen regent until a queen can be chosen." She decided not to mention her mother's suggestion about her candidacy for the position.

"Truly?" Master Vita said. "Azura would return to the throne?"

"Yes," Kai said, with a certainty she did not feel.

That seemed to be the assurance Master Vita needed. He straightened. "What resources do we have?" he asked.

Kai looked around helplessly. "You. Me. Quitsu. Maybe Maaya and Emi. Maybe my mother. Maybe Ryu, Hiro's seishen."

"That's not a lot. It's going to take more than an old man and one errant moonburner . . ."

"And seishen," Quitsu piped in.

"And seishen," he added. "To overthrow the queen."

"We know where they are keeping him. Or at least, I know a place I suspect they are keeping him. And they are keeping others there against their will. If we could get them out, the sunburners could help Hiro escape. The moonburners might even help too. Or could act as a diversion."

Kai pictured the angry pregnant moonburners pouring from their underground holding cells. Yes, the queen would likely have some questions to answer if that happened.

"So we need to figure out a way to help the prisoners escape," Master

Vita said thoughtfully.

"I suppose so," Kai said. "I wish there was a way to get sunlight down there. They would be able to burn their way out of those cells in no time."

Quitsu chimed in, helping with the brainstorming. "Could we break open the rock above the facility? Or . . . mirrors? Or some sort of storage device?"

Master Vita whirled to look at Quitsu. "What did you say?"

Quitsu sat up. "Break open the rock?"

"After that."

"Mirrors?"

"No," Master Vita said impatiently. "After that."

"A storage device. A way to transport sunlight into the cavern."

"Yes, like a moonstone, but for sunlight." Kai looked at Master Vita, hope blossoming in her chest. "Does something like that exist?"

Master Vita nodded, a smile growing on his lined face. "Don't you remember your History lessons, Kai?"

"Madame Furie hated me," Kai grumbled. "I tried to get through that class as fast as possible."

"When the first two burners were born, Taiyo and Tsuki crowned them with the celestial crowns."

"So?" Kai asked, not tracking.

Master Vita looked at her, exasperated. "Don't you remember the legends about the crowns?"

Kai searched her memory. "They glowed with the light of the sun and moon, even during the night and day?"

"Exactly!" Master Vita said, expectantly.

Kai shook her head in exasperation. "So? They glowed. Who cares?"

"They stored the light of the sun and moon, even during the opposite time of the celestial cycle. They were storage devices."

"Are they real?" Quitsu asked. "I thought they were just legend."

"They are real," Master Vita said, quietly. "The queen wears the lunar crown."

"So all we have to do is steal the queen's crown off her head?" Kai said, rolling her eyes. "Why didn't you say so?"

"No," Quitsu said. "If we want to help the sunburners escape, we need the solar crown. We need to help the sunburners burn their way out during the day, when the moonburners are at their weakest. That's the only way they stand a prayer of escaping."

"So we need to steal King Ozora's crown?" Kai asked. This task was seeming more and more impossible.

"Yes," Master Vita said. "And no. King Ozora doesn't have the solar crown. The citadel does."

CHAPTER 35

"In my younger years, before I worked as a tutor and librarian, I was charged with cataloguing the royal treasury," Master Vita explained. "I spent a lot of time down there, and saw all sorts of interesting trinkets."

"Down there?" Kai said, wearily. "Where is it located?"

"It is underneath the wing that contains the queen's chambers and guard's quarters. The entryway is located in the queen's antechamber."

Kai threw up her hands. "You must think me far more capable than I do, Master Vita. How are we supposed to sneak in and out of the queen's chambers undetected? They are crawling with guards and servants. Not to mention the queen herself."

"Let me finish before you get all doom and gloom," Master Vita said. "All the underground complexes under the citadel were built with at least two entrances, for air flow and fear of cave-ins. No one wants to be trapped underground, especially a sorceress whose power is derived from the moon."

"So where is the other entrance?"

"It's in the Oracle's tower."

Kai chewed on her fingernail absentmindedly as she thought. "Not a lot of people in the Oracle's tower. We could get in. Is the treasury guarded?"

"It has not been guarded in recent years, due to declining population in the citadel. But it is warded with some nasty tricks. I know how to disarm all of them, or at least I do if they haven't changed," he said, with a touch of pride.

"It's a risk we'll have to take. We don't have any other options," Kai said. "You will have to explain how to disarm the wards."

"What do you mean?" Master Vita said, crossing his frail arms in front of him. "I'm coming with you."

"Master Vita . . . I don't doubt that you would be a valuable addition to the team," Kai said. "But I am worried about your health. Are you honestly up to the task?"

He straightened, tossing his cane to the floor. "I have spent my life dedicated to Miina, this citadel and the moonburners. I have seen what I loved twisted into something it was never meant to be. If my last days can be spent ensuring that Queen Airi does not destroy all the burners left in this world, then I will move heaven and earth to do so." He looked intently into her eyes.

"I believe you," Kai said, softening. "And it means everything to know I am not alone in this. Thank you."

"Now hand me my cane back," Master Vita said.

Quitsu chuffed with laughter.

They decided that the best time to attempt the infiltration would be during the daytime, when the Oracle and any curious guards were likely to be asleep. They still had a few hours left until daybreak, and so Kai went to visit Emi.

Kai found her in the hospital ward, sitting up cross-legged on the bed, flipping through a book.

"Kai!" Emi exclaimed, leaping off the bed and flinging her arms around her. As Emi pulled back from the embrace, Kai saw that the whole left side of Emi's face, ear and head were still swathed in white bandages.

"Oh, Emi . . ." Kai said, her heart going out to her friend.

"What, this?" Emi said, with a nonchalant flip of her hand. "It's just a scratch. Builds character." She grimaced, pressing a hand to her bandages. "It hurts to smile."

"Are you okay?" Kai said, sitting down on the bed with her.

"Yes," Emi said. "I have a few bruised ribs and bad burns on my face and neck. But I'm lucky. I'll recover. I'll still be a moonburner."

"Of course you will" Kai said. "You're the strongest woman I know. How long . . . until the bandages come off?"

"Weeks. I'll still look like a hideous monster on one side of my face. The damage was too bad to heal completely," Emi trailed off, looking away for a moment. "You know, I'm relieved in a way," Emi said.

"What do you mean?"

"This is going to sound ungrateful and conceited, but all my life, people always wanted things from me because of my looks. They wanted me for my face or my body. I was expected to be a certain person, to act a certain way. It wasn't until I came here that I was able to be me. But I still worried that when people looked at me, all they saw was a pretty face. But with this," Emi gestured to the bandages, "I can finally just be me. Whatever I earn or accomplish from here on out will be because I earned it. I'm free."

Kai gripped Emi's hands, marveling at her friend's strength. "You've always been you," Kai said. "But I'm glad you can see it now."

"Me too," Emi said.

"Although . . . you're still going to look way better than me in a dress," Kai said. "There's no getting around that."

"Obviously," Emi said. "You have absolutely no fashion sense." They both laughed, but Kai's smile faded.

"What's wrong?" Emi said, sensing Kai's change of mood. "I was just kidding."

"No, not that. This doesn't feel right without Maaya."

The perfect side of Emi's face fell. "I know. But . . . she knew the rule and she broke it. She chose him over us."

"It's a stupid rule," Kai said. "And completely hypocritical."

"What do you mean?" Emi asked.

Kai looked around and lowered her voice, explaining the facility she had found deep under the throne room.

Emi's half-face went from shock, to horror, to anger as Kai finished her story. "So you are telling me that Maaya gets whipped and enslaved for the rest of her life for the crime of falling in love, but beneath our very feet the queen is forcing moonburners to mate with sunburners?" Emi asked, her voice tinged with hysteria.

"Keep it down," Kai said, waving away a nurse who was starting to walk their way.

"I'm sorry," Emi whispered. "This is wrong. We have to stop them. Who can we tell? Nanase?"

"I don't think she's involved, but I don't trust anyone at the citadel. If we tell the wrong person, we could end up in there ourselves."

Emi paled. "Stela. Leilu has been to see me a few times, worried sick about Stela. She just vanished after begging for Atsu's life in the courtyard. You don't think . . ."

"I do," Kai said, grimly. "It would be exactly like the queen to use the facility as a convenient place to hide dissenters."

"What do we do?"

"We have . . . a plan. Not a great one, but a plan."

"We?"

When she left the hospital ward, Kai jogged to Nanase's office for her orders. "You arrived hours ago," Nanase said, not looking up from whatever she was reading. "Where have you been?"

Kai swallowed. A half truth was probably better than a lie. Nanase seemed like she could sniff out a lie from one hundred paces away.

"I went to see Master Vita. He was very sick before I left for the mountains. I didn't know if I'd find him alive."

Nanase looked up, her face impassive. "And?"

"He is much improved. Pura saw to his care while I was gone. He is moving to the hospital ward."

"Good," Nanase said. "Pura has a soft heart. But these are dark times for the softhearted. I fear it may be too much for some, before the deed is done."

It seemed like an opening, and so Kai took it. If she had an ally in Nanase . . . she needed to know. "The queen shared her plan with me. About the eclipse. It seems . . ." she chose her words carefully, like a goat picking its next step on a rocky cliff face. "It seems like it should not be up to us—whether the sunburners are destroyed forever."

"It is a heavy thing. But the queen does not take it on lightly. The sunburners are bent on destroying us. She believes it is us or them."

"But is it?" Kai asked. "When I was a prisoner in the sunburner camp, I spoke at length with the crown prince. He wants peace. If we could just convince the queen . . ."

"Kai," Nanase held up a hand, silencing her. "I don't doubt that the prince was very persuasive. But what you say could be taken as treason within these walls. Speak not another word."

Kai wanted to protest, but she knew Nanase was right. She was walking a dangerous line even speaking to Nanase.

"I see that you take the weight of these things upon yourself," Nanase said. "It is an admirable trait, but misguided at best, and dangerous at worst. Your role is to obey orders. You must have faith that those who lead have the best interest of the moonburners at heart."

I've never been very good at faith, Kai thought.

"What are my orders?" Kai asked.

"Report to Pura's division, she will give you further instructions."

CHAPTER 36

Master Vita had changed into a dark set of trousers and shirt. He was ready for action. Kai almost laughed at the sight of him, at the thought of wearing all black for a daylight break-in. This was probably the most excitement he had seen in years.

They nonchalantly strolled towards the Oracle's tower and made their way through a garden around back, to a cellar door would lead them into the lower floors of the tower. With a brief bit of burning from her moonstone to melt the lock, they made their way into the cellar. Kai was nervous to attempt the break-in during the day, when she had no burning ability, but she had been forced to admit Master Vita was right when he pointed out that she wouldn't have any ability underground either way.

Master Vita had snagged a moon orb from the library that lit their way as they carefully traveled out of the cellar through the dark corridors.

Quitsu stalked ahead to scout for guards or people, but their route was deserted.

Before long, Kai found herself standing before an alcove, Master Vita holding the moon orb before him. There were two flickering candles on the wall, and between them was a grid of unlit votive candles hanging on the wall. It looked like an altar, similar to those one would find in Tsuki's temple. Unremarkable.

Master Vita lifted one of the lit candles off the wall. "Now let's see if I can remember the pattern."

He began lighting a few of the votives, seemingly at random. "Ursu. Hmm." He almost lit one, and then stopped, lighting another. "Septix." Another. "Cassia." Kai held her tongue, though she was dying to ask. Finally, he lit the last one. "Bellaru."

Kai had heard of that one. "The north star?" she said.

Master Vita grinned at her. "Stand back and look at the pattern."

She did, but still could only see what appeared to be a random selection of lit votives.

"Tsuki!" Quitsu said. "I mean, her constellation. I see it!"

"Very good, Quitsu." Master Vita said, slipping into teacher mode without realizing it.

Kai stuck out her tongue at Quitsu behind his back, who waggled his fox eyebrows at her.

A grinding noise before them pulled her attention back to the wall in front of her.

"It's opening!" she whispered.

Master Vita nodded. He ushered them through the opening in front of them, and then quickly blew the candles out and slipped inside. The door closed behind them with an ominous thud.

The white light of the moon orb lit a narrow corridor before them.

"Stay behind me," he said. "If I remember correctly, there are two other wards before we get into the treasury."

They walked slowly down the corridor, allowing Master Vita to lead the way, his shuffling steps and cane echoing off the stone walls. They soon reached another door.

"Is there a trick to this one?" Kai asked.

"I don't remember this door being here," Master Vita admitted.

"Great," Kai said. "Well . . . I guess . . . we just try it. I'll do it."

Master Vita raised his cane to block her way. "No, I am older. I'll do it."

"But you're not expendable. We need you to get through the next wards."

Quitsu rolled his eyes. "No one in the group is expendable, save me. And I don't have opposable thumbs. Kai, just open the door."

The two humans suitably chastised, Kai sidled up to the side of the door, and reached for the door knob. Her hand wavered slightly, and she closed her eyes as her hand closed around the knob. Nothing happened.

She turned the knob, and the door swung open. She waited. No loud noises, no arrows, no fireballs. Nothing came out the door. She moved her head to the right, trying to peer into the darkness.

"It seems clear," she said.

She walked through the doorway, and Master Vita and Quitsu followed her into the center of a circular room. Master Vita held up his light. No, not circular. Octagonal.

Kai slowly turned in a circle. Each side of the room contained an identical door. And then, a heavy thud echoed through the room. She whirled around. The door they had entered through had just swung shut. From the inside, it looked just like the others. Oak lintel, oak door, black iron hardware and doorknob. She kept her eyes on it, turning her body towards it.

"The door closed," she said. "It's that one. We can't get confused." She began walking towards it. She would tear off a strip of her uniform and tie it around the knob to differentiate it from the seven others.

Before they reached it, Master Vita's moon orb winked out.

The darkness was total, palpable, like a living thing. Kai froze, willing herself to stay in place. She could hear her heartbeat rushing through her ears.

"Kai," Master Vita said. In the darkness, his voice seemed small and thin. "Over here," she said. She tried to edge sideways in the direction she thought he was. There! She moved her hand down his arm to grip his hand. It was clammy and cold.

"There is an enchantment here to extinguish all light. It must be. I've never seen a moon orb go out."

She pulled in moonlight from her moonstone cufflink, trying to send up a light into the darkness. Nothing, and now her cufflink was drained. Nice.

A sound like a giant piece of metal grinding upon metal rang out in the darkness. It reverberated through the room, through her very bones.

"What is that?" she asked, turning about uselessly.

The room began to move. It was an odd sensation. She could only tell they were moving because a breeze tousled her hair. Her hair began moving more, whipping across her face.

"Get down," she said. She crouched to the ground, getting onto her hands and knees. She could feel Master Vita do the same. He released her hand. The ground they were standing on seemed to be spinning, and it was moving faster. She closed her eyes to the blackness and clung to the ground with gripped fingers, praying for it to stop.

After a time, it seemed to slow and finally creak to a stop. Kai let out a breath and climbed unsteadily to her feet. She grasped Master Vita's arm and helped him stand as well.

There was still no light.

"What was that?" Kai asked.

"Well, it appears to be some sort of mis-directional trap. Now, we don't know which way is out, or even which way we came in."

"And where do the wrong doors lead?" Kai asked, already guessing the answer.

"To horrors and death, I'm sure. I remember a nest of jackwasps being ordered for something while I was assisting on the project. I never did find out what those were to be used for."

"Great. So we can't see the doors and don't know what door to enter, even if we could."

"That's not entirely accurate, Kai," Quitsu chimed in. He had been silent since they had entered the octagonal room.

"Which part?" Kai asked.

"I can see. Foxes are nocturnal, remember?"

She was familiar with Quitsu's "Kai, use your brain for five seconds" tone.

"I can see you sticking your tongue out at me."

She pulled her tongue back in, smiling. "I guess you *can* see in the dark."

"Can you see anything unique about the doors?" Master Vita said. "Any markings?"

She didn't hear Quitsu move towards the doors, but his voice sounded from the side of the room.

"No . . . I don't think so. Wait. There might be something, but it's too high. I can't quite see."

His voice came from beneath her now. "Kai, I'm going to jump in your arms. I need you to hold me higher so I can look."

Kai held out her arms, feeling silly in the darkness. She felt Quitsu's soft fur against her forearms as he jumped, and she tucked one arm under his paws.

"Turn slightly to the right. A little more . . . there. Now walk." Kai did as instructed.

"Slow down now," Quitsu said. "We're almost at the first door. Okay, stop."

She complied.

"There is just a symbol. It is a vertical line, with two cross hatches from right to left."

"That symbol doesn't sound familiar." Master Vita said from across the room. "See if the other doors have symbols on them. We need to find a pattern."

Quitsu instructed Kai forward like a marionette without the strings. "This one is another vertical line, but with two lines slanting out of the top, like a tree."

She walked further.

"Vertical line with three parallel crosshatches from right to left."

She frowned. The symbols seemed familiar. One of the few books her parents had owned had been a primer on smithery and metals. Her father had at one point imagined that he could shoe his own horses and save himself the expense. When he had realized how complex the art is, he had given up, and the book was one of five Kai had read over and over.

"I think . . . I think I recognize them. They are the symbols used by blacksmiths to represent metals. The first is iron, the second, copper, the third is also iron, but the third crosshatch represents a better quality. More pure."

"Of course," Master Vita cried. "I should have seen it myself. Very good, Kai!"

"Now, we just have to figure out which metal represents the right door."

"If you were hiding a treasury," Master Vita mused. "Which metal would you put on the door?"

"Gold," she said, realization dawning. "Quitsu, see if you can find a door with a vertical line with two crossing lines intersecting it, like an X laid over it."

"Keep walking," Quitsu said.

She did so until Quitsu exclaimed, "Stop! There it is."

Kai turned and put one arm in front of her, slowly walking towards the door. When her hands connected to it, she put Quitsu down. "Go bring Master Vita."

Soon, the three of them were standing in front of the door. Kai took a deep breath. "Here goes nothing."

She turned the knob. The door swung open to reveal another corridor, flanked by glowing moon orbs set into alcoves. The light seemed downright cheerful compared to the blackness of the room.

"Does this seem right?" she asked Master Vita.

"It has to be," he said. "There is only one way to find out."

The corridor was not long. Kai could see a doorway at the other end. She took a step onto one of the large stones of the hallway. Nothing happened. She relaxed and took another step. When her foot hit the pavement, a shock radiated through her from her foot. Her body convulsed, shaking as she fell backwards through the open door. The shock stopped, and she lay still, gasping.

When she opened her eyes, Master Vita and Quitsu's concerned faces peered at her from above.

"Kai? Are you all right?" Quitsu asked.

She coughed, forcing air back into her lungs.

"I think so," she sat up, gingerly, her body painful and creaky. She put a hand to her head, checking ruefully to make sure her brains were still on the inside.

"Do you think it's the wrong way?"

Master Vita frowned, and peered into the hallway. "No, our theory is sound. It should be correct. I think this is the next ward."

"If this is the right way, I hardly can imagine what would have greeted us down one of the wrong doors," Kai grumbled.

Master Vita ignored her. "There is writing on the ground. A word on each stone."

He pointed to one. "You stepped on this one?"

"Yes, that one. " Kai looked at it more closely, bending down. "There is writing on it. A word. 'To.'"

"Two? Like the number?" Master Vita asked.

"No," Kai said. "Like going to market. "

Master Vita approached the edge of the stones and peered over his glasses. "They all have words on them. "

"Step on the 'to' stone again, Kai, " Master Vita instructed. She did so, body tense. Like before, nothing happened. "What are the words on the next set of stones?"

Kai crouched down, careful to touch only her stone. She looked. "Hunt," "sing," "cook," and "catch." She looked back at him. "Sing is the one that is not like the others, perhaps that is it?" She stood.

"No!" Master Vita called, stretching his hand out as if to physically stop her. "Hold on. Can you see the next group?

"They are just single letters. A, O, and I."

"Can you see the next?" Kai peered at the fourth row of stones before her, willing her eyes to focus. She shook her head. "I don't think so. They are too far."

"Can you see if the word 'maid' is on one of the stones?"

"I can't. Quitsu, you have eyes like a hawk. Maybe if I hold you up, you can see."

"I have eyes like a fox, actually," Quitsu said cooly. "But I will see what I can do."

Kai rolled her eyes as Quitsu jumped into her arms again. She stretched her arms out in front of her, holding Quitsu as close to the latter row of stones as they could. She was sure they looked ridiculous. After a minute, her arms began to shake from the weight of him.

"Can you tell? I can't hold you much longer." Kai said, strain creeping into her voice.

"I see it," Quitsu said as Kai pulled him back to her chest, arms shaking in relief. "Maid is one of the words on the fourth row."

She put Quitsu down and rolled her shoulders a bit to loosen them. Master Vita started chuckling.

"That sly bastard. I can't believe he got away with it."

"What are you talking about?" Kai asked.

"One of the other men who worked with me on this project was a fellow by the name of Colum. He had been everything in his day, a mercenary, a scholar, a medic, an astronomer. He didn't have much love for the queen." Master Vita smiled fondly. "In fact, shortly after the project was complete, the queen ordered him to be executed. I was never sure what that was about. He escaped shortly before his sentence was to be carried out. "

"Master Vita . . ." Kai said, trying to hide her impatience. "The stones?" "Of course. The man was endearing and funny, but undeniably lewd. He bragged that he would get a dirty joke into the treasury."

Kai raised her eyebrows expectantly. "I still don't understand."

"Have you ever heard the song "To Catch a Maid?" He began humming a tune that did sound familiar to Kai. "It was one of his favorites."

"I think so . . ." Kai said. "I can't remember the words."

Master Vita started to sing, the gravel of his voice contrasting with the cheerful melody of the song.

"*To catch a maid*
You need spirit brave
A chest like a rock
And a twelve inch . . ."

He trailed off.

Kai put her hand to her mouth, blushing. "I have heard that one."

"The words to the song will get us through the hallway."

Kai laughed. "He made a dirty tavern song the key to the treasury? No wonder the queen wanted him executed!"

"I never knew why the queen was so angry with him, but that is a good theory," Master Vita mused.

"All right." Kai said, "Here goes nothing."

Kai followed the stones marked by the words to the song. With each new stone, she held her breath, bracing herself for a shock to jolt through her body. But it didn't. It seemed that they had figured out the key. She shook her head as she stepped on the last stone, etched with the word "cock." That man must have had some nerve.

She turned the door knob, and the door opened to reveal a huge glittering room.

CHAPTER 37

The three of them gazed at the wealth of the room, wide-eyed and slack-jawed.

"How . . . this is . . ." Kai trailed off.

The room was long, with a central aisle-way flanked by stone columns. Each column held a moon orb that lit the center of the room, but left the shelves in shadow. To the left and right of the columns stood rows and rows of shelves stacked neatly with treasure. There were piles of gold, jewels, statues, scrolls, weapons, lamps, carpets and beautiful carved wooden furniture. The room contained more opulence than Kai had ever seen in her life.

"How will we ever find it?" she wondered.

Luckily, Master Vita had an answer to this. "The treasury is divided according to time of acquisition. The solar crown was acquired four queens ago, when Queen Athita met King Othio in the Seven Days War."

Kai vaguely remembered Madame Furie droning about the Seven Days War in her History class. She really should have paid closer attention.

Master Vita moved through the rows, seeming to understand the organizational system in a way she didn't. She and Quitsu trailed behind him.

A scraping noise sounded behind her. She whirled, peering into the darkness. Nothing. Probably her imagination, jumpy with the excitement of their break-in. She turned back to Master Vita, but as she did, she saw a shadow flicker across the well-lit room.

"Quitsu," she whispered. "Do you hear anything?"

He was standing with his tail outstretched, the hackles on the back of his neck raised.

"Yes," he whispered back. "It sounds like . . . scuffing feet. Multiple feet."

"Ah-hah!" Master Vita cried. He had pulled a golden circlet off a shelf, and held it aloft triumphantly. "I found it!"

Kai inched closer to him. "That is wonderful. Now let's get out of here!"

"Oh yes, yes," he said, turning towards her. "There should be a door at the end of the room. It can only be opened from the inside. It will lead us to a tunnel that we can use to circle back to the Oracle's tower."

"Kai." Quitsu said behind her, his voice even but tight.

"What?" she asked, turning. And she froze. There was a spider at the end of the row. It was unmistakably a spider, with a black carapace body and eight legs covered in fine hair. But it was big. Bigger than Quitsu.

"Oh dear," Master Vita said. "I was hoping they had abandoned the idea of using spiders."

"How do we kill it?" Kai asked. Her knife had found its way into her hand. She looked around for other weapons, trying not to make any sudden movements. There! A sword on the shelf, close to where the spider stood, blocking their path to freedom.

"I don't know how to kill it," Master Vita said. "I wasn't privy to that part of the treasury plans. I imagine, though, that you kill it the usual way."

"On my mark, we run for the door." Kai said. "Stay behind me. Quitsu, stay with Master Vita."

"Go!" she cried, and ran forward, grabbing the sword off the shelf. She swung it with all her might, knocking the spider out of their way. Its skin was thick and hard, the sword reverberated in her hand as if she had struck a wall. Kai doubted she had done the spider any serious injury.

As they got into the main aisle of the room, she stifled the urge to sprint for the door. Master Vita wasn't moving very quickly. They needed to stay together.

"Kai!" Quitsu called, and Kai raised her sword just in time to block the mandibles of another spider leaping at her. The force of its attack threw her to the ground, its heavy weight pressing on her. Her thoughts went blank as she focused on the spider viciously biting at her blade. She managed to get her foot up and kicked it away from her.

It went sliding across the polished stone floor, legs scrambling for purchase. Another one was coming from the left, and one from the right. She glanced around and saw at least five more spiders scurrying down from the ceiling and the aisle-ways. There were too many to fight.

She swung her sword again and again, hacking a way towards the door. They were getting closer. They might make it.

A spider leaped onto her back, its heavy weight crushing her to the ground. She felt its sharp mandibles bite into her shoulder, and she screamed in agony.

Quitsu was on it in a flash, shredding the spider's eyes with his sharp claws. The spider reared back, an inhuman scream ringing out. Kai managed to turn over as it reared up and grasped her sword, which had fallen to the ground. She pointed the sword up as the spider came back down. The sword pierced its stomach, and black liquid squirted over her.

Kai scrambled up, slipping in the spider's blood.

"Master Vita," she cried, half to herself and half to Quitsu. He was surrounded by spiders and they were closing in, toying with their prey.

She had lost the sword under the collapsed body of the other spider, and she didn't think she could lift it. She looked around wildly for another weapon as she dove into the circle of spiders, swinging wildly with her fists. If only she could moonburn, she could light them all on fire. But there was no light down here. She reached out mentally, searching, grasping for any stray wisp of moonlight that might be stored within the treasures of the room. She had exhausted her moonstone link. But there . . . she felt it . . . a well of moonlight. She yanked it to herself without thinking, drawing in the moonlight and sending it out, a mental movement so quick it seemed as one.

The spiders exploded in flames. Fire jetted from their backs and their bodies, consuming them. They rolled and screamed and scrambled, a mass of legs and smoking hair.

"Come on," she said, pulling a stunned Master Vita towards the door. Mercifully, it opened.

Kai slammed the door closed behind her and sagged against it, breathing hard. She tousled Quitsu's head, thankful they had escaped largely unscathed. The wound on her shoulder stung fiercely, and Master Vita and Quitsu looked like they had gotten a few scrapes themselves. But they were alive.

"My, my." A female voice rang out from the darkness of the hallway in front of them. "Doesn't it look like you've been up to something."

Kai froze. Was it the queen? The speaker moved into the light of the moon orb in the closest alcove, and Kai felt some small measure of relief. A tiny measure. It was the Oracle.

Kai scrambled to her feet, and when she did, she looked down at herself. She looked like she had been through battle. Black spider blood covered the front of her uniform and her own blood coated the back. There was no way she could talk her way out of this.

She straightened her back.

"We have orders. We cannot speak of them to you." Kai tried to sound as authoritative as possible.

The Oracle laughed, that strange tinkling laugh that Kai had heard before. "No you don't. If you did, you would have been given the instructions for how to deal with the treasury . . . guards without having to kill them." She strode closer to Kai. "Try again."

Kai weighed her options. She could try to fight the Oracle, knock her out, and tie her up until they accomplished their goal with the crown . . . but the woman might scream, or fight back, and Kai had no idea how formidable an opponent she was. She could try to lie again . . . but her lengthy silence was already enough to cause suspicion. So, the truth then. She took a deep breath.

"Kai . . ." Master Vita said with a note of warning.

"The queen's plan is folly. You know the one of which I speak. It will bring the end of the sunburners. I believe the battle the queen plans is unnecessary. The sunburner prince is ready to declare a truce."

"And here we have the truth of it," the Oracle said, sounding pleased. "But the truth of it is much worse. If the queen's plan comes to pass, I see a day with no sun and a night with no moon. Our victory will mean our defeat."

Those words. It was the Oracle's prophecy, spoken to her the day she first met.

"Yes," Kai said, the pieces finally clicking into place. "Not just a day of no sun and a night with no moon . . . the prophecy you gave to me, when I was first here . . . do you remember it?"

"The moon cannot enslave the sun, nor make the day its mistress.

Or victory shall spell defeat, a crimson sky its auspice

The sun and moon must shine as one, or all will be undone."

"I finally understand," Kai said with a mixture of awe and horror. "The queen's plan to capture the sunburners and enslave them, it will fail. It will be the end of us. Only by working with the sunburners will we find a victory."

She had known in her heart that trusting Hiro was the right choice, but she savored the validation.

"You see the truth," the Oracle said.

"Haven't you told the queen this?" Kai asked. "If she won't listen, why don't you tell everyone? Expose her plan for the folly it is. The citadel would listen to you."

"The queen does not want to hear the truth that I speak. Her obsession with destroying the sunburners has consumed her. And as for why I do not speak to the rest of the citadel . . ." She curled her hands into fists. "She is too powerful. I will not risk challenging her outright until I am certain my efforts will be successful."

"It will be too late by then. The eclipse is happening, and the queen will execute her plan. You have to help us stop her."

The Oracle sighed. "I will do my part, in my own way. After all, the queen's plan is a matter of precise timing. But I will not challenge the queen, as you so foolishly suggest. It would be suicide."

Kai ground her teeth, wanting to argue further, but she could tell it would be a losing battle.

"I will help where I can. For now, let's get you cleaned up. And you will need to charge that crown."

Master Vita had been holding the solar crown behind his back during the exchange. He sheepishly brought his hands around to his front. The crown seemed dull and dark.

"It needs a full day and a full night under the light of the sun and moon. Just enough time to fully charge it before the day of the eclipse," the Oracle said. "And then you can free your hero, daughter of Azura."

CHAPTER 38

The Oracle led them up a set of winding steps to the top of her tower. Her chambers were open and cheerful, with the last vestiges of daylight pouring in through windows on the west wall.

Kai wasn't sure what she had been expecting, maybe some petrified animals or dripping wax candles, certainly not the tidy crisp furnishings tastefully decorating the chamber in shades of lavender and blue.

"This tower was built to reflect the phases of the moon. It is astrologically perfect," the Oracle said. "Not that I get to use those features much."

Master Vita sat down in a plush chair while the Oracle pulled a fresh set of moonburner blues out of a large wooden wardrobe. Kai changed into the clothes gratefully, tossing the bloody tatters of her uniform into a trash basket.

Giselli, the Oracle's seishen, began darting around the room, flying into the air under the high ceiling before sweeping down directly before the Oracle's face.

"What's wrong?" the Oracle asked.

"Someone's coming up the stairs," Quitsu said with a hiss.

Kai and the Oracle looked at each other with wide eyes, quickly surveying the room for a hiding place.

"The wardrobe!" the Oracle said, hurrying to help Master Vita out of the chair.

They lowered him into one side of the wardrobe, moving aside silken shoes and scarves. Kai and Quitsu tucked themselves into the other side of the wardrobe, and the Oracle closed the doors.

"Roweni," a haughty female voice said. There was light coming through a crack in the wardrobe doors. Kai could not see the speaker, but the voice was undeniable. The queen.

"We need this room for a few hours," Kai heard Geisa say. "With Tsuki's temple burned in the attack, this tower is the next best place to worship."

"As you wish," the Oracle said.

Kai opened the door ever so slightly, so she could get a glimpse of what was happening. The Oracle exited the room.

"Are you okay?" she whispered to Master Vita.

He nodded slightly and then his eyes widened. She looked back out the crack and saw a man materializing on the floor. They must have cloaked him in shadows to transfer him. He had tattered clothes and was covered in dirt and blood. He lay on the floor, unmoving. Despite his filth, she could see his close-cropped golden hair. A sunburner. But not Hiro, she thought with relief.

Geisa rolled up the rug and began retrieving candles from a bag and placing them in a circle. She dragged the man into the center of the circle and then pulled an ornate knife from her belt.

They were going to sacrifice this man. And Kai was in a wardrobe, with the power to stop them. Maybe he was a murderer, the worst of the worst offenders. But what if he wasn't? What if he was a father or a husband, just an honest, hardworking sunburner in the wrong place at the wrong time? As if Quitsu had sensed her thought, he drove his claws into her foot.

"Ow," she mouthed to him.

He jumped nimbly into her arms, and whispered into her ear. "Do. Not. Leave. This. Wardrobe."

"They'll kill him!"

"If you leave, they'll kill us. And then him. We can't fight both of them."

"We can't just do nothing."

"We're not doing nothing. We are living to fight another day. How can you help Hiro or Chiya if you get yourself killed?"

Kai bit her lip and opened her mouth to argue, but felt a vice grip on her other ankle. She looked down at Master Vita, who vehemently pointed out the wardrobe. She looked out the crack and saw that Geisa was approaching.

God and goddess! Geisa must have heard her and Quitsu bickering.

Kai pulled in as much early evening moonlight as she could and wrapped them in an illusion. She had only practiced minor illusions in moonburning class with Pura, projecting shadows on the wall or a dark face over her own.

She had never attempted anything like she was doing now, trying to create nuanced shadows to match the dark wood of the wardrobe. She prayed it was enough.

Geisa threw the doors wide, examining the contents.

The three perched wide-eyed and frozen, waiting for her triumphant cry of discovery. None came.

"Contemplating a different sacrificial outfit?" The queen asked from across the room. "I doubt anything of Roweni's will fit you."

"I thought I heard something," Geisa said.

"Well, it's empty. Let's get on with this."

"Very well," Geisa said, closing the doors.

Kai sagged with relief. She was about to drop the illusion when the doors flew open again. Geisa's triumphant face turned to disappointment.

"Enough with the wardrobe," the queen said.

Geisa closed the doors.

Kai held the illusion the whole time, thankful for something to distract her from the wretchedness she felt. They heard the man awakening; the chanting; wind howling through the room. They heard Tsuki's strange echoing voice. And they heard the sunburner's final cry when a knife was plunged into him. It was almost worse, not being able to see it. Kai's mind supplied plenty of vivid detail.

When it was over, Kai opened her eyes, which she had squeezed shut despite the utter darkness of the closet. Her cheeks were wet with tears. She was a coward. She should have done something.

She heard Geisa's voice.

"He didn't deserve it," Geisa said.

"What?" the queen asked, sounding surprised.

"To meet Tsuki in death. To be honored by her. He deserved to die like a stray dog in the street, with no ceremony."

"You hate that we need them," the queen said. "As do I."

"You weren't there . . . you don't know what they did to me when I was their prisoner. Those ten years. Tsuki . . . she found me. She fed me her blood and she made me strong. Strong so I could have my vengeance, not let them sit in some cell like pampered prisoners." Geisa's voice was half-crazed.

"Geisa," the queen said gently. "I am grateful every day that Tsuki brought you to me, and that you showed me her true face. But don't forget . . ." Her voice hardened. "This is not about your vengeance. This is about my reign, my legacy, and my moonburners. I am Queen."

"I beg your pardon, Your Majesty."

"You have it."

Kai and her companions waited at least an hour after the room fell silent to crack open the door of the wardrobe and peer out. The room was empty. It looked like the Oracle had been performing some spring cleaning; the rolled carpet was the only sign that anything unusual had happened. But Kai knew. Master Vita squeezed her hand tightly.

Both Quitsu and Master Vita tried to talk to her after they extricated themselves from the wardrobe. She didn't want to talk. They offered her justifications and explanations, but she knew the truth. She had let that man die. She held his face in her mind, her memory tracing the contours of his dirty features. She would never forget what her cowardice had cost.

Kai threw herself into planning the next phase of their rescue. What else could she do? She was getting good at carrying on despite a mind numb with shock and sorrow.

The Oracle's news that the crown had to charge for a full day and night was a setback. The eclipse was in three days' time, which meant that the soonest Kai could get the crown to Hiro was the day before the eclipse. That was assuming that she was successful sneaking into the facility undetected. She presumed that her lock-melting trick on the city-side door had been noticed, and security had likely been increased on that side. Her best chance of getting in was through the throne room, which carried its own problems.

The queen had called a meeting of the moonburners in the central courtyard at daybreak the following day. That left Kai a few hours to figure out how to get through the throne room and facility undetected. That would be her best chance.

Kai found herself lurking behind a tree outside the throne room. She watched for an hour, and saw one set of guards pass into the building on the hour. The minutes stretched on, but finally the guards finished their rounds and left the building.

Kai strode into the front of the building, knowing that skulking would look more suspicious. The antechamber was deserted. She breathed a sigh of relief, and reached for the handle of the huge wooden door leading to the throne room.

"What are you doing?"

Kai whirled around, heightened awareness flooding every fiber of her body. Her mind raced to find a suitable excuse. Even in the time she watched the building, she hadn't been able to come up with an excuse that didn't fall flat.

But when she saw the figure that spoke, fear left her.

"Maaya?" Kai asked, running to the other girl and throwing her arms around her.

Maaya hissed as Kai's arms encircled her, touching her back. Maaya had been flogged. So much had happened in just a few short days.

Kai pulled back. "Sorry," she said. "I forgot myself for a moment."

"It's okay," Maaya said dully.

When Kai really looked at Maaya, what she saw twisted her heart. The girl seemed pale and flat, a dull version of her former bubbly self. It was as if the life had been sucked from her. Her skin was sallow, and she had deep purple circles under her eyes. Her hair had been pulled back into some semblance of a ponytail, but clearly hadn't been washed in days. Her signature braids were gone. She was wearing a white servant's uniform.

Kai tried to keep her dismay from showing on her face.

"Are you all right? I'm sorry I have been gone, they made me go to the mountains for testing . . ." Her excuse sounded lame even to her ears.

"I am alive," Maaya said. "Which is more than I can say for Atsu."

Her voice choked at his name. "But I have been stripped of all rank and privilege. I have to serve the citadel for the rest of my life. I'm a slave. I suppose it's what I deserve for disobeying."

Kai shook her head fiercely. "You don't deserve that. What they expect us to do . . . to give up . . . It's wrong. I just wish I would have seen it sooner. You can't be blamed for wanting something more than death and destruction. For wanting . . . life."

Maaya opened her mouth to say something more, but then closed it, her face a mask.

"What is it?" Kai asked. "You can tell me."

A tear leaked from the corner of Maaya's eye. "They put lusteric in my food. I can't moonburn anymore. I don't know if they'll ever let me."

Kai's anger flooded inside her, a raging river searching for release.

"It's wrong," she hissed. "This whole damn place is wrong. The queen needs to be stopped."

Maaya's eyes widened. "You're talking about treason. If Queen Airi does this to fornicators," she motioned to herself, "what do you think she does to traitors?"

"I don't care. Someone has to do something. If we are all too afraid to stand up to her, she wins, and we all lose. I won't ask you to put yourself at risk, but tell me. Is there a time where the throne room is completely empty? When I could slip inside unnoticed?"

"The guards do rounds on the hour. The maids clean twice a day, once after daybreak, once just after nightfall. I am only here because I forgot my cleaning bucket."

"How long do the maids clean for?"

"An hour."

"Thank you," Kai grasped her friend's hand, squeezing. "Things may change here very soon."

Maaya smiled, but it didn't touch her eyes. "I wish I could believe you."

CHAPTER 39

The next twenty-four hours stretched to an unbearable length. All around the citadel, preparations were being made for the coming battle. Pura's only orders for the time being were to eat and sleep, which Kai grudgingly followed despite her anxiety. She had to admit that after a bath, a hot meal and a few hours' sleep, she did feel like she could think straight once again.

Quitsu had found Ryu near the waterfall behind the citadel's walls. Ryu was furious and worried sick about Hiro, but Quitsu had convinced him that Kai had nothing to do with the moonburners descending upon the sunburner camp. Quitsu had sent Ryu to join the sunburner army that was rapidly making its way across the Churitsu Plain towards Kyuden. Kai prayed for Hiro and Ryu to be reunited after the queen was overthrown. Assuming they weren't all dead. There were so many things that could go wrong.

Like the fact that Quitsu had not found Hanae. Kai had been clear with her instructions to her mother—they were supposed to meet by the waterfall. But she wasn't there. Had her mother been harmed somehow? The thought of losing her mother a second time threatened to paralyze her. Kai didn't think she could go through that again. Not to mention everything depended on her mother. Without a legitimate ruler to step in after the queen was dispatched, Kai would be dooming Miina to sunburner occupation or civil war. Kai wasn't sure which was worse.

As light began to dawn in the east, Kai stood at the window, ready for the day to finally begin. Her nerves were jittery and her stomach flipped like a rabbit. Kai had a one hour window of time just after dawn when the maids and guards would be out of the throne room. Queen Airi would be giving her speech in the courtyard, detailing the coming battle. Kai knew from the Oracle that the moonburners would attack at nightfall, hoping to decimate the sunburners for as long as possible. Then, soon after dawn broke and the sunburners thought they were safe to mount their own attack, the eclipse would begin. With the sunburners drawn out and defenseless, the moonburners would attack. Kai prayed that she could stop it from happening.

"Are you ready?" Quitsu asked her.

She smiled. He always knew her thoughts before she voiced them. "You know I'm not. But we must do our best."

"The plan is a good one. It will work," he said.

Kai wasn't sure if he was trying to reassure her or himself.

"I know," she said with more conviction than she felt. "We've come this far. Further than I thought we would. There's nowhere to go but forward."

Kai and Quitsu walked the long way to the throne room in silence. They came this way to avoid the gathering in the courtyard. Kai bore the solar crown in a leather satchel slung over her shoulder. It felt heavy. Perhaps the weight she felt was just in her mind.

She ducked behind a tree near the entrance of the throne room. "Quitsu," she said, kneeling down. "I need you to promise me something."

His fox face was impassive. "What?"

"If something goes wrong, run. Get out. Don't try to defend me. I need you to escape."

"I'm not going to abandon you if something goes wrong!"

"You have to," she said, stroking the soft fur of his head. "You are the only one who could get Master Vita, or my mother, or Maaya to help us. If something goes wrong, you need to expose what Queen Airi has been doing, and what it will mean. You are a seishen. Revered. They will believe you."

"I am not going to leave you if you are fighting for your life."

Her stomach tightened. Nothing would go wrong. She wouldn't be fighting for her life.

"Please, Quitsu. I command this of you."

His face grew stormy. "That's not fair. Besides. If anything . . . happens to you, I die too, remember? So your little plan to 'get the word out' would be for nothing."

Her brow furrowed. "I know. But, if I get caught, they probably won't kill me, they'll just throw me in one of those cells to use for breeding. You would be my only hope. The only hope for the future of the moonburners. And who knows, maybe the future of seishen. I don't know exactly how the seishen are tied to the burners, but I think that if we go, you go."

"Really? You're playing the end of the species card with me now?" Quitsu wore a hint of a smile.

Kai broke into a grin. She had won. "I am most definitely playing that card."

She picked him up and hugged him, her face buried in his silver fur, all decorum forgotten. "I don't know what I did to deserve you, Quitsu. But I am grateful for you every day."

"I don't know, either," he said, as she put him down.

A beat passed, and his eyebrows waggled.

Kai opened the door to the antechamber of the throne room and breathed a sigh of relief to find it empty. She wiped her sweaty palms on her uniform. She wasn't cut out for this suspenseful stuff. She pushed open the next door into the throne room and started when she saw two moonburners standing there.

"You weren't going to leave without us, were you?"

Kai sighed with relief. It was Emi, dressed in her moonburner blues, white bandage on her face. Leilu stood at her side.

"I didn't know if we could get you out of the hospital ward," Kai admitted. "Well, just your luck, I sprang myself," Emi said. "There is no way you're doing this without me."

"Or me," Leilu said. "You should have told me. We're family now."

"How did you know I would be here?" Kai asked.

"Master Vita," Emi said.

That old traitor, Kai thought fondly.

"I didn't want to involve anyone else," Kai said. "What we're talking about is treason."

"Emi explained to me what the queen is planning. The queen forfeited our loyalty when she decided to use our sisters as brood mares. And if there is any chance that Stela is in there . . ." Leilu curled her hands into fists. "We have to get her out."

"We're with you. To the end. Whatever end comes," Emi said. Kai's throat grew a lump as tears threatened. She nodded.

"Thank you," Quitsu said for her. "We're lucky to have such friends."

They padded across the empty room. Even their soft leather boots sounded thunderous on the empty marble floor. She moved aside the rich tapestry hanging on the back wall, woven in the blues and silvers of Miina. The door was there, just as she remembered it.

They made their way down the steps they had once come up. Everything was eerily quiet. Kai prayed that she would find Hiro below unharmed. At the thought of him, her chest tightened. She wanted to see him again. To see his golden hair in the firelight, the curve of his smile as it broke across his face. To hear his deep laugh that warmed her to the core.

She willed herself to force the feelings down. The last thing she needed was romantic notions clouding her judgment. Hiro thought she had betrayed him. He might never trust her again.

The stairway opened into the room lined with cells housing the sunburners and moonburner test subjects. The room appeared empty. She straightened and they walked into the room, trying to pretend that they belonged. She passed one moonburner who was swollen with child, and another who appeared normal. Perhaps the experiment had not worked on her.

Emi and Leilu were unable to disguise the horror on their faces, looking around at the burners.

Kai continued forward, peering into the cells. Most of the inhabitants appeared to be sleeping.

One silver-haired woman jerked upright as they passed her cell, her face a mass of bruises and cuts.

"Stela!" Leilu cried, rushing against the bars.

Stela, clothed in white, pressed herself to the other side of the bars, tears in her eyes.

"Thank the Goddess," she said. "I thought I'd rot in here forever."

Leilu stroked Stela's hair through the bars, and the two women clung to each other, foreheads touching through the cold metal. The moment was strangely intimate and Kai turned away, meeting Emi's eyes.

She had a sad smile on her face. "Let's find your man," Emi said.

They passed another cell, and Kai's breath caught in her throat as she saw him. He was dirty and disheveled, but appeared unharmed. He was lying on a stone slab, one arm thrown over his face.

She approached the cell, wrapping her hands around the cold bars. "Hiro," she whispered.

He was on his feet in an instant, like a coiled snake waiting to strike. She stepped back in surprise.

He approached the bars, radiating menace as he looked down at her. "What do you want? Here to gloat?"

Her tongue felt thick in her mouth. "No. I am here to help you. I didn't betray you," she said, dismayed at the desperation she heard in her own voice. Her heart felt as if it would shatter under the pressure of his displeasure.

"Then how did those moonburners find my camp?" he hissed. "People I care about were lost, Kai. People I swore to protect. I failed them. Because of you. Because I was soft." He was practically spitting at her.

"I didn't know they could track me. You have to believe me. I've never lied to you."

"I don't have to believe you," he said, turning his face from her. "And I don't know why I should."

"Because I'm on your side," she stepped forward. "You can trust me. Trust us." She motioned to Quitsu. "Ryu trusted us."

The venom returned to his face at the mention of Ryu. "And what did he get for it? To be some moonburner's trophy?"

"No," Kai said. "He's alive. He's on his way to your camp. I didn't kill him."

Hiro placed his hands over hers, tightening her fingers against the bars painfully. He looked into her eyes. Their faces were just inches apart. "Don't lie to me. Is he alive?"

"Yes," she said, willing every bit of sincerity and truth into her voice and her face. Goddess, what would she do if he didn't believe her? She couldn't unleash him to wreak havoc and possibly kill her.

"And I think that's all the confession we need." A triumphant voice rang out behind her.

CHAPTER 40

Kai whirled around, her back to the bars of Hiro's cell.
Geisa stood at the base of the staircase, flanked by four moonburner guards.

Kai's mouth went dry. There was no way she could talk her way out of this. If she insisted she was loyal to the moonburners, she'd lose Hiro's trust. If she admitted she was on his side, she'd be taken prisoner. No good options.

Another figure came into the light behind Geisa and her guards.

"Maaya?" Kai asked, crestfallen.

Maaya stood behind the moonburner in her servant's uniform, head bowed.

"How could you?" Emi hissed.

"Oh, yes," Geisa said with relish. "Your good friend Maaya came to us as soon as she heard about the treason you were planning here. She understands the cost of opposing the moonburners." Geisa looked at Maaya like a master might look at a dog who had just retrieved a duck from the field. "Excellent work, Maaya."

Tears welled in Maaya's eyes as she looked between her former friends. There was regret there. Kai's bitterness at Maaya's betrayal softened. Maaya had been broken. Kai should have known not to place too much on her shoulders.

"Arrest them," Geisa said.

The four burners approached Kai and her friends, spears leveled. Kai pulled out her knife, and began slowly backing away from the women, towards the other end of the facility. Emi and Leilu seemed to have the same idea, pulling out weapons and taking up defensive stances. Kai hadn't wanted it to come to this. Moonburner against moonburner. They were outnumbered.

In desperation, a plan sprang into Kai's mind. She had to do what she came here to do. Free the prisoners. Even the odds.

"Burners," Kai cried, her voice reverberating through the stone room. "We came here to free you from this place. Your captors have come to keep you here, to use you up like animals. Do not let them. Fight with us!"

She drew moonlight from the crown and burned it, melting the locks on each cell door. Splitting the moonlight into that many streams was difficult. She fell to her knees under the strain.

One of the moonburners darted behind her, wrenching her arm behind her painfully. Kai fell forward onto the ground, face in the dirt.

"You are free!" she cried. "The locks are broken!"

Another moonburner smashed the butt of her spear into Kai's face.

The world turned black, and Kai's ears rang.

When her vision cleared, Kai saw chaos. The prisoners had swarmed from their cells and were attacking with fists and nails and teeth. Geisa and her moonburner guards were fighting back, slicing at Emi, Leilu and the prisoners with their spears and knives, desperately trying to keep the press of bodies back. It wasn't working. One of the moonburners went down, disappearing behind a closing circle of unwashed bodies.

Kai tried to pull herself to her knees and saw Chiya, in a white robe and leggings, fighting furiously with Geisa. The two twirled out of the way of stabs and slices of the other's spear blade, the shafts of their spears meeting with deafening clacks of wood. Where had Chiya gotten the spear? Even in her condition, Chiya was fast, but Geisa fought dirty, landing a punch straight to Chiya's belly. Chiya doubled over, falling to one knee, and Geisa moved in for the kill.

"Chiya!" Kai cried, her voice sounding strange to her own ears. But her warning was too late.

Geisa's killing blow fell . . . landing not on Chiya, but on Maaya who pushed Chiya aside to receive it.

Time seemed to slow as Geisa's spear tip buried itself in the soft flesh of Maaya's stomach.

Chiya exploded upwards, burying a knife blade in Geisa's own stomach. Kai hadn't seen her pick one up, and Geisa seemed just as surprised, eyes wide, hands feeling at the dark blood beginning to flow down her front. The spear fell from Geisa's grip but stayed embedded in Maaya's body, the long wooden staff waving like a macabre flag above her.

As soon as it had begun, it was over. Geisa's moonburners lay on the ground, blood pooling around them.

Kai staggered to her feet, leaning against a nearby cell for support. She made her way to Maaya, pulling the spear from her friend's body and throwing it to the stone floor with a clatter. She gathered Maaya in her arms, smoothing her hair over her clammy brow.

Quitsu sat on the other side of Maaya, his furry face a mask of sorrow.

"Maaya," Kai said. "It's all right. You'll be all right."

Blood bubbled from Maaya's lips and her face was pallid.

Kai's heart twisted as she tried to ignore the truth her medical training shouted at her. Maaya's wound was too severe.

"I'm sorry," Maaya managed, coughing.

"Don't be sorry. You saved Chiya. Whatever you think you did, we forgive you," Kai said, the tears beginning to flood in earnest. She held her hand over Maaya's wound, but her dark blood continued to bubble forth.

Maaya lifted a bloody hand towards Quitsu, hovering over him.

He moved forward so her hand touched his silver fur. She stroked him, smearing her life's blood along his coat. He licked her face.

"So soft," she said, with a smile.

Her hand fell from Quitsu's side and her eyes fluttered closed. She was gone.

A sob wracked Kai's body, and she closed her eyes, trying to hold it in. Maaya hadn't deserved this. She was the kindest and most innocent woman Kai had ever known.

"Kai."

She heard a voice, distant and buzzing.

She couldn't look away from Maaya's blood, vibrant on her white uniform. "Kai!"

There it was again. The voice. She pulled her eyes away and looked down. Quitsu. He was looking at her intently. "You have to stop this!"

Her thoughts were sluggish and she looked up at the scene before her through a haze. When it came into focus, she understood his alarm.

Sunburner and moonburner prisoners were standing across the room from each other in an uneasy detente, tensions high, blood lust in their eyes. Emi, Leilu and Stela stood between them, wide-eyed.

"Now let's all just think about this . . ." Emi said.

Chiya gripped her knife tighter, preparing to spring.

"No," Kai said. She had tried to shout, but it came out a croak. Blood trickled down one of her temples and stung her eyes. She blinked it away. "No." This time was louder. "Don't fight each other. We have a common enemy. The same person put you all in this place. Queen Airi. We need to stop her."

The sunburners looked to Hiro, who nodded.

"Yes. Stand down. The sunburners are preparing an offensive outside Kyuden as we speak. We must make it to camp. We will find refuge there and can join the fight."

"Prince Hiro has agreed to defeat the queen, subdue our army, but leave Kyuden and Miina in control of a Miinan authority," Kai said, lurching to her feet with the help of Geisa's spear. "That is . . . if our agreement still stands?"

"It still stands," he said. "General Ipan will convince my father."

The moonburner prisoners looked to Chiya, who exuded deadly power, despite her advanced condition.

"Queen Airi showed me no loyalty when she put me in this place and so I have no loyalty to her. The world must know what she has done to her own people," Chiya said. She shook her head, as if she couldn't quite believe what she was saying. "If the sunburners will help us defeat her, then I fight with them."

The other five moonburners murmured their assent.

"Can you guarantee our safety and freedom in your camp, sunburner?" Chiya asked, turning to Hiro. "I will not trade one prison for another."

"I can," Hiro said. "If you ally with us, you will be treated fairly and with kindness."

"I don't give a seishen's ass about being treated kindly," Chiya said. "All I want is a pair of pants and a sword so I can stick it right between the queen's eyes."

Hiro chuckled. "We have those, too."

"Then lead on, burner," Chiya said. They grasped forearms and shook, once.

Kai couldn't help but feel chills. Here in the dark, where no sun or moon could shine, an alliance was born.

Kai led them up through the facility towards the city. They reached the top and the sturdy door loomed before them. Still weak from her captivity, Stela leaned on Leilu for support. Chiya had found her seishen and now carried him lovingly in her arms, as he was still groggy from lusteric. Hiro had picked up Kai's bag after her fall in the facility. She motioned to him to hand it to her. She pulled the solar crown out. There was a little bit more moonlight in it, she could feel it.

Hiro took the crown from her, his eyes widening in recognition. "Is this . . ." he trailed off.

"Yes," she said. "It was in our treasury for many years. It holds more than sunlight, though. It holds moonlight too."

She opened her mind and drew the last bit of moonlight from the crown. When she did, something remarkable happened. It was as if a golden door, into a world she didn't know existed, opened to her. She could feel Hiro's qi like warm, buttery light, and beyond that . . . something else. Sunlight.

Through him, she could reach for it.

Hiro's eyes widened in shock when she reached for the moonlight; his mouth hung slightly ajar. He must be experiencing the same thing she was. Was it possible that through this crown, through the two of them together, a man could burn moonlight and a woman could burn sunlight? Kai reached towards the door. Sweet sunlight beckoned, warm and golden . . .

"Not now," Hiro said. His eyes flickered to the others. "Let's get through the task at hand."

He was right. Now was not the time to explore a possibly ground-breaking magical discovery.

Kai pushed her spinning thoughts from her head and burned through the lock with the crown's last bit of moonlight. She shoved at the door with her shoulder, and the lock gave easily.

"Let's go," Kai said. "We need to try to get out of the city and find the sunburner camp."

She pushed open the door and stepped out, a crown of ivy above her. Instantly, she knew that something was very, very wrong.

The warm spring air was punctuated with the sound of explosions and screams. Pungent smoke billowed over the tops of the nearby buildings.

Hiro looked at her with alarm. "What is going on?"

A woman ran by with a baby in her arms, dragging a young child in her wake. Her eyes were wide, her face pale. Kai grabbed her arm. "What's happened?" Kai asked.

"The sunburners have attacked. They have already breached the city walls. They are assaulting the citadel." The woman moaned with fear. "They'll kill us all." The woman wrenched her arm away, continuing her flight.

When Kai turned to Hiro, his face was grim. "My father has attacked preemptively, so the moonburners lose the benefit of the eclipse."

"So we're too late," Kai said, dismayed.

"Maybe not. My father will be located back from the main assault on the citadel. We need to find him and ensure he doesn't get too . . . aggressive . . . with his campaign."

Emi nodded. "I know the way. Follow me." She began to jog off. Their ragtag group followed.

"Hiro," Kai said insistently as they took off after Emi. "The Oracle . . . She said . . ."

"I know, the eclipse. But it's not until tomorrow, according to our sources. The sunburners will be fine."

Kai struggled to grasp an elusive thought with her mind, but it was like a fish slipping out of her hand. Something the Oracle had said.

"Things are in motion. We will take Kyuden and we will install a regent. Some moonburners will be lost, but I'll do everything I can to minimize the damage."

Kai waved his voice away, still wrapped in her own thoughts. "The Oracle said that if the sun and moonburners battle, none will survive.

There will be a day of no sun and no moon." But what else had she said?

Hiro opened his mouth to speak, but Kai motioned him to be silent. And suddenly, things clicked into place. Her eyes widened in horror. "She said that we had just enough time to charge the crown. One day and one night. That would mean that the eclipse is today. Your information was wrong."

"That doesn't make sense, our informant clearly said the day after the equinox."

"That's what the Oracle told the queen as well . . . I heard her. But . . . why would she tell me something different?"

Quitsu chimed in. "The Oracle said that she was opposing the queen in her own way. That it was all a matter of timing."

"Do you think the Oracle told the queen the wrong day, so she would miss the eclipse?"

Hiro had grown pale. "Let's go," he said and sprinted off after Emi and the others.

By the time Kai and Hiro caught sight of the ornate armor of the king's guard, they were winded and panting.

King Ozora sat on the back of an impressive palomino stallion, with a golden hide and a snow white mane and tail. His armor matched his horse's, or perhaps his horse's armor matched his own, with engraved sunburst designs. His helmet was off, and Kai glimpsed King Ozora for the first time.

She had spent so much of her childhood hating and fearing him, she half-expected him to have his own set of horns. But he didn't. He was a handsome man with neat golden hair streaked with white. His face was tanned and lined as if he had spent much of his life outdoors in the sun. His eyes were the same vivid green as Hiro's, she noticed, her stomach tightening.

Next to him, on horseback, sat General Ipan, in his own golden armor. Kuma stood beside him. They made for an impressive sight. The king's seishen appeared to be a great golden leopard, its spots vibrant against its golden coat.

"Father!" Hiro called. Their group must have looked strange to the sunburner soldiers. They were dirty and dusty from their flight through the city, with sunburners in rags and several pregnant women wearing white robes and leggings.

The King's face brightened when he saw his son. He dismounted, handing the reins of his huge horse to a nearby servant. He strode over to Hiro and wrapped his armor-clad arms around him in a bear hug.

"Taiyo has smiled upon us today my son! A victory soon in hand, an end to our ancient enemy, and now my son returned to me."

They looked so alike, standing across from each other—like mirror images. They were the same height and had the same strong jaw and earnest demeanor.

"Father. There is something we must tell you about the battle." Hiro beckoned Kai closer.

"This is Kai. She is an ally. She freed me from the moonburner facility."

The king's face was guarded. "This is the one we held in our camp."

"Tell him, Kai."

"If you continue forward with the battle, all of the burners will be destroyed. It . . . it . . . will be the end of us all." Kai's voice sounded small in her own mind, her words weak. That wasn't how she wanted to say it. She had to convince him!

"I'm not one to retreat from a battle I am clearly winning at the insistence of one girl of questionable loyalty. Or two, I should say. Your . . . mother appeared at our camp a few hours ago, demanding something similar."

"Father . . ." Hiro said, a warning tone in his voice.

The King crossed his arms. "How do we know we can trust these women? Azura apparently faked her death and abandoned her kingdom, not to mention my captain. And this one! Perhaps they ordered her to rescue you to get her right here."

Hiro looked at Kai. A sliver of doubt crept into his intelligent eyes.

"I serve no queen or king," Kai said, her anger rising. "I serve the burners. All of them. I am trying to keep our race alive. The Oracle has foreseen that this battle will be the end of us all. It is folly . . ."

The King interrupted her. "Your oracle! A whore of Tsuki like the rest of you."

Kai ground her teeth together in frustration. "If you don't care to listen to the prophecies of a whore of Tsuki, as you so eloquently put it, perhaps you won't care to hear that the eclipse is today, not tomorrow."

That got the king's attention. "What did you say?"

But it was too late. The sky was already beginning to darken.

CHAPTER 41

Instead of calling the retreat like Kai had hoped, the king strode away, yelling at his messengers to tell the captains to pull troops into defensive positions. She understood. It was too late to flee. The sunburners would be exposed until the eclipse was over, and when it was, the vengeance of the remaining burners would be swift.

Kai turned to Emi. "Go find my mother. Her name is Hanae. I think we will need her before the day is done."

"I'm on it," Emi said, jogging towards the sunburner tents.

"What should we do?" Leilu asked, motioning with her head towards the other moonburners.

"Find arms," Kai said. "And rendezvous here. If it comes to it, we'll need to fight."

She prayed it didn't come to it.

Kai pushed through the crowd to Chiya, who had somehow acquired a sword in the time it took Kai to talk to the king. Chiya looked ready to fight, her fingers flexing on the hilt. Tanu had awakened, and stood, snarling, at her side.

"I have an idea," Kai said. "It may be crazy."

"What type of idea?" Chiya asked.

"We need to stop the fighting. Make them declare a truce. Otherwise, this is going to be a slaughter."

Chiya's face was hard, her eyes deadly serious. "I don't care if every single sunburner is slaughtered."

"You can't mean that," Kai said. "Do you want this to be our future?" She motioned to Chiya's swollen belly.

"As far as I'm concerned, the world is better off without burners in it. Maybe this is our fate. What we have become. Let us slaughter each other and leave the world better off without us. Just let me take down a few on my way out."

Kai put her hand on Chiya's shoulder and looked into her eyes. There was hurt there, buried deep beneath the anger. "You don't mean that. The moonburners were your life. Your pride and joy."

"Look where it got me," Chiya spit out. "I was wrong."

"You weren't wrong," Kai insisted. "There is good left. There is a part of the moonburners worth saving. Once the queen is gone, we can start rebuilding the moonburners into who they were supposed to be."

Chiya closed her eyes for a moment. "You are so damn naive. But . . . somehow it makes people want to trust you even more." She put her hand on Kai's. "Tell me your plan."

Kai made her way back to Hiro, who was standing next to his father and General Ipan. The sky was darker now, turning a sickly shade of red. A crimson sky. The Oracle's words from so many months ago floated to her, unbidden.

"The moon cannot enslave the sun, nor make the day its mistress.

Or victory shall spell defeat, a crimson sky its auspice

The sun and moon must shine as one, or all will be undone."

Kai's understanding deepened. The queen had already tried to enslave the sunburners and she'd try again. But it wouldn't work. The crimson sky . . . if the queen was victorious today, it would mean the end of sun and moonburner alike. Kai didn't know how it would come exactly, but she felt this truth deep within her. The sun and moonburners needed to work together, or none of them would survive this battle. The weight of her realization settled upon her shoulders like a heavy yoke. She had to get this right.

"I can feel the moonlight," Kai told Hiro. "They will attack soon."

As Kai's words left her lips, a mighty cry rose up from behind the citadel walls. Koumori and riders launched over the walls and fire began raining down from the ramparts. The koumori riders lay down cover as the citadel gate swung open. Navy-clad soldiers poured forth like water through a floodgate. They crashed against the Kitan soldiers who had been battering the gate.

The soldiers panicked and their hastily-made line began to break.

Kai ducked as fireballs exploded around them, throwing men and horses into the air. Lightning struck the ground in jagged bursts. The onslaught was relentless. The sun was almost entirely covered now. She looked around for Hiro and saw him across the cobblestones, directing the retreating soldiers.

"Hiro," she cried, the noises of the battle stealing her voice away. He turned to her and his eyes widened in alarm.

Something crashed into her back, throwing her sideways like a rag doll. As she hit the cobblestones, the searing heat from a blast of lightning struck where she had just stood. Pain lanced through her arm and shoulder where she had met the hard ground.

She rolled over groggily, to see what had hit her.

Quitsu lay limp and unmoving on the ground, his silver body smoking from the lightning strike. Kai's vision narrowed to a black pinpoint, every fiber of her screaming in alarm. She couldn't breathe, couldn't move, couldn't think. No, no, no, no.

She dragged herself to his side, arm protesting in pain, rocks and grit digging into her elbows.

"Quitsu," she choked, tears threatening.

His side was blackened where the lightning had struck him, a starburst pattern across his silver fur. She gathered the leaden weight of his body into her lap. She stroked his fur and drew in moonlight, beginning to probe his body. She couldn't find any spark of life in him.

Hiro knelt by her side, running his strong hand down her back. "Kai," he said urgently. "We need to go."

His voice was a tiny buzzing in her ears, his demand an unwelcome intrusion into her focus. She had to find a way to heal Quitsu. Couldn't he see that?

"The moonburners are coming," he said, tugging on her arm. "I'll carry him, but we have to go."

Somewhere in her awareness, she could tell that the battle raged on around them.

Hiro ducked as another explosion blasted just feet away from where they knelt. Dust and debris rained over them. Moonburner soldiers drew close to their position.

She continued to explore the pathways of Quitsu's body with moonlight, trying to find somewhere that she could latch onto with the light.

"We have to get out of here," Hiro said again. "Or his death will be in vain."

The royal guard was coming out of the citadel gates. That meant the queen was on the battlefield. A small voice in Kai's head told her that Hiro was right, that they needed to stand and get to safety. But this voice was only a whisper amongst the resounding, overwhelming need to heal Quitsu. Somehow, she could fix him.

Hiro gently tried to pull Quitsu's body from Kai's grasp, and she snarled at him, like an animal protecting her own. A koumori approached, sweeping around for another pass. Kai could see the rider's gaze, intent upon them, and her arm, poised for the throw.

Kai buried her face in Quitsu's soft fur, oblivious to the danger. She didn't want to live without him. At least this way, they would die together.

Seconds ticked by. The killing blow didn't come.

Kai slowly raised her head and opened her eyes. What she saw amazed her. Before them was a shimmering field of gold undulating in the air. It was covering much of the sunburner force as they retreated. She had never seen anything like it.

"What is that?" she asked, breathless.

Hiro's face was scrunched in concentration—a bead of sweat ran down his forehead.

"Sunshield," he said, as if it was the most obvious thing in the world. His voice was laced with strain. "I can't hold it for long." Another blast rocked off the shield. The moonburners seemed to be drawn to it. The shock of the remarkable sight drew her back to herself.

"The sun and the moon must shine as one, or all will be undone." The Oracle's words echoed in Kai's mind, and a wild idea sprang to life.

The shield flickered as another blast battered against it. Hiro looked pale. She knew the sunlight in the solar crown must be almost used up, it couldn't hold much more than he was using. His father and his guards were the last group of sunburners remaining on the battlefield.

Kai reached her hand in her bag and grasped the crown. She opened herself again to the moonlight, streaming through the strangely lit sky of the eclipse. There it was again. The strange golden door. A form she knew was Hiro's, standing in it.

She said a prayer and quickly linked with Hiro in the way that Pura had taught her.

Hiro's drooping eyes widened as he realized what she was doing.

Kai pulled in as much moonlight as she could hold and burned it, weaving it down the path that led to Hiro's shield. She had never burned sunlight, but somehow it seemed intuitive—her qi knew how even if her mind didn't.

When the moonlight hit the shield, it exploded with light, a white light so pure and clean that it made Kai's tears flow anew. The power of the sun and moonlight together roared between her, Hiro, and the shield, raw and magnificent.

The shield shot out, growing exponentially, covering the battlefield, separating the sunburners from the moonburners. It was as if all fighting ceased, awed by the sight of the pure, radiant wall of light. Kai and Hiro looked at each other with wide eyes. And then she split the light, dimming the shield only slightly. Hiro's brow furrowed, but he turned his focus back to the shield. She pulled the light into her, the pure complete spectrum of sun and moon together, and poured it into Quitsu's body. She flooded every bit of him with energy, praying to Tsuki and Taiyo and every god and goddess who ever lived to save him. His body jerked and spasmed with the power flowing into him.

And then she felt it. His life force was sweet and pure and playful and expanded to fill him, retaking ownership from the white light. She withdrew her stream of light, her breath caught in her throat.

His eyes flickered open.

A choked sob escaped from her, her relief so palpable it was like a living thing.

The brightness of the shield washed out the scene around them, but as Kai looked up from Quitsu with watery eyes, she saw a single bolt of white light shoot into the air. It was the sign they had agreed on. Chiya was in position.

"What . . . are you just sitting around for?" Quitsu rasped.

A giddy laugh bubbled from Kai's lips. She kissed Hiro on the cheek and started running back from the front line. She grabbed her knife from its sheath as she ran. Right through the sunburner guards. Right past the king's seishen. Right to the king. As she approached, she withdrew her moonlight from the shield. It winked out.

For a moment, it was as if the world was colored in only black and white, a stark remnant of the bright light that had divided the burner forces. Those on the battlefield stood blinking, clearing their retinas of the residue of the image.

King Ozora's men looked around for their King. He stood a few paces before them, still as a board. Kai's dagger was to his throat.

"King Ozora!" a voice cried across the battlefield. It was Chiya. Kai let out a shuddering breath. This plan would not have worked if Chiya hadn't been in position. It just would have ended up with Kai dead.

Kai had wrapped the king's arms with hot bands of moonlight, so if he moved too far, he would be burned. She looked up at the eclipse, which was already waning. She only had a few minutes to pull this off, or she would be dead.

"Queen Airi. We are here and ready to talk of a truce," Kai said.

"What?" the king snarled under her. She tightened her knife.

Kai could see Chiya's distant form, her strong arm wrapped around the queen's body. Leilu and Stela flanked her, weapons at the ready, holding the nearby moonburners at bay. Chiya had promised to wrap the queen's limbs and organs so tightly in moonlight that she couldn't even draw in a sliver of moonlight.

It seemed to be working . . . the queen was not fighting or trying to burn her way out of Chiya's grip. Her face was a mask of rage.

"We have fought for hundreds of years," Chiya said, her voice strong and unwavering. "For so long that no one remembers why. Our monarchs have used the burners as their weapons. Our numbers dwindle to nothing. On the current path, you will destroy us all. We demand that you declare peace, or we will find a king and queen who will."

The battlefield was silent as Chiya's words rolled over them.

Kai added her own words to Chiya's. "You put your petty war in front of the good of your people. You take their crops, their livestock for yourself, and leave them hungry. You slaughter babies, you steal children from their parents, you kill your subjects for having the audacity to love each other. And you exploit us, using us like cattle to be bred. No more. Declare a truce, or we will find rulers who will!"

There was murmuring around the battlefield now, murmurs of assent and agreement. Kai could see fists that had been tight on swords beginning to loosen, even among the sunburners.

Chiya continued, "What say you, King Ozora? Will you give your people peace, for the first time in your reign?"

Hiro had approached while they were talking, his feet dragging, Quitsu in his arms. His skin looked white and clammy. He fell to one knee as he approached, sitting back on his haunches.

"Father. Your people are tired of death. We're tired of fighting." Kai felt some of the radiating tension leave King Ozora's shoulders.

"I will agree to a truce," his deep voice rang out over the heads of the gathered people.

A glimmer of hope blossomed in Kai's chest. They were so close. "And what say you, Queen Airi?" Kai shouted.

Silence hung over the battlefield, a collective holding of breath as they waited to hear what their future would be. The eclipse was almost finished; the sun was shining once again. The queen's rout of the sunburners had failed. Kai prayed that she would be reasonable. *Agree to the truce,* Kai thought. No need to know that then the sunburners will arrest you and the regent will charge you with crimes against your country.

Airi's response rang out, hard and shrill. "I would rather die."

Kai hardly had time to register Queen Airi's words when the queen exploded into action. She twisted from Chiya's grip, elbowing the woman in her swollen stomach. Queen Airi reached a hand up and a bolt of lightning shot from the sky, striking Chiya's doubled over form. She fell like a stone.

"Chiya!" Kai cried. She released the king and began to run towards the fallen woman.

Chaos broke out, cries and screams and soldiers picking up the fighting where they had left off. Everything was falling apart. Kai was knocked backwards by a sunburner shield swung in her direction at the wrong time.

The queen rose in the air, her white dress whipped around her by an invisible wind. Kai gaped as the queen's eerie floating form made its way towards them. She threw lightning bolts from her hands as she passed, striking down sunburners and soldiers in her path who tried to flee. The woman must have had a moonlight well of some sort, because the moon had entirely disappeared. The eclipse was over.

But that didn't stop Queen Airi's horrible progress. She had almost reached Kai and the king. Kai scrambled to her feet and stood before the king with his guards, knife up, ready to protect him. She'd be damned if she let the queen kill him after he had agreed to peace.

The queen was laughing, her beauty twisted horribly into a gruesome mask. The queen pointed at Kai as she raised her hand to throw a lightning bolt. "You will die first."

"Stop!" A voice cried from behind them. Kai knew that voice. Its normal kindness was gone, only a hard edge remaining. "Airi, stop this. What has become of you? What has become of my sister?" Kai's mother stepped forward. She wore a simple gray dress, her hair down around her shoulders, waving in the unnatural breeze. Despite her simple garb and face lined with age, she stood tall and proud. She looked every inch a royal.

Airi faltered, landing on the ground. "Azura?" she asked, her voice very small.

Hanae held her arms out to Airi. "It doesn't have to be this way. Let's end this war. Once and for all."

"But you . . . you died. I saw your body."

"It was a trick, Airi, a ruse. I didn't want to be queen."

"A trick? A trick?" Airi's voice gained a hysterical edge. "How do I know you are not a trick? An evil, cruel sunburner trick?" She began to rise into the air again, the unnatural wind whipping about her. "This changes nothing! Tsuki has tasked me with the destruction of the sunburners. They must be brought to heel!" Airi raised her arms, and the air crackled with electricity.

Kai closed her eyes in anticipation of the strike, hope dying in her. They had done all they could.

But for the second time that day, it didn't come. Kai opened her eyes.

The queen, arms still partially raised, wore a look of confusion on her face. She fell to the ground, landing on her knees. An arrow protruded from her chest, blood beginning to pour from the wound, coloring her white dress scarlet. And then another arrow joined it, just a few inches from the first. Kai looked around, searching for the archer.

She caught her eye. Nanase. She lowered her bow, a grim look on her face. Her silver seishen tangled with the queen's dragon in the sky and bore it to the ground, ripping its throat with its razor sharp talons.

Kai's mouth hung open. The rest of the battle had stopped again as quickly as it had begun. The moonburners were staring in shock as their queen bled out onto the cobblestones of the street.

Hanae hurried to her sister's side and knelt, taking her in her arms. "I'm sorry I failed you, sister. I never should have left."

Nanase approached their party, and the sunburners leveled their weapons towards her. She held up her bow in a sign of submission and lowered it to the ground.

Kai looked at Nanase in utter gratitude, unsure what to say to her.

Nanase dropped to one knee before them. What was she doing? Swearing fealty to the king? This would be a disaster for Miina.

Nanase looked up, calling out in a clear voice that rang across the silence of the courtyard. "I swear fealty to Kailani Shigetsu, daughter of Azura, heir to the throne of Miina."

Kai looked on in amazement as across the battlefield, soldiers and moonburners bent to one knee before her.

EPILOGUE

Kai sat eating a breakfast of fruit and spiced rice, leafing through the first of three stacks of reports. Soldiers' rations, merchant contracts, trade reports, banking sheets . . . she could feel her eyes glazing over. No wonder the queen had gone insane.

"Why do we need a census of the royal forest? It's a forest. Can't we just let it be?" Kai asked her mother, who sat beside her at the long polished wooden table.

Hanae flashed her a look. "It's important to prevent poaching. And to do that, we need to roughly understand the numbers of game in the wood."

Kai sighed, "I know, I know."

Kai looked around the beautifully appointed room, still mentally shaking her head with disbelief. The room was decorated in white marble interlaced with cool, gray granite, polished to a shine. A huge mirror hung on one end of the room, making the impossibly long table look as if it went on forever. The thought of hosting a dinner party for enough people to sit at this table terrified Kai.

The other wall bore a long set of windows letting in the light of the setting sun, illuminating low clouds in vibrant colors of pink, purple and orange.

Kai herself wore a dress of soft light blue wool, decorated with silver embroidery that highlighted her silver hair, which now reached down to her shoulders, and was cut so it fell in soft layers against her neck. She hardly recognized herself in the mirror.

"Maybe we should talk about something more enjoyable. Like your coronation tonight?"

At the grimace on Kai's face, Hanae hurried to the next topic. "Or a royal engagement?"

At that, Kai flushed with both pleasure and embarrassment. She recalled the words King Ozora had spoken to her as he had departed with his retinue two weeks before.

"It's not every day that I meet a woman who both tries to kill me and sacrifice herself for me in one day. Just the type of woman Hiro needs to keep him in line," he had said with a wink and a friendly hand on her shoulder.

"I didn't try to kill you, I just threatened to. Huge distinction," Kai said.

General Ipan, who stood next to the king, guffawed, his loud laugh warming her. "Already mincing words. She is ready for the crown all right!"

Kai and Hiro had shared a few precious moments together before he had ridden off with his father, promising to return in a month. He had been appointed as the Kitan ambassador to Miina.

Hiro had taken her face in his strong hands and pressed his lips gently to hers. She had leaned into his warm body as her knees grew weak and her blood raced through her veins. The kiss set her heart fluttering even in memory. It held the promise of more.

Kai returned to reality as her mother cleared her throat loudly.

"It's far too early to talk of engagements," Kai stammered, trying to recover her composure. "There is too much to do. "

"Pace yourself, my darling. You have done so much already," her mother said gently. "You have repealed the laws regarding lifetime service for moonburners, and allowed moonburners to choose whether to serve or whether to have families or pursue other lives."

Kai nodded. "I think seven years of service is fair in exchange for training at the citadel. Of course, we hope they will stay longer."

"And you paved the way for Kitan moonburners to come to the citadel, and then return to Kita when their training is complete."

"That is true. And our sunburners will be able to train with Kita and return to us. We can't stay segregated like we are now," Kai said. "And no more gleaming," she smiled. "My life would have been very different under these new laws."

"Both of our lives," Hanae said.

"We'd still have Father," Kai said sadly.

Hanae nodded slowly. "Yes. But do not look backwards with regrets. Your upbringing made you who you are. Things unfolded how they were destined to."

Kai grasped her mother's hand and squeezed. "I think they did."

Kai's coronation that night was resplendent. The great hall was filled with the silvery glow of moon orbs and white string lights that had been added for the occasion. Everyone was dressed in their finest clothes, shades of blue and purple, green and soft grays and browns. Kai was dressed in a white dress covered in swirls of silver thread and crystals. Her hair was done in elaborate braids, and her face had been painted with rouge and kohl. Butterflies flipped in her stomach.

She turned to Quitsu. "How do I look?"

He had been bathed and fluffed; his fur positively glowed silver. He examined her. "Passable."

She rolled her eyes. "Great. At least I'll always have you to keep me grounded."

He chuffed his cheeks out in his signature laugh. "That's what I'm here for."

The coronation was a blur—Kai walked down the aisleway, surrounded by smiling faces. Master Vita, clutching her mother's arm, the Oracle standing in the front row, Emi, Stela, Leilu, Nanase and Pura. Faces that had become her friends and her family. Even Chiya was there, though sitting down and still looking pale and weak from her ordeal with Airi. Kai thought with a pang of Maaya, whom they had laid to rest in the royal crypt after the Battle at the Gate, as it had become known. She thought of her father, too. She wished he could see her that day.

Kai said the words that made her queen, and the lunar crown was placed on her head. The applause was deafening. She couldn't help but grin, despite the weight of the responsibility that now rested on her shoulders.

The women at the front released a set of tiny gray koumidi into the air, their soft wings and bodies swooping over the heads of the crowd as they admired the show.

But then one fell, dropping from the air like a stone. Its small, delicate body landed on the step before Kai with a sickening thud. Kai stared at it, mouth open.

A voice rang out, loud and methodical.

"And in the reign of Kailani Shigetsu, daughter of Azura, there will be a great war. A war of gods and men. For Tsuki and Taiyo are displeased with the lands of Kita and Miina, and only one side will remain standing when it comes to the end."

It was the Oracle. She had gone straight as a board, her head tilted back, her eyes glazed white. Giselli fluttered above her head in distress. Kai's mother clutched Roweni's arm, her face pale. There was no doubt that they were witnessing a true prophecy being told. As quickly as it had begun, the Oracle returned to normal.

She shook her head. "What happened?"

A deafening silence filled the room as the audience took in the Oracle's words.

Quitsu and Kai glanced at each other. Disturbing. Kai shrugged.

"I think we should head to the grand dining room for the royal feast," she announced, the audience still dumbstruck. If she was going to have to fight a great war, at least she'd do it on a full stomach.

And with that, she lifted up her skirt, stepped over the broken koumidi body before her and marched from the room, Quitsu at her side.

FROM THE AUTHOR

Thank you so much for taking the time to read *Moonburner!* I hope you've enjoyed reading about Kai's adventures as much as I have enjoyed writing them!

Reader reviews are incredibly important to indie authors like me, and so it would mean the world to me if you took a few minutes to leave an honest review wherever you buy books online. It doesn't have to be much; a few words can make the difference in helping a future reader give the book a chance.

If you're interested in receiving updates, giveaways, and advanced copies of upcoming books, sign up for my mailing list at www.claireluana.com. As a thank you for signing up, you will receive a free eBook copy of *Burning Fate,* the prequel to *Moonburner!*

Now read on for a Sneak Peek of

Sunburner,

the sequel to *Moonburner* . . .

CHAPTER 1

The stag was nothing but skin and bones. It moved warily through the sparse pine trees, its hooves crunching the dusty leaves and needles that coated the forest floor.

Kai notched an arrow to the string of her bow, her sweaty fingers struggling to find purchase. She squinted at her quarry, hesitating.

A horse jangled its halter some ways behind her, startling the stag. It darted away, disappearing into the brown camouflage of the trees.

She lowered her bow, relieved. At least she could help one creature today. She turned her horse to the noise and spotted Quitsu, her silver fox seishen companion, perched on a tree behind her.

"Not a word out of you," she said.

"You always were too soft-hearted," he said.

Kai made her way to join the other riders who had come into the clearing. The hunt had been one of her mother's lunatic ideas. Strengthen her ties with the noble families by taking them out into the royal game preserve for a hunt. Nothing brought people together like killing.

But despite Kai's protests, her mother had gotten her way, as she most often did. So Kai found herself in the middle of the dry forest underneath the sweltering heat of the sun looking for game to kill. At least her companions were not entirely unpleasant. Though the men and their wives came from Miina's royal houses, they did not seem as vapid as some of the nobles she had encountered. They were flanked by two master moonburner bodyguards, wearing navy blue uniforms and vigilant expressions.

Her friend Emi sat on a leggy gray mare a stone's throw from them, her fine-featured profile illuminated by the sun. From this angle, Kai couldn't see the extensive burns that covered one half of Emi's face, a permanent reminder of last year's sunburner attack on the citadel. She could see Emi's set jaw and hunched shoulders, her haunted dark eyes. Emi hadn't been herself since their friend Maaya had died in what had become known as the Battle at the Gate.

Kai turned in her saddle and watched as Hiro approached, stopping his horse next to hers. She reached a hand out and he grasped it, closing her hand in his warm calloused fingers.

"She'll come back to herself eventually," Hiro said, following Kai's line of sight to where it had rested on Emi. "She needs time."

"It's been over a year," Kai said. "I miss Maaya too, but I . . . I've moved on."

"You've had a kingdom to run. You've hardly had time to wallow in grief."

That was true. But as she looked at Hiro, the golden sun shadowing his rugged jaw and highlighting his hair like a halo, she knew that her duties as queen were not all that had helped her cope with losing her friend.

"Maybe she needs a romance," Kai mused.

Hiro raised an eyebrow. "Do you have someone in mind?"

"No," she said. "Not like there are a lot of eligible men around the citadel."

"Maybe one of those fancy nobles." Hiro nodded towards the nobles riding ahead of them, clothed in colorful linens and silks. They were like preening peacocks in a field of brown—colorful, decorative, and useless.

Kai rolled her eyes. "I meant eligible *and* worthy."

"You're right. Emi'd eat those fellows for breakfast."

"Maybe I should bring Leilu and Stela back from Kistana," Kai suggested. "They might be able to lift her spirits."

Their friends Leilu and Stela were serving as ambassadors to King Ozora in the Kitan capital city, which was an important post. But she missed them. She'd be happy to have them back as well.

"You sound as meddlesome as your mother," Hiro remarked.

Kai laughed and held up her hands. "All right, I'll let it go. For now."

"Speaking of letting things go," Hiro said, turning to her with a twinkle in his eye. "Ryu said he smelled a stag in the clearing up there."

She blushed. "Tell him to get his nose checked." She tapped her horse's flanks with her heels and trotted back towards the citadel.

The sun loomed large and red over the brown farmland as the hunting party made their way out of the forest. Cooler autumn weather should have settled over Miina a month ago, but sweltering summer hung on with a vengeance. Kai had dressed for the heat in a loose white wrapped top and light brown trousers, her silver hair knotted in a bun under a wide-brimmed hat. Nothing helped. She could have been naked, and it would still have felt as if she were riding through an oven.

The farmland around them served as a testament to the stark devastation of the drought. Fields that should have been filled with green crops ready for harvest instead sat brown and dusty under the oppressive heat. While the hunt was an opportunity for her to bond with her subjects, it also served a practical purpose. The citadel would need all the resources it could get to survive the coming winter without the crops and plenty it normally relied on. Every little bit helped. Kai thought briefly of the stag she had let go, but then banished it from her mind. The bony creature would do little to stave off the hard season they faced ahead. She was glad she had let it live.

It was as if their world itself was rebelling against them. Last winter had been bitter, cold, and long, and then the land had skipped spring entirely, roaring straight into a sweltering summer. It hadn't rained in months. Crops hadn't stood a chance. Her people couldn't feed their families. Frightened whispers of a new disease, a spotted fever, was sweeping through both nations. It was supposedly highly contagious—skin-to-skin contact was enough to spread the disease. Only a few cases of the fever had been reported so far—on the outskirts of Miina—but those cases had been fatal. These new enemies she faced were not flesh and bone. How could she fight them?

Kai had heard whispers already. Her mother and advisors had tried to keep them from her, but she wasn't blind. Her people were saying that the gods were displeased with Kai's ascension to the throne and the peace between Kita and Miina. Word of the Oracle's prophecy, spoken the night of her coronation, had spread.

"And in the reign of Kailani Shigetsu, daughter of Azura, there will be a great war. A war of gods and men. For Tsuki and Taiyo are displeased with the lands of Kita and Miina, and only one side will remain standing when it comes to the end."

People were whispering that the only way to break the unnatural weather cycle was to return to war with Kita. Kai wasn't sure what would happen to her in that scenario, but she didn't think it would be pleasant.

Emi slowed her mare down to match Kai's pace. "You wear your worry plainly, Your Majesty," Emi said softly. "Best to not let them see it." She nodded towards the nobles.

"A good reminder, Emi; thank you," Kai said. "And speaking of reminders, how many times have I asked you to call me 'Kai,' not 'Your Majesty'?"

"You think just because you're queen, I'll listen to you?" Emi said, a ghost of a smile passing across her face.

"I wouldn't dream of it," Kai said.

"This will pass," Emi said, growing serious. "It has to pass. Soon we'll stand in the rain and laugh about how worried we all were."

"I hope you're right."

Emi gave Kai a sympathetic smile and nudged her horse's flanks, rejoining the other moonburner guards, who were riding ahead with the nobles.

Kai rode alone for a while, Quitsu silently trotting at her side. It was how it was to be queen, she realized. To be surrounded by people yet always alone. She shot a furtive glance back at Hiro, who was bringing up the rear of their column, chatting with Ryu, his lion seishen. Maybe not alone. If anyone understood the demands of ruling, Hiro did, as crown prince of Kita. If anyone could love her as queen and as herself, it would be him.

They neared the farming settlements that dotted the land outside the city of Kyuden. To her left was a stout house, the wood of its walls faded and shrunken with age. The house was surrounded by a dusty farmyard, vacant but for one sorry-looking chicken. *It's much like the house I grew up in,* she thought wistfully. Solid and functional.

"Get off the road," a high-pitched male voice called from ahead.

"Please," said a sobbing female voice, hardly coherent. "My husband."

Kai urged her horse towards the commotion. There was a woman in the middle of the road sitting on her knees. Her dirty face was tear-streaked and wreathed in greasy black hair. A threadbare dress that once might have been pink hung from her thin frame, tied tight with an apron. The nobles' horses danced back from the woman, no doubt picking up on their riders' unease at being so close to a commoner.

Emi had dismounted and was trying to help the woman stand.

Kai swung off her horse and strode to join Emi, taking the woman's other arm. "We have to get you off the road. Then we can talk about your husband."

The woman nodded and stood shakily with their assistance. "He's sick. He's so sick." She was near hysteria, her eyes darting to and fro. "I thought you could heal him. With your moonburning. You have to help him."

Emi and Kai sat the woman down on a bit of brown grass at the side of the road, leaning her against a fence post.

"I have medical training," Kai said. "I will look at your husband, and we will send a healer for him if we can help." If the man was truly ill, there wasn't much she would be able to do without supplies or herbs. But at least she could evaluate his condition and give the healer she assigned her diagnosis.

"Thank you," the woman said, gripping Kai's hands tightly.

Kai wriggled from the woman's grasp, standing.

"Your Majesty." One of her master moonburner guards approached, an older woman with thick silver eyebrows. "I have to advise against this. We don't know what his condition is. You should not risk yourself."

The peasant woman's eyes widened as she realized who Kai was.

"Thank you for your suggestion, but I did not ask for your permission," Kai said.

"I must insist," the woman continued. "It is our job to keep you safe."

Hiro approached from behind her, putting a broad arm around Kai's shoulder. "You should know by now that the queen will not be dissuaded when she has decided upon a course of action. I will accompany her. She will be safe."

The moonburner guard's thick brow furrowed, but she nodded her acquiescence.

Kai ground her teeth in frustration. How was it that Hiro commanded more obedience from her own guards than she did? She knew he meant well, but she would have to talk to him later about undermining her authority. He was not in charge here. She was. And she didn't need him to protect her . . .

She was getting worked up now, and there was a sick man to see. She shook off her annoyance and smiled at Hiro. "I would welcome your company. Let's see if we can help him."

The smell of disease struck her like a stiff wind as they walked into the farmhouse. Hiro placed an arm over his mouth, breathing through his shirtsleeve.

"Open the windows," Kai instructed. "Let's get some airflow in here. Fetch some clean water. And the wife. I need to know his symptoms."

Hiro handed her the water flask that hung on his belt and saw to her other orders.

Kai sat gingerly on the edge of the bed next to the man. He rolled about in the tangled sheets, deep in his delirium. He was thin but wiry with salt-and-pepper hair and a face deeply lined from a lifetime of sun and hard work. His ragged trousers and worn shirt stuck to him, soaked through with sweat.

Kai felt his forehead and let out a gasp. He had a raging fever. Despite this, his color was pallid and his lips were almost blue, as if he were chilled to the bone.

Hiro returned with the man's wife.

"How long has he been like this?" Kai asked.

"Two days, Your Majesty," the woman said.

"Was he exposed to anything?"

"No, I don't think so," the woman said, desperation in her voice.

"Did he receive an injury? A wound or a bite? Could it be an infection?"

"No," the woman said. "But he does have some strange marks."

"Show me," Kai commanded.

The woman knelt next to the bed and unbuttoned her husband's shirt.

Kai hissed and stood up, backing away from the man into Hiro.

"What is it?" Hiro asked.

The man had red-ringed marks covering his chest and stomach.

"We're leaving," Kai said. "We will send a moonburner healer for your husband as soon as we return to the citadel," she told the woman. "Keep him well hydrated and as cool as you can until she arrives."

"Thank you," the woman said, still on her knees. She tried to grasp Kai's hands, but Kai jerked back involuntarily.

Kai swallowed a lump in her throat and nodded, striding from the farmhouse.

"Mount up," Kai called to the hunting party, who had dismounted and were fanning themselves by the side of the road. "We head back to Kyuden."

Kai swung onto her mount and trotted off, leaving the rest to follow. Her heart was pounding in her chest. She willed it to slow.

Quitsu leaped from the ground onto the saddle in front of her. This was a common enough occurrence that it didn't startle her horse anymore. "What's wrong?" he asked.

Hiro approached from the other side. He had put the pieces together. "That was the spotted fever, wasn't it," he said, his voice low. "I didn't know it had spread this far."

Kai nodded, refusing to look at him. "Neither did I." Her voice sounded hollow. "The only reported cases came from the outskirts of Miina."

"We'll figure it out," Hiro said. "We'll find a cure before it infects too many."

"We'd better," Kai said. "I touched him."

ABOUT THE AUTHOR

Claire Luana grew up reading everything she could get her hands on and writing every chance she could. Eventually, adulthood won out, and she turned her writing talents to more scholarly pursuits, going to work as a commercial litigation attorney at a mid-sized law firm. While continuing to practice law, Claire decided to return to her roots and try her hand once again at creative writing. She has written and published the Moonburner Cycle and is currently working on a new trilogy about magical food. She lives in Seattle, Washington with her husband and two dogs. In her (little) remaining spare time, she loves to hike, travel, binge-watch CW shows, and of course, fall into a good book.

Connect with Claire Luana online at:
Website & Blog: www.claireluana.com
Facebook: www.facebook.com/claireluana
Twitter: www.twitter.com/clairedeluana
Goodreads:
www.goodreads.com/author/show/15207082.Claire_Luana

Made in the USA
San Bernardino, CA
07 July 2018